# AROUND THE MAYPOLE
# AND BACK

## ELLEY FLETCHER

*To My Uncle Mike,*

*I dedicate this book to you. I can see your wide, proud beam and big arms outstretched for a hug. I hear your chuckle, and it warms me. Despite the madness this novel holds, I know how proud you would have been.*

*Forever,*

*Elley*

# Prologue

"EXCUSE ME, DOCTOR?" George Hartmann addressed, trying not to sound pushy, yet his tone was eager and pleading. The older, wrinkly faced smiling doctor turned to look up at him, taken aback to not be speaking to a child for once, it seemed. His hair was greying around his temples and was slicked back on top with a hefty layer of hair gel to keep it all in place. The doctor gave the impression of being skunk-like with his style of hair and crow's feet at the side of his eyes, joining those at his cheeks when he smiled at the concerned man before him.

"What can I do for you? Is everything okay?" he asked, adorning a smile.

"My daughter, Melissa," George began, straightening his posture while reminding himself not to fumble over his words. His palms flattened his shirt. "She's on a different ward, but I need to speak to you about her treatment. You see, I'm a junior doctor and she came in late last night and had to stay over."

The doctor pressed his lips together as he finished his first sentence.

"Which ward is she on? I advise you to stay by her side, as we've already treated young Melissa today." The doctor smiled,

1

pumping on some hand sanitiser from the fat red pump stationed on the wall of the ward, rubbing it into his skin nonchalantly.

George shook his head, persisting with his argument, deciding the doctor had not listened. He refused to be brushed off so easily.

The Doctor began to walk out of the ward, to which George strode beside him.

"She's on the Ladybird ward, but she doesn't look better than last night and is still woozy." The doctor stopped walking, turning so he was facing George, his lips yanked downwards. "That's because of the medications we have her under, and I am not about to discuss that here with you, Mr Hartmann."

His change of tone caught George off guard, making the father drop any false front he may have had up. Raising his head to catch up with his thoughts before being blatant, he took a second.

"You have to be joking. Tell me what's wrong with my daughter." Upon the locking of his jaw, a hiss came from behind his row of teeth and his mouth clenched tight. George swallowed as the doctor looked to him with a blank, yet surprised expression. The silence angered him, making him almost become embarrassed with his persistence, but being too frustrated to care otherwise.

"I'm not going to discuss that with you, now. Please, I'm a busy man." The doctor excused himself, clicking away down the hallway in his polished shoes with his coat flying out behind him. George stood residing in his bubbling anger, in the hallway of the children's ward, paralyzed. ҃ He put his head in his warm palms and groaned, closing his eyes for a moment to gather himself and calm down. He took in a breath to the pit of his lungs.

George raised his heavy head when a few young nurses rushed past with panic etched onto their gentler features, headed toward a commotion coming down the hallway behind him. ⸗ He sizzled in the swirl of emotions, deciding it'd be best to move himself, rather than press any further and make a scene. George knew better. But worryingly, the state of his panic shifted once he strode back the way he had come.

Alarms blared and hurried footsteps squeaked on the floor as he hurried down, his heart racing— this was a children's ward. The gripping air became sweltering, beads of sweat gathering under his hairline.

George returned to the entryway of the ward Melissa was on, searching the space around him for the commotion he had passed. Lifting a hand to wipe the sweat from his forehead, he saw multiple nurses gathered around his daughter's bed, hunched over like vultures.

The sweat he had just wiped from his brow returned with friends in tow, ones that came down the side of his nose and would have dripped onto the floor if he had not raised his wrist to get rid of them.

Multiple pairs of feet huddled behind the patterned yellow and green curtain. Nurses were trying, willing someone, and urging, through the tones of their voice. The monotone beeps of the machines at the bed had never been more alive, they screamed around his head and pierced his ear when the noise regretfully reached him. The hollowness within left George barely breathing. He couldn't find Lauren; she was the only one not visible behind the curtain. She wasn't at the bedside but he heard a cry, and the pain resonated with him, too. He knew then, it was Lauren.

"Lauren?" He ran to her, leaning and cradling herself into a nurse's arms. Her face was blotchy, and she was visibly shaking. The nurse was trying the best to comfort George's wife, trying to walk her in to a different room away from where their daughter was. Lauren only stood there and sobbed; she wouldn't be moved. Taking Lauren, her husband held her up by her elbows. Trying to grip her was like holding melting butter.

"What's happened to my daughter?" The fear in his voice

was audible, the words shook as they left his quivering lips and hung in the air, akin to a bad smell. Lauren cried into his chest and her jagged nails caught on the fabric of his shirt, trying to grip onto him, but failing to find the strength in her palms. From all of her nail biting and gnawing, George felt the residual scratch on his skin when she flung her fingers at his chest and clawed.

The nurse led the parents away from the unfolding scene, ushering them out of the ward.

Melissa was transported into a private room by the same doctor with whom George remained angry.

Nurses were stonefaced, their complexion pale despite their rushing. He had never felt so out of control of his life, failing to grasp what was happening, although not for lack of trying.

The man was sweating profusely, his face glistening under the ugly hospital lights. George felt it appropriate to shout, but Lauren was a wreck—he clung onto her for fear if he let go, she may collapse. She could not speak and it was as if she was choking. His heart was battering against his ribcage and his throat threatened to close. Weakening under the weight of Lauren's persistent sobs, his hand remained clamped around her shoulder.

Unbeknownst to him, George's entire life was to fall apart that day. The shards of his heart shattered and gathered at his feet, and neither his world nor his heart would ever be the same again.

# Chapter One

EMMA NIBBLED HER BOTTOM LIP, as she drove through the split in the winding town to the hospital. The wheels of her small car bounced over the bumps as the striped barrier lifted high into the air. She felt her exhaust was going to fall from the machine. She gripped the steering wheel with clammy palms and held on tight.

She struggled to peer over the top of her car bonnet to peer for a parking spot. Feeling the engine sputter and hearing it groan, she yanked the gearstick down roughly to avoid a stall. It begged for kindness, but Emma gave none to her small, battered old car.

Westview General was the pride of a self-serving community in the middle of St. Gridgevey. The unremarkable town was a fair drive from the city, and nothing stood out like Westview General. Westview had undergone several transformations which took shape over the hospital's many decades. There were also a string of incidents which were more grisly and dark than most would admit to. All tales in St. Gridgevey focused around the old mental hospital.

Erected during the latter half of the dark Victorian years,

5

when mental illness, was viewed with an utter lack of understanding. Westview was one of a handful of asylums at a time when they were first opening. The open doors were thrust full of lost and poor souls, filling to capacity quickly.

During those formative years, it was not an act of boasting, but townsfolk would always reminisce when they gazed upon the hospital. The inhabitants of St. Gridgevey did not have a choice how the looming felt when gazing upon the towers of Westview.

Many residents felt they had suffered the leather boots derailing their jaw and kicks to the ribs, from the sadistic staff. They had grown to near dysfunction themselves by the lack of colleagues and sympathy for the job. Many folks in the town, were relieved upon learning their family members would be safe. The sources of social embarrassment to them could now be placed into a system made to help.

Some families felt the process was bittersweet. It was cruel to be kind in the long run, and the period of settling would be difficult.

The patients were often left to their own devices. Choices for treatment were frustratingly narrow. Often, doctors were uncertain what to do with the mentally ill. The mixture of sympathy and frustration brought to the surface a lack of realisation for the violence of the treatments. Science of the mind, and how to treat unseen illnesses was in its infancy, needing much more nurturing than it was receiving.

On the other hand the opposing opinion of many more wealthy families felt it better to altogether lock the dysfunctional members away. Those plagued by mental illness were of no use to those requiring useful labour, and so they would essentially be labelled helpless at the hands of disgruntled doctors and exhausted nurses.

Sympathy was hard to come by for the afflicted, as it normally comes from an understanding of which there was none to be had at the time. Becoming accustomed to a general understanding that in St. Gridgevey, Westview General was not a well-received subject at any family dinner table. It was hushed up, for it brought forth a deep shame upon one the majority. Harbouring guilt of locking away a family member, succumbed to great unseen pain, with no release. And so, it began with the small feeble nibbles at their sense of security.

Self-esteem, image, and confidence were washed away by the bleeding in, the invading of the illness. The nibbles became gutsy chunks ripped from the soul. Within the dysfunctional operation of Westview's early years, illnesses were free to grow large and ugly. Time wore on and the mental institution stood firm.

The townspeople of St. Gridgevey knew there was suffering, and ignored it. More known than guessed about, every so many months there would be an escape, and in the winter these incidents would be more commonplace. Escaping became easier when the sky began to darken at around three in the afternoon. Westview Mental Asylum housed thousands, and throughout both of the wars this remained a constant. Overcrowding was an issue only during the time after the wars. The hospital grew stagnant, as the fashion of throwing dysfunctional members away to become dependently institutionalised had fallen out of fashion. The next steps, the very few they could take at once, became up to that patient. As the times moved forwards in a massive shunt, Westview had a fallback in their new plans to let patients begin having choices in own treatments.

A patient on day release to St. Gridgevey had set alight to the town's vegetable shop. The stalls standing outside were made of wood and a blanket covering the various boxes of fruit and vegetables on the streetside burned quickly.

The patient was a middle aged man who had been on release for a day out by himself. He was trusted by staff, and a socialite. Curfew back at the Hospital was four that afternoon, because it was the winter months. Summer curfew was five in the evening.

St. Gridgevey residents butted heads and entered into disputes among themselves. Time, rearing its ugly head, ground on and the name of the asylum changed with the times to suit a more open- ended culture. It became Westview General Hospital in the 1990s, as asylums were fast becoming isolated and ridding themselves of the stigma surrounding such a title. It was not only St. Gridgevey that had been the victim of escapee's setting fires, and causing a degree of uncharted chaos.

The Hospital became changed for good, when George Hartmann came onto the scene. It had been late into 1996, and the chill in the air that winter morning urged any person to crave their bed as soon as they had left it.

Children entertained themselves by seeing their breath in the bitterly cold air. It did not stop the young George Hartmann from respectfully requesting to come in, knuckles rapping on the door at eight precisely. The young doctor was thrust in at the deep end, eyes widening at the shameful state of the patients lumbering at the windows, drooling onto the windowsills. Due to both lack of staffing and too many patients, he did not have a choice but to be thrown into the middle of it.

He vowed to make changes. And being a man of his word, he did not disappoint.

---

Emma's car puttered into a parking space, pulling a strained face as she almost hit the car on the left. Luckily missing the car beside her, she managed to not bump the doors. She exhaled, but cursed herself for being so careless. She wanted to be on her A-game today, and part of that was not almost hitting another car to fuck up her morning. She blamed it on her persistent headache, and told herself she needed to dig in her bag for a paracetamol, knowing there was a battered packet in there somewhere.

Yanking up the handbrake, Emma rested back, eyeing the white, vast building standing before her with a reluctant sigh, a sigh that said "I don't want to move just yet."

Emma was on a surprise visit, commonplace but never welcomed as much as when they are pre-planned. It sent everyone into a great flap, hurrying about, and stressing, and colleagues were found to be briefing each other on what to say if they were asked any questions. Emma had never been to this hospital before. She had the pleasure of the agency sending her straight back out almost as soon as she had walked in to the office this morning. Her boss, Bob, had wrangled her from walking through the offices. He lazily pulled his arm around her small shoulders and gave almost a "coaching" talk about where he suddenly needed Emma to go today. His worker had furrowed her brow, flustered, but Bob ushered her to his office for a quick briefing.

Only after taking his arm from around her shoulders, they strode to his office. Sitting across from each other with his messy paper-strewn desk between them, Emma crossed one leg over the other and began bouncing her left foot, awaiting the explanation.

Bob never did waste much time; it was a strong bonding point between him and Emma. "Westview General Hospital, the director of the old place is Dr. George Hartmann." He stretched himself out in his office chair, leaning back and slightly bouncing himself behind his busy desk. Emma swallowed, nodding.

"Alright, what's the problem then?" The young woman's boss smirked as he knew she was always one to be quite 'straight' with him, and it provided him with healthy bouts of entertainment, on other times he would find himself relying on Emma to "get it done, girl." The pair got on well.

"Ah, there's been no previous word of your arrival, so it'll be a surprise when you show up." He smiled. Emma tucked her hair behind the top of her right ear before lifting her head to lock eyes with him.

"Why this hospital?"

Bob shrugged. "Hartmann has been lingering under our radar for a while, with all of his strictness on confidentiality he has going on over there." Bob waved his hands about as he talked.

Emma raised an eyebrow, giving a slow nod.

"Element of surprise is all this time around. You'll have nothing to write back about, I suspect," her boss explained with a nonchalant shrug.

"Isn't that the old asylum?" Emma tried, tilting her head with a strain to listen keenly while trying to jog her poor memory. Bob chuckled, resting his intertwined hands on his stomach as he sat back in his battered office chair.

"That's the one!" He waggled a finger in the air with a smile. "I've not had time to print anything off for you, but you can get research done before you head in." Bob stood, stroking down his tie against his blue button- up shirt. "It's a pretty easy job, and you're my girl for it." He grinned.

Emma waited possibly half a second before then standing up, having all she may need to get out on the road and head off, hoping to make good time and again repeating to herself the name of this hospital she would drop in on.

Throwing a kind smile to her boss, Emma established that she was ready to leave. "Cheers, Bob. See you later." She strode off to snatch the shiny folder from the shelf in her office, about the side of half a shoebox before setting off. In her head, Emma was already planning to fill most of the boring paper- work out in the car once she had means to get her phone out and stalk this place up before diving in.

It was a good representation of her personality. Emma enjoyed knowing what she was getting herself in to before jumping in, whether it was her work or personal life. She worked to maintain everything she currently obtained in her life, but didn't ever seem prone to burnout. Her colleagues inside of the office wondered what it was that kept her going. She earned the respect from others through this demonstration of a consistent work ethic.

Pulling out the appropriate forms from within their plastic wallets with stretched out binder holes, Emma slammed the folder shut. Her hand reaching up to slide it back on the shelf with the remaining folders which now had a leaned precariously to the left. Flicking her eyes across the paperwork, turning them over in her hand, Emma's ears pricked when footsteps approaching her space made her pause.

"Emma do you have any spare training forms?" The perky voice came from the doorway of the room. Remaining bent over the folder of her own, Emma didn't turn but instead gave a nod of her head and pointed up to the right, further into the room, indicating the next shelf. She hadn't been startled by the sudden voice disturbing the comfortable quiet of her private workspace. The voice had come from a girl who was older than Emma, and resided a few offices down. Her colleague's name was Karina – who had always wanted to be a nurse but flopped out of university and had backtracked, or forward, into this career somehow.

It took Karina a long time to learn the job. Emma never bothered to pose questions, but Karina bugged her with a constant barrage. Her tireless questions of uncertainty and needing help with organising and filing paperwork appropriately, was enough to give Bob an aneurysm. Karina sucked up to Bob, but failing to ever finish a responsibility caused a feeling of disgruntlement from her colleagues towards her. Emma didn't care for the feelings of others when it came to

Karina., Emma just shrugged her shoulders and smiled, remaining unspoken of her own thoughts.

Karina half-assed her every day, but Emma may have been the only one who didn't run out of patience with her. On this alone, it gave Karina a good reason to forge a friendship of sorts with Emma, as if it was what she owed her for always helping her, or giving in to her begging.

"Orange folder, they're in there," Emma clipped with her forefinger outstretched from the rest, then relaxing her arm down, returning to fiddling with the sheets in the open folder on the desk. Flipping the plastic covered sheets of paper over and motioning her head up and down, side to side scanning, trying to find what she needed. Karina was offput by her friends bland reply, not entertaining the spurt of her high energy.

"Alright boss," she said, as if she expected Emma to laugh. The silence remained as it was before the remark was made. Emma never did appreciate her humour much, her sarcasm wore her out akin to how a child with boundless energy would. Eyes rolling in her skull, Karina stepped in next to where Emma was stood and retrieved the folder from the shelf, effortfully trying not to bump into her busying co-worker.

Emma flipped back through thick chunks of the plastic folders, closing it over and sliding it back in place next to all the others, regaining the neatness of the shelf. Rubbing her hands on her skirt she felt content, giving a pleased smile to herself.

"Where are you off to today?" Katrina asked, her brow paused in a slight wondering furrow.

Emma stood straight and her flat palms wiped down her pencil skirt as she was before being interrupted.

"A place called Westview General, doing a walk in," she said with a nonchalant shrug. Raising her head to meet her annoying co-workers gaze, she leaned against the desk and wrapped her fingers underneath to steady herself.

Karina raised her head and parted her lipstick coated lips, scoffing.

"You have to be kidding me, that's a dick move. You must be pissed about that first thing," Karina revelled with her mouth remaining agape, knowing she would think that Emma would agree with her and begin to slag Bob off.

Katrina annoyed Bob often, she had a poor attitude and it coincided with her work ethic around the office, as Emma and Karina's colleagues regarded her as lazy, whereas Emma was quite a workhorse. Emma smiled slightly, gaze downwards when she spoke.

"Not really, it's nicer to get out of the stuffy office," she said, giving another shrug and tilting her head.

Karina hummed in thought, tipping her head back in a slow nod with the papers she needed in her hands. The atmosphere loosened as the conversation reached a seeming end in Emma's eyes. She was unfailingly relieved.

Emma hurried herself, eager to become scarce from the poor company. Not finding herself in the mood for further chatter, she always asked Emma a barrage of questions. Good days and bad days, she guessed, but knowing that it was all a falsity for prying too deep could vouch Karina, who was younger than Emma, to land on some sensitive grounds.

It was slightly awkward or both of the two women, one who didn't enjoy small talk and beating around the bush, but the other who had to do just that in order to maintain a healthy relationship with her co-worker. Only inside of the office they both let the relationship be what it was, and it rarely escalated further than to only share the non-functional friendship outside of work. Emma would let her fingers loosen their grip underneath the desk edge, the seconds of silence were broken. "Have you been drinking lately?" Karina prosed in a hushed voice while casually leaned against the wall desk. At first, her heart gave a heavy thump but her ears perked up, Emma paused to look down at her feet - sucking her tongue momentarily. Feeling Karina's eyes on her, the question caused Emma to feel invaded and made her cheeks burn and her thoughts to gather at, "You've got a bloody nerve."

She kept her eyes on the brown slip on shoes she had thrown on that morning.

"I care about you, I was thinking we could get coffee tonight after you get back and hang out together, like we would do." When Emma didn't make a movement to suggest a liking to the idea, Karina leaned forward a little. "I thought it would be a nice idea." She shrugged, then looking down beside herself, but her eyes were visible under her heavy glitter-coloured lids. "I can't imagine your evenings at home would be too fun, all cooped up in the house all by yourself..."

Emma closed her eyes momentarily before lifting her gaze, giving a gentle huff and faced the intruding woman – whose eyes were quick to notice her shift in demeanour, putting an end to her monologue. It was hard to calm herself, as Karina had no idea of her struggle when she went home, and Emma for that fact doubted an evening with Karina would be of much better quality.

Karina's eyes focused on Emma's features, scrutinizing but only to fail to notice how Emma was trying not to flinch at her suggestion. Insulting Emma followed with a friendly invite out was a way of softening the mood, and offering her co-worker an olive branch.

Emma sniffed, and stopped leaning against the desk as she refocused, straightening with a purposeful abruptness. "See you later." She spoke in a hushed voice, then briefly flashed her co-worker a smile, gathering the folder and hurrying to get out before there was opportunity for questioning, which no doubt Karina would delve into upon gaining no sudden ripping off of her hand at the chance to go for a drink with her.

Emma felt the offended gaze of Karina's eyes burn into her back as she paced away, beelining to the lift.

"Emma!" She called out after her, now standing in the

walkway between office's, but her call was ignored and Emma continued to rush herself out of view before she could catch her and ask any further invading questions, or dare give her immature co-worker the opportunity to suggest that she was even capable of understanding her struggle.

In response, Karina's outstretched arms fell by her hips, a heavy sigh leaving her agape lips.

## Chapter Two

EMMA SAT in the carpark scanning over the expansive building looming before her. Her apprehensive hand wrapped around the keys, stabbed them into the ignition and twisted, the engine resting under her seat and yanking them out, holding them for a few seconds. Emma grabbed at her phone which was sat in the cupholder, turning it over in her hands with impatience. She was still reeling from her interaction with Karina back at the office, shaking her head at the annoyance her co-worker caused her.

A search on her phone provided her with multiple sources of information through the different published articles and blogs that appeared after a moment's wait.

Her thumb struggled to pick one, hesitating to press upon the glass screen. She discovered that Westview's history was one to revel at, as Dr. George Hartmann had revamped the abandoned building in the late 90's. Previously an asylum turned mental hospital before becoming a fully endowed hospital in 1996, all thanks to Doctor Hartmann. Emma dug further. Discovering the different sources about the "strange" practices which took place, one stuck out to be the paramount importance of confidentiality. According to the many websites, hospital policy practically left patients clueless of their own treatments.

Her thumb paused its scrolling for a moment, her eyes slowed their speed reading and instead started from the top left corner, being intrigued enough to thoroughly examine the article on the screen. Finding herself leaning into the account of an ex-patient's experience inside the walls a few meters away from where her car sat, she hummed. The first impression formed was that the hospital was eccentric and practices remaining old fashioned.

The ex-patient had written about not being told any form of diagnosis, but having to comply with treatments regardless. The patient was told this was part of standard practice as it was engraved into the ethos of the hospital, in effort to keep patients relaxed and stress free. The practice was not traditional at all, and concluding it to be completely unethical, Emma scratched an eyebrow, puzzled for the need of this anonymity. Emma brought the screen towards her face, a frown curling on her lips.

She began to stress, as this would become rather problematic if brought up in discussion – it was going to immediately be an awkward topic to ask about.

Emma thought of Bob's confident nod to her when she had left his office, and felt her lungs deflate, giving a hiss through her teeth. Her job load piled heavier atop her shoulders at that moment, hunched in the seat.

Tireless searching for documents, or a list of policies and procedures, brought nothing back. Emma was surprised to find the hospital didn't even have a website; there weren't any official published documents to be found online. She was uncomfortable heading in blind, only having formed a vague opinion based on a solitary firsthand experience. It seemed that whatever went on inside those walls of the hospital stood tall before her was kept completely private, almost like some construct of deliberate mystery.

The hospital was to be spoken about through formed opinions influenced by chatter and gossip only. It seemed to alienate those outside of the walls, maybe until you walk in.

Clicking her tongue against the roof of her mouth, she was annoyed that her research brought up nothing of proper use. Emma threw her phone into the vacant passenger seat wondering what it was she would walk into.

She released her seatbelt and kicked her leg to the door to stand. A slight wind tickled her, blowing out stray hairs from the yanked up ponytail when she dipped down to grab the folder from the backseat. Locking the car, its hazards gave a confirming orange flash.

Her head rose in the direction of the hospital's main entrance. The sun warmed her face pleasantly while making the walk to the expansive, painted stairs. The wide and long variation of windows allowed plenty of sun to stream inside. It was built purposefully long, the white painted building spreading out at the front, behind having conjoining buildings which linked together in closed off rectangles. The roofs of the different and adjoining buildings were visible over the flattened outer builds at the front.

The space left between these four building walls were gardens for patients to wander about on their ward. At either corner of the square building, there were Victorian-fashioned towers atop the roof, forming a conical shape atop of the mossing stone cylinders with cobbled tops. They looked like little gnome's hats to Emma. Next to the stairs which lead up to the main entrance doors, there were two statues of lions at either side to greet people as they approached. Their mouths were wide and green at the back, bearing teeth that looked ready to crumble. The manes were too, tinted with a dark green from the damp brought on by rain, which gave healthy, dark, thick moss room to flourish at the extremities of the stone animals' bodies.

Emma stood before the automatic glass doors, shaking

herself to smile. They were painted with a thick medical mint green stipe halfway up. Thinking it was a hideous colour, though, it bore into her eyes like a stain that threatened to never wash out. Inside, the shiny, constantly mopped floor had the fluorescent gleam of the light bars above bouncing from them. Emma entered and caught the eyes of the receptionist behind the large white desk, having been peacefully leaning over her keyboard, squinting her eyes at the glaring screen. The receptionist looked a little vexed before she had noticed Emma striding in, her teeth flashing upon making the initial eye contact.

The receptionist looked up from the rim of her reading glasses. "Good morning," she said, breaking into an uneven smile and nudging up her round glasses on the bridge of her nose.

"Morning," Emma clipped. "I'm from the medical council, doing a walk in, if that's alright."

The receptionist pulled a puzzled face, as if figuring out what to do with this surprise visit. The older woman tried to keep her cool, but Emma was able to see that the receptionist did not know what to do, and that Emma had suddenly caused her a bout of stress.

"Oh, yes of course, I'll have to find Dr. Hartmann. He's the administrator of our hospital." The receptionist gestured, walking from behind the desk to meet where Emma was waiting. "Come with me, I will try to find where he is, but he's most likely busy." She babbled with a twirl of her wrist, to which Emma gave a nod. Her eyes wandered around herself in the reception area.

The nervous small talk tired Emma somewhat already, feeling her patience wearing thin far too early.

"That's alright, don't worry about it." Emma smiled, switching the folder over to the crook of her other arm, following the receptionist down the hallway, passing different rooms. The clicking of the receptionist's heels made Emma feel she was following a teacher through the winding halls, giving quite a presence to the otherwise short stature of the receptionist.

"Dr. Hartmann can be hard to get a hold of, he's always helping somebody." The woman gave a short laugh.

Emma peered into the rooms she walked past, only half listening to the babble of the receptionist. By chance the doors were left open.

Her inquisitive peering had her performing strides to keep up with the rushing woman leading her through the halls of the hospital. The walls were painted white with one long hideous medical green strip running along the middle matching the automatic doors, and had a sharp odor of thick lemon bleach from the well-mopped flooring.

The shine glared so hard, people thought the floor itself was made of glass. Some of the rooms Emma passed had double doors held open on their hinges and were larger inside. At the back wall there were full length windows spanning from the floor up to the ceiling, giving patients views of the hospital's well-kept gardens. Emma appreciated the way the sun, beaming in, flooded the floor, warming anyone walking past.

Her mind wandered to the sun shining upon her face, reminding her of those arched windows, the ones Emma had in her bedroom. The old house had the most wonderful windowsills, and Emma was small enough to balance her small bottom upon them. With her button nose practically pressed up against the glass, she gazed down at the driveway that the two family cars stood on. Her writing pad bought from a bargain store upon her thighs, Emma maintained her balance for hours, content enough with the view of the neighbourhood to put up with the sensation of her bottom beginning to ache and go numb.

Emma's pupils dilated under the white lights interrupting the faded corners of her childhood memories. Looking back to the doorway, it appeared again that certain rooms along the hall were bigger, and looked to be socialising areas for patients. Comfortable armchairs were pushed up against the walls and tables and chairs in the middle, while other rooms she passed in the hallway were ward showering rooms. The receptionist rushing away in front caught the attention of a nurse who had bundled up some towels in her arms, emerging from the end of the hall, where it split open.

Being cautious to not make a conscious effort to listen in, Emma was handed over to the care of the nurse rather than continuing on with the nervous receptionist.

"I'll take you to Doctor Hartmann. I'm Nurse Jennifer, by the way." She gave a smile, having passed on her bundle of towels to the receptionist who was heading back up the way Jennifer had intended to go.

Hands were wiped on the front of her plain white pinafore. "Thank you, I'd appreciate that," Emma said, to which she nodded and led her further up the hallway.

"He can tell you what you'll need to know. I'm no good at that stuff," Jennifer laughed as she led Emma to stand by the door of a patient's room. Jennifer knocked with a curled finger, and awaited a response. She smiled while leaning in to the door. "Doctor Hartmann, there's a visitor that needs to see you."

Emma's heard the shuffling from the other side of the door, and a slight effortful metal creak. Her eyes focused in to watch when the white door handle was yanked down, then pulled back, revealing a tall older man, who Emma took to be Westview's administrator – Doctor Hartmann.

"Ah, thank you, Jennifer. Very good." Hartmann smiled wide at the young nurse while closing the door to step out of the room. His voice clipped with a purring German undertone, giving him a slight charm and air of heightened professionalism when he spoke. His voice was smooth, and creamy upon reaching Emma's ears. She decided it to be always pleasant on the ears of listeners who no doubt would do just that – listen.

Jennifer scurried off when Emma managed to refocus, leaving herself and doctor Hartmann in the midst of the hall. The doctor looked upon Emma as he pulled off a pair of white gloves. They snapped around his wrists, one after the other. He waited patiently for Emma to speak, and she almost forgot what she was there for.

With a slight inner shake, Emma managed to refocus.

"My name is Emma Merrick, you must be Doctor Hartmann, the administrator of this hospital?" she questioned.

Hartmann gave an entertained look, almost a smirk. Perhaps he was charmed at the politeness of the young woman before him.

"Yes, you would be correct," he said, his eyes shining for a moment, before duly returning to his point. "I was not told about a visit. May I ask where have you been sent from?" He began walking slowly, and she tagged along by his side, shifting the hefty folder to her other arm again to respond. The offhand remark caused a smile to appear, Emma having half-heartedly expected this reaction – she didn't want it at all, but it didn't surprise her.

"Only from the office down in Oxfordshire."

"Ah, I see. Well, unfortunately I cannot stop as I have to tend to my patients, they are waiting for me."

Emma shuffled from one foot to the other, deciding to cut things short while maintaining the doctor's attention.

"It's a routine inspection, but I will need these forms filled out by the time I leave," she said, lifting the folder held in the crook of her arm.

The doctor squinted, apparently sizing up Emma on the spot. "I need you to do that for me, Doctor."

Hartmann lifted his head in thought, resting a hand behind the space between the shoulder blades to prompt her forward a little, continuing to meander down the hallway.

"Miss Merrick, if your office had told me that you were coming today, I would most likely be available to help you, but

I am rushed off my feet," he explained with a tut while walking, his shoulders raising only to be dropped in a helpless slouch.

Knowing she would not be allowed back to work without the paperwork being filled out, Emma lifted her chin again.

"I'm afraid I have to go, but please walk around and watch how we do things here. You will find it fascinating, I do hope." Hartmann gestured around himself, pausing as he disposed of the crumpled gloves. He must have seen Emma's understanding, or rather irritation, because he stopped walking away in his elongated strides. He turned on his heel meters from her.

"I apologise, but if you want – tonight after I finish we can fill in the paperwork together over a few drinks," Hartmann said, giving her a kind and trying smile.

Within her chest, an echoed thump made her heart kickstart itself to beat faster in her chest cavity. Emma stammered forming words while, a nurse rushed up to Hartmann and his attention left her, turning instead to the nurse who stole his gaze. "Doctor, I need your help with Glen again, please," she pleaded to Hartmann. The nurse looked tired, her blond hair straying from the messy bun she had whacked it into, held together by a blue scrunchie to match her now wide eyes.

Hartmann tutted, closing his eyes in dread, as if to say internally, "Not again."

Emma refrained from smirking at the display of dread upon the man's pleasant face.

"Yes, I will come to his room in a moment," he said, raising his palm to the frantic nurse, who then became less panicked. Blue eyes dropped to his palm and turned on her heel hurrying back to tend to her patient, the thick ribbon-like fabric of the back of her tunic flying out behind her hips. Before he pulled away from Emma completely, he stopped.

"Will you join me in those few drinks tonight, Miss Merrick?" Hartmann smiled with his friendly proposal, his eyes twinkling as she fleetingly met his gaze.

The twinge of his accent when saying her last name gave it an alluring charm. Nobody had ever uttered Emma's last name like that before. Under his eyes, she found herself smiling from the way in which he had spoken it. Emma swallowed, but then began quickly nodding in nervous agreement, trying a smile to not appear as frazzled as she felt by the direct question.

"Yes, okay. I would like that," she said, and Hartmann clasped his hands together.

"Very good. There isn't much left of my day. Enjoy your exploration, Miss Merrick." With that, his pace quickened as the director left in the opposite direction of where she was stood.

That was that, she supposed. She stood alone in the hall-way, sighing, gazing down at the sad folder in her arms, thinking it wasn't wise to go out drinking, of not being allowed to. The surface of her skin had a wave of heat prickle, the increased body heat becoming trapped in her buttoned jacket.

Her shoulders wriggled in an effort to slide it off, folding it over in arm to begin wandering. Unable to help her curiosity, she looked up when passing under the wide double door arch-ways. Emma was slow to read the signs above, informing her of where all the different wards and wings were. The hospital appeared huge; it had to have housed thousands of people when it was an asylum. It seemed to go on forever with the shiny floors and glaring white lights in the long hallways.

The place almost made Emma succumb to a state of dizzi-ness, but she continued wandering through the hallways, watching nurses potter around and tending to patients with clipboards digging into their waists, scribbling away with heads down on their papers. She took in the small details of the patients she began to encounter as she traipsed further, noticing the hospital gowns had differing colours. Some were mint green and others she set eyes on were a light blue color – like a great, deep sea.

# Chapter Three

STRIDING to the middle of the hallway, Hartmann swiftly lead into his office, humming away to himself, continuing to do so when alone, having kicked his door shut with his heel. Edging forwards on his chair to meet with his desk, he crossed his feet underneath. He hunched over, fingers racing to type.

One leg wrestled free and began bouncing, his right hand cupping his chin to rest his elbow on his desk, scanning the screen as he clicked away. Hartmann accessed the medical files – having memorised that her last name was Merrick – and pressed down on the keyboard with a confident smirk.

Hartmann's eyes flicked over the screen when the open tab of hospital records loaded. Sucking in air between the space left by his lips, the screen loaded to reveal multiple women under the same name registered. Hartmann turned himself, so he was able to flick a look over his shoulder before refocusing his attention on his computer.

He scrolled with a hunger, clicking at each name, one after the other and scanning through the details that came in a list of paragraphs. Searching through the different women under the same name, he found one which made him slow his pace altogether. Hartmann paused to read. His lips stilled from their humming, his eyes squinted against the harsh glare from the screen.

Emma's medical history was grittier than Hartmann could have assumed. The young woman had been previously admitted into hospital two years ago, due to going into labour. The doctor sighed, rubbed under his nose with a knuckle, glancing sidewards to scratch the bridge of his nose before refocusing.

Hartmann's eyes set upon a document which revealed a death. His hands froze on the mouse and his eyes wandered to notice additional admittances for alcohol poisoning on a few different occasions only a few weeks after the date of a death was recorded.

Emma had lost her infant in a stillbirth.

The doctor flung back from the screen as if he received a punch in the chest. His eyes scrunched and his knuckles whitened at the curling of his fingers away from the keyboard.

He closed the tab, and leaned back in his chair, retiring his eyes from the screen. He bit his bottom lip, chewing at it in thought. A resonating sadness filled the man in his chair and weighed him down into the leather. Doctor Hartmann pulled himself back over his desk and forced himself to read further. There were multiple listed admission dates into hospitals, and he noticed with interest that the most recent one had been last weekend. The doctor scrutinised the small letters upon his screen.

Emma had been admitted due to an alcohol overdose, sinking into an unconscious and unresponsive state. Hartmann exhaled the wary breath he had been holding in. He licked his lips in thought, before flicking his eyes back to the glowing screen. Short and poignant notes indicated Emma was to keep on with her therapist for her struggle with alcoholism.

Emma had been showing very worrying signs of constant relapses and now increasing worries for the health of her liver functioning. The damage to her liver if she relapsed once more would be a violent kick, one of the few it gives before packing in. Hartmann tutted, resting back in his chair. Such a gorgeous woman plagued under her smiles, which he thought of as beautiful. He thought back on when he had asked her to have a few drinks over the paperwork she had asked him to do. A bundle of nerves began to unravel, twiddling his thumbs atop his stomach, internally struggling with the realisation. He looked to the screen, and stared at the typed up notes. The screen darkened, and the doctor reluctantly turned his eyes away.

Hartmann leaned back in his office chair again, the chair groaning out a loud creak. It was 4:45, fifteen minutes until he finished for the day. His fingers antsy, they began to absent-mindedly thrum on the armrest of the chair. He closed the computer tabs and the screen to shut it down. For now, Hartmann would resign in the darkening. The doctor stood, shoving his chair back. Twisting around to the back wall near the right side of the door, he yanked open the metal cabinet, stretching it out with a shunt, and revealing alphabetically ordered files. Tracing a finger along the tops of the papers, he traced up until he hit the "A" section.

Separating the papers to what he needed, he peeked at the contents when pulling the small plastic folder out, eyes rolling over the innards with a frown. He ripped out a sheet and strode back over to his desk to place it beside his keyboard. Turning back around, he kicked the metal drawer shut with the toe of his shoe and gathered up his belongings, which he stored in an automatic safe by the front wall of his office. Hartmann popped what he needed from his locked up possessions into his white coat pocket. While fumbling to shove his hands into his pockets, he mumbled to himself about having left his other coat in the back of his car.

Hartmann clicked the light off at the wall, pausing as he stood in the doorway before shutting the door. He continued on with humming to himself merrily, almost singing under his breath. The doctor tossed his office keys up and caught them mid-air after locking the door.

He straightened his jacket as he walked, headed for where he last saw Emma. He was eager to leave, for as far as Hartmann was concerned, his work would only become more complicated outside when getting around to filling in the paperwork with Emma. His dress shoes made an authoritative noise as he made his strides, which he never failed to find joy in.

Ah, it's the small things.

## Chapter Four

EMMA RAPPED her fingers on the white table in front of her while she sat in the empty dining room of the hospital. Her eyes flicked to her wrist and sighed, impatient and bored of her own company in the spacious room.

She found she was beginning to get worked up. It wasn't in her nature to be patient, and she found herself vexed by her own lack of such as she waited in the empty room. Emma knew why she was feeling so anxious. The back of her jaw clamped down and her wisdom teeth ground together in her annoyance.

Emma threw herself up from the chair and wandered through the vacant eating hall, heading towards the empty buffet area to wander a little less aimlessly, at least not circling the tables like some sort of a wackadoodle. All in an effort to ease her feelings of mounting anxiety, but she failed to calm herself.

"Ah, Emma," the voice came, echoing around her head from within the tall room. Her heart jumped in her chest, ripped from her winding thoughts. Emma instinctively turned around to see Dr. Hartmann approaching her with the corners of his lips upturned.

"Hello, Doctor, have you finished early?" she asked.

His hands by his side, he nodded as he stepped forwards, his pace having slowed upon closing the space between them both.

"Absolutely. I don't normally, but as you know it's been hectic and, as such, I took the pleasure of going home early today." He smiled, perching himself on one of the tables.

Arm aching, Emma lifted the folder and held it back into the crook of her arm after adjusting, beginning the slow walk out of the dining hall. "That makes sense, I appreciate you helping me out of hours." Emma looked up to doctor Hartmann as he walked on the right side down the illuminated hallway, noticing his lips pulling into a smirk.

"No bother at all, I'll be enjoying the beers you fetch me," he joked, laughing to himself.

At the mention of alcohol, Emma jerked out a sudden laugh, it having erupted from her throat in an eruption of nerves.

"Yes, ah, it shouldn't take long though, there's nothing too in depth." She rambled with heat in her cheeks, yanking the conversation back to the point of the affair.

Hartmann and Emma walked together to the receptionist desk where earlier she had met the skittish older woman, who was now chatting to a patient with his right arm held up in a sling.

When the man noticed Emma, he also looked to Hartmann standing at her side, and gave a kind smile. She widened her lips in a friendly beam.

"Are you off now, doctor Hartmann?" The receptionist greeted him with a relaxed smile as she neatened paperwork in her hands, banging it on the desk.

Hartmann nodded, resting an arm on the desk. "I am. Thank you so much for today, Andrea. A star as always," he praised with a bright smile.

Emma noticed the older woman's cheeks grow brighter in

colour, and she gave a wide, but shy, smile which made her eyes wrinkle at the edges.

The receptionist's smile showed no teeth, but perhaps her teeth were not as pleasant as Hartmann's. She flapped a hand at Hartmann and tutted, rolling her eyes in her display of flattery.

"You get off home, I'll see you bright and early, in the morning."

The receptionist smiled again with a nod, while Emma could not help but notice the woman enjoyed the attention from Hartmann, who already had his attention back to her.

"Let's go," he prompted, revealing his car keys from his pocket, curling his fingers around them.

Emma looked at the doctor, with his pinched cheeks as he met her gaze, and smiled. She could see he was excited at the moment, and felt something slightly similar building in her chest – which she assumed were just nerves.

Both the doctor and the smaller woman left through the automatic doors that one of the pair had walked through only a few hours earlier. Emma paused halfway down the few steps and dug a hand into her small shoulder purse, looking clumsy when digging for her keys.

Hartmann was patient, but he suggested something else while she dug around the bottom of her bag.

"Why don't you come in my car? I can drop you back here after we're done."

He was met with an adamant shaking of the head, Emma having grabbed the keys, tucking a straying few hairs behind her ear. Relaxing at having found her keys, Emma gave a smile. "No, that's okay. I'll follow your lead behind," she told him, walking from him down the steps to her car. Swinging her door open, she placed the file down and threw her purse onto the passenger seat. She turned as Hartmann gave a laugh.

"Ah, so stubborn, Miss Merrick!" he joked, waggling a finger as if to teasingly scold. His fist opened wide and flat.

"Are you certain? I don't mind one bit." He gestured towards his car with his open, upturned palms. Emma again nodded from over the roof of her car, holding onto the roof to steady her frame.

"One-hundred percent, I'll see you there," she said, to which he seemed to laugh, and left her wondering if she had offended him. Situating herself, she shook the thought from her head, and twisted her key into the ignition. Emma eyed Hartmann when his head ducked into his car, and she prompted herself to begin reversing. She had to pause to shove her seatbelt over her chest, calves aching from pressing on the clutch. With a thrumming heart, Emma left Westview General's carpark tailing behind the doctor.

As Emma followed behind Hartmann in his smart sleek car, the journey getting shorter, her mouth began to dry. She vowed to herself about levels of control, the control she needed to harness to continue on. The paperwork was the purpose, and she would not be giving in to the pangs of urge. This was going to be a professional chat, regardless of where it takes place. Emma told herself she would not break professionalism, and repeated her therapy vows under her breath.

Down a long country road, on the left hand side ahead, becoming larger loomed a red-bricked pub with brown painted windows, the car park packed. Emma slowed the car, pulling in and peering at the families sat on the different types of outdoor tables dotted around the beer garden, enjoying their assorted drinks in the setting summer sun. Emma pulled the handbrake up and removed the key from under the steering wheel, pausing for a second. She shook herself a little when her nerves had caused her to zone out, staring at nothing, just sitting in the car.

Her nerves sparked when she heard a car door slam, and quickly snapped her head to see Hartmann bent over, his hands digging around in the boot of his car. Her heart calmed. With a sigh, she pushed the door open and swung her legs out to stand. Turning around, she saw Hartmann approaching from where he had parked his car. She pressed hastily with her thumb on the button on the key, the flashing headlights confirming her car locking.

Doctor Hartmann adorned a smart black coat over his white outfit. He still looked like a doctor, albeit more lax, but not enough to let Emma lower her defences. This made her a little more relaxed, in a way – as it could be taken evidently that it was still a formal meeting. He wasn't wearing jeans and a top; he was still in his professional clothes. The sight of his outfit would pull Emma through this meeting, leaning on his formal attire as a reminder if her mind wandered away from the purpose.

"Got everything you need?" Doctor Hartmann asked.

Emma held out the folder. "Yep. I promise this won't take long, I've got to head back to the office after we finish here," she lied as he kindly held open one of the double doors for Emma to head in. She was already flattered by the simple gesture. Hartmann bypassed her comment, raising his head above the crowds to search the pub. A lurch in Emma's stomach forced her to breathe in the comforting smells of alcohol lingering, mixed with the upholstery of the chairs and wooden furniture. Hartmann walked to the bar and awaited for the bartender to finish serving his last customer, rapping his bank card on the wood.

Emma gave the woman a passing smile, moving out of the way as to not cause her to drop any of the three Prosecco glasses she held. Upon passing Emma, the woman adorned a wide grin and mouthed a "thank you."

Emma's eyes lingered behind where Hartmann stood, giving her view of the areas surrounding the bar. It wasn't busy to the point of overcrowding, but the day's afternoon hours had not passed by yet. The young bartender wrapped his hand around the lever of a draught beer keg and nodded towards Hartmann.

"What'll you have to drink, Emma?" Hartmann turned to her as the young lad stood opposite, trying not to watch the pair make a decision. Hesitating for a second too long, Emma tumbled out with a less than satisfactory drink choice, "A diet Coke for me please." Pulling on a smile directed towards the bartender, who nodded in response and knelt down to grab the correct glass. "Ice and lemon in your drink?" he asked, running a hand through his curly fringe.

"Wait, sorry," Hartmann interrupted, making Emma cringe. She felt her shoulders shrink. He turned to her, taking her by a shoulder so she was facing him too.

"Emma, I'm buying our drinks, and I did not come with a child. What're you going to have?" he encouraged, making her shift her weight from one foot to the other at his questioning.

"Just the Coke. Honestly, I have to get back to work after we're done here." Emma cut him off, standing her ground on the point of having alcohol.

Hartmann pulled an unimpressed face, and the young bartender was now serving another few people on the far right of Hartmann and Emma. Hartmann let out a healthy laugh. "Stop being so uptight, Emma!" he scolded again. "Now, what can I get you to drink?" he tried again, making her shrink under him, resonating in the humiliation, washing her cheeks to a blush.

Emma lowered her chin to swallow, peering into the fridges behind the bar. She wished to not see her reflection in the glass. Her cheeks cooled, and a hesitant finger pointed to the label of a fruity cider in the fridge. She threw a haphazard smile at the bartender as he yanked it from the rows.

Hartmann tilted his head. "What? No wine? You struck me as a wine lover, Emma," he joked, feigning surprise.

While he feigned surprise at her choice, Emma feigned contentment, scathingly flicking her eyes to the open bottle and a glass of ice beside.

Her shoulders raised in a mock-innocent shrug, giving a shaking laugh "I'm sorry to let you down on that one."

He turned to her, nodding away from where the pair stood as if to tell Emma to go. "Go grab us a table, I'll be over in a sec," he said as the bartender came back over to Hartmann.

Emma traipsed around the bar, which was shaped in a long curve, only straightening in the middle before curving around again. There were tables for two people to the right side, opposite the bar. The wall had a cute fireplace, and on either side there were two more tables, but suited to seat more people around them. Looking to the right there was a set of stairs with a battered wooden banister which led to another area, one which had a long plush fabric sofa running along the left wall.

There was a longer, wooden table at the far left corner of the sofa and she decided this was where they would sit. Emma slid herself along the sofa and placed her belongings with little care, throwing her purse and folder next to the arm of the sofa. Examining the space, looking around at the vacant tables yet to be filled, Emma opened her folder and began gathering together the specific documents she needed from the plastic wallets. Her actions were rushed and she took a second to calm her nerves. All on edge, she jerked her head when hearing the stairs creak, and she set eyes on Hartmann smiling away to himself.

He approached, placing the drinks on the table. Her heart collided with her lungs, providing her with a sensation akin to a hot punch in her sternum. Emma felt the walls crash around her, seeing he had ignored her request for the low alcohol drink she had chosen, and instead had brought her half a glass of white wine.

"There we go," he said, sitting himself down, wrapping his fingers around his pint and lifting it to his lips. Pausing before his lips set on the rim of the glass, he brought his pint forwards, stopping mid-air, and tilted the foamy head to Emma.

"Cheers."

Emma's right leg began to involuntarily bounce, straining not to bite down on her bottom lip. She avoided looking at the glass. Emma felt her resistance vanishing as Hartmann sat with his pint in the air alone, but the man retracted his hand.

"I know you said, but it's my treat," Hartmann said, giving a strained face.

Emma's eyes looked to him fleetingly, only to not allow the man to catch her wavering nerves faced with the glass. She tried to pull on a trembling smile, but finding her nerves electrified she couldn't hold her jumping muscles in place.

"Only the one can't hurt, hm?" He grinned, his hand resting around his pint which he now had back on the table.

His cockiness provided Emma with a feeling towards the man as if licking sandpaper. The sensation fuelled her to prove herself wrong on the anxieties that weighed on her so heavily.

Finding strength to rest her leg from its energetic bouncing, Emma took the wine glass in hand and held it up, smiling. Hartmann perked up in his seat, smiling back at her as he brought his pint to meet the wine glass. "Cheers." The pair of professionals went again. The glasses in hands clinked together, reeling to bring them to the lips. Emma hesitated on the first sip while Hartmann was grateful to gulp several mouthfuls down at once.

Tipping the glass forwards, it slid down the back of her throat, burning when swallowed. The young woman exhaled through her nose and placed the glass down, shaking. Emma grabbed the sheets from beside where she had left them resting out of their plastic wallets, and turned them over to Hartmann.

"Ah, is this everything?" he asked glancing over the papers.

Her head bowed and she offered a hum in a non-verbal agreement, flicking her eyes to the wine glass with her hands resting in her lap. Emma allowed herself to lay back, relaxing into the sofa during the silence. The music playing in the background was distasteful pop, emanating from the speakers in the ceiling corners of the room.

Emma plucked her pen from inside of the folder where she normally kept it. "Anything wrong?" she asked, eager to fill the silence. Her eyes looked to a family walking in behind Hartmann, having come in from the beer garden, and aiming to go out the front door, rather than around the back of the building. It was quicker that way.

"No, no, this is fine. I can fill this in for you no problem, Emma," he informed her, removing his black coat and hanging it over the back of the chair, then fiddling with the pen.

"Thank you, Doctor Hartmann. It's mainly health and safety stuff, plus minimal details on your staff," Emma explained, avoiding the impression of loading him down with a pile of awful paperwork to battle through.

Pausing from reading the papers to look over at her, he said, "Call me George." He paused before smiling, his lips falling. "Are you alright, Emma? You look like you have seen a ghost."

Emma straightened, loosening her lips to give a smile as he drew her away from her thoughts. "Sorry, I don't mean to be so rude; I had gotten distracted."

He put his head back down, turning the papers over and reading the back over. "That's fine, Emma. I'll fill this in for you, but first, let us enjoy our drinks," he announced, placing the paperwork to the spare seat at his side.

She eyed his hands cupped around the glass. She reminded herself he bought the drink for her, and that it was very kind of him to do so. Emma wrung her hands under the table, her mind racing to look at the chilled glass again.

"How is your wine? I was hoping you'd like the Chardonnay. I don't drink wine myself," he chatted with her, sipping from his pint.

Glancing to her glass, she nodded. "It's lovely, thank you. You shouldn't have done that," she continued when the doctor chuckled in response.

"Ah, Miss Merrick, it's the very least I could do." He smiled, and with his encouraging, bright smile Emma wrapped her fingers around the stalk of her wine glass.

---

Emma traced around the circular edge of her now empty wine glass with her finger as Hartmann turned his phone around to face her. She had ended up finishing a bottle of wine much quicker than he had managed seven pints.

"There's my daughter. You see her hair? It's just like yours." He nodded towards his phone screen.

Emma gazed upon the screen, gasping when she set eyes on a little girl with long brown wavy; almost curly – hair. Hartmann's daughter stood short at a kitchen playset brandishing a slice of plastic chocolate cake on a little green plate. She presented it to the camera with outstretched arms, a beautiful cheeky grin to accompany the dessert.

"Oh, George, she's beautiful," she whispered in admiration of his daughter.

Hartmann looked forlorn. His lips were curved up into a smile but his eyes looked glassy. He turned his phone off and shoved it into his jacket pocket, twisting back around in his chair to grab his pint glass. Without hesitation, he gulped down the mouthful of beer at the bottom, throwing it down his throat. When he put the empty glass back on the table, he wiped at the corners of his lips.

"She passed away twenty years ago," he said, scratching his stubble-lined jaw.

Emma's heart dropped, and she felt a wave of heat swelter her as heart rate increased after the drop within her chest. Emma leaned in, swallowing the acid from the wine zipping at the back of her tongue. "I'm so sorry," Emma apologised. "She has an amazing daddy."

Hartmann smiled half-heartedly, his lips loosely yanked up, but the motion was raw.

Emma felt a sudden heaviness inside herself, but swallowed to put a stop to the feeling.

"Ah, don't worry, I only wish to make her proud every day," he clipped in his German-tinged accent. He had his left arm bent on the table flat, and his right hand around his beer glass.

Emma leaned forward and placed a hand over his arm, feeling touched by this admission. Her throat tightened and eyes pinched with hot tears. "I know she'd be proud," Emma whispered, staring into his eyes, but he wouldn't meet hers.

Hartmann nodded, straightening in his chair, pulling his arm away and then throwing the remaining drops of beer back and slammed his glass down.

Emma's eyes dipped to her empty glass, biting the flesh of her lip. She juggled her thoughts in her aching brain.

"Another one, Emma?" he asked, now smiling and seeming to have rescued himself from the conversation becoming too emotionally upsetting and deep, leaving an uncomfortable dip in the conversation.

Emma knew she could put off that question forever, but at the rate she was going, a taxi home would have to be the price she paid. Emma didn't want to leave – she wanted to drink some more; she could keep going.

Quickly with two fingers, Emma plucked her bank card and presented it to Hartmann, who was already backing out of the chair and brushing down his shirt with his palms. She looked up at him, annoyed. "It's my turn, please." In her attempt to be stern, she met Hartmann with eyebrows furrowed,= but sounded more like she was pleading with him.

He put his hand up, stopping her argument in their tracks.

Emma's outstretched arm wavered.

"Emma, have another drink with me?" he smirked.

With a groan, her hand fell to the table in defeat as he strode to the top of the stairs. He winked at her when looking back, then disappeared from her view to join the crowd gathered around the bar. Emma let herself smile, shaking her head as it remained. Emma took her glass in hand and tried for the few gathered droplets of wine left before the glass collector made their rounds.

## Chapter Five

THE BUSTLING PUB moved in a blur; the tables surrounding them were now all full. Emma tried to focus on Hartmann, but within a matter of seconds he would have a twin, who liked to play a game of peek-a-boo behind his back, switching from peeking from one shoulder to the other behind his back.

Emma swayed, pulling her head back from poking Hartmann about and drawing in a breath. Her vacant eyes were dragged to Hartmann when he returned part of a silly argument that Emma had begun.

"Emma, look, there's my signature." Hartmann pushed a small piece of folded receipt paper over to her side of the table, and burst out laughing, the ripples leaving her bent over the table. Hartmann sighed, apparently tiring of Emma ridiculing him.

She pinched the sheet and held up the small paper to him, pointing to it.

"What's your doctory handwriting like? I can hardly make out your signature," Emma stated, becoming overexcited by the need to prove her silly point.

Hartmann took his glass of bubbling beer in hand and tipped some mouthfuls back before answering, eyes on Emma while he glugged. His glass banged down on the table before he spoke, the pint glass held now by an increasingly clumsy hand. Hartmann leaned back in his chair, smirking.

"You show me your signature then." He folded his arms.

Instantly Emma pulled the paper back from where it lay between the pair on the table and wobbled the bar staff's biro pen in hand, scribbling her signature down, drunkenly enlarged when she was finished.

"Look, see. You can read mine clearly," Emma argued, shoving the paper back in his face.

Hartmann laughed, shaking his head as he took it from her small fingers, holding it between his thumb and index finger. His eyes narrowed.

"That's because it looks like a ten year old wrote it out." He chuckled as he got his beer and held it to himself, smirking before he brought the pint to his lips.

Rolling her eyes, Emma's jaw unhinged in shock, clearly furthering his entertainment. With the bottle of wine almost finished – half a glass or so left in the bottom now – a live band organised for the evening began playing. Emma's attention span was snatched, leaning forward on the sofa to eye the band, rounding up for the second half of their songs.

Emma had been watching people rise from their chairs, to hurry to dance, in couples and groups of women wobbling around in their little cliques.

Without thinking, she shoved her folder and handbag to the other side of herself, the folder almost sliding from the leather sofa onto the floor.

Hartmann's head jerked up from looking at his phone, as Emma stood beside him.

"Come on, let's have a dance!" she said with a grin, grabbing at his wrist, and egging him on to join her on the makeshift dance floor.

Hartmann looked impressed by the confidence she exhumed, and a surprised smile formed on his face.

He allowed Emma to keep hold of his wrist. Other people sat around looking at them, laughing and smiling as they most likely understood what was going on by the scenario unfolding. Men sitting with their girlfriends and wives smiled and flicked their eyes from Emma to Hartmann, before turning to sip at their pints with a smirk. Hartmann felt blokes' eyes on him, with Emma pouting like a petulant, drunken child.

"Please, I wanna have a boogie with you." She pestered him with another pull at his wrist, having elongated the "please", and watching people gather to dance around the band all cheering and clapping. Those who were on the floor now shrank back to their tables that held their drinks safe.

An older lady in a flowery black and white dress dabbed at her shiny forehead, where sweat had begun to bead over her makeup.

"Alright, let's go then – you lead the way." Hartmann gave in, swigging from his beer and placing it back down on the table when Emma finally let go of his wrist, her arms flying up in celebration.

A small, excited noise, more a high-pitched squeal, escaped her mouth. Hartmann frowned at the carelessness she displayed.

Bounding to the stairs, Emma was careful to steady herself going down. She turned back to see her dancing partner leaned over the couple on the next table, figuring to look after the table so nobody would take their spot.

In front of the band there was space, the bar staff having moved two of the tables providing ample room for both the band, and space for people to dance.

The band of two men were in high demand of the pubs in the area, still. The last time that Emma saw them play was the month she went into therapy, but that was over a year ago now, and she was still seeing the same therapist. Next to the guitarist's brown leather shoes sat a pint of water next to one of the amps closest to the stairs. Feeling a smirk spread across her face, she thought, "You better not knock that over."

Hartmann came down the few stairs, and Emma reached out for his hand as other people began to crowd the space, beginning to dance around. Giving a cheer, feeling the music completely, Emma loosened up further with a tip of her head, laughing and dancing with Hartmann.

"My moves are better than yours!" she teased, sticking her tongue out. Hartmann paused, raising an eyebrow.

"I don't think so, Miss Merrick," he retorted, jiving with his arms and torso moving in sync.

Raising her arms above her head and hips swaying, she almost bumped into another woman beside her.

Hartmann wrapped his arm around Emma, laughing when she struggled to steady herself from her feet running away with her.

The doctor held her small frame up amidst the crowd. He stood before Emma, both dancing equally as mediocre as the other. Hartmann's cheeks flushed as he moved forwards, and Emma gave up an ear for him to whisper into.

Eyes widening at Emma's hips swaying, he leaned into her as she slowed. "You weren't kidding about those moves!" he hissed.

Emma laughed, standing there with Hartmann in the middle of the dance crowd, unsure of whether she was to take it as friendly banter or a nudging flirt.

Emma recoiled from leaning into him and turned to the band in appreciation, clapping along to the beat. She felt a weight snaking over her shoulder, and she stood up straight, seeing his white shirt sleeve draped over her. Emma pushed Hartmann's hand from where it lay on her shoulder, gently shoving him off. His gaze switched from looking cheerfully to the band to her at his side, still with a bemused look on his face. His features told her he expected a different reaction, and the one Emma had given wasn't the one he'd hoped for.

Emma left the dance floor, wobbling up the small few steps to where their still-empty booth was. Her eyes rolled back in aggravation, a careless hand swiping at the wine glass. Hartmann followed behind, her spine slumping against the back of the long, empty sofa. She eyes the bottle of wine and knew what was left in there.

Hartmann pulled his seat out from where he had tucked it before going for the dance, and watched her grab at the neck of the bottle.

"Be careful, Emma," he uttered, clasping his hands together in front of him on the table as she poured the half glass of wine.

Emma found it easy to ignore him, focusing instead on having the drink she had poured. Hartmann sat still opposite her, and he watched while she tipped the wine down her throat. Emma proudly, but a little violently, slammed the empty glass on the table and stood, staggering to the point she almost fell back down. She hedged her bets, turning and doing a jump down the stairs, elongating her legs out to skip the one in the middle.

Hartmann eyed people staring and meeting her with harsh looks. Continuing to scowl when she barged past, and through people who stood with their drinks in hand.

"Emma!" Hartmann called out behind her when she wandered out in to the dark, wet streets of St. Gridgevey.

Unsteady on her feet, Emma stood in the middle of the barren streetside, looking across the road to the taxi service building. She held back a scream when a hand took her wrist, having let her arms dangle at the side of herself. Rather than letting a high pitched, fear-fuelled scream out, Emma twisted around with a face like thunder to see Hartmann standing there. His face may have held concern, but she could only see his eyes piercing into her.

"Emma what are you doing?" he asked, searching her face.

He hunched his shoulders in a clear effort to gauge where her eyes were staring.

Agitated, Emma growled, as if it wasn't completely obvious. "What do you think I'm doing?" she barked, yanking her wrist free from his hand. His lips parted when the words struck him.

Emma stormed towards the road where the taxis sat waiting. She spotted a driver on his phone while he was parked. She charged into the road, without checking to see if cars were coming.

"Wait! Emma, stop," Hartmann's voice came, causing people's heads to perk up from the other side of the road, wondering what the commotion was. He jumped in front of Emma, getting in the way of her charging into the road to cross over.

Emma's arms froze at her side, fuelling a growing fire.

"You need to come with me," Hartmann tried, outstretching his arms at either side of her. He hesitated touching her, but his hands curled at her arms, willing to hold her in place.

Amidst her upset, Emma found Hartmann to be unreasonable in trying to control her rage. She felt her throat close and begin to ache, tears falling down her cheeks. She yanked at her sleeve to soak them up.

"Do you think you're the only person whose lost someone?!" Emma screamed in his face, anger getting the best of her, as mascara-streaked tears streamed down her cheeks.

Hartmann stopped, his hands lowering as he looked at the young woman, jaw falling open. "Emma, please calm down."

He seemed to beg, heightening her annoyance. In a swift move, Emma smacked his arm down from where it was outstretched to stop her again from walking into the road. She staggered through the street, past the closed coffee shop and high street buildings.

Hartmann once again jumped in front of her tiny figure as

she took massive steps into the street. Every step Emma now took, he took one in front, moving backwards and stopping her from moving forwards without him. His arms were outstretched again. Her eyes filled with tears.

"I want to go home," Emma sobbed, wiping at her streaked face again. Her eyes clocked a taxi pulling up on the opposite side of the road and she sprang out to the side of Hartmann, stepping into the road.

"Jesus Christ, Emma!" Hartmann screamed.

Jutting out the bottom of her jaw, Emma twisted around to shout at Hartmann. Before she could get a word out, her knees were slammed together as tyres screeched to a halt and Emma's frame was knocked onto its side.

Hartmann leapt out to the car that had knocked Emma over, cringing to see the small woman collapse so heavily.

Emma's skull smacked the road and the impact sent her skidding along the cold, wet gravel.

Emma saw her crumpled shadow elongated out on the wet gravel from the headlights behind, and she burst out crying again, trying to use her hands to push her torso up. Bits of gravel dug into the flesh of her hands and she sniffled, crying like a baby as Hartmann coaxed her in the middle of the road.

"Stay still, Emma do not try and get up," Hartmann's voice ordered, his voice echoing into her head.

Whoever had been driving the car had a poor reaction time, being a few seconds too slow, and Emma had been too fast to jump out in front of him. The road was soaking wet from the rain and he had knocked Emma such that half her torso lay in a puddle. Emma half heard muffled, but profuse apologies, but lay still on the gravel with tears rolling onto the ground. A lone thought told her she was going to throw up.

She saw Hartmann had an ear to his phone, jabbering away and pacing a few steps up, and then turning around to retrace them.

## Chapter Six

WHEN EMMA STIRRED, moving limbs she forgot she had through her slumber, the first feeling to overtake her was that of loathing. The loathing of self, piling atop her shoulders the minute she raised from the bed, arms reaching out in front of her and groaning, her head aching with the pressure.

The top of her tongue felt rough, throat dry, and she assumed that her breath must have smelt foul.

Emma's chin fell to her chest, lowering her head to feel the force of her aching brain throw itself against the walls of her skull. It pushed and throbbed, a grimace stretching her dry lips against the plaque coating her teeth. Failing to be surprised that when Emma had opened her eyes to see the bed she was in was that of a hospital's.

The wall in front was that horrible seventies green colour. Upon sitting, Emma looked around and all the rest was white. She lowered her head, looking at the thin white bedsheet which covered her, and rubbed her fingers over the fabric. She plucked it, and ripped the sheet from her body.

Next, her eyes set upon a pink, loose-fitting gown. The material was papery and creased, indicating it had been unfolded not long before. Humiliation flooded her, letting out a groan as the sensation of her self- loathing increased. In the silence of the room, Emma turned her head to the left of the bed to scan a white set of drawers with a glass of water which looked untouched.

Sighing, her brow fell and her neck grew clammy, turning again to look along to where the drawers ended. They met with the white wall which had a tall, rectangular window over to the side, the sunlight streaming in and aimed over where the bed was placed, letting that area bask in sunlight.

Under the thin sheet, Emma's calves were warmed. The hideous green wall in front of the bed had a small sink attached, and a tall mirror behind the two taps – next to it was a white wardrobe. Emma was grateful not to see her own reflection, thinking it would be best to avoid mirrors today.

Plastered on the wall beside the mirror, hung a white canvas with the image of a blooming lily on a dark green pad in the middle of a deep blue painted pond. The watercolours rippled to reach the edge of the canvas, and left the remainder for the imagination to continue.

Lifting a knuckle to her eyesockets, she rubbed an eyeball to see clearer. Emma stared at the painting on the canvas, her head tilting when she thought she saw the lily motion itself as if bobbing atop the water.

She blinked in the suffocating quiet, feeling her legs ache as her sense of confusion eased. Through the fuzz of memory loss, she began to piece together the events of the previous evening. She expected to hear voices through the walls, but nothing apart from the dead silence reached her ears. She was anxious to know what time it was, but was unable to hazard a guess from the surroundings of the room.

Emma ripped the cover fully from her legs, retracting her hand, her eyes fixated on a white plastic band which hung itself loosely around her wrist. Holding her wrist frozen in mid-air, she frowned. The band widened in the middle where it had written some of her basic personal details. Underneath those, it stated, "Dr Hartmann."

Emma examined herself then, noticing a cotton ball taped to her left inner elbow. She tugged at the corner of the white tape, before ripping the cotton ball off, seeing a small red dot of browning blood soaked into the cotton.

Lips creasing, she went to moisten her dry lips, sticking her tongue and wiping saliva along the drying surface. Her tongue was coated with a bitter film which rubbed off on the roof of her dry mouth. A groan escaped her, hunched in the bed. Emma clasped a hand to her forehead, motioning sweaty fingers back and forth on her aching forehead. She twisted around to stand, snatching the glass of water and gulping the water down.

Slamming the glass back down, she leaned against the chest of drawers, eyes closed upon feeling the blood rush through her ears. The water pushed her body into motion, eyes closed while she felt her insides welcome the liquid. The liquid was not alcoholic, and helped her feel better immediately. The hospital gown she adorned hung down to the middle of her shins upon opening her eyes. The floor seemed to have a heartbeat. Emma waited for the pounding behind her eyes to die down before attempting to move again for fear of being sick.

Emma's eyes wandered over to the window, the sunlight hurting her eyes while approaching, and peered out to see a vast and beautiful garden. The soles of her fleshy feet pulsed against the hard floor. She winced, for the sun was out in all its beaming glory.

Eyes adjusting, Emma must have seen a wind, as a great big oak tree had its smaller branches wavering back and forth.

The grass underneath the sprawling, crooked arms glowed while patients of the hospital sat on white benches. Some sat with legs folded at the knee, bouncing the foot of the leg on top of the other. Others sat side by side, leaning back against the metal. Emma could not spot anybody else sitting on the benches she had view of. The remainder of the garden curled out of sight.

Coming away from the window, she grimaced again, the corner of her top lip curling upon exhaling loudly. She looked upon the bed when she turned, but couldn't imagine crawling back between the sheets. Having lost interest in looking outside, she looked to the wardrobe next to the sink. Emma wanted to sleep her hangover off, but standing she felt unwell at the idea of her acidic stomach being thrown back when she would lie down again. The fear of being sick wracked her. Decision finalised, she would remain up for the day. Her feet unsure of how to direct her, hands flew out before bumping into the wardrobe. Emma's hands formed a grip on the handles and pulled open the tall doors, furrowing her brow to see shelves, and barren coat hangers.

Fingers loosening, she allowed the doors to close.

She spurred herself to go and find Hartmann despite her zombie-like state. Humiliation of her actions the previous night wracked her clouded brain, and felt her stomach burn in embarrassment, making her hesitant to leave the room at all. Her legs froze from making any movements, eyes shut while her breath halted. She focused on a deep churning sensation.

She had adjusted to being hungover often, but the one she was suffering from today was bringing forward a new, unsound type of pain and self-hatred.

She swallowed what little saliva she gathered. She struggled to erase the thought from her mind whilst wrapping a hand around the doorknob. Twisting it to the left with a shaky exhale, the confirming click allowed her to pull open the door.

She stepped out into the hallway, looking to the left and then to the right through squinted eyes. The hallway was bare and there were no nurses walking up or down, from either side when she turned her head. She understood why she had heard no voices – there seemed to be nobody else but her. Fingers pressed hard against her aching skull, she stepped out of the doorway. Emma wondered what ward she was on, if any at all. The hall behind her stretched far, so she figured she must be on a particular ward. Searching to the top of the closest double doorway for guidance, it only gave directions to the other sections of the hospital. Barely internalising a groan, she continued down the hallway, rubbing tirelessly at her forehead to ease the pummelling she was receiving.

Reaching further down, the white walls with the medical green strip along them changed to hallways having entirely glass walls. Daring to peer through them, the windows over-looked private gardens with four walls towering over them like the view out of the bottom of a cardboard box.

Feeling her stomach flip, she staggered back. Emma's face curdled seeing the garden was empty and devoid of anyone inhabiting it. She wandered on, understanding why in her cynical attitude. She thought it to be depressing being inside a boxed garden, but compared to the hallway Emma was stood in, anything would compare ten times better.

It was a strikingly neglected ward within the hospital and Emma tried not to focus on thinking too hard.

She sped up from her wandering pace beside the window, hurrying along the hallway to remind herself to find Hart-mann. Slowing only because she began to feel her stomach start to ache, drawing attention to that one specific area of her body. She took wide steps now, inhaling to only blow the breath out to try calm the aching, bubbling feeling. Her ears picked up the flat-soled shoes of someone approaching, and lifted her head from facing the floor, landing eyes on a nurse.

She managed to perk up, walking past to set eyes on the exit door she had come from on the right hand side before the end of the hallway, where it split in two again.

Emma stared at the door ahead. She had only noticed the nurse had failed to lock it upon leaving, unable to see the nurse reaching for her arms.

"Shall we go this way? Follow me," the nurse spoke, Emma straining to hear her exact words. Her smile was encouraging, and Emma's torso turned halfway before she realised she had no desire to go with the nurse.

Her feet stuck to the floor, resisting the woman trying to turn her around. "That's alright," Emma said, backing away. "I'm going this way."

The assertiveness she displayed threw the nurse from her, giving a wry smile. The nurse pointed down the hall they stood in.

"The way to the breakfast hall is straight, and all the way down the stairs. You'll find directions from there, no problem." The preppy nurse strode away from Emma.

Turning on the spot, Emma's head reeled at watching the nurse saunter away, manicured hands reaching behind her head to neaten her plaited bun.

She heard sets of keys jingling under her white apron when she sped away, the metal banging against her upper thigh. Holding onto that small detail for a moment when watching the nurse through narrowed eyes, she pressed her lips together.

Emma moved herself, swapping over to the right side of the hallway. Walking along the wall until she met with the outline of the door the nurse had exited through.

Emma turned to peer down the hallway, which the nurse was hurrying herself down now, soon to disappear out of sight altogether.

The door had a slim, silver rectangle on the top half of the door which read "Staff Only." Looking to the left and right of herself, nobody was around to see before Emma placed a palm on the handle, and pushed down.

The door released a confirming heavy "clunk" as the lock dropped from the inside of the painted door. Impatiently, Emma shoved it forwards with the brunt of her shoulder. Upon pushing her weight onto it, her feet stumbled forwards under the effort she had pushed the door with being exces-sive. Having thrown herself into the room, she kicked the door shut with a backwards thrust of a leg. The room enveloped in a sudden darkness. Images springing to her mind of terrible creatures coming to grab at her ankles, clawing at her skin and ripping into the muscles beneath. Claws that would pick at her muscles like guitar strings beneath her skin.

Emma squinted in the poor lighting while her chest thrummed and brought on an ugly sweat. A fluorescent light flickered on above revealing the elongated room. Her eyes adjusted to the light slowly. Now able to see, Emma focused around herself, immediately clocking the white metal rows of filing cabinets along the left wall. Her grimace left.

Beyond the cabinets sat another door, which would be opened towards oneself as a convenient exit through the room. To the right in the corner of the narrow, but long room, was a corner of huddled waiting room chairs. The kind with the soft play seating and armrests, also coloured hideous green.

On the left hand side beyond the corner of chairs there was a cornertop where stood a battered kettle. Above were light brown cupboards which she would take a knowing guess to have cups and mugs stored in. In the very end of the room, edging herself forwards with cautious, shuffling steps, Emma set eyes on tall metal cabinets.

Emma turned towards the filing cabinets, hoping the auto-matic light above would turn off to stop any unwanted atten-tion. She rid the silly notion from her head and then without much of a care given, decided against the worries of staff seeing her. Throwing herself at the metal filing cabinet, running a finger over the lock on the top right hand side of each individual drawer. Tearing her wide eyes away from the lock, Emma read the small emblazoned card above the handle, reading "Lab Results." Peering up to the drawer above it reading "Lab Requests." The final drawer at the bottom she strained to read, so stepped back and crouched down, squinting. "Patient Files."

Emma curled her fingers underneath the drawer's handle and pulled. The metal shook and bolts rattled like loose teeth, communicating she had failed in her goal, as the cabinet stayed clamped shut. She pushed at the cabinet again when she stood, making it rattle again, hissing out a breath between her teeth.

"Great," Emma mumbled under her rancid breath, standing in the empty room, feeling like an idiot.

"I better get out of here." She hedged her bets on the door in-between the rows of filing cabinets and the tall lockers being open, and so quickly pulled the door. Emma almost fell backwards when the door didn't budge. Letting out an overdue groan at herself, and instead shoving herself out of the room forcefully, she burst out into the hallway. The door's hinge meant it would close slowly to ensure safety, and she clocked nurses eyeing her as they walked down the hall, their paces quickening. Cheeks reddening, she didn't want to shove the door closed any quicker for fear of looming repercussions. She motioned her head back, conveying faux confusion as if the door had opened upon its own accord.

"Excuse me, what were you going into that room for?"

Emma jumped, putting a hand over her chest as a tall, lanky mean-looking nurse squinted down at her.

She felt a nervous laugh beginning to bubble, which she didn't appreciate, but found difficult to strangle.

Emma's spine straightened, rebuffed at the nurse's anger.

"That's private, do you understand what I'm telling you?" she snapped at Emma in a hardened tone, pointing a bony finger to the door she had come out of.

Emma narrowed her eyes at this nurse, recoiling. "Jesus, what's your problem?" Emma spat back while the sour-faced woman remained frowning down at her. The nurse's thin Vaseline-coated lips parted, fury flickering over her face. Emma smirked at her own little bite back at the sour old bag. As the many wrinkles on her face tightened, her lips opening, a voice boomed from down the hall, forcing them both to turn their heads towards it.

"Ah, Miss Merrick."

At the sound of Doctor Hartmann's bold, loud voice echoing down the hallway, Emma jumped again, her nerves on edge. The spike in her nerves shrunk and, she gritted her teeth while they calmed. She felt her jaw unclench when the lanky nurse shot off towards Hartmann without hesitation, tongue clicking to meet with the familiar face, and once again cursing herself for previous, humiliating behaviour. Remembering what she had to apologise for, it encouraged her to make a move towards him.

The doctor waved his hand and nodded to the nurse as she spoke to him. Hartmann stood in the middle of the hallway with the sun radiating through the panes of glass. He didn't look at the nurse, but rather straight ahead at Emma. Approaching, he seemed to "lend an ear" to the complaining hag, with eyes remaining on Emma until he turned his head.

Her cheeks burned, feeling an oncoming reprimand for her regardless. The sour-faced nurse left, Hartmann having then lost the serious look to his features, leaving him standing with a folder tucked under his arm.

He looked over at Emma, but his eyes were kind.

"Emma, good morning," he greeted upon walking up, then smiling for a moment.

She reached to scratch the back of her head. She took a calm breath before the beginning of a sobered apology fell clumsily out of her mouth. Emma shuffled herself to come closer to where the doctor stood. He didn't fidget like Emma did.

Emma aimed to ease off her visible embarrassment.

"Listen, I'm so sorry about everything last night," she began. "I was out of line, way out of line, and I don't know why I decided to do something so dangerous."

Hartmann's lips pulled a little thinner as he smiled, clearly bemused by her clumsy apology. His chest filling with air, he flicked his gaze to the floor before looking back at her. "I must admit, you are lucky to have had the car miss you, it was a fraction of a second but you could have gotten yourself killed," he said, hands letting go of their grip on the other.

Heat burned her cheeks, and she paused. "I know, I'm sorry to have put you in danger," she said, hoping to not sound as pathetic as she felt.

"That's all behind us now, because I was just on my way to get you for your first treatment." Hartmann gave a pleased look as he finished speaking.

The words sent Emma into malfunction, repeating that word to herself.

Doctor Hartmann began walking away with one foot outstretched and then the other following. Emma was slow to begin her meander with intention of following him. She hurried to catch up, tagging alongside him. Hartmann sped up to his normal pace of quickened, efficient walking through his halls. Releasing a breath she had been holding, Emma caught up again.

"I'm fine, honestly you don't need to worry, I only need to get home." Emma tried as he strut along through the halls, her indignance being of one many functioning substance addicts riddled off, naïvely hoping it was new to the doctor's ears.

Hartmann's face dulled, tutting. He stopped walking and faced her, his head turning to check both ends of the hallway before responding.

Panic flashed over her face for a split second.

"Last night I took the responsibility under a duty of utter concern for your welfare to run some tests on you, as your behaviour last night didn't just worry me personally, it worried me professionally," Hartmann told her straight-faced, his features serious as he spoke in a hushed tone.

Emma tried her best not to show her impatience with his

lah-de-dah professional chatter, managing to smile again only more falsely.

Hesitating wanting to tell him where to shove his worries about her behaviour, she knew last night was nothing surprising to see from herself, but resented the resulting melt-downs. Emma's state of being so drunk had suddenly triggered a detrimental one.

She swallowed her stinking attitude. She knew she couldn't have chosen anyone worse to have a drunken meltdown in front of. Emma knew it will have been bad irrespective of the fact she almost got herself ran over, but Hartmann being apparently "fascinated" by her meltdown was the last thing she wanted this morning. All she wanted was to go home. The absolute last place she wanted to be in her current state was in the hospital.

"Doctor Hartmann, all I need is to go home, I didn't need to be admitted," she argued, not maintaining eye contact.

"You need to come with me, this won't take long. Your test results will be back with us soon regardless."

Hartmann wore her down, with the little fight she managed to hold onto. Emma was sapped. Her shoulders sagged with the elongated sentences he spurred at her. She craved deeply to tell him to shut up. Emma was humiliated, only being able to reflect upon her poor behaviour.

Hartmann only smiled again, apparently having an incred-ible amount of patience, unlike Emma. She bit her lip in the silence that stood between.

"Let us go to your room," he clipped, the German twinge to his voice adding an allure to his professional tone. Emma sucked in her cheeks while he waited for her, his clipboard held at his hips. Walking alongside Hartmann, she realised she was retracing the steps to the room she left earlier.

"Ah, good," he said.

Dual footsteps echoed down the halls when turning back into the long hall where the room's door was on the far left.

Emma watched a nurse knocking on different patients' doors. She turned to see Hartmann approaching and gave a smile at him, her eyes creasing at the corners.

"Good morning, Doctor," a voice squeaked. The voice coming from a smaller patient, her curled white hair popping out from the doorway of her room, presenting a beaming smile.

"Good morning, Hilda," Hartmann said with a wide smile as we walked past her. Emma recognised the open doorway of the room up the hallway, and Hartmann continued with his strides. The pointlessness of the exhausting walk came to a head when Emma followed in behind Hartmann, setting her eyes on an IV stand.

"Emma," Hartmann clipped, holding open the door behind himself. "I will be back in a moment, okay? And then," he paused, "we will start your treatment." He gave another beaming smile.

Her eyebrows knitted together. "I don't understand what this is for."

He stifled a chuckle. "You need not worry, that is for us to do," he said with a smirk.

Hartmann left, adding unease to her cloud of confusion. His fingers on the doorknob, he pulled the door shut, leaving Emma standing in her room, alone once more. She sat on the bed and crumpled her face into her hands, her elbows perched on her knees.

# Chapter Seven

EMMA'S HEAD snapped up in surprise as the door behind her clicked open, signalling Hartmann had returned. Trying to refrain a yawn, she stood to see a full IV bag in his hand.

"You can stay sat there. I am going to get everything ready for your treatment, and we can get you better in no time," The doctor explained, pulling in the empty stand from the bedside.

"What am I being treated for?" Emma asked, watching Hartmann hurry himself prepping the stand, the bloated bag pulled onto the hook. Hartmann hummed away to himself, plugging in the long plastic rope and attaching a needle to the end.

"Miss Merrick, here at the hospital we do not tell our patients what we treat them for, in an effort to keep everyone calm and stress-free." He smiled, pulling on a pair of white gloves and letting them snap against his wrists. Hartmann looked to Emma as he yanked on the second glove.

"It's a part of the hospital's ethos. You need to trust us practitioners to take the best care of you." The doctor cooed, clasping his palms together as he stood in front of her with a caring look.

Emma's mind flashed to her prior confusion, when she sat

in the car wondering about the lack of information provided online. At least something was making some sense. Brow knitting, Emma was apprehensive when she looked at the bulging IV bag hung up on the metal stand. Pointing to it she shifted her weight from one foot to the other. Hartmann seemed to catch on to her apprehension.

"What's in the IV though?" Emma questioned, straining to make eye contact with the doctor. Hartmann fiddled with his gloves, pulling them down more, stretching the rubber over his hands.

"If you would sit down on the bed, we can begin the treatment for you." Hartmann gestured to the hospital bed with his gloved hands.

Edging forwards, delaying her steps, Emma slowly turned to sit on the side of the bed. Her toes scraped against the ground as she sat up straight.

Hartmann stood next to the IV stand with his hands clasped in front of himself, looking at Emma with something akin to endearment. "Please, lie down and we can begin," he encouraged, making Emma feel more apprehensive than relaxed.

In response to his prompt, Emma's body felt stiff. She went to lie herself back on the bed, but Hartmann grabbed the small electric controller to position the top half of the bed upwards, so Emma would be lying with her upper body at an upward angle. While lying back, Emma became afraid, her vulnerability forcing her chest to almost palpitate.

Her heart racing, Emma was able to feel the bed's frame shift underneath her. Her shoulders raised upwards, and then jolted to a sudden halt. Hartmann tucked the remote back underneath the bed, hooking it onto the side by the little plastic clip at the back of it. Propped up awkwardly, Emma turned her right arm over, exposing a blue vein which ran under her milky skin at the crease across her elbow.

Hartmann fiddled with the IV tubing and attached the

gauge onto the end, pulling a small white cloth from his coat pocket. He leaned over Emma as he held the pipe out straight in his hands, eyes squinting to focus.

Emma offered her arm up although her limb was shaking. She was not the biggest fan of needles. As a child, she was irrationally freaked out by them. Emma's poor mum had a nightmare getting the flu jab all those years ago, her daughter screaming and crying virtually having a panic attack at only about seven years old.

Emma fondly thought over the fuzzy memory, being yanked from the clouds of her memories as Hartmann tied the white bandage tight around the upper part of her arm. Only upon the tightening of the fabric did Emma zone back, then straining her wrist. Her glassy eyes peered at the doctor, but unvalidated Emma sunk back into herself. Emma looked to her arm, watching her vein pop up somewhat more prominently.

"Stay nice and relaxed for me, okay?" Hartmann said, ripping open a little white satchel, only to reveal a cotton ball. He provided Emma with a small smile as he began dabbing away at her skin with it. She barely stared at the ceiling of the room while Hartmann turned away from her, to fix the catheter needle to the end of the IV tubing. Acid resting in her stomach, she laid in the bed staring into space. Hartmann turned around from fiddling with the catheter, now with a needle attached to the end of the fat blue bit of plastic which he held in his gloved hand.

The doctor tucked his fingers under the skin of Emma's elbow and placed his thumb over where the most prominent vein was running under the crease, then pushed on it.

"Now, take a nice deep breath for me," the doctor instructed.

Emma' eyes closed, taking a deep inhale through her nose and then releasing, feeling the familiar sharp, cold stabbing on the exhale. She flinched slightly, but kept her eyes closed, only squeezing them a little tighter in discomfort.

"There we go, almost done now," Hartmann coaxed her.

Emma's cheeks warmed under his soft and praising voice. His thumb remained pressed down on the skin of her inner elbow as he pulled the needle out, feeling the slow tug of the tubing. Emma winced again, hearing Hartmann rip some tape off a roll and press it down against the tubing remaining. Opening her eyes and looking to her right arm, she felt a little calmer now the process was over, seeing the needle secured. Emma watched Hartmann's fingers squeeze the tube leading into her arm, watching the liquid begin to drip down, she saw him smile to himself.

"Now, this process should take around an hour, and I will be checking in on you periodically," he told Emma, untying the bandage from her arm and looming over the bed. He ripped off his gloves and held them in his hand. "If you would like, I can pull over the television for you, Emma? To help pass the time," he prompted kindly.

Emma hesitated, but nodded as to not be rude. She found herself to be grateful for the thoughtful offer, regardless of giving a shrug initially. "Yeah, okay." She hesitated while Hartmann remained, looking pleased.

He pulled the TV from the side of her bed, where it had been tucked away against the wall on the mount and switched it on. The screen blinked on with a reality show of some sort. An old fashioned laugh track infiltrated Emma's eardrums, irritating her. She pulled her lips and curled them into a smile, directing it to Hartmann despite her regret.

"I'll be back in a little while to check up on you," Hartmann said as he walked to the door. He motioned around the room with a pleased smile wide on his face.

"Relax, and enjoy the television, hm?" He glanced over his shoulder before placing his hand on the door handle, leaving the room and closing the door behind him.

Once he was gone, Emma's head flopped back onto the pillows and, staring up at the white ceiling, she exhaled. Laying there for a few seconds as the track of a sitcom played away to itself. Emma turned to the screen, the picture not being the best quality. She raised her hand to shove the screen away, taking no interest in the re-run of the show and feeling fed up with it already. Turning to the window where the sun streamed in over the bed, Emma felt warmth from her chest to her toes. She relaxed, feeling the sun on her body, basking with her, eyes closed despite the irritating laugh track. Irked, Emma resisted sleep for a moment. Straining to lift her head from the pillows, she looked to the needle in her arm before glancing back to the window.

Emma shifted, propping herself up taller in the bed, straining to be able to see out of the long window into the garden. The thin sheet under her slipped, and her effort to view the garden failing, she realised she was too short to be able to see. Reclining in annoyance, Emma instead listened to the faint sounds of birds outside the window in the trees not too far away. Struggling to pick out the individual sound rather than the TV – they seemed to mash together – Emma stuffed her head into the pillow and closed her eyes again, hoping for sleep to make this long drawn out hour pass by easier. Laying her face on its side, she blinked at the glass of water on the bedside chest of drawers. The glass was less than halfway full now, and she stretched a hand out to grab it, bringing the glass rim to her grateful lips and glugging down the two mouthfuls she managed. Emma placed the glass back before sliding back down and returning to the comfortable state of attempting to sleep.

She laid still until she felt herself drifting into the lull of sleep, aware and welcoming it, willingly sinking. Her tongue stuck to the roof of her mouth, and her breath tasted awful upon trying, and failing, to wet her mouth. Emma restlessly propped herself up and sat, feeling the familiar pounding against the top of her head.

Blinking in slow, groggy confusion, Emma looked around the room, and paused at the window. The frame around the glass moved, the window becoming fuzzy at the edges. The mix of the white and the glass blurred and Emma cringed, her eyes aching from staring. Her heart jumped, and then began to thrum while her eyes processed everything in slow motion. For all of her staring, she could not see. Her head turning to stare at the IV stand, Emma began to shake at the sight of the drained IV bag. Releasing a whimper, she grabbed the tubing that lead into the inside of her elbow, eyes closing as it took her a mere second to yank the needle out. Feeling the metal sliding from inside her vein, Emma's toes curled as the seconds of pain wracked her. She grimaced, removing the tape from her skin and letting the needle fall from her hands to hang close to the floor.

The tiny hole left behind from the needle began to ooze a small head of deep red blood. Emma twisted her legs over the side of the bed, and upon pushing herself off, she wobbled to her feet. She remained wobbling when walking over to the sink. Her legs were numb. Throwing her arm out before she reached the sink, Emma lumped her arm under the tap. She took her thumb and pushed under the needle's exit point; a thin trail of deep red blood dribbled down and dripped into the sink. It made small splotches of deep red against the porcelain, and Emma swallowed her uneven breaths at the sight. Her shaking fingers turned the tap, washing the blood from her arm, there being nothing in the room to stem the bleeding. Emma leaned forward, the sink managing to hold her upper body weight. Her mind ached and raced, but thoughts couldn't form, as if trying to pin clouds to a wall. She was panicked, but the logical reasoning of it, the emotional reaction, wasn't there. Only when she looked to her bleeding arm could she remember.

She held a hand over the inside of her elbow to mask the

spots of blood that oozed out. Poking her head out of her doorway, the ward was eerily quiet again, and Emma stumbled up from her door to the nearest adjoining hall, hoping to catch a nurse's attention. Every step forward resulted in a prominent thump from the inside of her skull. Laying eyes on the fuzzy outline of a nurse, Emma began to run, zig-zagging from wall to wall. Having rushed past an elderly man hobbling against the wall, she received a glare while he clutched the handrail. He stared at Emma, standing arched over the handrail, licking his dry, cracking lips. Her own lips stretched into a grimace to struggle while wobbling past him, feeling the blood press against her palm as it stayed clamped in place. The nurse began to break into a run , her hands cupping Emma at her upper arms and looking at her arm in panic, then to her face.

"Emma, what have you done," she pressed, more attacking than caring, stammering when the look of recognition flashed across her face. Releasing tension, Emma exhaled in her face, her nose wrinkling upon smelling her breath. Emma studied the nurse's face, in the fuzz of reality she perceived she couldn't place where she had seen her before.

"I don't feel well. Hartmann put an IV into my arm," Emma managed to breathe, then stumbled on the spot as the space around spun, lopping her sore arm to her side. The familiar nurse put her hand behind her shoulder blades, before then pushing Emma forwards, but she wouldn't budge from the spot.

Turning to the nurse, Emma snarled in her face. When the nurse recoiled from touching Emma's upper arms, she softened her voice to a plea.

"I need your help, please! I don't need to go back to my room, I need to feel better." Her voice on the verge of shattering, Emma weakened upon hearing her pathetic voice, working herself up while everything remained slow and blurry besides her state of panic.

The nurse's brow raised, she shushed Emma, flicking her

head over her shoulder, peering around the hall. "You're making an awful racket. Please be quiet and I can help you," she told Emma, leaning into her and rubbing her back. Emma was virtually inducing herself into panicked, overwhelmed tears in the middle of the hallway.

# Chapter Eight

HARTMANN BRISKLY SHUT his office door while eyeing his watch. Upon exiting, he was sure to take a second to lock it behind him. The doctor strode down the endless corridors and hallways of his hospital, smiling at his various patients and the nurses he passed. With his chest thrust up, Hartmann swung himself onto the staircase upstairs to Emma's floor. Her room wasn't far from the top of the stairway.

The white of Emma's doorframe was in sight as alarm bells rang. Hartmann noticed the door had been pulled wide open. From the window opposite the wide open door, sun streamed out into the hallway. Standing in the doorway, he scanned the empty space, then wandered in to see the neglected IV needle dripping out the remaining fluid into a puddle on the floor.

Hartmann's concern bubbled into frustration – his nostrils flared as he spotted small droplets of blood on the floor by the sink. Becoming aware he may step in some of the tiny droplets, he looked at his shoes and around his feet. Smacking the doorway with his palm, the doctor burst from the room. Eyes on the floor of his hallway, lips tightening when setting his gaze upon a smeared spot of blood, Hartmann stormed down the hallway, his forehead wrinkles remaining solid and unmoving. Turning the corner, eyes narrowed upon making out Emma's tiny figure, he tutted to himself before he set off down the hall.

"Please, I need a wipe for my arm," Emma went on at the increasingly frazzled nurse, who was trying to calm her down as best she could in the middle of the corridor. Trying her best to comfort Emma, the nurse herself seemed in a state of panic.

"What was in the IV Hartmann gave me, please? Come and look," Emma babbled, trying to gesture the nurse out of the hallway regardless of her efforts to calm her down.

The nurse shook her head, not understanding the level of panic over whatever was currently rushing through Emma's system.

"You need to calm down, and I'll take you to get sorted out, just calm down," the nurse tried, in a slow and low voice.

Behind her shoulder, Emma set eyes on Hartmann approaching fast in his white coat. She struggled to focus her gaze on his face. The nurse turned her head to see Hartmann and looked to her again, rubbing her forearm. She chewed on her bottom lip while Hartmann stood unavoidably in the way.

"Emma, would you like to come with me please?" Hartmann advised, his eyes flicking down to Emma's inner elbow clamped with her other hand over the wound.

Emma swallowed, but failed to wet her throat.

"Come, I need to sort your arm out." He gestured to her arm with a pointed finger, forcing Emma to look at her limp limb, and then back up at the doctor standing opposite waiting for her decision. Emma stood and her eyes looked to the young nurse, who returned a brief, small smile. Her eyes would not meet Emma's when she gave a smile. The nurse looked through her, looking instead over the top of her head. Emma wanted to be with her, rather than Hartmann. She looked to the nurse again, who had gone cold towards her.

Hartmann cleared his throat. "Nurse, I think it's best you

leave it to me," he said, flashing the woman a tight smile as he turned to her.

"I just need a bandage," Emma said, breaking attention from Hartmann. Again the bleeding woman looked into the nurse's eyes aiming to catch her gaze, but failing, only seeing how the nurse was side-eyeing Hartmann instead.

"Thank you, Mary-Ann. That will be all," the doctor clipped, his tone challenging.

Mary-Ann turned to Emma and tucked her hair behind her ears, stepping forward.

Emma momentarily felt her brow loosening in relief.

Hartmann watched from over her shoulder, his face unchanged and emotionless as he lingered. The nurse reached out to touch Emma's skin, letting her fingers brush her. Emma's skin formed a layer of goosebumps, but calmed when she looked into the deep brown eyes of the nurse. The nurse's orbs were wide and gentle.

"I'll come to check in on you, but you need to go with Doctor Hartmann right now. I have to go," Nurse Mary-Ann explained, peering into Emma's eyes, as if searching within them for the reflected look of understanding.

Emma swayed on the spot, giving the nurse a nod in the quiet which rested around after she spoke. The soft skin of her fingers moved from resting against Emma's upper arm, retracting back to her sides.

The nurse nodded, giving a gentle sigh.

"Good," Hartmann piped in upon sighting the progress of the situation. The young nurse left, walking past both Emma and Hartmann, beelining down the hall behind the two. Not turning to watch the nurse leave, instead Emma trailed her eyes from the floor to meet with Hartmann's piercing blue pair, with a heavier heart than she had a few moments ago.

"Now, let us go, hm?" he suggested as he turned on his heel, leaving Emma eyeing the back of his head in an angered, confused fuzz.

"Miss Merrick," the doctor called her, when she lingered behind, with no sense of urgency to follow in his every step. Emma was then quicker to join Hartmann, staying silent and watching her feet, one in front of the other, over and over. "How are you feeling?" he asked, giving her time to catch up to his slowing pace. Hartmann indicated to a white door with a sign at the top half emblazoned with the word, "Private."

He pushed the handle down and the door opened into a room with metal shelves full of medical supplies. Upon stepping in and the door closing, it revealed a small, old white table with the paint peeling off – those tiny bits of curling paint falling to the floor around itself.

"Sit, if you can please." He invited Emma to the table with his upturned palm. Emma narrowed her eyes as he brought down a box from one of the shelves, proceeding to dig through it. Releasing her hand from her inner elbow, it revealed her palm to be covered in a thin coating of blood.

"Don't worry, I will clean your hand too, Emma. Step onto the table," he prompted over his shoulder.

Upon climbing up, Emma's legs were left dangling with her feet a few centimetres from the floor.

"Doctor Hartmann," Emma questioned.

"Yes? What is it?" he said without hesitating.

"Why did the IV make me feel so awful?" she questioned while he filled one hand with small white and silver packages, pushing the cardboard box back onto the shelf where he retrieved it.

Hartmann ripped a glove from a half empty box with a small release of their white powder, and pulled it over his right hand, looking at Emma.

"Let me look at your arm," he asked, nodding towards where her bloody hand was again clamped again.

Upon his request, her hand slowly fell from covering her wound. Emma left her hand held upturned in front of herself, too apprehensive to smear her blood on the paper towel she was sitting on. Looking to Hartmann in front, his eyelids squeezing as he focused, he tutted when ripping open an antibacterial wipe.

"Please tell me, what was in that IV? It's made me feel disoriented, my mouth was bone dry and that's why I took it out, I wouldn't do that –"

Hartmann interrupted before she could finish. "Emma," he sighed, tiring visibly.

She watched his shoulders curl inwards and loosen as they dropped. She curled her fingers inwards.

His gloved hand took her wrist in his hand, wiping a thin alcohol pad over the bloodied area of her arm. She felt the alcohol sting her raw flesh upon the contact and tried not to reveal her wince.

"Emma, I am very busy, and you know we do not discuss treatments. You of all people should remember that," the doctor reminded, while he remained focused on her wound, placing a cotton ball in the crook of her elbow and taping it in place.

Her mouth fell open, then she gathered herself before he could notice her expression. "But I have never felt like that. If you give that drug to other patients here then I am trying to let you know it's not –"

Emma found herself cut off again when Hartmann raised his hand, letting her sentence trail off and hang in the air unfinished. Emma felt awkward, simmering in her lack of self-assurance.

The doctor stood back, lowering an eyebrow while removing his glove. Emma's train of thought dissipated.

"You're in need of some fresh air. I recommend you go outside into the gardens," he told her, his tone factual, grabbing the door handle to yank open the door of the small storage room.

Emma looked at the open door, and then back to

Hartmann.

"I have to tend to my other patients, Emma and you are holding me from my responsibilities, now please let us do the right thing."

Emma felt more embarrassed than she was moments before, and slid from the table. She walked out of the room, and Hartmann followed behind her, locking the door. She looked at the shoulders of the man under his coat, brow dipping when he turned.

And so she walked to the opposite wall of the hall as Hartmann closed the door behind himself.

She leaned against the wall while her eyes adjusted.

"It will do you some good to interact," he told her with a smile, but she avoided looking at him. She resonated with the feeling like he didn't believe her when she told him how she felt, brushing her off.

It struck her about going cold turkey while she was here, making a pit form in the base of her stomach. Emma's eyes flitted around the space in front as her mind raced. Again, she felt a motion of sickness wash over her, bringing up a sudden flush of heat. At that moment, Emma was beyond feeling lost. Out of touch with anything to make her comfortable. Her head turned when her ears pricked at the sound of Hartmann's dress shoes making their way down the hall, away from her this time rather than towards.

Emma looked down to the cotton ball taped to the inside of her elbow, letting her eyes roll upwards to the ceiling, tipping her head back and releasing an almighty sigh. Putting her head back down, with a push from leaning against the wall, she began wandering, in search of the garden. She walked up from her room noticing one of the lights above her flickering, making her wince when looking at the light struggling to stay on. Her upper lip curling, Emma kept her pace down the hallway peering into the doors of patients rooms.

More doors were shut than open, but the silence disturbed

her. Emma decided whatever ward she must have been in, it seemed to be devoid of patients and only hearing her own footsteps as she walked. She gazed into the uninhabited rooms with their bare mattresses yet to be made up for someone to come along to sleep in them.

Emma stumbled onto the courtyard of the garden, the stone slab pathway chilling her feet. She peered up to the walls stretching out at each side of her, and saw the windows for patients' rooms. Emma couldn't place which room was hers from where she stood, wincing to then raise a hand to cover the sun from blinding her. Lowering her hand and turning, the sun then warmed her back while it stood tall in the sky. She paused as she took in the scenery. From tall, flourishing trees came multiple songs, birds pausing to flit from one branch to another, the opportunities for nest-making plentiful. Emma watched a small blue-breasted bird chirping before stopping and flying off, its tiny wings becoming a blur of pretty colours in the sun as it flew away, and out of sight. Emma's eyes lingered on the small creature as if having never seen one before, and she wished another would stay still long enough for her to admire it.

Losing interest in the picturesque surroundings, she looked over at the other side of the grass. She noticed a separate area of the hospital, one which had large double doors wide open. Struggling to see into the entryway, Emma instead eyed the white decking which had tables and chair sets along each side of the doors. Many of the tables were filled by older patients playing card games or talking amongst themselves. She wandered over, eyes half closed from the sun beaming down in the heat of the afternoon. The grass under her feet refreshed Emma's mental slump, the blades sticking up between her toes while she walked. Patients, dressed in their assorted coloured gowns, were busying themselves with different activities. They all seemed to have friends, which was sweet to see, she thought.

Groups of three sat on the grass in a circle relaxing in the sun, and two older women were content walking along, chatting – although one was hunched over and the other could stand straight.

Stepping on the stone slabs, the hard stone warmed her, but felt less pleasant than the soft grass. Emma took herself off, up the white wooden steps onto the decking and passed a gentleman who smiled at her upon passing on the steps.

Turning her head around as he slid past, she watched him hurry off into the garden. Emma gazed over her shoulder before turning back around. Eyeing the wooden table and chair sets, she lowered her eyes to notice the hospital gown colours were all different. On her venture outside, she had seen blue and green, but nobody else was wearing pink, like Emma. The majority of the patients here were older, and Emma seemed to be the youngest person within the hospital. Moving herself from standing in the middle of the decking, her feet shuffled against the wall of the building behind a chair.

Emma drew in a breath and sucked in her small gut to squeeze behind the chair. Having squeezed past, she then pulled back, noticing a tied on blue cushion. She flicked her eyes up, seeing heads bow, and slowly she rested down into the deck chair. Overlooking the white banister of the decking in front, a gentle breeze tickled her neck, brushing stray hairs against her skin. The dizziness Emma felt had faded, and her head seemed to clear of the clouded confusion. Her nostrils flared, and she thrummed her fingers on the armrests of the deck chair. A leg began to bounce itself, as she felt heat build up behind her forehead.

Emma shook her head of images, and tried to listen to the bird songs and the chatter of the other patients. Apprehensive, she closed her eyes and tried not to blink. Her spine curved, and she was relieved.

"Oh, hello there, love."

Emma twisted her head, looking in the direction of the unfamiliar voice, having jolted upright in the chair. Meeting the eyes of an older woman, she noted a chirpy smile on her face. Emma tried not to show her annoyance while her heart calmed from the scare.

The woman began to pull at the arm of a chair that rested against the wall. Returning her gaze to the garden ahead, Emma broke her eyes away while the stranger nestled in the seat beside. Peering her eyes to the side without her head moving, she saw the woman was wearing a green gown.

Turning to the lady, the sun-freckled skin of her face looked soft when her cheeks wrinkled from her wide smile, they gathered in a mound at the centre of each cheek. The silence that was left between left Emma hesitating on her thoughts, wording the question before speaking it.

"Excuse me, but which ward are you on?" Emma asked.

The lady uncurled a finger towards the wide open doors.

Emma leaned forwards in the chair, her feet flat on the decking while straining to watch where the woman's long fingernail ended.

"Just over there, I am over by the ward at the gates."

Looking beyond the end of the decking to the hedges along the wall, and squinting, Emma saw the tall automatic gates beyond another area of grass, those gates being the ones which let in the staff first thing in the morning, and late at night to leave.

Emma's attention returned to the older woman beside her.

"You must be on the..." The lady hesitated, wavering her wrinkly hand about in front of herself.

Emma looked away from watching her throw her hand about, the woman shutting her eyes with a sigh. When her thought returned, her finger raised higher. "You must be on the Lilypad ward," the elderly woman said.

Looking at her, Emma leaned in.

"I haven't met anyone from that ward yet, we're quite literally worlds apart." She laughed.

Emma disguised a look of annoyance at the developing monotony. She jostled back into her state of attempting to relax, and the woman shrivelled, but Emma noticed she maintained her cheerful beam.

## Chapter Nine

EMMA COMBED her fingers through the top of her hair, feeling it begin to grease at the roots. She pulled her hand down.

"I'm not staying, I'm leaving soon anyways," she said. The older woman faced her, humming. "Are you certain? You're wearing a pink gown." She pointed to the long shirt-like gown, with the hideous patterning plastered all over it. Emma pulled back, her top lip curling. She fidgeted in the chair. "What do you mean?" she asked.

Her lips straightened. "The color of the gown indicates the treatment you're receiving, petal. Are you feeling okay?" she asked, leaning forwards with her small, wrinkled hand on Emma's forearm.

Emma pulled away from her touch.

The woman straightened her posture, eyes scanning over her. Emma's lips parted, realising her rudeness.

"I'm sorry, I don't understand what that means. Can you tell me anything about the gowns? I mean, their meaning?" Emma searched the woman's face, peering harder when she looked away. Her gaze dropped to her lap, digging into her sleeve. Pulling out a crumpled tissue from her long sleeve, she wiped at her nostrils with a loud sniffle. Re-folding the damp tissue, she pushed it back against her wrist, resting her arms folded over in her lap. She pulled at her gown, picking at the edges for stray strings of cotton.

"We don't see patients in pink down here much," she said, nodding her head to herself as she spoke. The woman pinched a string from the bottom of her gown, plucking it off and rolling it between her fingers.

Feeling her stomach tighten, twisting inside of herself, Emma realised she had no idea what she meant. Emma stared at her, eyes wide.

With an inhale, the woman flapped her hand in front of herself to jog her memory as she spoke. "I know the colours of the gowns are for different wards, and the treatments for each ward can be different," she went on, to which Emma gave a slow revealing nod as she was slowly gaining an understanding.

"Treatments are different? How?"

Jostling with a frown, she tilted her head. "I'm not a doctor, love." She looked at Emma tiredly. "Some wards are more constantly staffed than others. I think Doctor Hartmann does it for patient safety." She shrugged.

"Thank you, I appreciate your help," Emma said, pushing the deck chair back and hurrying down the few steps into the open space of the garden.

The elderly woman sat up, stammering and reaching out with a hand.

"I still don't think I'm right, but that's all I can remember," she explained, retiring back against her chair when her eyes met with Emma's.

While the woman strained her neck to watch her leave in a hurry, Emma inwardly panicked over what the woman had told her. She knew she had never agreed to any form of treatment, and it hurt to wrack her brain for answers while she paced through the garden.

Emma almost knocked two women over in her dazed speed

walking, spinning herself around to apologise, holding her open palms up as she rushed away from them.

She sped around the corner of the main outer building and fell onto a bench, slumping immediately and hunching her shoulders.

Palms fell to grab her head and pressed her fingers against her skull, rapping one foot on the path in front in an effort to release the growing tension.

Emma's chest filled with frustration while she stared at the stone slabs. The frustration morphed into anger, burning up with what the woman had told her, and how it linked to the way Emma had gotten herself so stupidly drunk. Thoughts swirled in her mind of humiliation at her failure with sobriety. Massaging her skull, she took a deep breath, but wished she was inhaling something rather different than air.

# Chapter Ten

THE OFFICE WAS A MESS. At the back wall sat Hartmann's desk, where he was furiously tapping away, hunched stiff over his battered keyboard.

On either side of him lay multiple piles of paperwork neglected in the metal cages where they had accumulated.

Hartmann was now upright in his office chair. His fingers tapped at computer, sipping from his steaming coffee with one hand while typing with the other, keeping the dual effort until his other hand could come back to rejoin the task. He held a steady hand, avoiding spilling drops of coffee on the paperwork. He placed his favoured coffee mug down, in the shape of the Tardis from *Doctor Who*. One of his receptionists had got him the mug for his birthday two years ago, and ever since then, Hartmann made sure to walk past her desk every morning with the mug in his hand as he said his chirpy, "Good Morning."

But now Hartmann stared at the screen in front of himself with dull loathing, leaning back in his chair and sighing, clasping his chin in his left hand. His eyes looked over the documents on the screen before him, humming. The printer beside him whirred itself into action, spurting out the documents and compiling them on the tray.

The doctor plucked the compiled papers, flicked through them with his lips tugging upwards when he peered over the finalised product of his work. Straightening the corners of the stack, he leaned over his desk and pulled out a plastic wallet, blowing into the opening. With ease he slid the papers in, separating them into the three different types.

Tutting, the doctor looked to his watch once more and stood, scratching the back of his neck with a stretch. He strode to the door, slamming it behind himself and making a beeline to the nurse's office up the hall with the papers clasped in his hand. Rapping his knuckles on the door, Hartmann's fingers then spread when he pushed it open. The door opened to three rows of five computers each, noting to himself that there were three nurses in the office.

The women looked up from their screens to greet Hartmann with a smile. "Afternoon ladies," he said, looking over their faces with scrutiny. After a moment to ponder, he made a beeline to Nurse Leah at her desk.

Leah spun around in the office chair with a surprised, yet pleased, look.

"Do you know where Emma Merrick is?" he asked. He lowered his head into the nape of her neck. "I've got her test results back and they're not looking so good. I'm thinking she needs more time here with us."

The nurse raised her brow, resting her palms on her lower thighs as she looked up to Hartmann. "I haven't got anything to tell you about her since you were last with her. She's been fine," Nurse Leah said with a shrug. "What happened with the triage?" she questioned.

Hartmann kissed his teeth. "She's going to be staying," he clipped, straightening up. He pulled the front sheet from his plastic wallet and passed it to the nurse. Upon taking it from his outheld hand, she looked over the front sheet.

"Lilypad ward, with you?" Nurse Leah then opened up a new hospital admittance tab, beginning to fill in the blank form.

Her fingers made quick work of typing away and filling in the details, flicking her eyes down to the sheet in her hand from time to time.

Hartmann mumbled an agreement, switching to leaning over the side of her chair. "Put them into her room, there are spare holders in that cabinet," Hartmann said, pointing to the other side of the room.

Nurse Leah nodded. "You got it, boss." Leah replied perkily, keeping her back turned, continuing her typing.

Hartmann rolled his eyes. "Thanks, Leah," he spoke over the room as he took his leave out of the office, being careful to close the door. The doctor beelined to the back of the hospital, knowing Emma would most likely, hopefully, be found in the garden. Halfway down the hallway, Hartmann passed a front desk, being sure to flash a smile to his receptionists. He bypassed an elderly lady in the hall who called out for him, but he was deafened by his own track of thoughts, completely ignoring his patient.

Hartmann was met with his body enveloped in the sun that beamed in through the wide open doors. His chest raised to gather as much sun as he could through the fabric of his clothes.

His eyes searched through the sea of faces, smiling at those who kindly greeted him from their tables. He remained looking for one patient in particular.

Pacing himself to the left of the steps, he looked over the hedges and squinted to spot Emma.

The wash of green and blue gowns failed to separate for the singular pink he was searching for. Hartmann sped towards the sight of the tall black gates, wondering where she could have gotten to in only an hour's time. Coming to a clearing of grass in the garden, he laid eyes on Emma sat on one of the remembrance benches. He could see a purplish bruise on her shin as he approached her.

———————

Emma rolled her eyes, groaning. She stood up, not willing to be cornered by the fast-approaching doctor. The heavy pit in her stomach let her know she was sick of the sight of him.

"Miss Merrick, I have your test results with me, and I would like if we can talk about this together in private."

Emma locked her jaw. "I don't care. I don't want to know, because I'm going home," she said, walking away from the bench.

Hartmann cleared his throat, in response to her irate stubbornness. "This is of much interest to you then, if you plan to head home," he informed her, his tone having deepened.

Emma froze in her tracks, and she saw him hide a smirk upon her body freezing on the spot. She turned around, and Hartmann displayed the paperwork in his hand as she narrowed her eyes at him.

"What the hell does that mean? I don't need to be a patient here, the treatment didn't bloody work and you're lucky I'm not having you arrested," she snapped, lifting her wrist to show him the admission band. She blocked his vision with her fist held up, breathless with anger.

Hartmann held his hands up, exposing his large palms.

"It's advisable you calm down, Emma. You need to listen to me," he said, slowing his voice down, clearly trying to calm the tension of the emotions Emma was restraining.

"Well, I can't discuss such a matter here with you. I will be happy to talk to you in your office," she said, sucking in her cheeks and licking the rim of her front teeth with the tip of her tongue. She kept her gaze stern and judgmental when staring at Hartmann.

"Just tell me what I need to know so I can go home," Emma argued again, folding her arms at her chest.

Hartmann straightened his lips, telling her she was testing his never-ending patience.

"Emma, do you not remember what the ethos of my hospital is? You need to adhere to treatments so I can help you," Hartmann went on.

Releasing a heavy sigh, her ribcage shrank upon her exhale of verbal defeat. Emma momentarily flinched, feeling her head begin to pound.

She winced, irritated by her body's miraculous ability to inconvenience her with sudden bouts of pain and discomfort. The inside of her mind fogged, and it brought a groan from Emma which she released with little care. Bowing her head, she massaged her temple with her thumb and forefinger in an effort to make the pounding ease somewhat in her optimism.

Hartmann kept his eyes on Emma as she became overwhelmed by a headache. "What is wrong, what is it?" he fussed, straining to look at Emma's face.

She hid from him, shuffling away and dragging her hands down her face. "Get away from me." Emma grimaced, looking up into the sun of the fading day with a frown. She stormed off in a quiet rage from him to run inside of the hospital's doors from the garden, shrouded by overwhelming anger.

Entering into an argument with herself that being inside the hellish place wasn't doing her any good at all, she had to argue her case to go home to Hartmann. Returning to the ward reduced the thick haze of anger as once again Emma realised the further away she went from the main wings of the hospital building, the quieter it became. She could only hear her own feet, and her increasing rate of breathing. Emma stood in the hallway of the ward, catching her breath from her marching and being left feeling eerily empty. She had not caught her breath completely when she heard Hartmann approaching behind where she was panting.

"Emma," he called out from close behind as he approached.

At once she felt trapped, to which her heart paced in almost a giddy excitement while the fight or flight instinct kicked in. All she could do was stare down to the floor ahead in confusion, trying to piece together the muddle of thoughts for a clear answer.

Hartmann nodded to the door of Emma's room. "Let us go into your room," he said, softening his face. Hartmann didn't recoil from Emma regardless of her state of fright.

Her efforts were pitiful, but before she could pull away from her mind, a hand laid on her shoulder. A shockwave erupted under the skin made her jolt, twisting around to back away as her gaze met Hartmann's. Looking to him, he nodded towards the end of the hallway. She turned her head and walked down, heading into her room like a robot.

The painted door of the room was closed, and she pushed it open with impatience as Hartmann followed in behind. Emma strode over to the window of the room, crouching and stretching her legs out in front as she managed to perch on the small windowsill, her back leaning against the glass. Emma looked over her shoulder and gazed into the courtyard. It was less busy as the evening approached and the sun began to fade. Her teeth nibbled the inside of her cheek in distant thought, only to be yanked back into focus when Hartmann spoke.

"Emma, you are not very well at all, I'm afraid," Hartmann said, grabbing her attention immediately.

With a glare that had terrified many before now, Emma's fingers gripped the small windowsill beneath her.

The doctor pulled the papers from the plastic wallet he had been clenching, his eyes flicking to her in the shifting of his focus.

Glaring at him with such intensity made Emma's eyes ache in their sockets, unsatisfied to have not made him uncomfortable. She stretched her leg out, blinking when she stopped her glaring.

"I have a headache," Emma then complained, rubbing her aching forehead again.

Hartmann stood near the foot of the bed, eyeing his trouser leg as if it would set on fire from the intensity of the anger Emma felt. She heard the tap running, perking her head to see him filling the bedside glass with water from the sink. Hartmann walked back over with the glass in his hand and held it under Emma's nose.

"Drink some water," he said. Emma looked at the glass in his hand and cupped her fingers around the glass, grateful for a few mouthfuls of water.

"Now, I took it upon myself to have a nurse take your blood for testing while you were asleep."

Emma stopped drinking the water, and stared at Hartmann.

"After the accident, in order to check that you were going to be okay, but they came back to me earlier today and I am very worried, Emma," he explained with a strained grin, perching himself opposite at the foot of the bed. Hartmann's face held a mixture of sympathy and sadness when she looked, but his voice remained serious. He crossed his legs over.

Feeling her mood worsen, Emma jumped up from perching on the windowsill and placed the glass of water down on the bedside cabinet. She leaned against the wall before the window, folding her arms at her chest. Raising her head to throw Hartmann a cruel stare, narrowing her eyes before changing her focus to the papers in his hand.

"Regarding the results about your general health I have some questions I need to ask you," he explained, moving his hand upwards so Emma could not peer and read what the papers detailed.

In a temper, Emma then threw her arms down at her side. "What the bloody hell for?" she spat, going on the defensive about whatever his results would now inform her. It wouldn't be anything Emma didn't already know, and so she did not want to hear it.

Hartmann tilted his head, while a tense pause grew.

The silence left Emma steaming, knowing it was an effort to calm her down. The doctor withdrew a breath before speaking again.

"For the treatment you will receive."

## Chapter Eleven

KEEPING HIS MATTER-OF-FACT TONE, Hartmann didn't wait for Emma to give a response before he continued. "There is an important difference between what you may want, and what you need, you see?"

Obviously only half-listening to him, Emma nodded absently. "What do the results say?"

"Emma, come on – you know the policy," he repeated, his wrist flopping to his thigh.

"But I am not a patient."

Hartmann raised a hand in the air. "Now, see this is where you are going to cause yourself all types of problems." His eye contact unwavering from being focused on Emma, he noticed her fidgeting. "I suggest you listen to me, for once." He tapped at the paperwork on his lap. His lips were pulled into a half smile, but it soon faded.

Emma turned her head to instead gaze out of the window.

Hartmann moved from the bed, hearing it creak from the release of his weight. The sky was darkening, the clouds melting away as the colours of pink and orange bled out behind the dissipating clouds reaching across the sky.

"Emma, look at me." Hartmann's face softened, his tone sweetening.

She was slow to meet his eyes. Instead, Emma looked to her fingers, rather than him, while she was still so clearly frustrated. She picked at a small piece of skin, tearing away from the side of her thumbnail, pulling at it to rip it off. Emma lifted her fist to her lips, and used her teeth to rip the skin off from the side of her thumb.

Emma having got the irritating bit of skin in her teeth, Hartmanns hand cupped her wrist.

Squeaking, she yanked her wrist free from being held by him. She shook her hand as the raw skin burned on her finger.

"Don't do that," he scolded while she cradled her wrist. His eyes lingered upon her gentle features.

Sitting herself at the head of the bed beside the pillows, a hand reached to snatch one, curling it over to hold to her stomach, slouching forwards into the softness of the pillow.

Hartmann held a hand to his lips in a ball, then coughing into his tight fist. He stood at the window, the evening light streaming in behind him, giving him an eerie shadow that cast onto the floor of the room.

"Your body cannot lie to me. Telling me that you are not healthy, or well at all for that matter," Hartmann said. "You will stay here for treatment until we have you better."

In obvious discomfort, Emma adjusted the pillow which she held at her chest and fidgeted, wanting to rest her head atop it, but apparently thinking better not to.

---

Emma had nestled into how her everyday life functioned the way it was. Finding that her complacent manner with her established day to day life was being threatened, she fast grew hostile.

It was as if coming to this hospital had doomed her from

the moment she stepped foot within, unable to handle the fact the threat to her routine was going to strangle her. Her fingers dug into the pillow she held at her stomach. She must have revealed her disapproval, because to her dismay, Hartmann began talking again.

"I wish to not overwhelm you, but we will need to do some scans soon, but we do this with all of our patients here."

Meanwhile Emma was ready to burst into tears, feeling her heart sink inside her chest making waves of heat flow through her. Her cheeks warmed from the heat which was released in uncomfortable waves throughout her body.

She sucked in her cheeks, but sat like a zombie. She feared if she would talk, she would break apart like thin glass and shatter on the floor. She felt herself shaking.

"Emma, are you upset?" Hartmann asked.

"I don't need to be a patient," Emma tried to argue, but her voice was monotone while she could not stop staring ahead of herself. "I have to go to work, I have a house to look after."

Hartmann tutted. "You won't understand now, but in time you will become better, and begin to feel it too. Patience, Emma," Doctor Hartmann chided.

Wanting to hold her aching head, she wished to go back to sleep. Bundle herself in the sheets and ignore the world. Reality had become a nightmare within the last ten minutes and she didn't know how to cope. She was dumbfounded at the amazing turnaround of events, and felt her internal organs swirling around inside.

"Let me call my office," Emma said, staring cold at Hartmann. He put a finger in the air. As her lips dropped and she clocked Hartmann, his face was lit up.

"Ah, thank you for reminding me of my next job, Miss Merrick!" he cheerfully said. Throwing the pillow from her stomach to the side of herself, Emma's lips pressed hard into a frown. Hartmann pushed off from the windowsill, taking a few tentative steps towards the door, the papers against his chest.

"Can I phone my family?" She tried not to growl her question.

Hartmann raised an eyebrow, continuing to the door of my room while he apparently thought on the question.

"Please, can I call my family?" Emma repeated louder, frustration building at her impatient assumption of being ignored.

His large hand on the handle of her door, he paused and retracted from the handle, turning to her.

"I heard you the first time, and they have already consented to both your stay here, and the treatments we provide." He gave Emma a look. "If that is what you were wondering."

Hartmann didn't flinch at her sudden jolt when she jumped up from the bed. He only blinked, his eyes carelessly gazing down at the side and then back onto her. He seemed to slow himself down the angrier Emma got. The doctors nonresponse to the obvious outrage she possessed was alien to her, morphing her anger into then, confusion. The racing angered pulse easing only when she glared into his eyes.

Emma felt the fire in her belly had met ice in Hartmann's stare. As such, the fire inside was put out. When she calmed from the anger soothing beneath her skin, it brought a film over her eyes. At once Emma was completely transfixed by the release of a memory.

As she met Hartmann's steady stare, her mind recalled the morning not too long ago when she should have been thankful not to have caused a fatal accident on her way to work, but was in too much of a bad mood to be thankful.

Like many times before, she opened the glovebox and down fell her box of paracetamol. Upon feeling the lack of weight in her hand, she knew it was almost empty. She shoved two down her throat and rested her thumping head upon the wheel of her car. Hunched over, she closed her eyes and gripped the wheel, releasing her grip on the leather to emit a loud groan.

With all of the reeking air from her lungs exhaled, she raised her head and grimaced at the sensation of her brain falling against the base of her skull. She wanted to wait for the paracetamols to kick in before she had to step one foot in that office, but didn't have the time to spare.

Emma kept her hair hanging down the front of her chest and made a beeline to her desk, smiling tired "Mornings" to the colleagues she passed. They were much more chirpy than she could be bothered to be. She dived into her office and dropped her bag on the floor beside her desk, slumping down into her chair.

She gathered herself, and processed what she had to get done today, and maybe she could slide by doing the bare minimum. Not talking to anyone unless spoken to first and keeping her gob shut while in these states was always a wise idea.

She didn't have a chance to touch her bag to retrieve her bottle of water before jumping out of her skin at a sudden interruption.

"Emma, you walked right past my office. I was just about to call you in when I saw you through the blind, but you zoomed right to your desk. Eager to get to the grind this morning?" Bob chuckled from the doorway of her office.

The bounce of his laugh pierced her eardrums. His voice was kind and warm, much to the added dread upon Emma's shoulders at that moment.

"I'm sorry, I was running late, I slept in." She gave a roll of her eyes, and Bob twitched his nose. He continued smiling, and kept his hands in his trouser pockets.

"Come on, I need you in my office." Bob tipped his head to the left of where he stood in the doorway.

Emma reluctantly moved herself from being slumped in her chair and followed behind, all the way back past the other offices she passed only moments ago.

Bob sat himself behind his desk, throwing a finger to the door. Emma pushed it closed and shuffled to a chair.

Her boss was pulling at his shirt, which was tucked neatly into the hem of his blue trousers. His shirt was white and patterned with tiny blue dots to match perfectly to the colour of his lower half.

"I was thinking you and me could have a little chat."

The statement lynched itself around her neck, and clawed, ripping at the sensitive skin. She would have clasped her hand to her prickling skin, but her lip twitched and she didn't. Emma raised an eye to meet Bob's, and he was making effort to fiddle with the various things upon his desk. He was sorting his papers, giving her time to think upon his proposal.

Giving her no chance to think of anything to return with, Bob continued, much to her relief.

"While it's only us, Emma, I've seen you struggle many times these past few weeks. You've come in to work with the perfume of vodka, or the acidic stink of wine."

The burn of guilt rested at the bottom of her stomach like a rock. New words he spoke after a sigh allowed the intensity within Emma to shift.

"And I am sensitive to your situation, but I am worried in the way you're choosing to deal with it." He looked across the desk to her again.

She tried not to shrivel away from his soft gaze, but frankly Bob's softer side made her uncomfortable with how to react. She wanted him to punch her in the shoulder and tell her to get to work, not be a shoulder to cry on. Emma knew in herself that she wasn't the girl for that soft stuff. Sensing her discomfort, Bob cleared his throat.

"I don't mean to come across being disrespectful, or conde-scending, but I see you every morning and can see the night before. You, alone in that house and left with nothing to do but –"

"Bob, stop, please," she whispered.

He did. He let his eyes roll over the uncomfortable woman sat across from him, ever wishing to make herself smaller in the rarity when moments like these came between her and Bob.

Her boss gave a sigh, flattening his tie again. "Have you spoken to your mum, at all? I'm figuring the answer is no."

Emma shook her head and cradled her elbows.

Bob raised a brow. "That is a good place to start. Drinking won't make you forgive her either, you know." He smacked his lips together as he finished.

Emma tucked her loping hair behind her ears at each side of her face. She straightened then, and shook her head once more, but only faintly. Bob was quick to catch onto her small movement, his eyes had not left her.

"I can't. Not yet." Her voice was small. Bob's lips tugged unheedingly.

"I know it's a damn hard thing to do, but you'd drink yourself to death before you'd forgive your mother and I know this to be true. If I know you at all." Bob flashed his wide smile across his desk.

Emma smirked for a second. "That is true. I hate what she left me feeling like. She looked to me with such anger in her soul, it flamed in her eyes, Bob. She looked to me like I was the perpetrator, she blamed *me*, rather than me being the victim of it." Emma wavered, and a finger ran under her nose as she sat back in the chair, staring to the side of her boss's head. With glassy eyes, she looked at her lap before rising her head again.

"I hate him, and I hate her. Both of 'em." She jostled in the chair at the heat spiking her spine all the way up.

"Anyway," Emma stood up and brushed herself off. Bob eyed her. "I'm having regular sessions with my therapist and am talking to her about coping mechanisms. I'm going to get better, okay?" she said to her boss and pulled at her skirt as she uncrossed her legs to stand. "Just bear with me while I get there." A curled hand reached to under her mascara-coated eyes and dabbed at a tear she hoped he didn't see, only the black residual smudge atop the pad of her thumb.

She left in a rush before Bob could reach out to her in the raw moment. With her rushing off, Bob smacked his lips together, and his gaze dropped with a residing sigh. He made a point to watch her every morning coming in, and she was well aware he was looking out for progress, but always seeing the tired expression from her previous evening, bound down at the shoulders by the anger and regret she lugged in with her. Poor Bob bore witness to both the good days, and her bad days during the worst period of her alcoholism. Emma never wanted to catch his eyes when she first came into the office every morning. She knew he would see if the previous evening was a success or a fail from the look in her eyes alone.

Emma's eyes were slow to refocus on Hartmann standing before her, transfixed by the power of her memory. Her ears seemed to re-open to his droning voice. The vivid imagery faded before her, leaving her confused as to what the voice she heard was telling her as she struggled to regain her mental bearings.

"Patients are not allowed to use the phones regardless, Emma," Hartmann sighed, turning to the frozen young woman with an unenthusiastic expression.

She blinked, feeling her nerves re-open as her eyes adjusted to the light her pupils widened. The sensation of swimming in another flashback washed over her, and left her reeling in front of Doctor Hartmann. She hoped he could not sense her initial confusion and repeat himself.

"You are a patient now, Miss Merrick. You will adhere to treatments and not ask questions, like you are so used to in your profession." He was now looking directly at her, and she felt the adrenaline leaving her system, draining into the floor.

"You also don't talk to anybody in here like that. Especially not me," Hartmann warned, lowering his watchful eyes.

His disciplinarian-like tone catching Emma off guard, feeling herself shrink under his gaze.

In the silence, Hartmann took the opportunity to hammer in a standard of behaviour to her. "Furthermore, I suggest you do as you are told." Hartmann walked away from Emma, turning his wrist over to look at his watch. "Now, dinner is in forty-five minutes. You missed breakfast this morning, so I expect I will see you promptly in the dining hall."

Hartmann put his hand back resting on the handle of the door, pulling it open. Emma stood in the middle of the room with her lips left open, staring ahead. Her dizzying anger had gone just as quick as it had arisen, leaving her unsure of what to feel. Emma raised her head from staring at the floor and looked around, releasing a breath. She jumped onto the bed with a grunt. The metal frame banged against itself under her, then quieting when Emma turned herself over, fidgeting.

Outstretching her arms so they hung over the edges of the bed, she noticed the ceiling of the room had swirls which were like tiny rainbows. Emma's eyes narrowed, seeing the swirls become a massive plait of hair, or the clashing of ocean waves in a storm. She strained her jaw out into a yawn and her eyes filled. Curling a forefinger and wiping her eye, she noticed a black smudge on her skin when pulling her finger back. Emma let her arm fall to the side, rolling over and squishing her face into the memory foam pillow.

She lay quietly, feeling herself sinking into the bed with her head vacant of any thoughts. Emma slowed her pace of blinking, lowering her arms to wrap them around her stomach. She watched the sky through the window, the colours melting as daylight faded into sunset. Emma's stomach rose, and she held her breath picturing a plate of hot food and tried not to gag. She rolled over to her side and was content to fall asleep, having no reason to get up – or to do anything. She felt herself deflate, and burdened with the label of being a patient. The heavy pull of sleep yanked at her shoulders, and Emma closed her eyes willing it to take over.

---

"Miss Merrick, wake up."

Emma's torso jolted, her state of dreaming penetrated by a voice outside of the ones swarming in her head.

The nurse who had awakened her pulled back from leaning over her, picking at the edges of her uniform, neatening it. Sleepily blinking, Emma propped herself up atop her elbows, the haze of the immersive nap retreating. She watched the nurse walk to the door, turning with her hand around the side, showing her manicured French nails to Emma.

"You're going to miss dinner," the nurse said before leaving, pulling the door in behind her.

At the mention of food, Emma was less than excited. But she moved to sit herself up, pulling in her legs and crossing them over. While she moved, she began to slowly piece together the images from her strange dream. Sitting there hunched over, a confused frown spread across her face while she conjured the images together of her strange dream. Emma had always had the most peculiar, bizarre dreams, and they were never quite pleasant – something bad or violent always seemed to happen.

Something horrible always would happen, like recalling events of her past which Emma would pay good money to forget. It seemed a cruel twist that no matter how successful she could be on a day-to-day basis that her thoughts and memories always haunted her dreams – her subconscious would not let her forget. In the dark of her mind when she would be trying to become well rested, that's when the memories would return. Emma knew that she was always highly driven by her emotions, it was represented seemingly in her dreams often, or rather – her recurring nightmares.

She clasped her hands to her face and massaged her forehead, staring up only to notice the hospital room did not have a clock on any of the walls. Emma grimaced, running a hand through the roots of her hair, reluctant to get herself moving. She strained to picture the way to the dining hall from poor, faded imagery in her memory. Unfolding her legs, Emma swung them over the side of the bed to stand. Staring down to her bare wrists while walking out of the room, she clicked her tongue in dissatisfaction at the hospital band. With little aim to her walking, Emma looked up to make herself possibly half-aware of the passing surroundings.

More than ever, once again Emma was drawn to the detail of how empty the ward was.

Pausing, she stopped dead in the middle of a long empty hall, staring at the reflection of the white fluorescent light bars gleaming on the floor. The doors of the bedrooms were all closed, and presumably not locked. Nibbling her bottom lip, she twisted her head to peer over her shoulder down the hallway, toying with a childish urge to nose into a different patient's room to satisfy a curious urge.

Moving herself down the hallway, she ignored the niggling impulse. She held her arms straight at her sides, peering out when she tiptoed down the stairs, and then coming to the double doorway.

Upon her creeping around the corner, Emma had a nurse brush past her while she leered on the bottom step. She turned, recognising the nurse from the haze of confusion brought on during the failed "treatment." That was the nurse who had the unforgettable panic-stricken face when Emma had begged her to help.

She led herself into the cafeteria area, but was fascinated by the other inhabitants of Westview Hospital. Upon entering, the air was poisoned by the stench of green beans and other over-boiled vegetables.

Emma didn't feel hungry. Along the far wall of the large

hall were patients hobbled into line with trays held out in front of them, shuffling with their feet not leaving the floor.

Her staring at the scene in front of her caused a man in a wheelchair to bump into her. Emma jumped quickly away to allow him passage.

"Sorry," she said, cheeks heating as he passed. Emma sighed, moving back from entering the hall, trying not to get anxious or letting herself get too into her own thoughts. Emma was uncomfortable not knowing anyone, and the feeling of being quite alone set upon her – deepening when she was forced to overhear the jovial chatter of tables she passed. Emma had remembered circling these tables deep in thought while waiting for Doctor Hartmann, for those drinks together, remembering how the night had gone sour.

Her body moved itself along on auto-drive while she dug back into that night, straining to remember if she had cried, and most likely knowing she had the sensation of tears streaming down her cheeks and the cold of the late night chilling her in the hall. Emma cursed herself for getting so drunk at the given opportunity, to the point of a blackout of memory after falling over the tipping edge. Emma thought that Hartmann, the intelligent doctor must think something sour of the woman she was. Sour, like being left to look after a child you are not too fond of. Emma's arms folded in, squeezing at her chest as she walked.

Emma wished to pull the whole night from her mind, to replay it in a sober state to try and make sense of the events, being told what she had done, said, and how she acted from another person's view was angering. Emma's alcoholism made her feel so out of control of her life. She could not handle herself drunk, and blamed it partially on being so highly strung.

The situation had reached a stalemate. There was no excuse for Emma on a "night out," to get pissed faster than anyone else in her friend group. She had done it a few times, and it drove her friends from her side, tired of looking after her.

She subsequently became a joke, and would dance the worst, stealing the microphones from the singers in the pubs, and sustain her drunkenness by being stupid with it.

At home, faced with a bottle of wine – she would sit in the same chair swigging it back, smiling to herself as her vision progressively doubled.

Emma had banned herself from joining staff nights out, and other adjustments she had to make to save herself from the anguish of her issue. The sight of the metal trays full of baked chicken and mushy, overcooked tomato pasta dismayed her, but she found herself holding out her ceramic plate for it to be filled with the items she was disgusted by.

Having gathered a small meal of different carbohydrate, she wandered into the open space between the assorted types of bread rolls and beige buns piled in the baskets.

Emma's ears perked to hear a laugh she recognised to be Hartmann's echoing from the front of the room. She searched where she had heard it emanate from, tilting her head to then set eyes on the doctor, cutting into his dinner with an appeased smile. It infuriated Emma that he was surrounded by nurses on the table, giggling around him. Her top lip pulling upwards in a curl of disgust, even Emma could tell he was enjoying the attention from the junior nurses who were bashfully swooning over him. Emma's eyes rolled in her sockets and she decided to make a point of sitting the furthest away from Hartmann's area. She stood, staring – she felt the eyes of many other patients on her. She made sure to once again eye Hartmann before lowering into a seat.

"You alright there?" a voice croaked, Emma's attention being placed across from her.

Attempting not to show her alarm at the hollowness of the cheeks of this man's face, noticing how frail he was for being possibly middle aged, at a guess upon seeing his features.

"Yeah, I'm fine," Emma said, thinning out her lips into a taped smile. His fork dragged along the ceramic plate when gathering his peas, making Emma wince at the scraping. She darted her eyes to stare upon her plate, not eager to begin eating in the least. She dug her nails into her palm when she heard someone smacking their lips. With a weak grip she picked up her fork, ripping off a shred from the lumped baked breast of chicken on her plate, and tossed it around her mouth. Her lips tightened as she eagerly swallowed the lump and allowed it to fall down her esophagus.

"You not hungry, love?"

Emma raised her head from staring at her plate, making eye contact with the woman opposite as she managed to zone back into the room. She had one half of her cheek full of green beans, her jaw clicking as she moved the mass around, clicking every time she bit down.

Her lips moved, but no words left. Emma was pulled from a halfway point of daydreaming, only physically in the room – mentally, she was miles away.

She gave a brief pull of her lips, flashing her teeth across the table.

"Ah, not really I guess," she said, letting out a small laugh, disguising her lack of confidence at having done so. Emma peered over the woman's head as she bowed to shove florets of broccoli into her mouth.

Hartmann was as content as ever, chattering away to the nurses and ignoring her – having not noticed Emma. Her view behind was blocked when the woman raised her head again, as she gazed around the table with a beam.

Emma registered her gown was green coloured.

"That's a shame, the food is lovely here. Not like the usual hospital food you'd get served," she said with a pleased grin revealing yellowed teeth.

Emma briefly looked at her plate. "I'm aware," she mumbled, but the others around the table had not heard her.

Emma placed her fork by the side of the plate and sipped her glass of water instead, retiring completely from the idea of eating. She remained frozen to her seat in the midst of the dining room, so out of sync with her surroundings. It seemed to blur around her, but Emma was indifferent and stared ahead.

"What happened to your arm?"

"Huh?" Emma quizzed under a lack of breath, but recovered herself, realising the man's question. Before he could place his knife and fork down on his plate to reiterate himself, she answered.

"I pulled out my IV needle by accident. I fell asleep," Emma lied with a shrug. But she felt, with the degree of elderly folk at the table, that she would scare them if she was to mention the drugs were the wrong type than intended.

Emma didn't need to, it seemed, go into any gory detail − because with the lie alone, the man recoiled in his chair, his lips wrinkling. He dabbed at the corners of his mouth with the handkerchief he pulled from his lap, giving a loud singular tut. Observing the others around the table, cutting at their various cuts of overcooked chicken or dried up beef with hands being too gentle to do so effectively. Emma dragged her eyes away.

"That's bad luck, but you'll be looked after here," he said with a wry smile. He then wrinkled up his napkin and threw it down onto his plate. Upon watching his movements, his eyes flicked to Emma and she jumped back in the chair. He smirked, but his brow wrinkled in a confused smile as he grabbed his glass. She looked around again.

Emma looked at the deep wrinkles at the corners of his eyes.

"You know," a voice interrupted the ongoing trail of thoughts she was having. Her eyes leered over to the woman at her right, raising her eyebrows to listen in. "Doctor Hartmann has a lovely bedside manner, why don't you get him to look at your arm for you?" She nudged Emma with a small smile.

"Oh, no that's okay. I'm going to go back to my room," Emma excused while nodding, reaching out for the folded handkerchief to wipe around her lips, although she had not eaten more than a bite of anything.

"You're not hungry?" The man with the crows feet posed to Emma, tilting his head upwards.

Swallowing, she then gave a false smile while her insides churned, washing a hot ripple throughout her body.

"No, I'm fine." Emma shrugged, curling a hand to wipe at her nostrils. She folded her arms and turned her head, leaning back in the chair. Her eyes flicked over the room in motion.

Emma paused her scanning of the room, noticing a patient had been attempting to cut a chunk of beef, and her hands were shaking. She watched as the woman dropped the chunk of gravy-dripping beef back on her plate, then begin the process over again.

Emma stopped leaning in the chair, eyebrows pulled down to focus in on the woman struggling with her meal.

"What's her deal?" Emma whispered into the ear of the man beside, looking ahead still, to the woman's head which bowed as if in a permanent prayer. Her hands struggled upon gripping her utensils with shaking arms, Emma licked her bottom lip, keeping eyes on the fellow patient.

The man beside her hesitated. "That's Hilda, she can't speak."

Eavesdropping, or his tone having been too loud, the patients sat around the table picked up on the topic and eyes remained fixated on their plates. Nobody looked up, despite Emma looking to see if they did.

Emma reeled her head back in a slow nod, tearing her eyes away from the woman. "But she can hear you," Emma stated, looking to his face blankly.

"She can," the man agreed. He looked to Hilda, raising his head. "Can't you Hilda?" he said a little louder, leaning. A noise of non-committal understanding left Emma's parted lips. The man sat beside her relaxed and lay against the back of his chair.

His head turned into Emma's shoulder.

"There's talk she's deaf. Nurses on the station say Hilda had a viral ear infection."

The skinny, fragile woman managed to place the tough beef onto her lolling tongue. Emma gazed inwardly before giving a nod, retracting from the conversation. The man pointed to Hilda with his fork, moving closer to the skin of her neck and pulling Emma back to the conversation.

"She's from your ward, up that way ain't she?" he whispered. Emma's lips pulled into a frown, turning to search his face. When she expected him to continue, he stopped completely, returning to his meal with a degree of nonchalance that irked her. Emma pulled her fingers through her tangled mass of hair, exhaling when she stood. Although her stomach tightened, her mind was a fog again, focusing on the man's words. Emma's eyes wandered to the gown Hilda was wearing, and surely enough – it was pink.

Emma looked at Hilda once more, who was barely able to feed herself. Wringing her hands, she shifted her body weight on her feet.

"Alright, well I'm off, I'll see you 'round." Emma did not raise her eyes. Two of the women raised their heads and smiled with closed mouths. Emma's nose twitched and reached with her thumb and forefinger to pinch the bottom of her nose to rid herself of it.

Lowering her hands and separating them from their grip on the other, Emma walked around the table. "Do you need some help? I can help you, if you'd like." When Hilda turned to look at Emma, who had a small smile.

With a rapid nod of her curly haired head, Hilda ushered Emma to sit with her.

With something akin to a severe lisp, Hilda's jaw lopped, but her tongue moved about inside her gaping jaw.

Emma picked up the woman's fork and gave her time to speak, leaning in with cheeks gathered.

Although Hilda's *th* came out as more of an *f*, and her tongue bounced outside of her lips in a fashion which was unpleasant to watch, her appreciation had been understood and Emma felt her chest warm at the exchange. Emma shook her head at the way the man had told her Hilda could not speak, and then dismissed her.

"That's perfectly alright, don't worry." Emma smiled, looking to Hilda, whose eyes gleamed although her knuckles jittered at her torso, now free of holding the utensils.

***

"That is very true," Hartmann said, tilting his head with a smirk, locking eyes with the blushing Nurse Jennifer.

"Thank you, doctor, it shocked me when I heard that, too," the nurse continued, looking around at her colleagues now seated around the table with her. Nurse Jennifer held the doctor's eyes for a moment more, a blush on her cheeks.

"Up on the ward, I think it'll become really important that we ensure patients are happy with..." Jennifer's sentence trailed off when she looked to Hartmann again, but seeing his eyes staring across the hall.

The doctor sipped from his water, but his eyes were watchful of another, his lips thinning in dissatisfaction. But Hartmann leaned sideways ever so slightly, giving himself view of Emma's wrist holding a forkful of dinner to the lips of Hilda. Throwing his dinner napkin from his lap over his plate, he studied Emma beginning to feed Hilda, and stood quickly.

"What's wrong, doctor?" A nurse leaned in.

"Ah, continue on with your meal please." He did not spare the effort to give a smile, eyes miles ahead of the many heads in the chairs. He went past the table, marching through the sea of chairs.

He did not remove his hard eyes from Emma, who seemed unaware of the fast approaching doctor.

"Ah." The lady at the side of Hilda raised her hand, then standing up, raised the attention of someone. Upon the hand wavering in the air, Emma jumped to see the narrowed eyes of the patients on her. Staring, frozen in their seats around the table. Raising her head with a look around herself for the first time since starting to help Hilda, she set eyes on a frowning Doctor Hartmann towering over her.

"Ah, Miss Merrick, would you like to come with me please?" the flat tone came.

The hand holding the fork wavering, her eyes flicked up from staring at the pool of gravy on the plate she was holding to Hilda.

Hilda had her chin almost in Emma's eye, her sunken sockets on Hartmann towering above.

Hilda's hands shook at her chest, and would not rest. Her eyes were stuck, both of them – staring up at Hartmann, lips parting to coil in over her sparse teeth.

Seeing how Hilda's upper body became rigid and stiff Emma sighed and dropped the fork onto the plate she held. She stood, knocking her chair over, and upon twisting to grab it, she saw that Hartmanns arm reached out faster than she had twisted, stopping the chair clanging onto the floor in a blur of his sleeve. The doctor pushed the chair back into the table.

She stormed past Hartmann, and continued to do so with little chatter heard from the tables throughout the dining hall.

"Emma," he called out bluntly. But she was lengthy strides ahead of him. "You are acting like a child," he scolded.

"You are getting used to treating me, and speaking to me like one." Emma quietened, eyelids pressing together. A clammy hand held her stomach, suppressing a violent gag through swallowing. She kept her mouth closed but the dreadful, violent noise of the undeniable gagging was audible in the empty hallway when she failed to swallow in time.

"Why'd you come to get me, anyway?" she asked between her small breaths.

Hartmann's voice was flat. "Hilda can feed herself. You do not need to go out of your way to help her. She is fully capable." He gestured with an upturned palm.

Emma's brow knitted, doubling over.

Hartmann's shoulders turned around and his eyes widened at the sight of Emma, his hand going to catch her before the small woman keeled over.

Batting him away, eyes spiking and welling up with her throat audibly spasming. In a blur, she thrust one hand out in front of herself while the other remained clamped over her stomach.

"Emma, calm down," Hartmann tried, sensing the hard skin of his hand resting on the small of her back.

At that moment Emma projectile vomited up the wall. Managing to spray the banister with her foamy sick, she let out a small defeated cry. Emma swallowed then grimaced, the acid at the back of her tongue obviously making the action painful. She cried aloud again, wiping her mouth remaining bent over, holding the banister to gain some balance from it. There was blood streaking through her sick.

She refused to let go of the banister at each side of her to stand unaided. Emma raised her head.

Resisting Hartmann trying to hold her up, she fell in front of her pool of vomit. He knew she wasn't listening to him, she instead lay on her side, curling into the fetal position – a rush of nurses barreling towards her.

Amongst all of the sudden commotion, he watched when a lopsided beam spread across her face.

# Chapter Twelve

HIS FOREFINGER TRAILED along the bloated bottles of medicines on the strained shelf inside of the old white cabinet.

Hartmann mumbled the words plastered on the white labels to himself as his eyes worked ten times faster, working hard to find the one he now required.

The nurse who then entered the office, stood quietly for a moment. Holding on to the handle of the door in order not to let it slam.

"She's stable." The nurse interrupted Hartmann's train of thought, pinning back a few straggling hairs with a bobby pin she had between her teeth. Having contained the straying hairs, she twirled them and plucked the pin from between her teeth to slide it against her skull, holding the hair back in place underneath the back of her bun.

"Good," Hartmann replied, keeping his back to the nurse. "Did you get me a report for Emma?" he asked, holding up a sealed bottle of medicine to the light, squinting his eyes in effort to read the small print.

The nurse stared at the back of his head. Taking a moment to think before being certain of having no clue.

"Who?" the nurse asked, shifting her weight from one foot

to the other as she stood in the background of the room. Hartmann gritted his teeth before turning half of his body around to face her on the spot, throwing his arm upwards and pointing above himself, his eyes glaring at the nurse.

"My patient." He gestured, to which the nurse immediately grasped who he was enquiring about.

"Yes, of course – I'll get you one," she said. A hand on the doorway, the nurse hovered. "Ah, just one thing, Doctor Hartmann, before I leave," she started.

Hartmann didn't turn away from the cabinet, flicking his eyes up to the very top shelf, taking a step backwards to strain his eyes at the labels.

"Yes, what is it?" he asked from where he stood, reaching upwards to read the bottle labels. "Gloria, on marigold, she has been having side effects from the trial of medication you have been giving her," she said.

Hartmann paused, his arm lowered from where his outstretched palm was reaching. He half turned his body towards the nurse.

"Oh? What side effects?" Giving her a moment's eye contact before returning it to the bottle in his hand. "You must write them down on the report sheets, make observations and then come to me." Hartmann began lecturing, upturning his empty hand.

"Yes, I have but I just feared you wouldn't get around to it – since you have been very pre-occupied," she excused, losing the doctor's half hearted shred of attention as he turned his back to her once again, scaling the shelves. She rolled her eyes.

Hartmann hissed through his teeth in impatience.

"Leah, I have asked you what side effects did the patient have from the trial? I don't need the paperwork to tell me, I am asking you."

Nurse Leah swallowed. "The patient suffers with drowsiness, nausea, she's more forgetful than normal, and has vomited twice today," she listed off without a breath in between listing the many side effects of the trial of medication.

Hartmann hummed to himself, flicking an eyebrow at the nurse. "That's no good," he said, shoving a bottle back onto the top shelf, barely paying attention to Leah dithering behind him. He pictured Emma, when she was sick and was suffering from a wave of nausea beforehand of throwing up.

Leah shifted on her feet, hands clasped in front of herself.

"Just take her off the medication, it's not working." He sighed.

She hurried upon being able to leave the claustrophobic room.

Back in his office, Hartmann turned around on the spot, and he was quick to stab a needle into the vial of liquid, eyes scrutinising the measures. He tutted under his breath, shaking his head at the incompetence of the nurse. The needle was yanked free, being placed on the worktop under the cabinets, taking a stride to the drawer behind him to get a needle cap. "This ought to work now, I'm certain of it," he mumbled under his breath. The doctor's mind remained pre-occupied, ideas and theories ticking away in his head while he fixed the cap over the point of the full needle.

Shoving the needle into his coat pocket he made his way through the halls, his many patients bustling in their gowns.

The front two legs of a walker came protruding from the frame of a bedroom doorway as Hartmann was speeding past, and he swayed sideways to avoid bumping the walking aid.

"Oh, excuse me Doctor Hartmann," the elderly lady called, raising her weak hand as she watched him speed past without turning.

Hartmann pulled himself up the stairs by the banister at each side, jumping up the stairs in front of him, unable to find the time to look around himself.

He looped his fingers around the door handle, pausing. Inhaling, the doctor relaxed his shoulders and pushed the handle down before making the singular step it took to enter the room. Upon his eyes setting upon the sight of his patient laid up in the bed, a smile spread onto his face.

———

"Good evening, Miss Merrick," Hartmann started, walking to where she lay in the bed, throwing an examining look over Emma residing under the thin sheet.

He brought the chair by the side of the doorway forwards, letting the wooden legs drag. A silence remained, his greeting going unrequited. He peered into the sheets, realising she was in a deeper sleep than he thought upon entering her room. Positioning the chair adjacent to Emma's sleeping face, Hartmann pulled up at the thigh of his trouser legs before he lowered down to sit, crossing one foot to rest over his other knee.

Before the doctor could admire her peaceful state of slumber, Emma's eyes fluttered open.

He saw how her eyes set onto his torso, then flicking her gaze down to see his foot rhythmically moving as a small spending of energy. While she slowly shook off the lull of her heavy sleep, his eyes trailed her small frame under the thin sheet while she warmed to the room. Hartmann clasped his hands in his lap, holding them together over the space between his thighs. He clocked the young woman's eyes wide staring at him without blinking, although she laid in the hospital bed looking worn out, he saw how her eyes darted to him.

"You fainted," Hartmann said, letting his eyes roam around the room, wanting to lessen the chances of her feeling uncomfortable. He eventually brought his gaze back to her.

Her upper body shot up in the bed, the sheet falling to her hips in folds. Emma turned her attention to Hartmann with wide eyes.

He smiled to himself. "I need you to relax, you need to focus on getting your strength back for now." He unfolded his legs and reached forwards, standing to lean himself over her.

Emma's fell back on her arms as he pulled the fallen sheets over her stiff torso.

Hartmann pulled himself back from where he was glowering over her, the smell of washed out hair products wafting up his nostrils as he retracted himself from her to sit back down in the chair. He wriggled a little, adjusting himself a few times before finally settling into the seat. His nose twitched while fidgeting, brushing his knuckle underneath to rid of the itch he felt.

"I noticed you hadn't eaten much at dinner, were you not hungry," the doctor quizzed with a gentle smile, tilting his head to suggest the possibility to his patient, but more so, wanting an answer.

In the quiet she left him in, he continued speaking.

"I am sure at your age I do not need to tell you to eat, Emma," he scolded in jest.

Emma eyed him from where she had now propped herself up on her elbows, letting the doctor catch her eyes hardening on him when he looked to see the joke had not been well-recieved.

He straightened in the chair and cleared his throat.

"I fear your fainting may have been due to the medication. It wasn't the correct type," Hartmann said. "You continue to mystify me, Emma. You will be under supervision until the medication has left your system, and so we can give you what you need."

Emma searched Hartmann's face, lips agape. In agreement, Hartmann gave a confirming nod, then holding a finger up with a smirk pulling at the side of his lips.

"I will be looking after you throughout this. After all, I am responsible for your care now. Nobody else but me." He finished with a smile, which loosened on his face when he saw Emma's look of devastation.

"This is ridiculous." Emma broke, ripping the sheet from her torso and pushing out of the bed.

Quick to react, Hartmann leapt from the chair to rush to the other side of the bed, wrapping an outheld hand around her flailing arm, tucking his palms under her arm, his grip hard on her instantly. Glaring at the doctor, looking to his hands grip on her arm. She gritted her teeth and pushed her face forwards, hoping instead that he would be the one to recoil but no such thing happened.

"I was fine before I came here, now look at the state of me!" Emma hissed, flecks of spit escaping through the space between her teeth. She yanked her arm to free herself from Hartmanns restraining grip.

"What have you done to me?" she accused, hot angry tears streaming her fast reddening cheeks.

"Emma, calm down. This is an adjustment, and I know it's scary," Hartmann coaxed, stood opposite, moving back to stand in front of the closed door. Scrutinising him stood in the way of the door, her forehead broke out into a sheen of sweat under the bright light of the room.

"You don't know shit about a lifestyle change. I am not your patient," she argued with indignance.

"Emma, you're trembling," Hartmann indicated, to which she shot her gaze to his eyes, peering at her hands as he had paused, loosening his grip around her arm. The adrenaline from her burst of anger had pushed her body to begin shaking.

Emma backed away, not saying anything to agree or disagree with the doctor. She withdrew a breath, an effort to calm herself down.

"Your skin is so pale." The doctor breathed, taking a step towards her and moving his arm upwards, fingers outstretched.

Clocking his movement she stepped backwards, eyeing his

hands with a glare that commanded what she wished to scream in his face.

Hartmann almost huffed, his hand recoiled and he looked unsure of why Emma was acting this way towards him. Edgy, and uncertain of his slow movements, seeing the fear in her eyes.

Hartmanns hand completely lowered. As his hand rested at his side once again he stood in seeming amazement with his lips parted to breathe. Closing his mouth, he rubbed his hands together beside himself.

Behind Hartmann the door was rapped on by unknown knuckles. He sauntered over and pulled it open.

Before anyone stood into the room, outstretched in the arms of the skinny, rude nurse was an off-white square of thick looking fabric, with dangling belts and long bits of rope-like fabric, too.

"Doctor," the pinched-cheek nurse addressed, her forehead wrinkled deep with her tensed features as she pushed the door shut behind herself.

Hartmann watched how her eyes flicked from Nurse Ruth to him, and back again.

"What is that? Doctor?" Emma asked, hunched over. Hartmann held the folded fabric, beginning to unfold it in front of himself, small belts falling out from the middle as he approached.

With fearful, glassy widened eyes she was left to numbly stare at the now revealed straightjacket dangling from his hands. Hartmann held it out like a towel, the nurse behind tapped her arms. Emma brushed the nurse's fingers from touching her shoulder, moving to turn and glare at her.

The arms of the jacket found Emma's hands, the nurse behind yanking at the collar ties to pull it up around the front, the itchy cuffs at the end of the arms itching at her skin, worsening when her arms were crossed over her chest as if giving herself a hug.

Hartmann nodded approvingly, to which the nurse moved from standing behind Emma, coming in beside him.

He could not avoid her obviously pained stare.

"You think I'm crazy?" she whispered, Hartmann fastening the belts at the back, almost choking her in the process of yanking at the ties and belts.

"Please stop!" Emma motioned sideways, her elbows jutting out in attempt to rustle Hartmann from restraining her any further.

"Stop it, you're hurting me!" Emma burst out in argument once more, yanking an elbow up with such irritation of being confronted with the jacket, her protruding bone knocked into doctor Hartmann's jaw. She clipped the bottom of his jaw with a such force, the man froze up completely as the pain wracked through him in waves.

While the realisation hit, Nurse Ruth was quick to continue on with her striding, almost ripping Emma's arm from its socket when she failed to notice Hartmann had paused.

Immediately Emma glued her eyes to his face when he rotated his jaw in a disturbing fashion – as if she had punched him, or gone out of her way to attack him. Fear made her freeze up entirely. The doctor's jaw clicked as he did though, and Emma was white with fear that the man she had accidentally hurt would pummel her to a pulp. The vivid imagery flashed through her mind while blood continued to drain from her face.

The two pairs of eyes laid on her. Doctor Hartmann hissed something in his harsh and aggressive German. In replacement for Emma being unable to understand him, his hand tightened on her to drive home the temper behind his words, if the anger was all she could understand, he would be content with that. Emma's lips dropped in horror, her bottom lip shivered with her mouth open.

"I didn't mean to hurt you." She allowed her sentence to

trail off meekly as she was dragged along. Emma sounded false, and her words hung in the air without meaning behind them.

His hands rested on her shoulders, giving a push to turn her around to face the door of the room, the sour faced nurse was now smirking. Hartmann wrapped his hand around her upper arm, motioning her forwards. She stared at his hand in alarm, trying to shake herself free.

"Thank you, Nurse." Hartmann smiled to Ruth stood now behind her.

"You are most welcome, Doctor," Nurse Ruth purred, slinking off after opening the door barely halfway for her skinny frame to slip out of, then pushing it wide open with a bony hand once on the other side.

Emma poorly concealed her disgust, her face soured by the nurse's suck-up behaviour and manner towards Hartmann.

With a roll of her eyes, nurse Ruth slid her bony wrist through the gap at Emma's inner elbow, where she also formed a hard grip.

"Where are you taking me?" Emma questioned.

"Stay relaxed for me," Hartmann responded nonchalantly as he led Emma through hall after hall. Out of the corner of his eye he saw how his patient was transfixed by the pretty murals on the walls, looking with what he could recognise as longing at the pictures of beautiful forest scenery or colourful, bright animals painted on both sides of the white and medical green ugly walls to brighten the mundane wandering. Hartmann and the nurse dragged her to the singular door at the end of the yellowing, moulding corridor.

Taking a stride ahead, the nurse unlocked the scarcely painted covered door.

Emma's eyes widened when the door was pulled back, revealing that it was heavy, thick metal with a shunting, tough lock. She saw it had taken Nurse Ruth a great deal of her body weight to pull the door open.

At the top half of the metal white door there was a thick

glass window. The nurse strode in front and remained standing there.

"Get off," she mumbled, pulling away but heading closer to the wide open door. On the inside it showed the door had a cushioned backing, and was a pale, off-white like discarded chewing gum. It gave the appearance of dampness beneath the cushioned walls having soured.

"Emma, you're staying in here for a little while," Hartmann clipped from behind, placing a hand on her shoulder to guide her through to the very inside of the room.

Hartmann's felt her push back against his hand as he went to guide her inside. Her eyes like saucers as he met with them.

"No, please," came the line of argument under her breath, pushing back again.

"Stop wasting our time, you need to step in," Nurse Ruth instructed in a snappy tone, taking paces towards where Emma stood. The nurse's eyes fell to her outstretched hands, almost bumping into Hartmann as she went to grab at the terrified girl.

Hartmann raised a palm.

"Ruth, please," he said, stepping forwards, bringing dual attentions to only him. The pinch-cheeked nurse Ruth stopped glaring at Emma, and retracted her gaze, easing the weight she felt on her chest. Emma could still feel the cold fixation of her glare when she was forced to look at Hartmann.

He stood against the open door, his eyes softening on hers, which were full of fear, he recognised. He watched how she did not blink at him, and looking down at her face reflected the imitation of a terrified prey animal.

Despite a passing look of of sympathy, the doctor's lips moved in such a way to show how one would mimic a "coo" to an infant.

Doctor Hartmann gripped her jutting elbow and walked into the cell. The skin where his hand tugged burned like his hand was on fire, the rough fabric dug in. He watched how

Emma's jaw fell open but a scream failed to leave her, which he was grateful for.

She wriggled her arms back and forth inside the jacket, causing her to fast become hot underneath the towel-like fabric.

"Emma, sit down please," Hartmann instructed, the nurse's pinafore visible through the space between his legs, hovering in the doorway like some sort of lanky bouncer.

"No, please don't put me in there," Emma tried, her face visibly reddened from the tireless attempts to free her restrained limbs.

Hartmann wouldn't let himself catch her gaze, instead looking over the top of her head, which was an easy thing for him to do. Upon being thrust onto the floor, Emma wobbled, trying to find her feet and afraid of falling over onto the filthy fabric below.

"Please don't go," Emma urged between shallow breaths, but Hartmann stepped out of the padded room, ignoring her plea. His head did not turn from looking at the floor, discarding Emma in the cell. Nurse Ruth moved out of the way for him to make a well timed exit.

Hartmann remained with his head to his feet as his arm outstretched to the side of himself, pushing the door to close.

Hartmann was able to hear her small whimpers and sniffles as the door closed. He brushed his palms on the front of his trousers, looking to the nurse, who smiled at him. He turned, Ruth following suite, and both doctor and nurse began walking back up the hall, leaving Emma to stir in the padded cell.

## Chapter Thirteen

IT FELT like many hours had passed. Her hair was stuck to her sweaty face, and having no use of her arms, she was unable to rid herself of the additional torture the irritating strands caused her. Her mixture of tears and sweat proved a good glue.

Emma had no way to tell the time and even a minute in the cell left her feeling tortured in the silence. So she had resorted to humming childish, comforting tunes. One from a film she had watched, perhaps? Or was it from an album she knew, but it was no hinderance that she could not think of the name.

She had no answers, but she was glad for whatever she managed to hum, stringing together her loose notes in their rises and falls.

She wasn't sure how long ago that was, as the concept of time had left her. The alienating sensation had begun to seep after Emma began to walk around the four walls of the cell, watching her feet traipse one in front of the other – like balancing on an invisible beam.

Soon she began to pace instead, getting frustrated at her pathetic wobbling due to having no arms to help stay steady, placing her toes behind the heel of the leading foot.

Emma felt she was putting herself through a test to do

both what she could to ease her boredom as time passed by, while also trying to keep a lid on her swirling intense emotions. They lurked under the surface – threatening to overflow at any given moment. Knowing what she was trying to avoid, inadequacy kept seeping in.

Pacing the walls, her toes reached the corners of each of the four corners humming away to keep her mind occupied. Emma pushed away thoughts about Hartmann or even the room she was in. She ignored her situation as best she could, going into herself more to try and keep secure her mental and emotional stability. It was a silent, painful fight.

Emma found herself interrupted when the metal door's heavy lock dropped.

At hearing the first sound in what seemed to be hours, she jumped. Her small frame was fuelled by a shaking instinct – and she was quick to throw herself in the corner as the commotion of shuffling feet and muffled voices was heard from the other side of the door.

Her legs were splayed out in front rather than hugging them to her chest, straightening her back.

Hot and cold, on and off. Black and white. She felt herself shaking, and was almost whimpering as she willed herself to sink into the damp walls.

A battle ensued in which she bounced from one extreme to the other. It left her craving to find a middle, a balance where everything was under her own control. As the padded door was pushed open by a gloved hand, she realized her hope was one filled with naïveté.

Emma eyed the small, square, bulletproof glass window at the top of the door, squinting at the dark hair which was angled forwards.

A single white trouser leg stepped in, followed by the other.

Emma's eyes looked to the side, avoiding meeting those of the doctor.

"Good evening, Emma," Hartmann said, walking across the small room to stand in front of her in the corner.

Emma's brow dipped, then furrowed.

"Is it? Oh." A shrug from her shoulders was given indifferently from where she lay against the wall.

Emma only moved her ankles to make circles with the front of her toes. Hartmann knelt down to where her eye level would meet his easily.

Upon his moving, Emma eyed his every action, wanting to fall back into the wall to distance herself as much as she could.

Doctor Hartmann's breath smelt of burnt coffee, only forcing Emma to lean further into the blank room devoid of anything apart from the off-white colour. The wall almost hugged her but it was too thin in the cushioning. His presence shifted the room to morph and contort, Emma unfamiliar now, with him in it.

"Now, I have your finalised medication here with me," Hartmann informed her, reaching down to pull out a small white bottle from his coat pocket. He held it in front of her eyes between his thumb and forefinger at the bottom.

It struck her that Hartmann thought that was good news. He brought it upon her as if it was.

She wanted to sneer at him. Emma focused on the small white label slapped on the side of the rotund bottle, squinting to be able to read what it entailed.

In his hand she was able to make out her full name and Doctor Hartmann's below it. The text was the same style as the one which was slapped on her wristband. Emma recoiled from staring at the pill bottle, looking to the doctor from her laid up position against the wall.

"Why?"

At hearing her voice, Hartmann's eyes dipped. When his head raised, a smile had spread onto his face, and Emma leaned back again.

Her top lip flinched at his smile, feeling the heat under the straightjacket spike again.

Emma felt she could not do anything to change how he perceived her, the straightjacket a stiff reminder of that fact. More than anything, it filled her with fear.

What he thought he knew, he could laugh at. She'd let him laugh. He did not know anything, Emma assured to herself, and at her self-assurance, her nostrils flared.

"Now please tell me you're going to be good and take your pill for me," Hartmann said, glancing down at his feet before refocusing his sturdy gaze back onto Emma, that smile still perking on his lips.

Her top lip curled in disgust.

"You've got another thing coming if you think I am stupid enough to take medicines from you anymore."

He looked down between his knees momentarily, before raising his eyes again to give her his sound reasoning.

"Emma, you have a choice to make. I only want to help you become better."

Her lips tugged wide in a grimace. "No thanks." Pulling in her knees to the front of the straightjacket, the clammy bottoms of her feet stuck to the floor. There was a tense pause and Emma withdrew from feeling his palpable displeasure at her stubborn arguing.

"Take one, for me? Or you will have to stay in here, as you are unmedicated, and we can't have that, can we?"

Emma remained with her knees tucked at her chest, miserable. He spoke with a purposeful slowness, it vexed her greatly.

She displayed indifference to the looming prospect of her staying in the padded room for hours longer, leaving Emma to another miserable existence trapped in Westview General. It all merged, the winding halls became one in her mind when she tried to picture them, as if rolling out like the floor was never ending before her. The colours of the walls melted, giving the image of thick wax and Emma thought they would bleed from her ear canal, as it flooded her head.

Doctor Hartmann took a knee to the floor, resting his one empty palm out on his other. He turned inwards on himself while turning, giving a small sigh.

Emma remained with her eyes distant from him as he knelt opposite her, too close for her liking and so she hugged herself that much tighter.

"Emma, look," he tried.

His tone had dropped its professionalism, with a clipped edge to his words, leaving Emma to realise the absurd nature she had the man in. On his knees inside a padded room in front of her.

Blinking slowly, Emma turned her head to look at him.

"They won't hurt you, you need to take only one," he said, holding a pointed finger in the air from resting on his leg, letting her see his up-raised digit before retracting his hand.

Emma let her head dip, wondering if she really had a chance to fight Hartmann. Upon the thought appealing to her, she gave an unmoving stare at the doctor. She wanted to get back at him, and toyed with the idea.

Hartmann's gloved hand began to unscrew the top of the white bottle, rattling the pills inside the bottle.

"Open up for me," he instructed, tipping the bottle onto his flat palm until one pill fell out, placing another two which had fallen out back in.

They were colourful, wrapped in plastic. Like her hideous long gown, the plastic pills were also pink.

Emma feigned a surprised smirk – a scoff – at the fact that the pills did not have her name on them.

She had never seen pink pills before. They were alien-like against the contrast of the inside of Hartmann's palm.

"I need to see an improvement in you." he urged, apparently switching from trying to bait Emma through niceness and pleas, to being professional and acting accordingly.

His good cop-bad cop routine gave her a slight whiplash, and she tilted her head upon squinting at the man.

When her eyes didn't move from where they were fixated, he tried again.

"Do you like the colour pink, Emma?" Hartmann asked her, the pill balancing on the end of his fingers with a small, encouraging smile on his lips. Doctor Hartmann dropped the remainders of the bottle back into his coat pocket.

Emma was confused by his futile attempt to engage her, to get something out of her verbally. Laying against the wall, she stayed quiet.

"I promise nothing bad is going to happen, Emma, so open your mouth for me and we can go outside."

To which Emma hesitantly licked her lips, going to relax her jaw to let the doctor place the pill on her tongue.

Sticking her tongue out slightly, her gaze flitted back to his eyes which then again had softened.

His gloved fingers unfolded and revealed the small pink pill again, revealing how alien it looked in the off-white of the room. It looked so ugly, Emma not taking a liking to the colour much at all – her having never cared for it. She instead liked deep red, the colour of flowing blood from an artery. And luscious green so rich that it glows, or blue like a droplet taken from the clearest sunny sky without a dash of white to interrupt the calm, serene peace. Pink was plain, and boring enough to make her feel distasteful towards it. Too rich or deep and it looked ugly, not complimenting anything around itself in a garish fashion.

He had the small pill between his thumb and forefinger still, and placed it onto the end of her tongue, taking his hand away while she closed her lips. She swallowed it, all the while her doctor watched.

"Open, please. Show me your mouth is empty," he asked, and Emma stuck her tongue out as her lips again parted. Hartmann keenly inspected all around inside her mouth before pulling back from her, satisfied she had swallowed the pill.

His lips spread into a smile.

"Good." He put his hands on his knees and stood up, grunting under the effort it took. He looked to her with his easing smile.

"Would you like to get a wash first, Emma?" he asked, leaning out of the half open door before turning himself back to her.

Emma nodded, jumping on the opportunity

She wriggled her arms inside of the straightjacket.

"You will stay in the jacket until I get you to the wash room," he informed her.

Emma stepped forwards to stand closer to the doctor, indicating her desire to be freed from the awful silent room. The doctor let her stand there a little longer than she found necessary, but he finally pushed the door open and the other side of the hallway was finally visible. She felt like a caged animal being freed, but hurried to rush past where Hartmann stood to the side of the door. She released a shaky exhale, feeling like she was finally having her jumping nerves calmed. She heard the lock of the door shunting across and clanging down once more, relieved to be on the other side of it.

"Why did you put me in there?" Emma questioned, catching her hitched breath. He paused, blinking.

Feeling her shoulders tense, she watched as Hartmann smiled from his turned head, allowing her to see the side view of his features.

"Why do you think, Emma? Please, come let us get you cleaned up," he told her, only providing a shake of his head in answer to her question. His one hand opened to guide her, reaching around to the small of her back. Not wanting him to make contact with her, she briskly jumped forwards, beginning the long-winded walk. Emma was unable to tell which she hated more, the long, winding halls of the hospital or the hellish, silent padded room.

They both were held in high regard to be torture to her. Unprepared to be vulnerable in front of Hartmann again, she stammered on her words, while he looked down his nose at her, like a petulant child.

"But why? I don't feel better," Emma said, trying to keep up with his pointed strides, but her legs only stretched half the distance he managed.

His strides stopped dead, and he turned to face her. His head lowered, an eyebrow raising. "You don't feel better?" Hartmann tilted his head. Emma looked at her toes.

"No, I really don't," she mumbled, looking back up at him. Emma dared to become fiery, and accuse him of unfair action against her, but she faltered.

He hummed.

Emma waited, under his gaze while he looked over her head to the hall behind, awaiting his verdict

"You need to get a wash first. I will see what I can do for you soon, okay? I have a lot to do," he said, continuing on. While she leapt with a small dash to regain pace alongside Hartmann, Emma whimpered, feeling her fall away into herself. Knowing Hartmann had ignored her, she slumped beside him.

"If you had adhered to treatment at the beginning, we would not be having these ongoing problems."

The words he spoke struck, leaving Emma's lips parted as her heart shrank, breath sucked from her lungs left her mouth gaping like a fish out of water. Whether out of frustration or as a backhanded insult, Hartmann's cruel words collided with her like a slap to the face, as if being unwell or unable to cope as he had expected was all her fault.

It was her fault she was not thriving and reacting well to a massive change in her normal everyday functioning. If Emma knew she had the nerve to hit back at him with her own swirling, raging words, she would have cut him into bits.

Emma felt an eyelid twitch. Gathering together her thoughts, she fought against talking back – thinking the wisest decision would be not starting to dig a hole for this man to later drop her in. Her hands clenched at the restraint it took her.

Emma decided he must have thought that she had not heard it as they continued to walk. That must have resonated with Hartmann as a throwaway comment. His mood was hard to gauge.

Hartmann threw his gaze over his shoulder, and Emma looked to the floor, cheeks still reddened by her residing anger. Quickening her pace, the walls were once again bleak and boring, lacking any colour to brighten the bleak walk. There was no breeze coming up or going down any of these halls and nothing open to allow wind to come in, nor birds to be heard in any of the gardens. The floors didn't even smell the same, being musty and dirty, and the smell that flew up her nose was mustier, like slight rusted metal and old wood. It was acidic and unpleasant, the smell of neglect lingered.

"Walk faster, I've no time to spare for your dilly-dallying right now," he ordered from behind like a dictator.

His voice irked her, but stubbornness being innate, Emma instead slowed down.

He stepped out to the side with his brow furrowed, giving her a hard stare, his lips crumpled.

"You cannot be tired, you have done nothing all day," he stated with an incredulous look, before shaking his head and hurrying her along into one of the derelict rooms.

Emma felt she had managed to lose all sense of her own ability as an adult to speak for herself without the fear of being either humiliated or trodden all over by Hartmann.

She worried she was becoming accustomed to losing moral battles to this man, only finding the reason to be because of the power he held inside of the hospital. He may have been the head of the hospital, but it didn't make Emma any less powerful in her own rights to speak or reason for her own botched, awful treatments. It disturbed her that she was likely losing her edge.

Emma was adamant she had never agreed on being a patient, furthering the thought that the treatments were against her will and non-consensual. Hartmann was breaking the law. Regardless of her logical reasoning, she still longed for answers. A deep sense of separation came over her shoulders and made her slump when she walked.

The wards were crusty like an old scab, itching to be ripped off and discarded. Emma's mind flashed back, eyes widening and feet stopping in their tracks when she recalled the information she had failed to find online about the hospital when attempting her research.

An idea, or a theory of her own rather, planted itself, rooted into her brain. Emma could barely hold onto it, but she willed the seed of epiphany to grow, straining for her clouded mind to clear and for events to become understandable for the possibility of two minutes as to not lose herself entirely once more.

She pushed to try and imagine the reasons why Hartmann didn't have any direct information about his hospital published online, but realising it was an easy answer – it would be full of lies. The outside appearance wasn't true to the inside of the hospital.

Emma was desperate for clarity, some extension of the sense she felt she had been able to make for herself.

She gritted her teeth, trying to think back to the overwhelming thought process and straining for her brain to expand on the idea, but it had dissipated. It left Emma to remain zoned out at the floor, watching her feet go one after the other like a machine.

All she was left with was the singular knowledge that Hartmann was a liar. It made her skin prickle with anger.

Emma felt a pit of sick in the bottom of her stomach. She laid a palm over her intestines as they bubbled. Hartmann would have never let her see this part of the hospital on an inspection.

Who else had been put into those padded rooms?

"Emma!" Hartmann pushed into her. His fingers lingered against the small of her back for a few seconds too long. Her thoughts then burst with the sharpness of his shrill voice, losing all sense of her surroundings before gathering mentally upon a delay.

Emma only thought one thing when she finally turned to look up at Hartmann. *You're a liar.* Her eyes bore into his with more sense of self than she ever had since arriving. She bounced back with emotions anew and refreshed from before, when she had emerged from the padded room like a shell of herself.

Glaring at Hartmann, he tipped his chin downwards into his neck, clearly trying to understand her facial expression, taking a few seconds to do so. His eyes searched hers, only to then carelessly dismiss her, and push Emma by her shoulder into a large shower room.

Emma fumed. Regardless, she thought it would be wise to keep her anger hidden. She spitefully thought of turning the tables on him. If she didn't already know Hartmann, her doctor, personally, then what was stopping her now?

She had other tools to use to her advantage. She wouldn't argue – he had the upper hand in this hospital and she could grapple her own puppet strings. Even though Emma was a patient, she had power too – and she would be sure to be utilising it from now on.

The shower room was all white. Old, damaged white tiles on the wall were thick and large with brown at the corners where the broken sides met. The grout underneath which had been used to slam the tiles onto the walls had grown old and worn by the ever-present dampness of the room.

Flecks of black mould dotted the wall corners where water had seeped in to such an extent that some of the tiles had fallen off from the wall and black had completely replaced the small space and protruded. It showed a significant bloat from the amount of water it had managed to hold over time.

Emma imagined if she was to touch those small square spaces, her fingertip would fast sink into the decaying wall behind.

With a shiver, she stood limp with Hartmann fiddling to her side, swearing she could feel his cold breath on the back of her head.

The wear between the tiles and black mould trailed off into smudges that became random gatherings of concentrated dots as it progressed further into the centre.

Emma swore she could feel the damp already making her dead hair begin to frizz from standing outside of the doorway. She was left to stare at the pathetic sight of a plastic chair sitting over a plughole in the middle of the huge shower room, where the floor sank to drain the water. She turned to watch Hartmann's hand wrap around the handle, forcing the lock to drop, feeling her heart thrum.

The doctor turned where he stood.

"You need to undress, and I can wash you," he said with a nod of his head.

Emma looked to her feet, half swamped over by the loping fabric of the gown. She grabbed at the hem, and gathering some spare fabric in her hands. Mentally preparing herself to undress in front of this man horrified her, but she reminded herself not to argue. Emma had little shame in her body, but this discomfort made her shake. She swallowed, trying to rifle herself up with the buried pit of spite she held onto.

Emma knew Hartmann must of seen lots of different bodies and excessive human anatomy, but it was different. He was her doctor, yet it somehow seemed personal, not professional. His hands remained bare, without the trademark white powdered gloves that would normally be covering his knuckles. She cringed, hesitating on lifting the hem of her gown.

Emma took a breath before raising the hem over her head,

bundling the collected gown into her arms. She stood, cradling her gown at the navel while he pulled the shower head from the stand on the wall, his fingers grasping at its neck.

He made a circle with a hand. "Hurry up, come on."

The spite-filled Emma stood behind the plastic chair, eyes on the shower head Hartmann held. Her thighs were shaking, and knees almost knocking together. Emma stood, not cold enough to have goosebumps on her skin despite deep discomfort.

Despite being eager to have the process over with, more so than Hartmann, Emma found herself delaying her movements as if her body was layered in glue. She looked down again while Hartmann waited.

"Can I have a nurse wash me, please?"

"Even better, I am your doctor," he said. "Do you want to wash, or not?" He lowered his head, flapping a finger at Emma's bare torso.

She looked to the hem of her cotton undergarments at her hips. Her hands were slow to grip the elastic fabric, and pull them off. She moved her shoulders in such a way to help with the straps of her bra loosening, eventually coming off and holding the small folded cups in her hand.

Hartmann's watchful eyes flicked against her frame, and Emma grimaced while a wave of prickly heat washed over her, forcing her eyelids to close when she wavered on the spot.

Her eyes flicked to Hartmann fast, who was looking at her, still waiting with the shower head in his palm.

Sitting down in the plastic chair, Emma kept still and sat straight, staring at the door ahead while listening to the goings on behind her head. She heard the sound of flowing water through the old pipe connected to the head choking behind.

His fingers trailed through Emma's mess of knotted hair, pulling at her scalp when his fingers got caught halfway down, causing her to scowl. Her anger heightened while humiliation wrecked her, fingers wrapping around the bottom of the chair she sat on to steady her torso, being pulled back by Hartmann.

Hartmann soaked her back with the lukewarm water, but it did not ease her from sitting stiff. "You're doing much better now. I am pleased with you," he murmured.

Emma heard the smile in his tone.

Her eyes were shut and she squeezed them tighter, her chest shaking and teeth clamping down on her bottom lip so hard she thought she would rip it off. Her fingers under the chair jammed into the grooves of the plastic. She wished his voice would not echo in the room like it did, words palming against her skin. In the awkward silence and the darkness her eyelids provided, her ears picked up on something mumbled over her head.

"Oh my, Melissa,"

At the mumbled words, Emma froze. She breathed in heavier, indignant of neither going to kick off or cry. Hartmann seemed to be humming to himself then, hearing the sound of rising and falling notes hummed around her head. She squeezed her eyes harder.

Vowing then that she would not show Hartmann her emotions, conveying true feelings under a shell, she tried her best to hammer together at that moment in her disturbance. Emma hated the feeling of his fingertips brushing against her skin, the lingering smell of his old, woody cologne infiltrating her nostrils.

It only made her weaken, and she had to swallow and force air through her nostrils to plug the tears.

The warm water trailed and fell from where it had gathered in Emma's hair that stuck along her spine. The doctor kept on combing his fingers through her hair, then allowing the shower head to be yanked forward to pour all over her front.

His breathing was audible and it made her stiff in the chair, not relaxed by the experience like she would have liked to have been, if things had been different. If Hartmann was not the one to wash her. If he was not the one whose fingers grooved against her skull, if he was not the one to see her naked. If he was not the one with eyes plastered on her with such softness that it terrified her.

It fuelled the spite she held onto, telling herself it would get her through the hell he inflicted upon her. Her time to relax would come later, but only doubled in the pleasure it would gift when it finally would. She knew it would be wise to bide her time.

Hartmann stopped towering from behind, Emma not sensing his eyes on her head any longer.

He stepped back to turn the shower's weak jet off at the decaying, moulding wall. She remained frozen in the chair, only making movements when he gave an indication to do so. From behind, he passed a small, white towel to her. Emma snatched it from his hand, throwing it over her chest and tucking it under her armpits after wrapping it around herself.

Emma scrutinised Hartmann's every action. She watched his careful movements and got to an understanding through squinted, narrowed eyes, but her brain couldn't form the connections between one idea, and another. It was frustrating as the pathways between two ideas would not come to her. She was unable to link together what she saw, even when it brought forward a great deal of disturbance.

Upon the anticipated exiting of the shower room, Emma wanted to do only one thing – escape. Hartmann was slow to hand over Emma's old pink gown to throw back on over her garments that she had been hasty to throw on.

The doctor did not say anything to her, and instead was quiet with only a small smile when Emma dared look at him.

It burned her throat and filled her with the sudden, undying urge to vomit.

# Chapter Fourteen

DRESSED ONCE MORE, soaked locks of Emma's hair dripped and left a trail from where she had walked.

They stuck to her pink gown, making it damp against her cooling skin. Upon leaving the shower room, she took in the drab surroundings once more, feeling connected with the old, neglected walls when making her way between the two of them.

Hartmann led her out, but she understood he was beside her the entire time. She was driven by thoughts of escape, as it had planted itself in her mind and she wasn't trying to fight against the idea.

"Let's get you back to your room," Hartmann said, as he led Emma up a flight of stairs, with her in front. She sensed his eyes on her back while she pulled herself up the stairs by the plastic-covered handrail, shaking.

"I want to go out into the garden please," Emma said when she reached the final stair. She waited, lingering without stepping forward again into the closed-off hallway leading into the normality behind the locked doors.

Hartmann's outstretched hand towards the door paused mid-air, flicking eyes to his face to see him pause. He let out a small breath through parted lips, a small smile forming, then turned to Emma.

She longed to see the outside, birds flying overhead with their wonderful, charming songs. To see, to hear the peace of the outside.

He pulled the old key from his white trouser pocket. "I don't think so, you need to rest," Hartmann's shoulder barged the door to pry it open, the old door hinge groaning under the rust.

Emma watched the sudden power he exerted, and she quieted. The door shunted open, and he pulled himself aside to allow Emma to leave first. Her head bowed when she walked out, clumsily into the middle of an empty hallway. Upon looking down again, she set eyes on another woman who was trundling along. Nobody had seen Hartmann, nor her. The air tensed in a boiling, stagnant silence standing between them.

"You ought to come to your room and rest up, do you understand me?" Hartmann interrupted her thoughts, shutting the door and locking it shut. The undertone of "secrecy" was eminent. It stank, and Emma's nose wrinkled.

Hartmann, a seemingly stoic man, was flitting his eyes around, Emma being able to recognise the signs of paranoia he displayed. His actions contrasted with the slowness which Emma moved. She smirked to herself, the smug grin spreading across her face at the man's animation.

Hartmann clocked her grin, and paused again. The air thickened, sensing the smirk which was then wiped from her face with haste, but her effort was far too poor. An emotion had slipped out, and he had seen it. She looked up to him, his eyes scanning her face and eyes hard as he looked. He looked panicked, fading into anger like a switch being turned over. Emma recognized by his facial expression that some moment of understanding clicked. It was as if his skin had become transparent.

Emma hesitated, but Hartmann's hand outstretched, landing the pads of his fingers at the space between her shoulder blades and pushed her forcibly down the hallway. His lips were tight, and the muscles above his eyebrows were square while he frowned.

Emma's lips crumpled when Hartmann exerted himself. Emma was forced to move from the area before, and more than likely the two were seen by any other patients wandering the halls. She understood, or knew he was angry, but she smirked again, knowing what he had done was outside of practice.

Emma hoped to quickly become wise to his actions, and grasp for a string to pull. She knew that at the very least Hartmann would not appreciate her efforts, and that alone made her happy. Reaching the end of the hall, he released his fingers from where they had been pressing into Emma's back. She looked to other patients, wanting to make eye contact with someone.

The ones Emma passed looked only to Hartmann with a smile or a kind greeting, a hand raised from the walkers, or giving a nod of the head in acknowledgement. He rushed behind while passing the residents, bee-lining to her room. All Emma could think about was her pang of desire for clarity, but the environment she was in stopped her constantly.

Emma was then grateful to head to her room, at least then she may be able to think clearly – or try to. She'd finally be able to have a moment to get her thoughts straight. Emma sped ahead of Hartmann, coming to see the room's closed door on the left hand side. She burst in, the doctor following behind. Her chest was tight and left her feeling pent up.

"Hartmann, why is that area of the hospital still here?" Emma quizzed, seeing the nonexistence of discomfort on his features.

"It's for special patients, and you are one of them. You

need a very different form of treatment than my other patients, Emma. That's all." He smiled.

Emma found it teeth-grittingly frustrating that Hartmann wouldn't give a straight answer, or the answer she wanted to hear. His tactics of avoidance irked her, seeing how easily he shrugged her off.

Emma would take straight bullshit at this point. He made her blood boil, feeling it simmer while being thrown through her veins.

*You're a liar, you're a liar. I know you are.*

Emma's shoulders only loosened when she allowed herself a moment without her anger. If she was the only one who knew about those old asylum wards, then surely she would see more of them now?

She knew a dark secret. She knew Hartmann was a liar. But then, the dread.

This would debilitate her, because Emma knew the layer beneath, and she posed a danger to Hartmann's hospital, and his position.

People with secrets shared are watched, and not trusted.

Emma looked to Hartmann, eyes wider than before upon the clouds clearing. He lifted his chin, his eyebrows raising.

She began to panic, her urge to escape deeper than before now coming to the realisation she had a valuable secret to expose Hartmann – either she would become trapped in this hospital or she would have to make a desperate escape sooner rather than later.

"What's wrong, Emma?" he asked, moving forwards.

She stepped back. Hartmann was to become her enemy, or her best friend.

The world drained of all colour when confronted with her choice. Black and white, there was no middle ground between the two options both being extreme in nature of actions and consequences.

"Nothing, I'm just tired," Emma lied, looking down to fake

a yawn. Her poor display was accepted by Hartmann, his face softening upon watching her jaw stretch to release her slow yawn.

"I told you to rest up, so let's get you into bed." His fingers tucked under the sheet and were brisk to pull them back. Hartmann folder over the corner, leaving the bed welcoming Emma to climb into. Behind the facade, her heart was racing. She had to remember she had power over this man and once she escaped, she would exert it to the best of her ability to expose this liar of a doctor. On the outside, nothing would be a barrier. Emma slowly laid herself onto the bed and flopped onto her side, Hartmann leaning down she squeezed her eyelids shut.

"Get some rest, I will have a nurse leave you what you need on the bedside table for when you awake," he said, throwing the blanket over Emma's upper body.

Laying in the bed, Emma heard the curtains being pulled over, the room enveloping into darkness.

Her back to the door, Emma only opened her eyes to hear the door close, and sat up a few seconds afterwards. A shiver tickled her spine, releasing a grimace to rid herself of the unpleasant sensation Hartmann left her with.

Emma looked to the stream of yellow light coming from under the door and kicked her legs out from the paper thin sheet.

She looked down to her legs, eyebrows dipping hard. Emma felt she could have allowed herself to laugh at the ridiculousness of herself. Anger burned inside her, but then she found it all so ridiculous. This place, the hospital of lies, gave Emma no middle ground where her emotions were concerned.

Every little action was scrutinised, Emma realised Hartmann stood as a very alternate individual to her, compared to how others viewed him.

It gave her space to question everything he did and looked for an ulterior motive to his every action.

Although she didn't look for one, she expected one. After all, he was a liar.

Emma was not sure of the time, but it had to have been late into the evening now. She didn't want to sleep, having way too much on her mind, plus it would not come to her easy regardless.

She struggled to think for herself, and became angry at the inability to be clear, anger rising to be impulsive or violent. Each time Emma would urge to run away and escape, it ended with her kicking herself at imagining her poorly clothed figure running the streets.

She clamped down hard on her lip, staring down at her knees while her foggy brain ticked away on a new plan. Emma failed to formulate a string of thought to follow which would go beyond her next two steps.

It seemed to fade into a fog behind her eyes and would be left grasping at nothingness, trying to pin a cloud to the walls which was running up and down inside her mind. She fell into a hole of racing thoughts, but from what she could pull at, nothing became clear.

It was like knowing you stood somewhere completely recognisable, but terrifying all at once, as the fog surrounding is so thick that you cannot see your hand outstretched in front of you.

Bringing her cheeks to flush, feeling she would drool like a zombie if she had remained inside of her insufferable head for a second longer. Emma swayed like being upright on a boat riding through a windy sea, and she snapped. She shook her head in imitation of a wet dog drying, splattering the bath water all over the walls.

When she rested, she thought she saw brain matter splattered like thin paint covering the white, but there was nothing. The walls were still pristine white, possibly the only defect now being tiny droplets of water on the paint.

Emma sat with the sensation of acid in the back of her

throat and wishing to collapse into someone's arms, to rest against something steady.

She pulled her lips thin and let the dual feeling of loneliness and that ugly, desperate pang of human longing wash over her.

The door of the room was closed as Hartmann had left it, but she found herself writhing for the environment to change. The walls were too tall and Emma resented the sight of them. Maybe that would help. Emma's mother had always been the one to tell her, whenever she could see her daughter struggling that it was best to go for a walk. It would always follow head outside, to clear her "muddled little mind," as Emma's mother put it. She would be the one to drill the small, but immensely helpful lessons, into her before puberty had chance to rip her apart. That would be when those moments would treble in the weight they were able to carry upon her shoulders.

With that in mind, Emma clutched the handle, hesitating on pushing down when her mind sent her to freeze over at the thought of Hartmann lingering outside.

The acid that lay at the back of her throat stung, and it drove her to push on the door, forcing saliva down her throat.

It was quiet, and the long light bars lit up the middle of the mopped floors like an entranceway all along itself, reflecting the weak outline of Emma's shadow.

She crept nearer to the left side of the hall, hurrying along to the stairs. Her bare feet were cold, slinking like a cat and fearing she would be scolded from behind, wagged a finger at, and told she should be in her room. Emma smirked while she crept.

Emma wondered just then, as she watched the stairs before her – where her confidence had gone? Her smirk faded at the thought heavy at her chest.

She was apprehensive about being caught creeping the halls and reprimanded by a duty nurse. Emma held the nurses in a lesser regard of her fears, and told herself she could handle that small scale if she did get caught. Managing to calm herself, Emma remained with a feeling of smug elation.

Most of the doors to rooms she saw were now shut, or left comfortably ajar. The yellow glow from a bedside lamp being the only thing to emanate into the hall, or under the space below the bottom of the door.

Emma hoped there would be soup left in the dining area, as she may indulge herself in a bowl – if there was, and that being chicken soup, Emma was already happier at the thought of it. The lack of dinner she had chosen to consume left her stomach grumbling now at the thought of salty, thick soup laced with flattened pieces of corn and the shredded breast of chicken.

There would be leftovers from dinner. It wouldn't be half as much of a waste that way. Hopefully, too, a basket of bread left out to dunk into it.

With the image of a bowl of warm soup in mind, she continued creeping the halls, albeit quicker.

Emma reached the double doors, peering in and dotting her eyes across the empty chairs. The dining hall which had earlier filled her with nerves, laid barren and empty. The tables were void of those nodding heads that gave her the image of children's toys.

In the quiet, Emma relaxed her back from its hunched over state, exhaling among the empty room. She bee-lined to a singular drum of soup upon a small square area which was earlier used for stacking ceramic plates on. Next to the large silver drum were soup bowls. She was eager to fill her stomach, and return to her room happier, feeling better with a belly full of hot soup.

The round tables had remnants of other patients having visited to gulp down a bowl of soup, as there were no members of staff who were visiting to tidy the used bowls and spoons away.

Small crumbs of stale bread sat atop the round tables in

different places, close to the metal drum. Its lid had a ladle handle sticking out of the top, but that didn't affect the temperature of the soup, as the drum was heated from the inside.

Emma jolted when she heard the clink of a metal spoon against ceramic from behind.

Emma searched, then spied a woman, who was also joining in on the late night supper of bread and soup.

The salty smell wafted up Emma's nostrils, relaxing her enough to bring a smile to her lips which she then presented to the lady. She had a spoon in her right hand and placed it back down into the bowl, and gave a quick tightening of her lips which Emma took as a tired smile.

"I didn't mean to scare you, I'm sorry," Emma said, regardless of the roles in that sentence being completely opposite.

The woman took a mouthful of the soup, looking down into her bowl, and trying not to miss her mouth.

Having put herself into a position that may have gave her a creepy air, Emma retreated to turn around to the bowls on the side. She bit down on her bottom lip while the embarrassment fizzled through her. Her limbs were stiff when she reached to the top of the drum and placed the lid to the left of her. She felt her cheeks burn.

She lifted the ladle and poured some soup into the white bowl she held.

"Ah, that soup is lovely. And, you didn't scare me." The lady smacked her lips together once she had finished speaking.

If Emma hadn't already been on edge enough, when that voice came from behind her, ending the silence in the hall she felt her nerves spike. The lady smacked her lips together once she had finished speaking.

Emma appreciated the confirmation of having not made it awkward or making the stranger uncomfortable. Turning around with her filled soup bowl, Emma smiled and gave a small laugh.

"That's good, I was worried."

"About the soup being good or having scared a stranger?" The lady smiled at her, raising an eyebrow.

Seeing her relax, Emma's panic eased and she smiled back to the lady.

"May I sit with you?" Emma asked, sensing a few answers could come of this encounter.

The woman wiped at her hairy top lip with a tissue and gestured to the remainder of the empty chairs around the table, nodding to confirm before she could verbalise it.

"Yes, yes you can, lovely."

Emma was happy to get over her bout of sadness in the company of the fellow patient, able to escape her own head, as insufferable as it had become lately.

She sat beside her new partner in conversation, eager to chat and enjoy her soup. She left a chair remaining empty between herself and the other woman. Her arm still bore the bandage from the IV incident, Emma becoming nervous to think she would have to lie to her new friend about what had happened. She masked her nervousness by clearing her throat when she lowered into the chair, feeling the lady's eyes on her movements as she settled.

"Which ward are you on? I don't recognise you." Emma swallowed, but tried to remain confident. "I'm on the Lilypad ward, how about you?" She perked in her chair, giving a pinched smile to the woman.

The woman swallowed. "Rosetta."

A silence came, vague, but powerfully. Emma swallowed her mouthful of soup, burning her tongue as it zipped down her throat as she strained her neck in an awkward attempt to ease the scalding.

Before Emma's mouth had relieved itself of the burning she had just put her tongue through, the woman spoke up.

"I'm Gene, and you are?" The woman's wrinkled palm was held out to Emma.

"Oh, sorry." She put a hand to her throat as she swallowed again. "Emma Merrick," she managed before lowering her head to cough into her balled hand. She rubbed her thigh and lifted her eyes to the woman.

"Where's that?"

"On the side of the main building closest to the road, nearest the entrance gates. Do you know it?" Gene asked, bringing her spoon down into her bowl to let more of the soup seep onto the utensil.

Emma shook her head. "No, I don't. I haven't explored that far yet, but the garden is nice."

Straightening from being hunched over her bowl, Gene furrowed her wrinkled brow and leaned back in her chair. Emma gave a thought to her honesty of saying such, eyes flicking to the table. "Actually, I don't think you are allowed to come onto our ward," the woman corrected, to which there was a pause.

Emma looked to her, lips parted to speak, but she hesitated.

"What makes you say that?" she probed.

Gene hesitated, just like Emma had seconds ago and a pit of dread formed at the bottom of her stomach.

Without shame, Emma watched the face of her fellow patient flinch along with her stammering purple bottom lip. Emma sat stiff, awaiting an answer, simmering while her eyes drove through Gene's skull.

"Erm, I think it's just the rules, darling. I wouldn't be allowed into your ward either, up where you are." The nonchalant shrug of Gene's shoulders came, but Emma was suspicious of Gene trying to ease her perking interest.

Emma rested from her hot glare at the woman's head. She instead filled her spoon again, sinking it below the surface, eager to bring warmth to her stomach in the discomfort of the quiet.

Emma shrugged, eyes on her soup. She put her spoon back down, having paused completely in her swirling thoughts.

"I don't see why I can't visit other wards. Patients are allowed to wander all around these hospitals, I should know that."

Gene looked panicked. Unsure of herself, she stammered out loud as she sat. She became unsure, looking ahead of herself with unease. Her freckled hands rubbed atop her small thighs and she gave a small laugh.

"We just have to listen to Hartmann, don't we all?" she laughed, placing her freckled hands atop the table.

At the mention of the name, Emma perked with a hitched breath. She looked around quickly for the sight of him leering somewhere in the dining hall, but nothing of him was to be seen and so Emma lowered her eyes back to the table. It brought an ease to the prickling sensation under her skin. Emma dragged her fingers down the side of her face, leaning back.

"Well, I'm not listening to whatever rules restrict me from exploring now. I'm a patient." Gene looked struck. "I think it's best you don't. He doesn't let patients roam far."

Again Emma found herself glaring at her. The words sunk in and she stopped leaning back. "I don't understand what you mean," she stated, eyes flicking at Gene's face.

Gene had taken a spoonful of her soup while Emma had been deep in thought, and so she was slow to swallow and answer.

"It's the way he has things, it's what's best for us all."

Discontented, Emma was bored of the conversation by this point – she thrummed her fingertips on the table and gazed around the hall. Raising herself from the chair, she stood behind it and pushed it forwards, tucking the bottom under the table.

Emma flicked her drying hair behind her ears, and looked over her shoulder to the doorway. "It's been a pleasure meeting you," Emma chided as she took steps away from the table, flashing a smile as to not alert the woman to the fact that Emma had forgotten her name entirely.

The old lady looked up, squinting behind her large rounded glasses, which she then pushed up the bridge of her nose.

"Oh? Alright love," she mumbled, pinching the spoon in her fingers again.

Emma turned on her heel after having gave the lady a parting wave before diving through the chairs. She bee-lined straight for the Rosetta ward.

Emma left the dining hall and turned left instead of going right.

It lead her towards the nurses' office, and towards the bedrooms which would have a view of the front garden if they were on the left hand side.

The signs above just before the doorways helped guide herself onto other wards, where there was little movement from people.

Apart from the rhythmic beeping of machines coming from behind the closed doors of the rooms, it was silent.

Her footsteps became steps in which she stood on her toes to ease noise, even though she made next to none – Emma was convinced of doing so.

Her skin prickled.

The hallway she found herself stood in was much wider, and the doors had clear glass instead of ones with skinny, crossed black lines.

In the middle of the hallway she crept down, looking to each side of the walls, being unnerved by the lilac flower murals.

As Emma crept, she hoped that the automatic lights above wouldn't alert any of the nurses – her exploration wasn't over yet and if she were discovered it would come to a screeching halt. It would stop before she even had the chance to begin.

She brought herself towards the end of the hall to an open

room where the reception of the ward lay. It was identical to the Lilypad ward. The reception was exactly the same as on the opposite side of the building. She wasn't sure what she had expected.

Her feet made a turn when she stood in front of the white desk, put at peace by the silence that surrounded herself.

Emma wanted to see the bedrooms, theorising that they must have been different. Not seeing anybody behind her, she continued walking.

The lights flicked on when sensing her small and creeping frame underneath, and then off again when she passed. Emma was irked to set sights on a communal area which stretched out from the left hand side of the hallway.

It had windows which reached the floor and comfortable looking armchairs, and there was a television propped up on the wall. Emma's top lip yanked upwards in disgust, looking at the blue shag carpet on the floor which sat under the seats, although it was flattened and old.

Her chin jutted forwards as she stopped walking. She turned her head to take in the homely little scene before her.

"There's nothing like this in Lilypad ward," Emma thought with a tensed face.

She wondered why the patients on the other side of the hospital didn't get to have TV sets and a communal area along their halls.

The scene triggered anger within her for the clear display of inequity. She pledged to raise this question to Doctor Hartmann, smirking at the thought of him struggling to answer her.

———

Back in the hellhole of her room, Emma wanted to bounce on the spot in her sudden rush of overwhelming emotions that threatened to drown her. Everything was overflowing. Her deep sadness, and gnawing anger became large rows of jaws full of teeth as sharp as a knife's edge.

She felt compelled to do something, like a spark had hit. She wanted to jump about the room and was compelled to wreck it completely. She wanted auditory confirmation of being able to do damage, like clay pots smashing or glass shattering. Emma stood in the middle of her room completely still, but her heart raced as if it would erupt from her chest. She was furious, driven by frustration mounting and now overspilling everywhere.

Black and white.

Glaring hard, Emma dived head first into the bed, her arms out at the sides of her head gripping the pillow while her body convulsed. She didn't suffer from panic attacks but the situation thrust her into one, faced with the mental block which angered her in such a way. Emma kicked and writhed like trying to expel a demon from underneath her skin.

With her nails stabbed at the sides of her temples and jaw tensed, her eyes rolled back. The ceiling swirled and seemed to move in front, like terrific rolling clouds above. Emma shut her eyes, squeezing them while waiting for her pumping adrenaline to die down.

Emma felt so out of control. It brought forth a great realisation of paralytic terror. She didn't understand what else to do but listen to her body and its sudden need to expel explosive energy.

With a hideous grin, she stretched her cheeks into cherubs and tipped her head back, wanting to scream. She turned back onto her front and grinned into the pillow, straining and kicking her legs out.

Emma lay there, frozen. Her breathing had only then became shallow and slow while her eyes dried as she stared into space.

Just as fast as she had felt compelled to bounce around, then felt drained, her limbs regaining incredible weight.

Had an invisible demon just thrown her around the room?

Leaving Emma exhausted, her limbs tingling as they loosened – the electric current leaving her body feeling like jelly when the weight invaded.

Her brain was empty, and she only remembered the desperate simple desire to escape. Emma didn't want to move from where she lay. Moisture was provided to her twitching eyes when she gained strength to blink.

She moved her gaze over to the closed curtains, head pulsating on the pillow like it was going to implode. Emma curled her bottom lip as her face crumpled, eyes filling up with hot tears – and she began to weep.

## Chapter Fifteen

BETWEEN THE PADS of both her forefinger and thumb, Emma held a pregnancy test with two solid blue lines. Looking up from the positive test she scaled her fiancé to look into his glassy eyes, creased at the sides where his proud smile was etched onto his face. Jason enveloped her into a big cuddle, his head resting against hers as he held her in the embrace – standing cuddling, the pair rocked on the spot in joy. The constant trying had paid off. They were going to be a family.

The dream came to her in flashes, like different cut scenes out of a student drama class project.

Emma was elated, Jason's smile made her heart melt, but so full at the same time. She felt like a baby herself as they stood in the hallway of their apartment, cuddling. Emma couldn't wait to be a family, her throat tickled with a warm rawness that pinched her eyes with tears. Closing her eyes with a smile, tears of joy fell down her cheeks. Jason's lips pressed against the top of her head, to which Emma could only squeeze her arms tighter around his waist.

Soft eyes set on her stomach which was fast becoming well rounded. One hand cupped the round curve above her pelvic area, somewhat hoping to ease the pressure of carrying their growing child for the past few months. The nursery was painted a soft yellow like ducklings' fur, and had light white curtains at the window opposite the doorway. Jason had left his paint-spattered stepladder in the nursery. Emma at once wished to move it, but it was too heavy for her to lift, it was too short of a time now before the due date arrived at the end of June, and Emma couldn't wait. She was eager to hold their little bundle, and utilise everything which she had been gifted and given – new baby bottles, outfits she had planned – especially the first outfit. That had taken Emma a week to plan out and pack into the hospital bag before Jason got fed up of her mucking about, and how he had playfully took her face into his hands and kissed her head.

"Stop your fussing, would you?" he said, feeling the quick exhale through his nose brush Emma's forehead when he laughed. His lips pressed warmly against her cool skin again, and Emma melted into his hands. Emma was ready to take so many pictures with her Polaroid camera, as her mother had bought her and Jason a family album to fill with their 'journey into a new depth of love,' as she put it. The album waited patiently atop the white chest of drawers, resting on the top to be filled out. Emma had already stuck in the first picture of her scan. Ready and waiting, she had decorated the last page, ready for the image of the last scan in the middle of the borders. Every kick to her inside and every wriggle late at night reminded Emma of what was to come, and she smiled each time when she felt the baby move. Emma sat in the comfy, white plush chair in the corner of the room opposite the cot with Jason on the floor, his hand on her stomach while the baby kicked. His eyes shone. She had never seen her partner so elated. With a contented smile, Emma ran her fingers through the top of his hair while he nuzzled her stomach, resting together and waiting for that anticipated day to come.

Waking up, the colour of the dreams draining through her, Emma knew the day was ruined before it had begun. She sat up, pulling her knees into her chest.

Her hands met and clasped at the middle of her shin, replaying moments from the dream.

How Jason embraced her with such adoration, the elation Emma knew she always felt cuddled in his arms. Flashbacks of the separation rode over, and she crumpled – feeling her spine curve when it toppled on her shoulders.

From the inside she felt empty. Hollow, at the very start of her day already drained from the dream, the emotional weight of those moments of her past weighed her down. How Emma felt his large hands brush against her, and the warmth emanating from his body exchanged with her own.

It was so real. Emma had tried so hard to forget and move herself onwards healthily, but her dreams were betraying that aim, and how hard she had been working to achieve it.

Her unconscious betrayed her. It is said that dreams are representative of what we desire, or what our unconscious is troubled by beneath an outward image. Dreams mean something, and Emma was a believer in the meaning of dreams, but it distressed her greatly in the instance when it was reflected at her.

It stabbed her heart, and Emma had that awful restless urge to drink to feel numb and not so overwhelmed by the waves of uncontrollable emotions.

It was like going into a lockdown to protect herself, what little she had left within to treasure she wished to keep fighting off the demons of insurmountable guilt. Anger, and then coming down and sinking into a depression. The thin sheet stuck to the prickly hairs on her legs.

Emma was stiffened by the fabulous disturbing bright colours draining from inside and leaving behind the bland reality of those awful walls. Upon exhaling, her eyes dropped to the sheets, slumping her shoulders and letting her ribcage relax. Emma wanted to know the time, but within her room she hadn't been given the privilege of a clock. She ragged a hand through her hair, growing restless and feeling a simmering bitterness, irritated by the circumstances of her stale situation. Her feet swung out from the bed and she slid down to meet the cool floor with the bottom of her warm feet. It wasn't late enough into the morning for it to be warm yet. It was calm and cool before the sun had managed to rise properly, or rather before the clouds from the night had dissipated, allowing the sun's rays to warm her skin.

It took Emma only a few steps to reach the window of her room, overlooking the garden. There was nobody around to fill the natural space, indicating it must have been very early. Emma had almost forgotten that in summer the sun rises much earlier than in the winter months. It was daylight, but the warm rays were still hidden behind residing clouds. Her brain pulsed in the quiet, sinking back into her cloud of thoughts, leaning against the wall at her side. She fidgeted on the spot, flicking and scratching the top of her nails.

For a while, Emma had been developing a habit of "rubbing," when she had something on her mind. Preoccupied, she would rub the dead skin from areas of her body such as the bottom of her feet, chest, and her hands until the collected sweat and dirt from those areas collected, forming small black bits on the surface. Emma did this habitually at the joint of her thumb on her left hand, imagining herself running down through the grass and hopping over the fence surrounding the garden. The fence had the road upon which she had driven up on the other side of it, leading up to the automatic barrier and carpark.

She desperately pictured escaping while she stared longingly out of the window, convincing herself of the reality so close. Her breathing almost became paced, rubbing at her thumb joint.

As she ran to escape, the grass would tickle the hardened bottoms of her feet. She wouldn't look back over her shoulder, not once during her sprinting. What would she do that for, everything she wanted was ahead of her. Within her mind she had a plan, the first step was all she needed and after that she was home free to get out of Westview General, and return to where she craved to be. Where she belonged. She clasped her hands at her temple, skin prickling as her head became enveloped into the thick blinding clouds of her imagination.

Lifting her head, Emma turned on her heel to face the white door of the room, having wrapped her hand around the door handle. She leant in to push it open, but paused for breath which she didn't manage to catch. Waiting, she stood there trying to control her body's quickening pace versus her calm mental state.

Taking a breath, she held it in the tension she had created around herself, paranoid of someone knowing what she was doing. Emma was in her firm mind, being able to recognise that this place wasn't benefiting her. She blamed Hartmann, but he would not let her go from his watchful gaze and his haunting grasp, and so she longed to run.

Westview brought Emma's face to pucker, looking like she had finished sucking on a lemon when thoughts about Hartmann's treatment of her came to mind. He may have been a doctor, but he didn't actually have a clue what he was doing to her, she theorised. He read her body, not her mind. It all accumulated and tortured her. But it spurred her footsteps to be faster, and lighter on stepping.

She had to escape this awful place to save herself.

Doctor Hartmann – whatever the hell he would pull out of his sleeve for Emma next, she was adamant to not be here to participate.

Emma thought she could slip away, simply discharge herself without the fuss. A self-confirming nod affirmed the pull of the grand idea becoming a reality. Emma came to the open doorway of the dining hall, gazing to see the patterned, swirling ceiling. Squinting, her eyes became clouded with the concentration of moisture, giving the ceiling the appearance of clouds. Feeling as small as ever, she made a conscious effort to not make any chairs scrape on the floor as she breathed in to move around them. Her ears pricked to crockery being placed onto tables, ceramic plates fresh from the dishwasher stacked in a large metal bin.

Leering, she saw plates carried into a divider separating two stacks of plates ready for breakfast. The chef placed down the piled up crockery in his arms and turned his back on her. She knew she needed the dining area to open up properly yet, as she haplessly wandered between tables and chairs being careful not to bump into anything.

Emma's eyes observed the empty room with a kind of peacefulness, the knowledge of knowing she was alone – away from Hartmann and the other patients, whose compliance and seeming blindness she found increasingly irritating.

She thought that being alone in the spacious, barren room she would become uncomfortable and jumpy, like she had the last time.

That seemed a vivid memory by now to her, thinking back it was fuzzy around the edges of the imagery in her mind and threatened to dissipate altogether. Like so many of her other prominent thoughts. Her throat itched, she needed to cough but swallowed the urge as her eyes became hot and panicked tears trickled down her cheeks. With her forefinger she wiped them away and dabbed at her darkened undereye. Emma didn't wish to draw attention to herself.

Rather than discomfort though, she found peace of mind being in the empty room with only herself. The sudden few tears wiped away after almost choking herself to stifle a loud few coughs. Restraining them left her cheeks reddened and face looking flushed. Forming a knuckle to rub her eyes clear, Emma set sight through narrowed, watery eyes on the tall hand of the clock which was propped on the wall.

It read half six in the morning.

Emma traipsed through the divided jumble of tables, analysing each one, tipping her head up and then back to the attention of the tables – she had to sit at the right one. Would it be best to sit nearest to the exit, or furthest away from Hartmann? The sun had begun to stream in through the few windows which dotted the room and allowed the sun's morning rays to stretch over the tablecloths.

Emma raised her head to determine out which table Hartmann would sit at, preparing to distance herself before he arrived.

One after the other, the servers and chefs came marching through the floppy double doors of the kitchen with the individual hot trays of food in their arms.

Emma watched in silence, content to watch someone else go about their business without paying her any heed at all. The servers' faces conveyed content, while some looked overtired. She was glad to be causing no worry or damage by being stood there like a child in a daydream, on the cusp of being mystified by such an ordinary event. And with the indifference of chefs and servers, Emma continued to do so.

Staring eyes gave way to blinks and she returned to the attention of the tables around her.

Stimulated by the surroundings she wished to soak up, the invasive thoughts within her head made it difficult to keep focused. She didn't know what time other patients in their zombified states would make their appearances in the dining hall. She was apprehensive about the arrival of other people coming around anytime soon. The loneliness of the dining hall became creepier with the thought of elderly ghost-like figures leaking in. Emma made a hasty beeline for a table, and threw herself into a chair she yanked at.

Now sitting at the head of an empty round table, she would wait, feigning a relaxed state. She waited for the other patients to accompany her.

Emma's eyes never remained still for longer than half a second as her spine poked the back of the chair. Her fingernails were nibbled at the edges from where her thoughts took over the night before, absent-mindedly making her fingers bleed as she ripped off the nails and took a thin layer of protective skin with it.

Emma scolded herself for biting at her stubby fingernails – it was a dirty habit performed through nerves.

Sitting alone, fidgeting in a chair at an empty table, in the barren room, Emma feared the clock was incorrect. Her head swirled with doubts.

Was it breakfast time? Was the clock wrong? What if nobody else came?

Her fingers rubbed the underneath of the edges of the chair she sat on, licking her lips, then curling her tongue back to make room for her teeth to nibble. Looking again at the clock, her hair tickled her nose and she shook her head with a push of air through her nostrils. The tickling hairs moved. Emma simmered in her tense nerves, telling herself as soon as someone else would arrive – they would leave her alone.

# Chapter Sixteen

THE CLOCK in the hall seemed to never move in front of her but time would make jumps each time she looked at the face. Five minutes gone. Then another five. Emma felt resigning herself to bed would be a productive way to regain energy. She decided not to look at the clock anymore as the confusion it provided her gave a sense of dread for another headache.

She fidgeted less when the patients began to drip-feed in.

Emma had sat herself at a table near the back wall of the dining hall, the stretch between her and Hartmann would span a good fifteen meters, as he would most likely be sat in the centre of the hall.

She watched the patients in their different coloured gowns flood in a little at a time, the smell of greasy, fatty meat wafting through her nostrils. She was fast to expel the smell from her nose with a huff. When she looked again, the clock read it was fifteen minutes past seven.

It seemed that from the empty room she had come into an hour earlier had come alive in front of her. Tongs left in the metal trays of food used to grab at thick grease laden sausages, and the legs on the floor of the dining hall scraped harshly against the floor.

It was busying, more and more people queuing and bustling about with plates outheld.

Hartmann failed to appear where Emma had imagined him to be. She saw several nurses in the growing crowd of gowns, but not him.

Her toes met with the floor as she slid forward on her chair. The floor was made of stone slabs which kept heat inside in the winter and cool in the summer. Among the hungry bedheads Emma sat, too timid to move for fear of people looking at her and the everlasting hate she had of drawing attention to herself. She stammered and rubbed her hands together on the idea of needing the plate of food in front of her as a prop.

Emma felt hungry regardless but knew there was little point — she would waste most of the food that sparsely filled her plate. Standing from the chair she felt glued to, she pushed it back so it was pressed against the wall — slinking along and chairs pushed into other tables at the right hand side. The nerves she felt were changing every other second, not being able to make her mind up over what she was so nervous about. Emma could not choose from a multitude of topics. Feeling she was the only one who was deeply unhappy inside of Westview, but also knowledgeable of a dark truth about Hartmann. How his practices were covered in lies and secrets — she itched with vengefulness to be the one to initiate the shattering of the facade like a clay pot.

It fuelled her. Emma was now faced with the various trays of hot food before her, quick to get herself a plate and sit back down. The patients bustled, women in their green gowns chatting and tipping heads in exchanged laughter bouts.

Emma resented their happiness. She was angered because they didn't notice how much she hated the damned place. Her face was painted in a scowl. The patients didn't interest her to speak to, as they all would raise alarms to a nurse or Hartmann, and for that they were not to be any acquaintances of hers.

It was Emma, fighting tooth and nail on her own and she was going to win. Any interaction with anyone other than Hartmann would not be worth it. She would be solitary on her mission, and that way, successful.

―――――――

The white ceramic plate soon was filled with a round of dry toast – the crusts of the brown bread burnt at the edges from the dodgy toasting machine.

The next item of food Emma shoved on her plate was bacon, two rashers. She got herself two hash browns because she knew she'd eat those. While everyone else around her hurried to shove multiple different foodstuffs on their plates, Emma watched as they looked over in thought. It was etched onto their wrinkled foreheads.

Seeing the pondering behind their skulls, what they might like for breakfast this morning, something different than yesterday, or something they hadn't tried yet? It gave the illusion of something akin to a hotel, not a hospital. It was difficult to comprehend the massive difference in what Emma had seen in the past day. It brought a deep fracture to what she saw happening before her.

It wracked Emma with a deep distrust and resentment for everyone around her that was brainwashed, or maybe plain blind. She smirked at the literal thought upon the sight of a squinting eighty-something year old woman.

Those stupid white slippers and gowns gave even the fattest person plenty of spare fabric to be swamped in, and the comfort of knowing they don't have to be high maintenance, or worry about the little things like what to wear. Everyone else was content but Emma remained to be seething with frustration. She almost dropped the plate when she saw the man himself stride in, hands in loose fists by his side through the propped open double doors. That prim, little smile on his face with his quiff of slimy hair, Emma could smell his woody cologne from where she was seething the sight of him.

Back then it had allured her to him, intrigued the young woman to see if the pleasant smell was as lovely as the sight she would see. Now it made her stomach perform flips inside as she knew who smelt that way.

She knew she had changed much in such a short space of time as she stood in the midst of the room spacing out.

Between thinking about the past and her present, Emma was thrown back into reality when an older hobbling woman brushed her side.

"Oh, sorry," Emma whispered, shooting off to her table with her cooling plate of breakfast, more awkwardly uttered than much of a genuine apology. As she rushed back to her table, she cursed herself inside her head for sounding in-genuine. She didn't mean to sound so but was caught off guard by it happening. Something so small, had caused her to shrivel within herself.

Emma was struck then with the memory of helping feed that old woman. She wracked her brain to remember her name, and didn't have to strain for more than a few seconds. Thinking of Hilda needing aid to feed herself, Emma searched the room for the sight of the small woman hunched in a chair in her gown, but couldn't find her. She slowly lowered her head, having scrutinised the room enough to retreat with a residing disgruntlement.

Emma seethed watching the patients chatter away around the remaining five seats at the table. They all chatted away with glee, eating their glowing yellow toast and overcooked scrambled eggs, covering their full mouths to let out their laughs. It was almost perfect, sickeningly – Emma's teeth ripped into her burnt toast.

Their happiness and unrelenting chat made Emma want to bury herself six feet in the ground.

She was eager to see the back of the hospital. Every giggle and shared laugh made Emma cringe, angered – only to be then calmed by the thought of her escape.

The patients ignored her. Sitting with a face like thunder, she didn't appear the ideal conversationalist and didn't care for giving the appearance of one either.

Every positive remark of Hartmann or the hospital which left the idle mouths of the people around Emma made her sour mood sink lower.

She internalised her disgust when an elderly man accidentally let some mushed-up toast spit from his bottom lip and eject into the centre of the white cloth. She stared at it, as if smelling faeces.

As much as Emma desired to not care about the fact that the patients around her were obliviously happy, making talk amongst themselves as if she were never there at all. It bugged her that they were unaware. Unaware of something she was merely scratching the surface of. Out of spite, Emma allowed them to ignore her and did not voice herself once or make any bother about what she thought. Instead, she narrowed her eyesight past the heads of the many patients to focus on Hartmann himself for seconds at a time, being careful not to catch his eyes, though. Emma was certain they must have been playing the same idle game of "don't let the other person see me eyeing them," but for polar opposite reasons.

The situation was different but the chemistry Emma radiated and her reasoning for not being caught were similar. She recalled high school, the daunting halls and thick glass windows to peer through to the different rooms, and the rushing teachers' shoes on the hall floors, the teachers you'd hide from to avoid even making eye contact with.

Was it really all that similar? It even fit the fact that Emma, akin to her high school life many years ago, did not fit in. And knowing she still did not, her joints tightened up.

It made her top lip curl in disgust if she was careless enough or brass enough to reveal her emotions for her strong, stinking internalised dialogue.

Her eyes flicked to Hartmann, and being unsure of herself, she did it again.

Quickening each time, she checked to see Hartmann with eyes on his plate, knife and fork paused in each hand, as he listened to the swirling conversations.

From a point of observation, Emma noted his aura in the room had an effect on those around him. He attracted people with such a magnetic force, and held much respect with his nurses, who giggled and smiled at every chance they got – swooning over the man.

Emma's hatred weighed heavy on her shoulders and ensured her tongue was laced, ready to spit out her fouling thoughts.

She'd rip that man to bits if she could. She wanted to listen in to what was entertaining Hartmann so much.

Eyeing the doctor's hands, Emma took her burning gaze from Hartmann to sip at a glass of water. Little did she know he was keeping a steady eye on her that morning, as he had noticed she was up very early. Hartmann theorised she was the earliest to be walking around the hospital out of all of the hundreds of patients. It made the man ponder, while eating his breakfast that morning – what had driven her to be awake so early.

---

Hartmann was acting best he could manage, feigning joviality. He had to make sure to himself he was joining in with the conversation around him. Both Emma and Hartmann were focused on something else and only half putting in effort with their immediate surroundings.

While Hartmann's focus strayed to Emma more each day, he observed her behaviours become stranger, and deepening his forehead wrinkles while his concerns followed suit.

The previous evening, Hartmann was up late, and he couldn't find himself resting in any way, no matter what he tried. As a result of his lack of sleep he knew he was performing under his own standard the next morning. The previous evening Hartmann had been lying in his bed, staring at the ceiling and hands intertwined laying over his stomach, just waiting for sleep to take him over like a blanket. It never came.

Shifting his position from laying on his back to his left side, when that failed he tried his right side but hated facing the wall. Hartmann hating having his back to the door of his bedroom and knew he never consciously fell asleep that way, so why did he even try?

Hartmann couldn't clock off from his head in which one thing above all swallowed his headspace – Emma. For once he would stop faking his restlessness, as he knew exactly what the reason was he could not fall into the lull of sleep. His subconscious wasn't even tempted to let him try, for he held unresting thoughts.

Emma had been acting different towards him, reflecting on the first time the two had met it was evident that she was changing, but not in the way he had hoped. Hartmanns thumb and forefinger pinched the bottom of his chin, rubbing the small cleft and keeling over – giving a groan.

He had sat up in his bed among the mountain of pillows, but he sat there hunched over his legs rubbing the heel of his palms against his eyeballs. So that morning, he had gulped down two cups of black coffee to fuel himself for the stint of the morning. It was yet to help.

Emma placed the glass before herself, swallowing the small mouthful of water she had swilled in her cheeks. Removing her fingers, she looked up at Hartmann again. His head bowed. Emma couldn't see his expression. She looked back at her plate, and it would not come to occur to Emma that Hartmann had let his watchful gaze slip from her, on which it had been constant throughout breakfast.

That was the only reason she got as far as she did, between her standing amidst the dining section to walk with her plate in hand as a prop to say outwardly, "I'm just going to get more food."

Emma was careful to ward off any watchful eyes on her, of which she figured there would be a good few pairs.

Silencing her thoughts, she swam through the tables and lead herself to the heated trays of food at the back wall, closest to the exit.

She walked alongside the trays, being careful to walk with a purpose but not too slow to arise any suspicions. Her heart would only begin racing when she put the plate down on the wooden space between the metal trays of food, and walk out through the wide open double doors as she had entered just as before.

And it was on.

Once she had left the dining hall, Emma began to run. She broke out into a frantic run, her adrenaline fuelling her small legs to whirr that bit faster.

The route to the garden came to her like a jigsaw, piece by piece the route before became clear. Leading her to freedom, beyond the tall metal fence before her now as she bolted towards it, fearing she'd stumble and fall.

Under her hairline small beads of sweat accumulated, giving her already greasy face a shine too. Emma jumped over the few steps of the decking, hurtling to the fence that was quarter way covered by the hedges.

She threw herself into the fence, fingers gripping through the metal slits. Throwing a glance over her shoulder, she expected Hartmann to be somewhere close, glowering with rage at her audacity. It was an ecstatic relief to her when she didn't see him where she had fuelled herself to believe he would be. She exhaled. Emma looked to the bush. The fence lay behind. Under the pressure of her thudding heart and racing mind, Emma jumped and gripped her fingers around the mesh.

Her legs were clawed at by the limbs of the bush as her foot failed to grip at the metal the way her hands did.

She hissed, feeling a painful scratching drag across a calf that was forced to dangle in the sharp branches.

Emma began to scale the fence, the joints between her fingers aching from gripping and entangling with the thin metal by the time she reached the top. She was relying heavily on what work her skinny arms could do for her. Her desperation increased, pulling herself up once more, her chest coming over the top of the fence, her toes finally slipping in place within the mesh to support her. The mesh wobbled under her, making her upper body shake.

Emma kicked a leg up, bending at the knee to get a leg over the top of the fencing. She wobbled when she desperately willed her torso to follow, using the muscles in her thighs to sustain somewhat of a balance.

Looking down to her side, she slipped her leg over to the desired side of the fence. A cruel wind blew up her hospital gown, straying hair across her eyes as she clung to the top. Her fingers ached from the sustained stress of her grip. Having to kick it out behind her and dangling, before she grew tired, and let herself fall onto the road.

The pavement was beginning to warm from the sun beating down, getting stronger with each minute that passed.

Emma looked at her calves and saw a few ugly scratches, and on the fleshier, more muscular backside of her leg there were thin smears of blood.

Throwing a look over at the grass and then the pavement ahead, Emma's jaw was left gaping. She pushed herself to break into a lazy, wobbling run. Her legs were aching, but she managed to run for a good while until she thought her lungs would shrivel up. Only allowing herself to stop running and slow her pace to a jog, she then slumped into a hurried, panting walk.

The fence soon became covered by trees and tall, looming hedges which she figured to have been recently trimmed, as not a leaf or bit of greenery out of place.

Emma wobbled along on the winding road, looking down at the state of her calves, but grinning like the Cheshire Cat. This was half because it made breathing easier with her mouth wide open, and it felt appropriate for Emma to no longer care. The quivering ecstasy flowed through her, that familiar buzz knowing this is where it all begins, wherever she chose to take it from here.

She was free to do as she wished. Amidst her panting and trying to regain her breath, Emma faced the tall building looming over the black metal fence and hedges to raise her left hand, curling every finger into her palm apart from the middle one. Emma turned on her heels to continue down the road which would lead her out into the comfort of normality. Each step she took was one which lifted the feeling inside her, going from desperation, to glee.

# Chapter Seventeen

FROM THE OTHER side of the dining hall, Hartmann had been watching Emma throughout breakfast.

Every couple of minutes his eyes flicked up to her little bedraggled head sat amongst the table of chattering mouths. Those seated around her forked large amounts of breakfast into their mouths to quiet them when not talking. Emma's wavy hair lopped down at the sides of her face like curtains – how he wished that she would tie her hair back, so he could watch her features, clock her gaze. Hartmann, when asked why he was so 'quiet' at breakfast came out with a half-hearted smile. He simply responded, "I'm tired." It wasn't a lie, anyway. Hartmann was tired. Every time he bowed his head to his plate to receive a forkful of food he raised his head to look at Emma, who was looking lost. He was contented with the image he kept seeing when he checked. His patient lost at the other end of the spacious and noisy room – it fulfilled the lust he had for her and gave the man reason to erase the creeping paranoia.

The doctor, watchful as he felt he was being, would have been a few moments too late in giving one of his senior nurses a nudge and saying into her ear, "Go and see where Emma has gone."

Becoming aware of the chances she may begin to take, he grimaced to himself. His demeanour at the table changed, and he stiffened, his frame having gone rigid, lips pulled into a frown with eyes on the nurse rushing off.

Hartmann cleared his throat. Friends at the table bustled in their chairs and fidgeted without talking while he didn't choose to involve himself. He withdrew from the conversation, looking over the heads of his co-workers to peer at the nurse having run off, sickened to sit without answers. Elbows placed upon the table at each side of his plate, he rubbed the clasps of his fingers together and drew in a breath when his head dipped down.

The doctor raised himself from the chair, a hand placed over his stomach. "Please, excuse me," he said, standing in the hall and addressing his co-workers with a brisk nod. His eyes searched the hall, seeing her chair was vacant and the small figure was nowhere to be seen – most likely wandering around in the gown that swamped her.

Inside of his chest a thick, hairy rope wound around his oesophagus, tightening as he stormed through the hall. His hands outstretched at his side while he paced, leaving only mystified onlookers behind him wondering what had caused him to leave.

The nurses looked to each other, giving knowing glances, but only those who worked on Lilypad ward understood why the doctor had fled the hall.

Hartmann beelined to Emma's room. He forced air through his nostrils like a bull, pushing himself forwards through doing so. Emma not being in his sight threw the doctor off course, but having seen her leave made his paranoia worsen. Maybe it was the lack of sleep, or his evolving infatuation with the young woman – but the only thought in his mind was Emma. His main focus was her, and he prayed her room looked touched when he threw himself up the two flights of stairs to reach Lilypad ward.

The door was closed, and he paused. Her door was closed. His hands straightened, his fingers being curled into his palm, stepping forwards to wrap a hand around the handle, the metal cold against his sweaty palm.

Bursting in, the scene unravelled before the doctor. His chest tightened.

The nurse was folding back the sheet to reveal a clump of plumped pillows in the deceiving shape of a curled up sleeping woman, who he would have hoped to be Emma. The walls caved in, and his heart dropped in his chest. Dread fuelled him, feeling almost faint at his world caving in.

She was gone.

The nurse turned to him. "Would you like me to check the toilets?" she offered, obviously unaware of the effect this was having on Hartmann.

While small beads of sweat began to line on his brow, he thrust his chin. His chin then clenched in retraction, eyes staring around the room and wanting to set it on fire from the power behind his eyes, his throat closing up and restricting his ability to swallow.

The nurse paused, straightening her back from where she had been leaning over the bed, pinching and pulling at the sheet.

"Doctor?" she asked again, watching Hartmann enter the space around the bed, throwing a hand and grabbing at the bedsheet.

His knuckles turned white as he gripped the sheets and yanked them off, throwing them aside to let them bundle in a pile on the floor. His nostrils flared with a fierce exhale.

The nurse's eyes darted to watch where his hand focused, taking steps backwards, her hands rushing to her side. The nurse withdrew from interfering any further, side-eyeing Hartmann in his fury, towering over the bed, glaring at it. He glowered, his left hand swinging out in front of him and releasing a loud, guttural shout.

His arm swiped the water jug and two glasses beside from where they stood, smashing the glass into pieces which spread out all over the floor. He clenched his eyes closed, fists shaking at his side.

The nurse yelped and jumped back, fear etched onto her face at the sudden outburst of anger. Hartmann's burst of anger left the nurse with shimmering shards of glass spread out on the floor of the room. She clasped her hand to her chest. Tucking the straying hair of her fringe behind her ear, she side-eyed Hartmann.

He stood, seething with his chest being the only moving part of him. He hadn't moved from glowering over the bed, heavy amounts of adrenaline pumping around his system.

She froze there, apparently too afraid to dare move an inch.

Hartmann remained fuming while the nurse took a step backwards, her hands shaking as they loosely held the other. Flapping around, looking unable to decide as she looked from Hartmann with his veins popping in his neck, versus the shards of glass on the floor. Through a pair of shivering lips, the nurse managed a weak attempt to calm the doctor.

"I'll go outside and see if she is there." She made no bones about wanting to rush off.

Hartmann only moved from glowering over the empty bed once the nurse had left him alone.

He allowed the nurse to scurry away. The squaring of his shoulders combined with his breath having hitched since he remained holding the growing ball of tension. He felt like tight ropes around himself had become unravelled, leaving him in pieces all over the place much akin to the shards on the floor. His brow heated, and his shirt stuck to the inside of his armpits. Hartmann managed to conjure the dreamlike state in which Emma was shown glancing over her shoulder before running for it. The fuzzy imagery left his mind, feeling his heart race in reaction to something that was made up on the spot. He couldn't handle the idea of the fantasy, so the reality of the bed laying empty before him had him swaying on the spot. Doctor Hartmann's Adam's apple bobbed in his throat when he would then bury his thoughts, ripping into action.

The useless nurse could search the gardens all over, but Hartmann would chase this one himself, determined to have Emma return to his care.

"Clean up the damn glass. I'll deal with her," Hartmann instructed to the dazed nurse with a pointed finger at the glistening floor.

Emma wasn't safe out there on her own. He tapped the small pill bottle he had in his long white coat. In the hall, he pushed himself into a run, jogging down the halls with the back of his coat flapping behind his calves. His brow shining under the luminescent lights as he dashed underneath.

Nurses knew not to ask Hartmann what was going on, as he wasn't in the frame of mind to be poked with questions. They bowed their heads if they passed the stormy man, and hurried their pace.

It wasn't difficult to see, his forehead speckled with beads of sweat and his eyes were glaring. He was running through the halls and having not informed anyone of where he was going in such a rush, or what had happened to elicit such a change in the doctor.

The women saw he was in a raw panic. His feet thudded on the floor much to his irritation, bringing undue attention from patients giving him funny looks when he ran past. Under his breath he uttered curses in his native tongue. Unable to help but notice patients eyeing him and some ushering themselves out of the way for him.

Emma's feet began to hurt just as she reached the main road, where the winding country entrance to the hospital spread wide out into bustling life. Her heels ached from the constant treading on the poorly paved road. There were many potholes and gravel that bore and dug into her feet. She hobbled, and then paused, flicking the digging gravel from her flesh. Emma's shoulders slumped upon being able to view normal people going about their lives. She envied people walking along without the one of three different coloured gowns adorned.

Without any protection from the ground she was treading on, the balls of her heels ached and she willed to rest them.

The paranoid, restless state Emma resided in cracked at her exterior, threatening to ruin the stability or the mindful peace she tried to embrace from having escaped the hospital.

The walls were no longer around her, but she felt somewhat crippled. Looking to the road again, and the kind faces of the many drivers became mean, hard stares.

Emma swallowed, looking at her dirtied feet on the pavement. Everyone that passed in the cars were looking unmistakeably at her. She hated the eyes on her, why were they watching her, staring and glancing at her like they were?

The world became concave, and it curved around her head.

Emma bowed her head and eyes to remain fixed on the pavement, feeling immediate judgement fall upon her, heavily.

Should she have been kept in the padded room to rot or the hell of her stupid Lilypad ward bedroom?

Emma became aware of her thoughts leading her to realise a cowering inability to cope outside of Westview.

Her neck warmed despite the cool wind blowing leaves down past her ankles. In a flash, the sinking embarrassment turned to a pit of anger. The bottom of her stomach burned as it began.

Nobody understood what she had been through, and it spurred her mind to the reason she had needed to escape in the first place.

Deciding to stick with that reason alone, she picked up her sore feet and began treading down the road. Emma quickened her pace, meandering past the small trees with the black fencing around them that decorated the pavement. Emma felt pressure to run out of her growing thoughts that only whirred around her head like a thousand voices shouting over each other all at once. For a moment, she had the thought to consider having grown a second head.

Overwhelmed to the point of screaming, she staggered on the side of the street. She wobbled behind the planted trees in front of the rows of houses. The passers-by sat in the cars were still staring at her, feeling the eyes burn and leaving her unable to stand being watched. Emma broke into a sprint past the last five houses on the street and dove into a side-road.

She struggled to regain her breath as cars rushed past her. Her chest rising and falling from panic more than the sprinting, she was scared people had eyes on her from windows in the houses. Emma peered fearfully up into the side-windows of the red- brick homes, waiting for a curtain to flinch. She half expected to see the glaring eyes of cruel strangers burning into her but found there were none.

In the midst of the backstreet Emma wandered, eyeing the walls and fences which surrounded the gardens, fearing the judgement of other people which may set eyes on the unfortunate sight. As she walked she waited for the pacing of her chest to slow down and stop, but it showed no signs of calming down. Her mind fuzzed. She gazed down, and knew she needed plenty more help than her exhausted legs could provide. Spurred on by her racing mind and restrained by her aching lower half, she made a lazy, dizzied travel to the train station.

The glares and stares of strangers hardened when Emma rocked up, finally at the train station. She had forced her feet to drag herself there. Hoping to conceal herself, she sat on the furthest stairs from the platform closest to the entryway. She ambled closer, waiting to see if anyone was coming out. Emma could only see narrow shelters otherwise, and the stairs were her best bet at being able to remain unnoticed.

She avoided other people as much as she could, until it came to those moments of certainty, where those unpleasant incidents became insignificant. She was certain she must step onto the next train that would stop at the station – only then would she be content to be around the public. At least with a smidge of confidence in her darting gaze. Then the stares, glares and overlooking the tops of phones would be worth it.

Once Emma was aboard the train, and could rest with her head leaned against the shaking window that provided view over green fields and the backs of houses.

Until then, Emma stared at a tall handrail of the footbridge. It was painted green each side, and Emma scaled it with haste. She pushed onto her toes to peer over the middle of the footbridge, looking down at the tracks below. Her head raised and followed the tracks along, the green fields glowing at each side. Silent, Emma continued along the bridge, and came to the steps down to the left hand side.

There was nobody at the platform ahead of her or having entered, but she double checked as the thought niggled at her. Her head went around each shoulder again.

Stepping halfway down the flight of steps, she knelt and sat, shuffling herself up against the barrier. Finally able to rest her aching feet on the metal stair and sit on the next, she hunched over in a more private space. Her head collided with the barrier at her side, inhaling again and filling her lungs with the fresh air. Emma thought of where she would end up, but she idealised the city, outlining the tall glass buildings on the painted green metal beside her. The image, which she fitted herself into so perfectly – elated her.

Her nails got to work picking away at the clip of the wristband, bringing her wrist to her teeth and gnawing away at the plastic in hopes to rip it through. Holding her wrist in place she tugged at the plastic band, biting and chewing until a hole had been ripped through. When Emma pulled away, she felt her jaw clamp shut on itself. The plastic strained as she pulled again, willing it to break in half, gnawing away at it with her molars. When she successfully made a tear at the side, Emma pulled at it until the plastic stretched enough to be pulled completely over her hand.

She then stood, throwing her hand out over the side of the steps, discarding the hospital tag without care. A content smile spread across her face as she watched the band fall on the rubble below the tracks and rest there. Emma sat back down, retiring with a release of breath, hoping a train would come soon as she laid eyes on the never ending line of track ahead.

The cool of the day brought on a wavering chill over her skin. She brought her hands up and crossed them to rub the opposite arm.

Just as Emma felt a benefit to her efforts, the warmth transferring from her hands to her chilled skin, her heart leaped, feeling the floor under her shaking. She buried herself, hunching her shoulders when her ears perked at hearing voices. She cowered and it made her insides weaken at the sound of the different voices becoming louder.

Two voices. One female, and one male. A couple, she guessed with an inward shrug. Or possibly good friends – best friends? Their jovial laughter bounced from her, hunched against the side of the stairs, trying to make herself as small as possible. She stared at her feet, looking at the stairs anticipating the strangers passing.

The sensation of their shoes in sync of the walk reached the corner where Emma was sat. The gentleman recoiled as he stretched his leg to turn, the toe of his shoe almost making contact with Emma's spine.

"Jesus Christ," his female counterpart hissed, then released an awkwardly received laugh, pulling him by the arm to go around the back of Emma.

They were a couple.

Emma eyed the backs of the pair as they came around her right side.

The young man threw a look over his shoulder upon passing, and Emma raised her head. He turned his head forwards upon her catching his eyes. Emma straightened her back and unfolded her legs, coming away from resting against the wall.

Standing together at the platform, the male whipped his phone out. The girl stood before the young man, peering at his face rather than the screen that captivated him. Emma's eyes whipped up and down their bodies as they stood facing the other, sizing their relationship.

Did she want his children? Did he want to marry this girl, grow old with her, watch the wrinkles appear on her skin? Did either one plan for their future, of which was intertwined in the other, as if it had always laid there? She pictured a thread through a needle.

Emma sat, watching while they weren't looking at her – she took advantage of the power in her own vision, like a spiralling artist at the desk. Possibly, more perverse, though.

She hoped the two never argued, or had many hardships. They have been together, not long – but Emma squinted, and came to the guess of over six months. The girlfriend's style of dress was immaculate, but he was childish, dressed for something like a night out in a Marvel shirt and blue jeans. Old vans, the white thick sole blackened. They were both so young, but the pair oodled the innocence of love at its finest – the lack of clear thought, or vision. Like the saying, love is blind. The parents of each counterpart were yet to meet. Emma didn't have to half heartedly believe the saying for she knew it was absolutely true.

Staring at the couple provided Emma a blank on which her memories drew into her consciousness. Her eyes glassed over and eyes froze in their sockets, transfixed – she stared ahead.

"I won't be here, I've got to stay in late, I owe them time now."

"Oh, and that's my fault is it?"

"No, for god's sake it's not. Would you stop making me seem like I'm attacking you every time I open my mouth?"

"Please don't stay late." Emma sucked her cheeks, trying to hold back tears coming from her watering eyes. "I need you here."

Jason looked to the floor before speaking. With every quiet second, she feared she was getting closer to losing the man she loved the bones of. "I have been here, Emma. You've seen me, I've been here constantly but I have other responsibilities."

At that moment Emma could have simultaneously ripped him to shreds on the spot, diving into him with nothing to spare but malice – but knowing she would do anything to see him stay, just so he would not walk out the door and leave gracious time to reflect on how she was behaving. Emma knew she was never like this, and he was more frightened than anything. She knew in his mind he had made a perfect plan in alignment with hers, and the fact that it had all gone suddenly so wrong on her end only, had left Jason with a heavy heart. It made his shoulders slump with the weight Emma had given him in his chest. Emma wished she could stand him up stock straight and fix his tie and kiss him on the breakfast counter like those mornings a few weeks ago. Even if he had to fake the entire thing ,Emma was a hair away from screaming at him to straighten his back and demand him to give her a kiss before he left. Like he used to do.

Like any decent man, Jason did not outright blame his partner for the stillbirth of their daughter – regardless it left him heartbroken. A man with a cracked exterior. His pride was gone. Emma perceived his grief to be something deep inside his image of her that had changed. Something inside of her. Something to do with her anatomy. It left her terrified, white hot petrified, and Emma failed him in the only way she couldn't fix.

From then the relationship had become a sinking ship. Emma couldn't express her need and desire to save the relationship, and how he looked at her as a broken woman fuelled her into a mania. She cried, screaming out how he was needed at the house. At their home. Needed? For what, stupid woman? You failed to bring him a family. Emma was poisonously hostile towards the man who she held nothing but adoration for.

In her eyes, Jason's view of Emma had undoubtedly changed. It destroyed her, leaving her with only depression or desperate adoration for the man she loved. Thrown off by her ever-changing bout of hormones he was practically paralyzed, while she charged around him like a whirlwind. The raging emotions that trapped her washed off him, while she was desperate to grasp for some control. His indifference left Emma with no surface to grip at.

"So I'm just a responsibility now, am I? Am I that much of a problem?" Emma sobbed now, tiring Jason greatly – his jaw shut tight and leaving Emma to notice how his cheekbones stuck out slightly as the muscles in his cheek strained. His eyes flicked to the floor and she knew she had made his insides burn with anger. Emma watched his nostrils, the ends flared while she stared at the top of his head. His silence made her only cry out louder, trying to erupt something as extreme in return from him, making herself louder in a growing panic. Emma hoped the burning of anger elicited a fire in him, but she had failed.

"Emma, I can't *not* go to work. I can't cope with you being all up and down, you need to stop this manic behaviour."

Emma wanted to jump up and down on the spot and scream until her voice went hoarse, feeling she had the full capability to destroy the entire house. Her stomach tightened and her palms closed tight.

"Listen to me, I'll be back before you know it and we can talk but I am not speaking to you while you're in such a bad state," he tried, walking those few steps to the front door. He pulled the set of car keys from the box on top of the radiator cover. Taking a deep breath, her lungs in a panic, she almost had to forcibly gasp and hold her breath to calm her erratic breathing.

Without Emma having spoken, Jason continued. "I love you, but please stop all this."

Enraged, she found herself wanting to laugh and call him a hypocrite. Even an outright liar. She wondered how he could say those words and then in the same breath tell her to stop hurting so much? Emma was in agony. He was blind to her hot pain and the cycle was stiff with little change from either of the two; unbearable.

She wondered after he left if she had scared him into that finalising step of the separation.

Emma saw herself as having become unsafe for him, emotionally and physically. She wasn't safe to touch again, or connect with for fear of her outbursts. It was all fractured. Jason was a man who wanted a baby − seeing the bump grow made his smile wider each morning as he laid a palm open across Emma's growing stomach, kissing her belly before coming up to meet her awaiting lips. Emma had spoken about adoption but half-heartedly expected the reaction which she received from Jason, but wanted to voice at least what they had as a second option in mind.

It left room for paranoia. Maybe he left her for someone younger, who would be easily impressed by him. Reboot his esteem after Emma having inevitably destroyed it, along with any hopes for a family, too. The impressionable girl would be taken easily by the dates to the places which Emma had been strung to a few dozen times, drove down those same roads together in turns − maybe his new partner couldn't even drive. A fresh, fertile partner to reinstitute all hope within them both. Jason having begun his own fresh start left Emma in a pit of worthlessness at her stunted phase of grief.

Waving a hand in front of her hard stare to break the fixation she brought upon herself, Emma managed to snap back into the grey of her reality. A cool wind whipped the gown against her bruised calves, and she clicked her tongue as she blinked for the first time in several minutes.

While she had been staring, she barely noticed the couple's eyes wandering all over her while she lay vacant to the imagery in her mind.

"Elias, she doesn't look well at all, we should help her."

"I don't think we need to, she'll have people looking for her, what would we do for her at this point, Molly?" her boyfriend said. "She's waiting for the train just like us, alright? Take it out of your mind." He shook his head, wiping at the stubble loosely dotted around his upper lip.

Molly gave a sideward glance to the woman in the hospital gown, sat hunched on the steps. Her glancing at Emma was pained, and a clenched half smile pulled onto her soft lips while she weighed up her words.

Molly paused before nudging her boyfriend, biting her bottom lip she glanced over at Emma again. She swallowed before going to speak.

"Please?"

Looking at his short girlfriend with disbelief etched into his features at her pointedness, he raised a brow-as he hissed at his girlfriend. There was a moment of hesitation in Elias before he spoke.

"No, I said no. She's escaped a hospital, or a facility of some sort," Elias hissed into the listening ear at his shoulder height. "Either way, we aren't going to help her even if we offer. She's escaped for a reason," he whispered to his girlfriend, willing her to take his caution into account rather than continue on her wave of empathy. Elias' eyes darted while releasing an impatient huff. He remained watching Emma's movements from where they stood together.

In the background of the two whispering to each other, Emma stood up. Looking to the train billboard, she read that the next train was in nine minutes, leaving her feeling stranded. Nine minutes was way too long and it wore at her optimism.

Nobody else had arrived to fill the emptiness that still remained in the station. As much as it benefited Emma's state of paranoia, the emptiness of the station also forced her feelings of desperation to heighten. The desperation to get help, before the train arrived, she had to take advantage of the shrinking window.

Emma figured she must have been outside of the hospital now for an hour. She thought about Hartmann wondering where she had gone, flustered about what she was up to.

She thought about what he would be doing to find her, or if he was trying at all. Emma secretly hoped he would be, as the thought of doctor Hartmann – panic-stricken by her running off on him pleased her. Having put a crack in his professionalism, breaking his control. Her lips pulled into a smirk at the thought, making the one eye crease at the corner. In her mind, she made a fantasy he would be absolutely dreading who she'd tell. Like a child with a secret, she'd rat on him to whoever she could find outside of that horrific place. With that thought of revenge, Emma wiped the smirk from her face and looked to the couple. The back of their heads were facing her, while they cuddled and stared down the track stretching out ahead.

Emma mustered the courage to take the few steps down to land her feet one after the other on the platform. Standing at the foot of the steps, Emma noticed the boyfriend shroud his girlfriend, stepping forwards to avoid her looking. Emma thought steam might have been coming out of her ears, rehearsing what she might say, how she would come out with it.

"Hey, do you need help, are you okay?" Elias asked.

Being yanked from her racing thoughts, for the first time her eyes met with those of the young man who had stood huddled with his girlfriend.

He stood facing her, with his girlfriend watching behind his shoulders.

Emma's heart jumped, wanting to grab the loping hospital fabric in her hands and crumple it in her palms to ease their growing clamminess. Her chin lifted while her mind went blank, the ominous buzz of thoughts having left upon being confronted by the stranger before her. Her almost vibrating brain then seemed to upturn itself and empty at once, as if her mind sucked up the thoughts bleeding out to leave her be with the stranger.

Emma's pupils dilated, trying not to let the flush of her cheeks show. "I'm okay." She breathed a little too heavy, wincing at herself. "When does the train arrive?" she asked, trying not to stare at him. The young man kept his eyes on Emma after she had spoken, unsure of what to make of her.

"It arrives in six minutes. Where are you heading to?"

"The city. I hope the train is on time." Emma released a nervous laugh. Around them the wind dropped, letting her fidget with her mop of hair and feeling herself rot in the tiny silence that lingered. The top row of her teeth clamped on her bottom lip, and in the silence between the two strangers her thoughts grew louder. It allowed her head to refill with the pressing desperation of her situation. She fought the niggling urge to smirk, entertained by her own ironic tragedy. The way her thoughts cowered away entertained her, they tortured her so, but were utterly useless when she wanted to express them.

At the thought of exploding on the spot, her slimy intestines splatting against the concrete. Her blood would trickle onto the tracks and paint them red for miles after a train ran over the remainders of her. Stain the world with her suffering, hopefully everyone would be sorry – for only then after some massive tragedy would the onlookers bow their heads in shame.

God, ain't that always the way? Again, Emma smirked to herself.

Hartmann would rot in his office, deceased at his poxy little desk. The paperwork would curl at the browning corners like the padded cell she had been locked in.

"Are you alright?" The voice managed to pierce through the smoke of thoughts which poisoned her.

"My name is Emma Merrick and I need to speak to the police, do you have a phone on you, please?" Coming out clumsily with it all at once, the words collapsed in a pile like she had vomited everywhere. Her nerves didn't ease by the breaking of her silence.

The brow of the young man wrinkled.

He was apprehensive, the girl beside him was spurred on by the admission Emma gave. Rather than cowering like her male counterpart, Molly pushed past her boyfriend replacing his narrowed eyes with her wide orbs.

"I really need your help. Westview, do you know the hospital?" Emma continued to the young lady in front of her, the boyfriend becoming a blur behind the girl's fuzz of flying hair. Molly's hand fiddled in the zip of her jacket to produce her phone, and she hastily passed it over to her boyfriend.

"No, have you ran away?" she questioned, as Emma's eyes stared at the screen watching his fingers press at the glass to dial the emergency contact.

"It's a terrible place, and I need everyone to know what really happens there, it's not normal," Emma rambled, fuelling her own pace of breathing which became quickened at the pace of her speech escaping, inhaling hard when she paused.

Molly flinched. She edged slightly closer to her boyfriend, not quick enough to let Emma know she was uncomfortable, just the right moment to break away from the conversation and submit an end to it. The touch of Molly's shoulder to

Elias' chest being an indicator for him to shield her, or to make her boyfriend aware of her growing discomfort.

Sensing the sudden drop of interest, Emma continued in effort to try and regain the dual attention while the boyfriend had his phone to his ear.

"There is one man, Doctor Hartmann, he put me into a straightjacket, you know. Who does that to their p-people anymore?" Emma declared, stammering her words and entering a state of fuelled ranting all by herself. Her eyes glared and bulged at the fast retracing of her words. She stood back on the platform but maintained her eye contact with the couple before her.

Emma wanted to pace back and forth to expel her growing adrenaline, mixed in with a degree of freeing and growing excitement. Combined with the tension of the situation her attention had diverted, she grabbed the opportunity she thought she would not reach. The couple eyed her, the boyfriend protectively holding his girlfriend's hand, standing before her. And although they eyed her, Emma did not maintain she cared for a pretence any longer.

She watched his thumb dragging across the glass screen. Being shrouded by the gown, the small woman was pacing on the spot. The factor of heroism in the gesture of caring about the woman in the gown had vanished. Emma saw that both Molly and Elias kept tabs on her from the corners of their eyes.

Emma couldn't care less, she meant no harm to them and she consciously knew that was an absolute – regardless of anything else that worried them, whether it was her appearance, how she spoke, or represented herself. It didn't matter, if it hadn't five minutes earlier then now it surely didn't one teensy shred. The boyfriend kept eyes on Emma as she stared ahead of them at the concrete floor, he turned his head with his ear pressed against his phone. He raised his head.

"I told you she was a bloody loon."

When the young man hissed to his girlfriend cowering behind his back, she briskly thumped him at the base of his spine, standing beside him with an angered frown. He gave his girlfriend a wink, to which Molly glared at him.

"Do you think this is funny, Elias?" she remarked in a horrified whisper, recoiling her head from his chest.

His brow furrowed under his fringe and shook his head. His eyes shot to Emma, who was looking at him piercingly.

"I need the police please," he said firmly.

His voice collided with Emma's ribcage, and raised up through her throat while her lungs filled with air. Her feet ached a little less upon realising her fight was coming to an end.

"Thank you, thank you so much," Emma said while relief flooded her, smiling at the cowering, nervous girlfriend who avoided meeting her eyes.

Elias ran a hand through his fringe and turned on the spot when the call continued.

"Yes, I'm at Saint Gridgevey train station," he said.

Emma's head twisted. "No, Westview General," she corrected.

The young man pulled away from her interruption, taking a few wandering steps further down the platform. As he strode away a couple of feet, she turned to Molly. Elias' voice became less audible as he paced away, leaving the two women standing in proximity to each other. Emma looked to the girl, watching her stare at her meandering boyfriend on the phone.

"Honestly, I do appreciate what you two are doing for me."

Searching her face, Molly smiled and looked at the concrete. She sucked her cheeks. "It's okay, don't you worry," came her soft reply.

# Chapter Eighteen

HARTMANN'S INSIDES hollowed and his palms were wet with a panicked outburst of sweat brought on by the news of Emma.

He wished to know exactly how long ago she had run from his care, but he had an estimate in mind. His teeth gritted, his molars locked in place, arms by his side as he ran through his halls. As he ran, he imagined paying out good amounts of money to put walls high around the entire hospital, electrified ones, barbed wire on the top, lining it all around. Guards on watch of patients in the gardens since his favoured couldn't even be trusted. That little brat of a girl got all of his attention, ninety percent of it all of the time, why was she so determined to ruin everything he had worked for? Why didn't she see all of his efforts, why didn't she want to get better?

Spitefully he cursed Emma over and over for running on him, and actually escaping. She had been the first.

Images ran through his head of gripping her face in his rough hands and crushing her cheeks, tears streaming down her face as he shouted and screamed, humiliatingly reprimanding her.

The images he conjured up did little to soothe the doctor,

although he wanted her to crumple in front of him and become completely limp; that would satisfy his anger.

Running into the reception, Hartmann thrust out his arm with a pointed finger as he strode up, coming up and leaning over the desk.

"Get me Ruth. Where is she? I need her with me right now," he snapped. Being met with gawping jaws, and when the receptionist failed to move quickly as he needed, Hartmann snarled at them. "Urgently."

To which the leading receptionist picked up the telephone to her ear, the dialling tone ringing out. Her lipstick-coated lips shook as her eyes darted to the desk in front of her while the doctor fumed.

The receptionist's fingers were shaking as she pressed in the numbers on the phone's keypad.

Hartmann stood on the other side of the wall with his arms folded, eyes narrowed watching the woman's every move, disapproving. A shaking finger pushed up her glasses at the bridge of her nose. She almost fell to bits under Hartmann's glare. Her hands flapped about on the desk when the dial tone came back through to her as a long delayed beeping – the line was in use.

Smacking her lips, she pressed a key once more, only picking up the nerve to make eye contact with Hartmann when the monotone noise ceased.

The receptionist jabbered into the receiver, turning as the wiring came across her stomach.

Moments later, the phone was dropped back onto the holder.

"Doctor Hartmann, Emma is at the Saint Gridgevey train station, Platform two."

Hartmann was grateful when Ruth rushed out from the automatic doors, having been on the wards furthest from Lilypad.

Without a word between the pair, they ran through the winding hallways together. Doctor Hartmann's palms gripped the leather steering wheel. He took a breath and shoved open the passenger door.

Ruth was quick to shunt into the seat. Pulling the seatbelt over her chest, her eyes locked on to the road ahead.

The engine growled, and Hartmann twisted the wheel over to the left. Despite her almost gaunt face, Ruth's cheeks flushed, pulling back the straying hairs behind her ears, licking her lips to soften the drying skin.

"She managed to escape, huh?" Ruth stated, breathless. Hartmann hummed, pushing hard on the accelerator as the car park barrier lifted, the winding road elongating in front. His face broke out into a smile at her question, then scoffing.

"Oh yeah." His eyes flicked to the left before pulling out into the road. "She isn't going to get very far." He then grumbled, tossing his eyes over to the nurse beside him, leering forwards and the car lurching. The main road come closer, the road splitting in two, houses being in front on a neat row, neighbourhoods coming in force one after the other as the roads split off from each other.

"This is unbelievable, does the girl not want your help?" Ruth asked, giving Hartmann a glance to only see his eyes focused on the road.

Hartmann clasped a hand to his forehead, then throwing his hand onto the gearstick as he pulled up to a junction. He could tell Ruth was watching him, but he ignored her staring from the seat.

His arm outstretched from his hand's grip on the wheel, and a finger pointed to the window.

"Keep looking," was his sole instruction.

Hartmann's eyes did not stray from focusing on the street coming ahead of him.

"I'm sorry but I need her back in the hospital. I've never had a patient escape before, you know that." He gestured with an open palm, keeping the other on the wheel.

Ruth sucked her cheeks before answering, raising an eyebrow in the silence. "I'm surprised she is the first, you look after her so well," Ruth quipped, shifting up in her seat at the comment.

He released a long sigh.

"I know, all I do is help people and she makes a run for it – and actually escapes." He laughed to himself in disbelief. His smile disappeared and he shook his head. "I've still got a long way to go with her, evidently."

In the passenger seat, Ruth hummed in agreement.

Hartmann's car sped through the roads, coming down one and up the next before finally, breaking onto the main one that ran through St. Gridgevey.

"Are you thinking the city?" Ruth posed. "She wouldn't have made it that far." Hartmann said with a click of his tongue. "Are you looking? Be on the lookout," he instructed.

The need, and desperation, of the situation unfolding forced a great deal of stress upon Hartmann, as it reflected in his voice having come out more pleading as he berated his needs to the nurse beside him.

The street became the primary focus for the pair, practically hunting, as when they found who they were trying to look for they'd pounce. Hartmann's mouth was dry from the breathing he was doing between his agape lips.

"I'm heading to the station, she may still be there." Hartmann mumbled.

The car then swerved into a junction on the right hand side, leading down a quiet road of cottages. On the right stood a fence line, until the road came to another turn where the car park for the station began. Behind it was a footbridge over the alternating tracks, just above the high stone wall.

Hartmann's face etched with intensity as he pushed hard on the brake, pulling up behind the public house of the station.

Parking the car near the entryway to the tracks, Hartmann kicked his door open while Ruth had to strain not to whack hers on the back wall. She edged her way out, but pulling her lanky legs out of the car one at a time proved to be a struggle when she almost fell over. Hartmann slammed his door shut and strode around the back end of the car, while Ruth was forced to side step along the wall.

Hartmann ducked under the entryway to the platforms and stepped onto the concrete. It took him too long to set eyes on the figure of Emma on the opposite side, the dual tracks separating the pair.

The doctor threw himself up the footbridge, with Ruth following him close behind. The bridge clanged under their heavy steps. Hartmann was the only one to watch a man and woman, squinting his eyes to assume a couple, listening to Emma's shaking voice.

Emma's crooked neck and jutted elbows gave him the understanding that she was on the phone.

His desire to put an end to her little "daytrip" expanded tenfold. He scoffed in his pause. His arms were out by his side while he strode, anger pulsing through him and it was exposed in every movement he made, escaping him in deliberately hardened movements.

Coming down the metal stairs after crossing, his toes turned outwards as he ran down them, his shoes making the metal cry out.

The couple stood before Emma then glanced over her head of fuzzed hair. They stood frozen, but Hartmann gave a reassuring smile to the couple as his pace didn't slow until he stood behind his patient.

The heels of Hartmann's shoes rested directly on top of the faded yellow line of the platform, confident no trains would come down the line any time soon – before this affair would be over.

Emma did not turn around, her back was to the doctor and Nurse Ruth. Before he spoke, Hartmann locked his hands together behind his back, inhaling almost as if hoping to catch the scent of her skin in a private moment before he opened his mouth.

"Emma, we have been looking for you everywhere."

---

She wanted to clamp her hands hard over her ears, squeezing her eyes shut. She hoped in the next second she could open them again and the train would have arrived.

Her skin bunched tight when she screwed her eyes shut.

The doors of the arriving train would slide open and she would run to the very end, screaming for the conductor to shut the doors, to which he would nod and give a shout towards the front of the train. The doors would shut tight and Hartmann would be left staring with his jaw agape as she sped off behind the safety of the glass.

Emma knew in her vivid fantasy, her eyes gleaming at the sight of Hartmann chasing the train and ordering it to halt, but her words being stronger than his – the train did not stop.

A hand on her shoulder made Emma scream, violently awaking from a fantastically satisfying fantasy scenario where she managed to block out everything around her at once, if only for those few seconds. She saw the train approaching on the tracks before she spun around on the spot to face Hartmann and Ruth by his side.

Emma backed away, the couple standing far in the background now.

Hartmann pulled his eyes down disapprovingly, and looked

to the couple with a sympathetic, and apologetic smile.

"I do hope that my patient hasn't interrupted your travelling too much. I apologise sincerely." With a shake of her head, the young lady gave a glinting smile.

"No, no. We understand," Molly said with a wave of her hand, then letting it rest atop her purse beside her hip. Hartmann smiled at the couple.

Emma watched in horror as they conversed between themselves in front of her. The smallest of winds would have made her disintegrate and fall up into the sky in tiny shreds, carried off by the wind.

Emma almost began flapping her arms.

"Her boyfriend phoned the police," Emma blurted, staring at the side of Hartmann's head. Her eyes stilled, then glared at him head-on when he turned to face her with a snarl. The doctor's eyes fell to the side of himself, his face softening and he exhaled, straightening his stance before the small woman.

"Is that right?" he quipped with a flash of sarcasm. The doctor pressed his lips together. "Let us get you back to the hospital. Come now. I won't let this escalate further."

He went to reach for Emma's shoulder, but she flinched away from his touch, being the only one able to see the anger in his fleeting looks.

Emma's confidence wavered, the smirk on her face wobbling. Hartmann's hot fury was palpable. She avoided his hard, insulted stare.

The control Hartmann was able to muster from that simple line was more than able to inflict doubt in herself.

She snapped to the young man who was holding hands again with his girlfriend, eyes on the train coming down the track. Emma washed in panic once more. She felt violently unwell when the couple ignored her, withdrawing themselves from the affair unravelling before them. More than happy to allow Hartmann and the nurse to take control over the woman that had approached them in the hospital gown. She resented the couple's ability to become so uninvolved that fast, that she could no longer touch them. It angered her, the freedom they had to dip in and out of her life like that, especially at such a crucial moment such as her escape from Westview. Little did they know, though, Emma spitefully told herself, they were dumber than dirt.

Emma poised herself to run.

"Emma, are you listening to me?" Hartmann posed, tilting his head like he strained to keep his eyes on hers when they darted around the tracks.

"No, I'm not letting you take me back. I'll have out what I need to say right now," she spat, darting her eyes from the nurse to Hartmann. He stood there with a frown, while Ruth was poised to strike.

The train was fast approaching, but began to slow as the head passed the couple, who followed the carriages when they continued down the track, until the train came to a complete halt. Time slowed, and she became increasingly desperate.

"It can wait until we get you back, you're doing your mental state no favours here," Ruth snapped, shaking her head at the spectacle unravelling before the public came ushering off the arrived train. Emma jumped back on the concrete, smiling widely, jabbing an accusing finger at her.

"What makes you think being back at that hellhole is going to magically make me better? Better than I am here, and now?" Droplets of poisonous spit flew from her lips.

Ruth went to step forwards, backing Emma up to the carriages behind her. Before she got her second leg to follow her first, Hartmann clamped onto her arm. The aggressive nurse froze at once.

Hartmann released his grip from Ruth's arm.

"Emma, what is going to make you better is listening to me," he stated.

Hearing how his voice had softened, Ruth's face contorted.

"Doctor Hartmann, I believe it is in the patient's best

interest that we do not allow her to cause any further damage."

"Ruth," he growled. Hartmann's eyes darted to the train doors having now shunted to one side, looking to her feet, and then her eyes which did not meet his own.

"Emma, talk to me, I have always been here to listen to you," he tried, eyes on Emma.

Hartmann had to fast convince himself that wasn't going to be anything possible, she wouldn't be stupid enough – unstable, uncertain – yes, but stupid enough, absolutely not. Emma would not jump the train.

When Emma didn't make eye contact with him, he searched her face but grappled with the feeling of having very little control in the situation. Everyone paused, Ruth was staring at Hartmann's eyes from the side on, seeing him focused in on primarily Emma, but she could see an underlying panic.

Cornered on the edge of the platform, Emma's top row of teeth clamped onto her bottom lip. She turned into the train, looking up and leaving her back exposed to Hartmann. In that moment, only a foot left the ground and Hartmann lunged.

One hand grabbed at a wrist, and dragged her back from the shunting carriage. On the edge of being exasperated he pulled at her like a ragdoll and convinced himself he wouldn't yank her arm from its socket. His exhale was hard through the minimal space between his clamped jaw. When the train gathered its shunting speed from the station platform the doctor's palms yanked down hard at her arm. Emma released a staggered cry, but with a vice grip he fast clamped around both arms, securing her to his front in a restraint hold. As the train sped off Hartmann grit his jaw when he let go of her arm after throwing her away from the moving train.

Ruth jumped back from the effort at which Emma came flying from Hartmann's restraint.

"You stupid girl," he hissed, eyes hard on the agonized girl bent before him.

Emma bawled aloud.

"What are you doing?" Ruth's voice came, looking at Emma unsteadily falling about on her feet, between her streaming tears Ruth saw the way her cheeks pinched with the pain he had erupted upon her. He looked to his nurse, fury remaining on his face for the few seconds after when she stared at him.

"Stopping her from getting herself damn near killed," he grumbled with a sneer.

Emma hunched over and turned to the tracks, sobs leaving her in short bursts. Upon hearing her cries, Hartmann softened himself as he had to remember who he was dealing with. He wet his throat and took a breath. She was still being held close to his body as she was left to contend with the situation.

"You should not be here, it is dangerous," he explained, looking at the tear-stained face of the woman before him. Her eyes were reddening at the corners.

Her hands ragged up to the sides of her head and gripped at her hair, her bottom jaw lopped open. A guttural, deep moan left from deep within her chest.

"Miss Merrick, calm down," Ruth instructed while she writhed on the spot, muscles contracting and loosening like a slow motion seizure. Ruth watched her unravel, and then watched the patient raise her head and stare at the pair of them.

"That's real funny," The young woman grinned, giving a laugh, despite her flowing tears. Hartmanns brow tightened watching her face contort in such a fashion.

"I'd rather be here than your cursed hospital," she seethed, her arms flailing at the pair before her, pointing to Hartmann. "You're suffocating me, I can't fucking escape you, no matter how hard I try," she spat.

"Emma, listen to yourself, you're not acting right," Hartmann said, earning another loud cry out at the remark, weakening Hartmann when it resided with him. No wind chilled him, but he bristled.

He cleared his throat, his gaze dipped. He slowed himself, raising his eyes to see nobody at the station.

Doctor Hartmann flexed his shoulder blades under his suit jacket at the sensation of himself weakening to the singular cry.

"Emma, I genuinely don't mean to up –"

"Acting right?" Emma laughed, the shine from her cheeks from the stray of tears drying "I can't stand you, and you definitely don't have a clue what's good for me!" she shouted, her voice laced with venom.

The doctor took a step towards the girl and she jumped back with a wide grin. Her arms were held behind her back so he was unable to reach and grab her limbs.

"Before you go shitting all over my coping mechanisms, would you like to know the ones I had before you knew me? Even had a clue I existed? And, guess what?" she egged, teeth gritted. She gave her hard glare to Hartmann, wishing to rip into his heart on the spot. "They do me much better than your barbaric treatment," she seethed.

Ruth raised an eyebrow, sneering at the girl. At the end of her screaming, doctor Hartmann put his hands down and recoiled, swallowing. He slowly blinked, sizing Emma then and looked to her for any hook of control. Emma's chest was visibly straining for air, she breathed through her lips with her teeth on show just below her lips.

"What do you think I am? Some monster?" he remarked.

Emma nodded. "Worse. You're a doctor."

Hartmann sighed, pinching the bridge of his nose.

Emma broke out into a grin, but it fast faded at the sensation of a needle piercing her hot skin. Turning to the nurse whipping her hand away, it gave Hartmann opportunity to then lunge, wrapping his arms over her upper chest. Emma gave a choking sound, a half- assed scream turned into a gurgle at the back of her throat.

"Thank you, Nurse," Hartmann said as the pair worked together to then hold Emma up as her muscles became useless.

With a wince, her eyes filled with hot tears that trickled down her cheek when the doctor and nurse pulled her up before she had chance to fall.

"Please don't take me back," Hartmanns patient creased, hair straying into her pained features when she doubled over. He looked her over as Ruth tucked away the capped needle in her pinafore, choosing to ignore Emma's remark.

"She's taken her wristband off, we'll get her another when we get back," Hartmann mumbled to Ruth when he took Emma's shoulder in his palm to aid her walking. Her legs were slowly buckling. The nurse aided the doctor in lugging Emma back to the car. Her feet dragged on the ground rather than having the ability in the muscles of both her calves and thighs combined to enable her to lift them from the floor.

"What have you done? Please, I just want to go home," Emma begged, slumping forwards.

Hartmann tuned himself deaf to Emma's pleas. From her lips came argumentative grumbles, letting the pair of medical professionals hauling her gain the understanding the loss of her upper body didn't render her any less capable of voicing her distaste.

"I only wanted to go home," Emma whispered.

When confronted with the steps down to the opposite side of the platform, she was debilitated by the power of the drug. Behind the wall as she gave a wandering look she saw the unmistakable hatch of Hartmanns car. From the side, Hartmann watched her eyes lolling about.

"You overdosed her, Ruth," he stated, shaking his head after his eyes scanned over the drooping girl. "You always overdose my patients."

His arm let go of Emma's shoulder as she became too weak to hold up her own body weight under the relaxant's hold on her frame having loosened her too much. At the doctor releasing his hold on her Emma almost crumpled into herself. She was not crying or screaming anymore, and he could see she was fatiguing fast. Ruth stood aside while Hartmanns hand slipped behind Emma's knees and gave a small grunt to lift her from where she was threatening to fall down the steps.

Ruth looked at the director incredulously, going to stop him, but retracting a wary hand back to her hip. Hartmann's hand wrapped around Emma's limp shoulder, only looking up in disgust to the sight of doctor Hartmanns stubbled chin, wriggling on his arms and he gripped her.

"Stop that immediately." The scolding voice came from above her head. He reached the bottom of the steps and continued to walk with her floppy in his arms, under the walkway of the station.

Emma was carried to the car, where Ruth took the keys from Hartmanns pocket and held the door open while Hartmann ducked in, sitting the drugged girl into the back. She stared when Ruth and he sat in front of her and nestled into their seats.

Hartmann hadn't fastened his seatbelt before he pressed hard onto the accelerator and the car sped off, flicking his eyes into the rear view mirror to look over Emma slumped in the backseat. He took a deep breath watching her dull orbs laze about in her skull.

She knew he was looking, seeing out of the corner of her eye the way his head turned ever so slightly to view into the rear view mirror. Emma looked only out of the car window.

Hartmann watched, swerving his car too many times when he struggled to gain the understanding of something he could not allow himself to give to Emma – that being what she fought for so desperately.

At the unmistakable drive back under the brush of the trees above, Hartmann saw the return to Westview earned a tear to roll down Emma's cheek. She closed her eyes tight.

# Chapter Nineteen

EMMA'S BODY contracted in a violent jolt that awoke her when her head fell forwards. She curled her lip to find she was back at Westview hospital, in the middle of those long hallways she ran down the day prior. Her mind fuzzed, but she wanted to claw at the walls and will them to collapse. She wanted to rip the place apart at being returned. Maybe she would have tried if her wrists would not have been bound to the armrests of the wheelchair she was in. Pulling at them, her wrists ached when the tight binds stopped her hand getting through, it pulled at her skin and made her wrist ache. Both of them, one after the other – bound tight.

The ugliest picture was coming up the hallway, bearing blue and green, the white in the middle splayed out all hideous. The awful floating lily plant resting atop the pad on the deep blue water rippling around it. Emma closed her eyes when she was wheeled past the mural, but was relieved Hartmann wasn't speaking to her. He wheeled the deflated young woman around the halls like a trophy. The soles of her feet were not able to touch the floor and she couldn't drag them to stop the process, so she kept her eyes clamped shut.

The silence Hartmann chose to leave her resting in made

the skin on her arms prickle, and she hurt alone.

Ruth was gone. Turning, nobody was to either side of her and it made her heart bounce like a panicked animal in her ribcage. "Back home now," Hartmann finally mumbled.

Her toes came to the foot of the door of her room, Hartmann pushing it open and wheeling her in, the side of the chair catching the weight of the door for them both. Catching onto the word "home," Emma butted in.

"I don't live here."

"I do apologise, it was only a nicety, Emma," Hartmann said.

The chair came to a stop at the foot of the bed.

Emma would dare to smirk at the sight of the made up bed if she wasn't so angered. She threw her thoughts away, ridding herself of any care for the gesture. The bare sides now had white metal barriers which stretched along the length of the bed. Emma thought they were to stop patients rolling out of the bed by accident, like the elderly she had seen so many times. It was a safety precaution, but for her they were elongated and restrictive, she knew they were meant for something different.

She still couldn't move her legs. Setting eyes on the bed again, the middle had cross-sections of straps meeting in the middle, at the foot and at the upper section of the bed. Emma was exhausted, a small grin coming to her at the unimaginable sight of the restraints she recognised.

She looked up at Doctor Hartmann from the wheelchair.

"Don't you think I'm too tired to fight you, Hartmann?" came her voice, watching the man.

"This is for your ongoing safety, not for your behaviour today. This is not a punishment," he answered, rubbing the wrinkles that appeared just then on his forehead. "You must understand what you did today was nothing short of foolish. You must never pull something like that again, do you understand me?"

Emma recoiled.

"I thought you said this wasn't a punishment." She glared at him.

His lips yanked into a frown. Hartmann snapped the bars at the sides of the bed down as he began.

"It isn't, but I need to tell you it was wrong, don't I? Otherwise you risk doing it again, giving us all a mighty scare like you did today," he said, turning to her with palms held in front of him, leaving her to stare at him from the chair.

Humiliation again coursed through her suffocated veins.

She looked away, digging her dirtied fingernails into her palms at the suffering she felt agonise her.

It was still painful to stand on her feet, Emma found. When she winced in pain, Hartmann told her he would be bandaging her feet later on. Her running through the streets had stripped the protective layer of skin to nothing, feeling like she was treading on the bones of her heels.

He looked to the back of her calves with a frown as his fingers lain over the scratches inflicted by the innards of a bush. "You must rest, do you understand me?" Hartmann said, getting to work with the restraints of the bed.

Emma's eyes bore into him when he gripped her floppy wrist with the white tie in his hand.

Hartmann slid off the biggest restraint which lay open awaiting her at the middle of the bed.

Emma lay quiet while he worked around her bedside, continuing to fix the restraints around her ankles and wrists. All that occupied Emma's mind was the maddening, rotating thought of utter despair at the hands of the man restraining her.

As he finished securing in her final limb, he stood at the side of her ankle, a flash of pity coming over his face for half a second upon the sight of her.

The doctor strained his neck, clearing his throat.

"When a patient does not listen, they put themselves in

extreme danger of damaging their health, as your care is completely my responsibility, you see?" When she lay there unbothered he tried again. "Emma, are you listening to me?"

"What does it matter if I listen to you? You've got me tied down to a bed for christ's sake. You do what you like with me and if I don't want to partake, it doesn't matter a toss. You're the all- knowing professional," she spat.

Hartmann raised a brow. "Stop that." His hand dug into his pocket, and he pulled out the small white prescription bottle.

"You must listen to me, your behaviour inside my hospital is unacceptable," he snapped just then, gripping the bottle so his palm engulfed it.

"You will need fluids, so I'll prepare what you need. Are you hungry, at all?" he asked, placing the bottle on the bedside table.

Emma knew her stomach was hollow and would have much preferred it to be filled, for it would begin growling at her in the hours to follow if she were still awake. She let the silence linger, wanting it to fill him with discomfort, but it infiltrated her instead, feeling herself wriggle on the bed. "No."

Hartmann looked down his nose at Emma.

"I'll get a duty nurse to bring you some fruit, that way it will bring your fluids up, also," he said to himself, Emma making no effort to listen. She turned her face into the pillow, staring out the window.

The sky was greying, possibly promising rain over West-view if the clouds didn't pass – but they were thin and streaky so if rain did come, it would only be a light shower. It would pass.

She withdrew from Hartmann, allowing him to talk away to himself as he normally did when chattering about her care. Emma felt he went on power trips all by himself, and she let him fall over his own words, hoping he'd trip into a massive black hole.

"You must be exhausted. I will see to a nurse getting you what you need. Rest up, and I will be back later on."

Emma only closed her eyes to try and shut out his voice, or the image of his lips moving to make them, his mannerisms imprinted in her tortured mind even in the darkness. She bubbled with irritation, irked that this was akin to a scene out of a film, the sensation of a deja-vu – knowing this had all taken place before now. Emma was convinced of it, like those moments that stay with you before awakening from a dream. The moments that are easy to replay in your mind throughout the day, they stick there at the back of your skull. Sometimes they don't ever go away, good or bad – not having that choice. It stuck.

Hartmann's feet were heard making tracks away from where he had stood by the bed. She jumped when the sheet at her feet was brought up over her by him, having opened her eyes to see him tending to her like an overgrown doll. His chin threatened to graze against her cheek, and it unnerved her laid up in the bed, the sight of the restraints covered by the thin sheet he placed over her. He didn't speak, but his breath smelt like his tongue must have been burnt with the residue of sour coffee. His smell was unpleasant but his presence felt better than the fear she'd be left to dry out with the drugs bleeding into her once more.

It was like her blood would be replaced with drugs, foreign substances of Hartmann's knowledge to keep her going, to sustain her state of dysfunction. And oh god, was the drugging consistent, never ending, it threatened to swallow her up entirely like a vicious dog.

Emma closed her eyes again.

Hartmann's breath stopped tickling her and in that tense moment when he finally pulled away, she opened her eyes.

The bed creaked when she moved her legs along the mattress, the cuffs around her ankles tight and scratching at her skin.

## Chapter Twenty

DOCTOR HARTMANN'S hands balled up tight at his sides, then relaxing and spreading his fingers out on his thighs.

He uttered irritated tuts under his breath, sinking into the chair at his desk. His brain was able to gain a singular moment of peace, allowing the rest of his body to relax, releasing the tension from his pacing thoughts, and then turning over a painful blank.

The glare of the computer screen made him eager to have some glasses on hand, to slide onto the bridge of his nose to ease the ache behind his eyes from the harsh white light boring into him.

It was quickly darkening outside now. He retracted his hands from hovering over his battered keyboard, turning over his wrist so he could see the face of his watch.

Hartmann felt his brain pulsating as if giving out its own heavy, tired breaths from inside his skull. His brain was threatening to tap out on him.

Underneath his fingertips, he felt the small heartbeat pumping under the surface, from his non- stop typing, hammering away at his keyboard. Hartmann's hand clasped his chin, holding his head steady as he stared at the blinds of his office window, elbow resting on the arms of his chair.

Locking eyes with his biro pen, he plucked it from sitting next to his keyboard placing it between his teeth, his jaw pressing down on the fragile plastic.

Hartmann's hand held the pen in place between his teeth, toying with it rolling around along the tops. He yanked the pen from between – defeated, he released a tense hiss. His gaze hardened, not making a motion while he wracked his aching brain. The tireless freeze frames of deep thought brought back nothing to fruition. He had nothing to grasp at or which to ease the burden of the end of his own knowledge.

Hartmann thought he had quite a lot of ideas, or knew what his next steps were to be – but for once, he drew blanks over and over. The defeat piled atop his shoulders and became trapped in this hideous cycle without answers or a visible end. He sat at his desk, imprisoned in the maze in his mind. Again, the pen's end went between his teeth. The doctor bit down on the end and let it roll along the tightening space between his top and bottom row of teeth.

From behind, the office door's lock twisted, allowing the outer sound from the hallway to reach his. He remained still, and the nurse who had entered jumped at the sight of his hunched shoulders in the chair.

"Jesus," she breathed, her open palm resting on her chest, then slipping down to have her hand back at her side. Hartmann listened but he didn't turn.

The nurse shook her head. "You scared me." She gave a staggered laugh.

"Oh, I'm sorry I was just lost in thought," came the spaced out reply from Hartmann, who upon flicking his head to the side then turned around completely, pulling his ankle to rest over his knee with his hands resting over his ankle. He was relieved to see that it was only Mary-Ann who had come into his office. Mary-Ann gave a small smile when he watched her stumble about in his office.

"I haven't interrupted you, have I? I was only coming in to grab a few forms for the nurses over in Rosetta."

Hartmann's lips parted, giving a small head tilt backwards.

"I haven't printed any in a while, so I apologise now if they aren't in the filing cabinet as it's probably gone a bit sparse." He shrugged, scratching the stubble lining his jaw.

The nurse hummed and was quick to fumble under the cabinet's handle. She pulled at it before using a key from her lanyard to render her access. Nurse Mary-Ann hunched over the open drawer and flipped through the plastic folders inside. Her Vaseline-coated lips parted as she searched, eyes darting across all of the labels as she sifted through them.

With his eyes on her back, Doctor Hartmann tilted his head to the ceiling in thought.

"Emma, on Lilypad ward," he interrupted on a whim, his own voice being the one able to yank himself out of his thoughts.

## Chapter Twenty-One

MARY-ANN'S HEAD was pulled from staring down into the cabinet, turning her attention to Hartmann. A manicured hand resting over the top of the cabinet drawer so that it would not slide in and shut itself. Mary-Ann tried not to frown on the mentioning of the young woman's name.

She paused, scanning over the desk space which laid before Hartmann.

He never allowed his personal workspace to get as messy as it was now, through her mascara coated eyelashes she squinted, and refocused her eyes on the doctor. She flicked her eyes to the clock on the wall and bit her lip. Her hair was a mess, evidence of having no time to touch or neaten it. The foundation caked upon her face was shiny, the sweat under the layer of the paint-like substance breaking through to give her perfect skin a look of greasiness.

"Has she been giving you any trouble, Doctor Hartmann?" she asked, breaking the silence. Mary-Ann, like most nurses and other doctors in Westview, all knew about the young woman's botched escape attempt.

Hartmann hesitated but coughed into his balled up first as

a reflex for his hesitating. He rested his hands over his stomach, fingers loosely interlocked. "I wish to do something for her," he said, ignoring her question.

Making it tense, he looked at his staff member now, making sure to meet Mary-Ann's gaze to drive a serious connotation home. It made any irritation at him ignoring her question fade instantly.

Her face ashened, knowing his eyes were on her hard, she let her fingers slip from hanging over the edge of the filing cabinet drawer, letting it clunk locked again. There was a pause in which Mary-Ann scrambled for how to answer him.

"What do you mean, Doctor?" she asked.

Hartmann stiffened in the chair, pushing his chin out a little as he ground his jaw. Mary-Ann watched his features.

"I mean, I wish to do something nice for her," he offered as a way of further explanation.

"Well, you could let her contact her family, let them visit her while she stays with us."

Hartmann winced at the idea, smacking the inside of his cheeks.

"Ah, I contacted her family earlier this week," he lied.

The nurse's small smile wavered. She almost put a hand on her hip, but stopped herself and instead fidgeted on the spot.

"Buy her things to relax with while she's going to be here with us, then," she prompted with a shrug.

He just gave a nod, taking it into a silent consideration – she could only hope.

"That's a nice idea, say," Hartmann paused, eyes on the ceiling above. "Proper slippers, chocolate, some flowers for her room, to brighten it up."

Mary-Ann recoiled, shifting on her feet to swap the weight of her body from one side to the other. A weak, tired smile came onto her lips.

"Give her a rest, why don't you focus on other things rather than driving everything you've got into this one patient?"

Without pausing, she continued. "I will be the one to oversee her care, I know the medication you've put her on and if you see fit I would love to read her file for myself."

Hartmann's eyes flicked to where the nurse stood in the space of his office before him.

"There is no need for that, her medication will begin to work as she needs, her dosage needs to be upped is all." He gave a shrug.

Mary-Ann pulled at her bun with a pull of her lips, grabbing at each side and pulling it tighter at the back of her head. She folded her arms over her chest as she leaned on the cabinet.

"Sometimes drugging people to high heavens isn't going to magically fix everything, if you want to know my honest thoughts her. The girl needs some intense therapy. She's hurting inside," the nurse said. "Why don't you invest in that, instead of medicating her up so much?"

Hartmann brushed a knuckle under his nose, sniffing as he twitched his nostrils. He looked to his lap, then back at the young nurse with his lips pulled thin on his face. She shifted her weight from one foot to the other again while Hartmann sat there unmoving.

"I'll most certainly have to go buy Emma those flowers, then," he said with a brisk release of breath. Mary-Ann's eyes dropped to the floor.

She did not relent.

"I would be more than happy to give her a therapy session myself and see how she responds to it."

"No." Doctor Hartmann shook his head as he brushed his knuckle against his chin. "Even if you were to do it, it wouldn't help her any." He brought his hand back to his chin when he finished speaking, eyes vacantly gazing at the floor.

"You need to let us help her too, you know," Mary-Ann said, her tone flat.

Hartmann didn't think it was that difficult to understand,

when it came to personal feelings – he had a stubborn attitude of "that's that," and the disgruntled and snappy expectation of people to get over upsets sharp-ish. He was not an emotionally-driven man, but on this occasion, when it came to his patient, he shrouded her with a great selfishness. The internal fight could rip him in half, but outwardly only one thick eyebrow was raised.

"Get out of my office, please," came his flat voice. Hartmann was hunched over himself, slumped into a sulk.

Mary-Ann looked to the closed door of the doctors office.

"Get out, nurse."

Mary-Ann did just that, allowing herself to loosen when out in the hallway. She headed up the lit up hall to print the forms she needed, as Hartmann hadn't any for her to take. She had almost forgotten what she had been there for in the first place, Hartmann having washed a whole new mound of problems over her.

As she walked, she bit her lip again and rinsed her hands, shaking her head.

Once the door shut, Hartmann remained still, staring at the door as if trying to set it alight with only the pure annoyance he was left residing in.

Pulling his tired eyes away from the door, he spun around in his chair back at the computer screen with an unimpressed huff.

The black of the screen showed his outline, his own face staring back at him as he rolled his eyes back. Jabbing a finger at the power button, the screen jumped on, his reflection disappearing. Only for a second his eyes looked upon the screen again and his jaw fell open, a the hand which rubbed his beard now clasped to his face as a hurried noise of defeat came from deep within the doctor's chest. His forefinger and thumb got to work massaging his temple again.

Inside his skull, his brain continued to pulse. He felt he

would never gain any respite from the constant train of thoughts that kept hitting a wall over and over. He couldn't rest his pacing mind, the wires kept pulsating the same stupid thoughts and ideas that lead to nothing, over and over again – he felt his head would explode.

Tired eyes flicked at the screen, resenting what he laid his gaze upon. The screen showed a failure, the medication he had created all those years ago wasn't working, it had been missing the outcome he wanted. Selfishly, Hartmann was already thinking to simply heighten the dosage Emma was receiving. But he shook his head soon after the idea formed, thinking of the dangers it would bring to his door.

Confronted with a dilemma in the darkened space and limited privacy of his office, Hartmann's gaze roamed to the seam which covered the zip of his white trousers.

His brow softened for the first time in the span of hours upon an idea creeping over his shoulder. In the glow of his computer, his eyes barely had time to flick over to the door before a straying hand landed over the seam of his pants. His thumb rested directly over himself.

The doctor felt himself perk immediately, his back straightening as he dared tease himself.

His breath hitched, lips parted dryly while his gaze longingly looked upon the straining zip of his trousers. He toyed with a cloudy idea, tempted, he muscled his eyelids with a wishful imagery in mind.

The buzzing from his restless brain began to soften when the idea appealed further, revealing itself completely to the man.

The toes of his shoes pushed the chair letting himself begin to swivel on the spot as he pondered thoughts. His spine slacking as a sudden intensity began to drain away.

The doctor flexed his nostrils and his chest expanded with a heavy inhale, then releasing it. Hartmann plucked the silver zip between his thumb and forefinger. He was dumbfounded he had restrained such an urge.

His head twisted over to stare at the thick glass in the top half of the office door before returning his focus, still clutching the zip. His top row of teeth fell down hard on his lip, pulling the skin back into his mouth, wetting the skin when his tongue ran across.

His pinched fingers fell open over his bulging zip, feeling his ache, the desperate need for release under the fabric. His clouded mind strayed to the image of Emma laid up in the hospital bed, knowing full well she'd still be there for him if he wanted to check in on her. The thick plastic straps tight on her tiny wrists laid limp at her hips.

Hartmann's lips trembled.

The apple in his throat bobbed, throwing himself up from where he was sat in his chair. Hartmann circled his shoulders when he sat upright, pulling at the gathered fabric atop his thigh. "Shit," he uttered under a staggered breath, moving about in his chair. He rested his head in his hands, letting them take its full weight. His momentum was lost on himself, rubbing his hardened palm into his sockets, dizzying himself when he again raised his head, groaning. Trying to think better of his urge, he stood, observing his office which was neglected, a state of disarray.

The frustrated man flexed his hands, willing to grip onto something to allow his eyes to clear of the mist. His hand collided against his clammy temple, sucking his cheeks to ease the tenting at the centre of himself.

He searched the office. The images of Emma flashed through his eyes, but he willed them to be forgotten at once. He winced, bouncing a leg as his mind paced.

He laid eyes on his pigeonhole, knowing he had gotten extremely lazy. He should have organised his various piles of paperwork weeks ago.

Hartmann ran a hand through his hair where he gripped the top of his skull, pulling hard on himself for a moment as he strained to think clearly. Stumped on the spot, he yanked his cuff up his arm, folding it over and darted out of his office, almost headbutting the door as he sped to leave.

The sky was beginning to bleed like various inks in milk when Hartmann reached the wing he and the nurses kept all of the medications. The halls were barren, and the air sat unstirred. Held in industrial boxes in a massive backroom, shelves were laden heavy with whatever practical items the professionals may need.

Hartmann pushed the door open once the lock shunted from inside. A confirming mechanical noise emanated from behind the wood planks of the door. He gripped a bulging IV bag from a plastic packaging and two syringes, one's barrel being considerably larger than the other.

---

Hartmann returned to his patient's room the next morning. Upon setting eyes on the sleeping Emma, he was relieved to see the IV was still embedded in her arm where he had placed it meticulously the night before.

He pushed the door closed behind, taking his time to stroll to the side of her bed. His eyes strayed from her sleeping face to examining the lack of liquid inside of the hanging plastic pouch. Pulling at his lips with a nod of approval, the doctor was pleased when he looked over the sound asleep Emma again.

Tensing his palms when his zip threatened to begin straining, he raised his chin in the air and looked away, freezing on the spot. He released a cool, steady exhale to gather himself.

The evening duty nurse had closed over Emma's curtains, the two thin layers of practically see-through fabric coming together to leave a greying window looming over the bed. It was replaced now with the early morning sunlight streaming in.

Emma's hair glowed as it lay splayed out against the contrast of the pillow beneath her sleeping head. Doctor Hartmann relaxed his hands from their clamped position behind his back and rubbed his fingertips together. His eyes trailed along Emma's hair, and in leaning forwards gingerly, the space between his fingers was warmed by the sensation of her hair. He sat beside her while he ran his fingers through her hair in her slumber. Looking upon her face so calm, the small rising and falling of her chest and his fingers in her strands, his eyes gazed on her translucent skin, his breath catching in his throat, his Adam's apple bobbing at the sensation.

He then recalled the events of that terrible day years before.

"I am a doctor, I can save my own daughter!" George Hartmann argued, but the doctors tending to his daughter's care put their palms up to their shoulders and nurses burst between the men. As the situation unfolded, nurses came between to stop the distraught man from interfering.

"I know I can, you're doing it all wrong!" George cried, tears streaming as he yanked and pulled from the grips of nurses and bodies of the gathering doctors to the unravelling scene. The fabric of his shirt was strained near to ripping by the many hands and palms gripping him.

"Please, Mr Hartmann, you better calm down, this isn't helping your wife's state either."

His cheeks discoloured by his shouting and crying, George gritted his jaw as he stood. His top lip twitched as he shoved his thumbs in his eyes to rid of the emanating flow of tears. His vision cleared of the irritating blur, but his chest did not of the thrum his heart pumped through him. "Let us do our job, Mr Hartmann. Everything will be fine if you would just calm yourself."

He turned to the perpetrator of the voice.

"If you would just tell me what the hell has happened. You haven't told me anything yet and Melissa is my damn daughter." His voice was delicate, quieting at the final word and he swallowed uncomfortably, the action spiking tears to well again. His sobbing wife hunched in a blue chair against the wall with a nurse whispering consoling words into her ear and rubbing a shoulder. His wife was too distraught to listen.

"Let me see my daughter," George asked, the cries behind him becoming louder. His voice wavered but did not break when he spoke.

"I'm afraid I am not at liberty to share what we are doing in effort to treat your daughter right now." The doctor shared a sympathetic smile.

George's chest burned with anger. At that moment he wanted to rip the doctor's face to shreds.

The physician clutched his clipboard tighter in his hand. "I apologise, I am not allowed to share treatment details with you, Mr. Hartmann. We are doing all that we can."

The doctor avoided brushing shoulders with George when he passed, his eyes on the floor when he walked away with his head low. George felt his heart palpitate with fear, a residual sheen of sweat on his forehead, his wife still gently sobbing behind him.

Doctor Hartmann was released from his entrapping thoughts and he pulled his hand out of Emma's hair, straightening his bent posture. His throat burned and he stepped over to the window when the corners of his eyes pricked with salty tears. His finger curled to wipe them away, exhaling hard on the window so a sizeable imprint of his breath remained on the glass for a moment. He blinked to clear the remaining tears, wiping again with a small unintelligible murmur, hissing under his breath when the tears kept coming in their pathetic trickles. His fussing clouded in annoyance was interrupted when the bed behind him began creaking, indicating Emma was stirring, or awake.

Hartmann's shoulders rose in the jacket he wore. He stayed staring out of the window until he was certain of his patient being awake. Still facing the window, he spoke aloud to rouse her completely.

"Good morning, Emma."

It was near to the second that Hartmann finished speaking when Emma, in turn greeted him with a groan. The unpleasant noise prompted him to then turn, pulling away from gazing upon his wandering patients like ghosts under the morning sun.

Hartmann fully expected her to have turned over in the bed if the restraints weren't there. He smiled in good humour, patiently awaiting a proper response from Emma. The doctor balanced on the front of his feet.

"I said good morning to you," he repeated, taking steps towards. "How are you feeling? Much better I suspect." Hartmann's heels were hard on the floor when he looked over her.

His judging attempt at posing Emma a rhetorical question failed to elicit the desired response, and he stretched his palms behind himself.

"I can't believe you kept me chained up here like a dog all night," she remarked lowly from the bed.

Hartmann blinked slowly, allowing the comment to wash over him. He did not tense, although his voice was hard.

"Do not take that tone with me. You were told this was not a punishment, and it isn't." Hartmann stepped forwards to remove the straps from each corner of her limbs at rest. He went to handle the restraints, but Emma shot him a hard glare.

"Don't touch me," she demanded, the straps pulling up the metal bars when she yanked herself away from his hovering fingers.

Hartmann raised an eyebrow at her.

"I beg your pardon?" His face darkened. "I am your doctor, Emma. I am only doing what is needed. You were a great danger to yourself yesterday. I don't think you realise that."

She was silent for a moment, apparently pondering a response. There was a scowl tight on her lips.

"You have not made me better, if anything I have gotten worse. I blame you for my worsening."

Hartmann retracted his hand, his cheeks hollowing.

"If you want to get out of this bed, you'd be wise to stop that talk," he quipped with a flash of impatience escalating, catching himself before growing too heated.

"I don't think you're hearing me. I do not want you to treat me any longer."

Hartmann sighed in exhaustion with the defiant young woman, frankly insulted by her careless remark. "And who would that be, to treat you, Miss Merrick?" he asked, his response quick and flat, his eyes glaring when he looked at her.

Emma's normally puckering bottom lip was sucked in as a crutch while she simmered. Hartmann looked to Emma's wrists clasped tightly by the restraints. He dismissed the state of distress she displayed.

The doctor's chin raised when a smirk spread across his face.

Hartmann hummed.

"Do you think, if you would stop the fighting and arguing with me, that it would become somewhat simpler for you as a whole?" he asked, walking in front of the foot of her bed as he went to continue. Emma had no choice but to strain her head to maintain her eyes on the man pacing at the foot of her bed.

"That way, we can come to resolutions easier, and you would feel the benefits with all I am doing for −"

"I am not the goddamn problem here," she said.

He stopped his slow pacing.

"You have been making excellent progress under my care,

do you not see?" he asked. "You have been doing exceptionally well," he praised with a tilt of his head.

Emma lay in the bed without responding.

"Emma." He stood with his hands behind his back again. "What do you suggest we do, to move ourselves forwards?" Hartmann proposed with a shrug of his shoulders, and upon having turned the tables to her he met with her gaze.

"I warn you to make the right choice." Hartmann raised an eyebrow, but his face was relaxed and saddened by her stubbornness.

Emma gave a nod.

"I want your treatments to stop," Emma breathlessly said.

Doctor Hartmann's chest bounced with a singular exhale, shaking his head with a careless smile, thinking the girl was ludicrous. His head tilted to gaze into her eyes that were staring ahead.

"I am the best here, nobody else can do more for you than me." The doctor looked directly at her with his lips parted.

Emma, although, seemed firm. "If all you can offer me is more of what I have suffered already, I want much less than you."

In the rejection, Hartmann's face soured. "You fail to see the progress," he remarked, pulling back from Emma. "I warn you, this is not a wise idea."

"I cannot get better around you," she argued with a sneer.

Hartmann's jaw jutted and he shrugged, feigning his wariness. He inhaled fast through the space between his teeth.

"Ah, so be it," he clipped, stepping forward again and resting his hands on the metal bar at the side of her bed. Just below his hands, the plastic wriggled about where Emma was fidgeting. He stopped his fingers manipulating the plastic ties.

"If you feel you are not making progress with me, Emma, this leaves me little choice in what else I can do to help you. Your condition is very serious."

When what he had said failed to elicit any sort of panic

from her, Hartmann waited in the silence until she would make a reply.

Her head turned to where he was looming over her bed, his shadow stretched out lanky behind him, hands holding onto the bars to listen in.

"How can I improve when all you do is pump me with concoctions of drugs and I'm getting worse after every treatment you give? Pardon me if I'm skeptical, but all I want is to do is get out of here." She finalised with a tone of authority that resonated with Hartmann standing at her side. "And for whatever reason, that sure as hell isn't happening with you," she snapped.

He half smiled at the ceiling when he tipped his head at her small amount of understanding. He lowered his chin and managed to wipe away his smirk.

In the silence between the two, Hartmann's weight lifted from the bars and they released a creak when he took his own weight from atop. He frowned and pulled back, gathering himself to look only over her and become a little more undone. He inhaled, eyes closed, before opening them to speak clearly, almost in a tone which was robotic in his explaining.

"You need to go downstairs, breakfast begins in an hour. I recommend you go outside while I have a talk with my nurses." He snapped off the plastic ties at her limbs.

Hartmann moved from Emma's wrists, lifting the cuffs to make a note of the time, although tutting when he noticed small red marks that remained around her ankles. He had to be quick to move himself, the young woman kicked out much like a skittish cat when he was slightly too slow to pull the ties from under the back of her heel.

Emma pulled into herself, sitting up to scramble and stand beside the bed. Hartmann did not speak, folding the plastic over in his hand and neatening the bedsheet which lay wrinkled atop the mattress she jumped from. He went to watch her leave but had turned to find that she had already left him there alone in the room. His nostrils flared, staring longingly down at the cuffs gathered in his hand while his thumb rubbed the plastic, warming it.

The doctor's hand clasped over and his arm flexed at the force of his grip, releasing a large, wracking exhale.

# Chapter Twenty-Two

HARTMANN GRABBED at the phone on his desk and dialled. At the tone cutting off, he practically shouted into the receiver.

"Doctor George Hartmann," he breathed, curling into the phone at his ear.

Ripping a hand through his tangled mess of hair, he threw himself down into his chair in the growing chaos of his neglected office.

A peering face came into view through the glass of his office door and he put a finger in the air to indicate to the nurse she was to not interrupt.

His lips continued moving with eyes avoiding meeting the nurse, although she was holding paperwork in her hand. The woman's face sheened with old sweat. She stepped back and waited at the wall, lingering while the paperwork weighed her hand down. She held her wrist carrying the paperwork, it taking the effort of both hands to avoid a dull ache coming on.

Hartmann's figure came to the door with his hand holding the phone to his ear when he saw the nurse was waiting for him.

He opened the door of his office only to give a small

gesture with his fingers bending towards him, indicating the nurse was to pass him the paperwork while he continued talking on the phone pressed to his ear.

She limply held her hand out which held the stack of paperwork. Hartmann did not gaze upon the nurse. He did not spare her the courtesy. Instead he slammed the door and turned away to tread back over to his desk where he dumped the stack of stapled papers. They became another mass to add to the collection atop the desk covered in the splay of disorganisation.

Hartmann would have sensed the irk he left the nurse with, but his mind was much further away from even coming close to considering how the she felt. He turned behind his desk, waiting in the gathering tension. Making a non-commital hum, he rustled through the arrayed mess of papers, struggling to find what he needed. Cursing under his breath while the other end of the line went silent in waiting, he grew heated under his jacket. Fingering through the endless plastic wallets in growing stress when he failed to find the documents, his forehead took on a stressed shine.

He sighed in exasperation and stood up straight, tossing the phone over to his other hand. The doctor pinched the bridge of his nose.

"I'll have to email you the documents, I don't have them here with me at the minute."

There was a pause in Hartmann's movements while he listened in to the handset. He wandered a few steps ahead, looking down at his feet and watching them lead. The doctor mindlessly paced in his stuffy office, back and forth scaling wall to wall for a good half hour.

When he paused again, his eyes looked down to gaze beyond his jaw. He raised his eyes. The skin between his teeth was sucked into his mouth, his lips pursed.

Hartmann began pacing again. Pulling his arm up to nibble at the nubs of his chewed fingernails.

Hartmann pressed his thumb and forefinger against the wrinkles on his forehead and got to work spreading them apart.

---

Emma's anger fizzled away inside when she managed to remember the way outside. Residing in the feeling she was never to leave the hospital, the gate around the garden became much more solid when looking at it from how she felt at that moment.

Hartmann lingered on her mind. Much like how a flea lingers upon the thick coat of a dog. Digging, ripping, careless about the knowledge of causing hurt to their host. She pained with every flash of his smirk that came before her vision, the sound of his voice trapped in her head.

Emma didn't understand what to do about being cut off from all the drugs he had been giving her in their multiple forms.

When faced with the sun's glare from behind the trees, she raised a cupped palm out in front of herself. She turned her head away when walking down the stairs to step foot onto the concrete path before ever reaching the grass.

How Emma wished she could numb herself. The evening's close were as difficult as the morning's rise. She busied herself with work during the dull, grey bit in the middle of the day. Starting her day with the demons and finishing with them. It was the same at Westview but without her normal crutch of a bottle beside her. The draining, heavy misery she lugged at her ankles remained.

It was cruel that despite the apparent treatments, Emma remained with the pang of unfulfillment at the bottom of her hanging guts.

It drove her to near insanity that she was fuelled so much at times but only to bounce up and down on the spot or scream until she fainted. From the hysteria, she would fanta-size to physically exhaust herself and run desperately up a vertical hill or through a forest – fuelled to do nothing but vent her own suffering and pent up emotions.

It beckoned the pain of realising, if the multiple forms of the dreaded treatments would not cure her of the biggest affliction she suffered from, what would they cure her of?

It made her reflective to the way she was numbing to other aspects of the routine in the hospital. Emma would wait like a discarded doll for these moments to wash her over, at the mercy of her suffering in her head. Soon after entering the wormhole, her blood pressure would shatter through the roof, her porcelain teeth gritting, knuckles white with clenching and grabbing for something real to hurt. Something to break through her skin, bring her feet back onto the floor. Some-thing to tell her she was alive, and real. In her hysteria, she craved that confirmation.

The world through her eyes became fuzzy and discoloured, the green of the grass melted and the sky swirled above. It all bled together, swirling in a kitchen pot she boiled and drowned in. Once or twice, Emma had become convinced she heard echoes of deep laughter breaking through the clouds.

She was unsteady on her feet and feared if she was to look up she would fall flat on her face, or be pained at her spine greeted by concrete. The world was luminescent and ugly, the shine of the sun blinding her.

The patients draped in their assorted coloured gowns were tiny. She looked upon them with a sneer, but her terror crept in and she wavered in her grin. The wind threw a chill that rippled through her and under her skin, leaving goosebumps along her legs and arms. The wind took the remaining of her sneer from her face.

"Are you alright there, love?"

Emma jolted, her arms retracting defensively against her chest.

With a degree of caution, Emma turned to see a hunched woman watching her from the steps. "Of course I am," came her unwavering reply.

The hunched woman shrivelled and shuffled away from Emma with a residing glare. Emma curled herself forwards, turning her back to the doorway where the stranger stared.

She looked to her left and was quick to hurry away. Thinking the woman was a nosy old hag, her questioning having interrupted the flow of her own bitter thoughts so abruptly. A world where it was all electrifying. The looming threat of being electrocuted at any minute, finding the buzz was coming from deep inside herself. Emma paced through the garden in her stumbling blur. The same feeling of an uncontrollable vibration that shook her reality in front of her eyes as she was laying witness to it. It was a surge that shot through her. She was elated, but with her mouth wide and arms outstretched at her sides, she was exhausted – she found her ribcage was nearly jumping to regain her breath.

Her outstretched arm muscles loosened upon hearing a small batch of chattering voices behind her. She straightened her arms again and felt her muscles pull taut under her skin. She again closed her eyes and embraced the residual buzz from within.

The voices behind her would not stop interrupting her, and Emma twisted on the spot to give a hard glare. Her brow softened, and her arms dropped. Her chin fell to her chest and eyes scrutinised the sight before her.

Emma planted her feet the way it was seemingly anticipated by the two before her, only one of the pair she recognised, but it was not so with warmth.

Standing with quivering limbs curled again at her chest was Hilda. Emma's face tightened, and she looked upon the shaking woman with eyes that bore on the sight.

The counterpart to the duo stood much taller than Hilda.

With an encouraging smile, the tall counterpart introduced

herself. "My name is Helen." She paused and leaned inwards. "And Hilda has something she wants to say to you. We didn't mean to interrupt." Helen gave a nervous laugh when gesturing with a finger between the pair of them.

Emma's eyes narrowed. "How? She can't speak."

Helen then snaked her pudgy arm around Hilda's shoulders. Emma looked upon Hilda's face with a slight upturn to her nose. Her eyes dropped to the ground and she leaned back, kicking at the grass beneath.

"She can. Oh, but she can. People simply don't give her the time of day to let her even begin. But, whereas most people fail to see that, I do not. Hilda's a dear friend to me."

Helen's pudgy frame then lumbered forward, looking down at her shoulder to ensure Hilda was aware to walk forwards with her.

"The effort required of Hilda now is too great for her to speak often, but I have ingrained the message to you within my brain," she revealed, Emma seeing the proud smirk on her round lips as she put a finger to her temple. "Honest to god, she has something she wants to tell you."

Emma felt much less kind to Hilda and displayed impatience with the two women, who had, in fact, interrupted her.

Helen went on, leaning in to Emma.

"Hilda, she likes you. She can see good in people, and saw it in you."

Emma winced at the distant memory of feeding the hunched woman who struggled to do it herself that dinnertime. Bristling, she flicked her gaze to Helen, and Hilda stood shaking beside.

"And so, she wishes to share something personal with you."

Emma's eyes stayed on Hilda, who raised her head upon her tiny neck to look directly at the unmoving figure before her in the garden.

Hilda's lips began motioning like squirming caterpillars, her tongue again was lolling about, seeing cogs turn to lazily form sounds from her fading memory. Emma's brow furrowed as she watched Hilda use her entirety of her facial muscles to make a singular sound. Trying to reign in control over her lower jaw was incredibly difficult for Hilda.

"I am the," Hilda had to pause to pull in her lopping, yellowing tongue. "Result of..." Her bottom lip gave a dreadful tremble, and it shook for multiple seconds of accord all its own.

Emma sucked in her cheeks, cruelly mirroring the facial muscle control Hilda could not muster. Seeing her friend struggle for what became a pregnant pause, Helen jumped in.

"The experiments," Helen finished.

Emma's eyes dipped, but Helen continued in an urging tone.

"And she wanted to tell you, as you are on the Lilypad ward, too. She trusts you with that fact. She gets awful lonely."

Hilda made a mustering noise but Emma did not look at her again. The sensation of her ribs closing in on her major organs was overwhelming her, wanting to only be alone.

Emma's eyes welled, but behind her temple a tremendous heat had built up. She hung her head to stare at her feet on the grass and was completely blank. She blinked while Helen continued.

"We figure we are not the only ones here to be done by like this, and we need your help," she said. The pleas collided with Emma's skin and fell among the blades of grass.

She closed her eyes as failure weighed her down, pulling her to the ground like many enormous hands all over her arms. Eyes welled full, but tears did not fall. She swallowed and tipped her head to fight against them.

"I can't help you," Emma whispered, lifting her head to meet her empty pair of eyes with their pleading ones.

Unable to handle the eyes on her as Hilda and Helen's plea was met by deaf ears, Emma stepped out to the right of the pair of women, and made effort not to brush the shoulders of Hilda when she hurried behind them.

Rushing back into Westview, Emma reflected on the woman only several minutes earlier asking if she was alright. As her stomach contracted, and lungs struggled for air under a stream of electricity through her skin, she thought to herself, "No, actually, I am definitely not alright."

Just when Emma released a loud, wobbling gag, she threw herself into a disabled toilet in time to catch a stream of thick saliva emanating from her throat, having been thrown up by the reflex.

Leaning over the toilet bowl and spitting out all of the saliva she could muster, it took Emma only seconds to recoil from her head in the bowl, and it dawned on her.

*So, that's why you pulled me away from her.*

She yearned deeply to be held, comforted, and told it would all be okay. Her breathing grew panicked. Her fingers gripped at the porcelain bowl feeling a deep unrest in her guts. The acidic burn at the base of her throat then prompted a violent stream of yellow, bubbling bile to be ejected into the bowl.

# Chapter Twenty-Three

THE NEXT MORNING Emma had managed to stop the incessant electricity running through her bloodstream when it rolled around to breakfast time. She shrugged, thinking the electric within had calmed after forcing herself to sleep.

She cringed at how she behaved with Helen and Hilda. But she buried any feelings of sympathy, if Emma couldn't help herself, how could they expect her to help them?

She awoke sapped, and felt more hollow, like she now carried significantly less weight since the previous, unpleasant evening. Emma had calmed down enough to return to the feeling of her skin being attached to her body – rather than buzzing as if flies chewed at her under the surface.

It just filled her with questions, she wanted to speak to somebody to see if these surges' of mania, and thoughts over-crowding her skull to near suffocation like a white-out, were a warning of something far more terrifying. Emma feared more that the suffering inflicted would barrage her without warning. It being out of her control and leaving her sluggish and drooly, reigned an overarching terror.

Deep in thought, she came to realise she carried symptoms

both physical and mental, existing at the exact same time – it was too awful to not be important. Emma stiffened.

The image of herself cowering at being mocked for her weak, child-like helplessness came to mind. Battered with nothing less than her own limbs, she was left helplessly shrinking from self- inflicted blows.

In a wrack of paranoia, the image of Hartmann's held out palm flashed to mind, on it was a pink pill laying upon the stretched white powdery glove covering his palm.

Emma's thrumming heart clenched in sync with her jaw tightening. The thoughts continued when she loosened forcefully.

She didn't want to sit at the table, it was draining, and becoming increasingly difficult to be false.

So Emma sat limp seated at the table full of strangers.

The chat overhead wound her up, wanting to insist the topic to change, but instead remaining silent. She became more absent, not touching the faces of those around her with eye contact, but staring ahead.

Emma only moved her head to keep eyes on the tables. She allowed her eyes to roam to side- eye someone and her ears perked keenly to where conversation was the loudest. Awareness spiking of eyes on her, people who were sat at the tables were discussing, chatting, laughing – at her.

She sank, trying to shrink in the chair. Managing to become fast convinced of it, needing no looks to confirm or neither hearing it to know. Emma's head fell, resulting in her chin becoming pressed into her chest to block out the eyes all over. She felt them burn and warm her flesh to break into a clammy sweat.

Emma jumped from her chair and lowered her head when making a beeline for the double doors. quickening her pace to almost fall over her tangled feet when she pictured a straying hand grabbing at her hair and dragging her back.

She fought back a giddy smile, her lips quivering in a bout

of excitement. Inside her mind she was entertained by fantastic images of Hartmann running after her, and she pictured how she would practically bounce off the walls of corners she sped around. Practically throwing herself into the wall opposite when she failed to slow down. Hair flying behind and Hartmann in close pursuit, reaching out but never able to grasp her. Not caring when alarmed residents would give glares at Emma grinning and throwing herself around the corridors. Nurses couldn't catch her either, they'd shout after her but she would continue to run without stopping. Maybe Hartmann would bellow, shouting out a low warning and receiving only a squeak in reply, forcing her feet to move that tiny bit quicker.

---

Every time her brain began to wander back on her, she swigged from her glass to restrain the ability it held, only allowing her thoughts to wander so far. Or better yet for a result, think of anything else. The house was sparse. Jason had left hours before, and fled to his mother's house rather than stay in with his fiance. Fiance, although neither of them were wearing the rings anymore. It had not been spoken, but since the pair had come back from the hospital, it didn't need to be. Emma was not prepared for an evening on her own.

It was only the next evening, and everyone she knew had been "touch and go," since the news broke. Dropping off flowers at the door, and stepping back when she would pick up the nerve to open the door without breaking into floods of fat tears. Regardless of her loneliness, nobody would stop in to see her. She felt untouchable, and even her family were less than supportive. Being at the brunt of Emma's stubborn and argumentative nature, they figured she had managed to see "this one" off for good.

Emma still hurt from the birth. It was a cruel reminder of what she did not have, and what she had been so prepared for.

Being alone brought forward the realisation that she could now barely handle herself, let alone how Jason would handle her.

He was cowering at his mother's, still. At the brink of her crisis, she turned to the alcohol in her cupboard that sat tall beside the fridge.

Having not drunk a drop for nine months was something to behold. After only two glasses of wine, Emma stumbled around the house and her eyes saw double.

Emma's phone buzzed on the arm of the couch but she only grimaced and turned the phone over. She knew it would be messages from friends on Facebook sending their sympathies, and multitudes of heartfelt emojis.

Emma got herself paralytic that evening.

Turning on some idle watching crap on the living room's TV, she slumped on the couch with her glass sat on the floor, the bottle beside it. That was the only thing to illuminate the otherwise black of the living room. It pulled her mind away from her situation, at least = made the tragedy more of a comedic point with the alcohol swirling her system.

Her mother called. Emma hesitated picking up when her Apple ringtone echoed through her dazed skull. She resented thinking of hearing her own mother's grating voice. She felt unable to face what she was, and what she had failed to become. She watched the phone screen turn black as the ringer sounded off. She gulped from her glass.

Emma mumbled aloud to herself in a rant about how Jason was a spineless bastard. She put on some music, and ended up listening to Coldplay, and finally allowed the tears to come flooding out.

Emma had only her bottle of wine to weigh her down. She was completely lost.

She did not know what to do with herself apart from drink the contents of the bottle she clutched.

When Emma had finally picked up the courage to answer

her mother's phone calls a few days later, she had already begun her drinking – it hadn't rolled into the evening yet.

"Where's Jason, Emma? Where is he?" her mother breathed down the phone. "He's at his mum's. I don't think he'll be coming back."

"Oh, Jesus. Have you rung him at least?"

"No, Mum. Why would I?" Emma looked to the empty bottle at the side of the couch she perched on. She wandered forwards, rubbing her thumping temple and closing her eyes. "I don't think he wants to be my fiance anymore."

Emma's voice went hoarse at the admittance, and she swallowed to ease the pinch of tears at the corners of her eyes. She exhaled fast in a hiss, cursing herself for the tears that welled up behind her eyes again.

The phone was quiet, and a slight rustling was heard. "Have you argued with him?"

"No," Emma wiped at her eyes with the wrist of her cardigan. "The complete opposite." Emma took a breath before continuing. "He didn't say anything to me."

"I think it'd be good if you would call him."

Emma felt her throat grow raw. She began pacing again. "I'm not going to."

"Let me come over and we can phone him together."

"No, you're not listening to me."

"You scared him off, didn't you? Are you lying to me, Emma?"

At this accusation, Emma's battered heart shattered and she gave a loud cry as her legs seized up beneath her. The phone clattered as it collided with the floor, and Emma's hands were fists that banged against the wooden planks. She collapsed onto the floor of the living room in a writhing heap.

"Emma? Emma?"

Tears pooled before her and she let out several agonized cries. Her chest seized, and her tears would not stop. The grieving woman curled into a fetal position, and her wails wracked the house.

She wailed, and then gasped, filling her lungs with air and seizing into small sobs. Then wailed like a banshee again. Emma had never felt so barren in her entire life. Her body was left uncontrollably shaking, eyes were wide upon releasing her heart-aching screams.

Emma felt all she could do was scream until she fainted. She screamed for the undeniable failure she had managed to become.

At the fading of the imagery that hypnotised her, she had no clue how much time had passed. She rubbed her temple, desperate to be alone.

Emma's palms unballed to press hard against the door on the left, the other one remaining shut. The effort required made her feel like the door was pushing back against her. She was dismayed at the lack of strength behind the tremendous effort it required of her.

Entering the room, her nose was assaulted by a sour smell, a stinking sourness which emanated strongly from the carpet she stood on.

Emma hoped it didn't cling to her when her nose wrinkled, and she pinched her nostrils, turning her gaze from the moulding floor to the room spread out before her.

Before Emma could take in the rows of chairs coated in dust her eyes settled on a singular head. A woman was seated in the front row of the auditorium.

When the door shut behind her, the woman did not move an inch, she didn't turn around to concern herself with who had entered.

She stepped down the aisle separating the first and second block of chairs. Apart from the door shutting, Emma's feet on the floor did not make any noise as she approached the back of the woman's head, cautious not to startle her.

The side view of the woman's face came into view as she walked further up the aisle. Emma tilted her head to see the woman in a trance-like state and her eyes lolling up on the stage. She was glued to the barren stage as if watching dancers – her irises slowly made circles and she blinked.

There was no music playing, but the woman swayed in the seat to a rhythm only she could hear. The absence of music and interruption proved the woman would not have been startled. Her state of daydream, possibly of what at one point would have been erupting on the stage before the pair, was too strong.

Standing at the front of the aisle, Emma looked from the woman to the barren stage. The curtains yanked at either side of the pillars were discoloured. They were covered in a thick dust where the fabric gathered in folds, bound to the pillar at each side by a thick, mustard rope bound in plaits.

Emma's face wrinkled in her wondering, having the thought of how long the woman had been the only one to inhabit the deserted auditorium. Her greying hair pulled in a ponytail that trailed down her curved spine as she leaned into the deserted stage, she sat entranced in the seat. Emma watched the hands of this woman, with the wrinkled skin decorated with moles, some darker than others – not to miscount the abundance of them. The hands of the woman rose, and fell like conducting an orchestra, or wishing to rise from her seat and begin dancing herself. Shaking, but moving to an inaudible rhythm of music, her hands swayed in the air, fingers together and palms being the guide for how her head would follow. Dry lips that seemed unable to close in awe of visions, of the magical sounds sought after.

Inside her mind, the keys of a piano were bleeding through Emma's fingers. The vision which was vivid through the woman's consciousness and brought her withering body to break in to graceful movements. Softened, Emma sized up the height of the stage compared to her frame, looking to the door of the stage. She was fast to run over to grip the handle and give another heaving push. To her pleasant surprise it gave way for her to then be greeted with three steps at the side.

Looking up, they lead her to the floor of the stage behind the curtains. Emma clambered the steps, having a kindly determination to seek for the shared reality of what once was a great joyous sound to fill the hall.

The elderly woman remained entranced, having not paid Emma any heed despite her movements creating otherwise disruptive noise.

The patient's feet were covered in dust, the bottoms being blackened by the dust- covered stage. The thin blanket coating the wood being walked on with caution, for Emma did not know whether the wood of the stage was thin and would break under her. No noise emanated from the panels of wood below, and so Emma's sights were free to be set on a grand piano.

Its lacquer once shone brilliantly, but was now neglected. The keys were exposed, just left at the side of the stage. The picture was tragic, the lonely instrument of such honour to play upon with skill discarded with little care. The black and white keys were fluffy with the same thick dust that clouded every area of the hall.

Taking a glance over her shoulder, the elderly woman sitting before her remained with eyes absent.

Emma returned her eyes to the dust- coated piano. With a delay, her hands raised from where they hung at the sides of her hips.

The patient flinched upon her fingers pressing on a key, the deep internal groan of the keys being forced to move for the first time in what must have been years. At the tiniest echo of the pitched- up key being heard, Emma scanned the remaining keys at each side of where her finger rested.

It pleased her, bringing a new sound to the repetitive environment of Westview and a near shiver through her, a small ripple of pleasure. Her brow lifted and she bent over the keys to study them, tentatively hovering. When Emma finally built up the courage to play a small, simple and gentle tune it made the silence of the room that remained, uncomfortable. The silence allowed her to simmer in the comfort she soon after triggered. The warming relaxant of the keys' tune brought a calm deep from within herself.

Something so neglected and alone for such a long time can still be beautiful. Its loneliness had no effect on the piano's ability to give pleasure to others. Emma longed to harbour the same resilience as the instrument.

The few melodies Emma knew from years before, echoed through the hall, the only source of happiness she was able to grasp and keep all for herself. The reality of her situation was able to drift away from where it clung to her. The way she pressed upon the keys in a rhythm she developed, fast becoming engrossed in the beautiful sounds emanating from inside the wood. Upon pressing on the keys, the note ran through her fingers and Emma felt she got lighter with every key she played.

Emma's heart lurched when an ear-splitting scream wracked the hall. Her hands shot away from pressing upon the keys any further, immediately recoiling to her sides. Her eyes focused on the old woman who had lurched from her seat, hunched over to reveal a large lump at the top of her spine, visible behind her narrow face. Emma shuddered at the way the woman threw a bony finger at her, fearing it would detach and fly at her.

"Be quiet! That godforsaken racket you're creating is ruining my day," the hunchback woman accused, throwing her flapping arms up and out at Emma. The woman moved so aggressively despite an obviously uncomfortable ailment, it gave Emma the impression of a witch.

Flecks of grey saliva dribbled from the corners of the

woman's wrinkled mouth when she spat at Emma for the racket she caused. Disturbing the elderly patient in such a way clearly made her ~~plain~~ outraged. The accusations stopped, and Emma stood like a figure of humiliation upon the stage.

The audience of merely only one was not impressed. She didn't think the piano made a racket, and had not intended to do any wrong by playing music upon the instrument. In the face of being reprimanded her heart could have fallen, rolled out from the space between her ribs and landed on the dust coated floor where it would rot upon the stage.

A fine show that would be, hm? Maybe finally at the sight of a tragedy, it would begin to fill the vacant seats.

Just like every other damned thing in the hospital, Emma thought her heart would fit in perfectly in the auditorium among the dust bunnies and dead bugs. She trembled, eyeing the accusatory woman when she curled her ugly finger back into her palm, as if withdrawing a weapon. At once, Emma felt those enlightening feelings drain from her, losing hope and confidence simultaneously, it left her unsure of what to do with herself.

The woman turned with a huff, expressing her extreme annoyance outrightly directed at Emma.

She failed an audience of only one. Deformed, grinning, laughing faces appeared at the failure Emma felt burning in her throat. Dragged deep into a pit where all above, the only source of light to shine on her = was dimmed by the heads of those who laughed.

Hot pinching tears were swallowed and bitten back, but the upset caused her frame to rattle on the spot, like recoiling from a blow to the back, having winded her.

Emma did not feel she wanted to play the piano again after the cruel woman had left. A small seed of resentment narrowed her vision when moments before she was watching the shuffling feet of the old woman make haste out of the auditorium. Anger fading, Emma was mystified to drag her eyes from searing into the back of the woman trudging out. Her walk was funny, as if weighed down by the lump on her back. She hobbled side to side and did not move her legs in front of herself. Apart from the rightful thought of thinking the elderly woman was something along the lines of an asshole – Emma pondered a reason for the outburst.

The fantasy in her head is perhaps much preferable than the reality.

## Chapter Twenty-Four

EMMA GAZED BACK to the piano again, the imprint from her fingers on the keys leaving marks in the dust. The doors to the auditorium had closed. It sealed her alone, in the hall.

She hunched herself over to continue with her playing small melodies, ones which brought her a tiny bout of happiness – private and now alone. Shrugging to ease the tension, Emma turned back to the keys under her fingers again. She hurried to play with the knowledge that it would stop the shaking that bit quicker than if she withdrew herself from the instrument.

The small shakes in her hands subsided when the music floated up from the keys again. Releasing another small rhythm from the tips of her fingers, she found a synchronisation and became very agile.

The feelings of warmth erupted from the bottom of her stomach and flooded to her arms, forming goosebumps atop her skin. Her fingers darted to continue the light in her lungs.

Bending forwards further, her collarbones poked out where the gown slacked. Emma at once becoming intertwined with the piano, the tips of her fingers not leaving the keys once to rest or become halted by a lack of thought, or no memory of a song to play. So invested in the sounds she was playing to an audience of ghosts and piles of dust, Emma did not hear the door shut. She didn't hear the interruption, her music surrounded her like a fortress.

Emma was deeply immersed in the tunes of the piano she lamented over, becoming more and more in tune with a rhythm of her own making.

The music had stretched and whispered into the ears of a gentleman wandering the halls with hands clasped behind his back. He burst into the auditorium, his wrinkled face emblazoned with a wide smile.

The gentleman seemed amazed that another patient was labouring passionately over an instrument otherwise forgotten. His eyes went wide, and the smile on his lips expressed his astonishment upon staring at the stage.

The gent in question beamed, hearing the playing of the instrument with such ease, the notes rising and falling. With his wrinkled face emblazoning a beam, he was quick to walk down the aisle to the foot of the stage.

The fellow patient had a spring in the way his feet would lug from the floor, one after the other with a degree of speed he had not had access to in years.

The man angled himself in sideways to rest on an aisle seat. He tilted his head in effort to help his deafening ears remain equally able to hear the keys that jumped in a beautiful array of notes that allowed the astonishment to melt over him. The two patients had not noticed one another.

It was only when the music stopped flowing into his ear canals that he shook himself awake in his chair from the state of peace he had sank into.

The gentleman's knees creaked as he strained to heave himself up to stand. He stammered to catch his breath. He looked upon the stage at Emma where she stood.

"I have never seen a piano inside this place," he began with a breathless glance. His hands gripped the backs of the chairs before him when sidestepping out into the aisle to approach the stage.

Emma stared at the man, squinting to get a clearer view.

"I was attracted," he began sweetly, but catching himself and pausing to slap a hand to his wrinkled forehead.

Emma watched cautiously, her fingers intertwining at her stomach.

"D'ow, no, I mean.".. He became breathless again with the dual effort of walking to the stage, and talking to Emma. The man stopped at the end of the aisle. His eyes looked up from under the pile of wrinkles above, and below his thick eyebrows that raised when he spoke next. "I mean to tell you, your playing is a stunning sound." Then he smiled, his somewhat odd grin unnerving Emma, but charming her too. The man gave off an air of eccentricity, an impression of being someone upper-class.

The man stood before her winked with a haughty smirk. "Thank you, I haven't played since college. That was quite a while ago now."

The man was not looking at her when she went to make eye contact with him, rather, had turned to look at the door of the stage where Emma had entered.

"May I come up, and you can play me some more of that beautiful music? I'm no good myself, getting forgetful, you see." He tapped the side of his skull.

Feeling pity, she shrugged. "I'll play, but I'm not the best." Jostling her shoulders to loosen them as she looked at the piano again.

He held a hand up to her to stop Emma from speaking further.

"No, no. What you play is quite splendid, I assure you of that. Now continue while I battle these menacing stairs," he said with a smirk, pointing to the door to the side, his wrist waggling at the inanimate set of steps.

Emma's cheeks gathered when she smiled at the man,

deciding he was comical – that eccentricity the man had about him providing her entertainment. He was properly spoken whilst his body language was small and odd. A character with certain 'isms' about him, particular grand and wide gestures and methods of tending to his own interests. More waggles of the wrist and twitching his nose, maybe. He would suit a walking stick, she decided. He'd be the type to circle it around in front of himself when walking downstairs, or turning on a street corner. Perhaps he was like that at all times, no matter what, and the thought of it entertained Emma. The eccentric man presented himself to be someone not to have his bright and optimistic character dampened by everyday inconveniences.

With a small beam remaining, she turned to the piano and laid her fingers before her, looking up to see the top of his balding head make its way up the stairs.

Emma could hear him struggling, so she was patient and held back from playing, until he joined her on the stage.

"This auditorium has not been used in years, and it is so pleasing to me, the entire premise here," The man paused as he got one leg up the final step, the other to follow. Emma looked over the empty rows of seats again before he reached the stage with a grand smile.

"I missed the sound of music being played," he said, approaching Emma and gesturing to the empty auditorium. "The nurses don't allow music."

"Why doesn't the hall get used anymore?" came her burning question.

The man's face dropped, sticking his tongue out to wet his lips for his jaw was slack. He took a breath before answering her.

"Doctor Hartmann didn't see any clinical use for the space, I believe. In the early days he gave it a shot, but it sort of, dissipated." The man looked away for a moment, beyond the top of Emma's head. "He shut it off from patients. My friends and I asked but never properly got our answers."

The air became still between the two, and the older man refocused on Emma.

"That's terrible, I think this is to become my newest escape while I'm here." She visibly perked, struck with an idea. "I could suggest bringing it back, the music, the use of this entire hall." Emma paced, becoming excited at the idea of the dust being cleaned and the piano loved by someone who knew how to play, much better than she did.

The older man's face lit up, arms outstretched and joining her in the shared excitement building.

"Imagine, oh, oh now – that would be the day." The man leaned back with an admirable twinkle in his eye as he gazed, refocusing on Emma with the same expression.

Emma perked, feeling a twin flame of excitement in the man, his eyes shining despite little light in the room. Any chance of the natural light having been blocked out at the curtained over windows under the barrier of the tall ceiling. When she looked back at the man, he had interrupted her from gazing ahead of herself in a fiction.

"My name is Henry, Henry Allen," he introduced cordially.

Looking at him, she smiled. "Emma," she clipped, turning her eyes away from the man to give way for her fantasy which was fast evolving. The light of music touched between the ribcage of every person, picturing it almost lifting the audience from their seats.

"It would be just the thing this place needs, I could maybe teach myself songs to play."

Henry gestured to Emma as if having given him a ground-breaking idea. His jaw went slack with amazement, showing his colourless tongue when he seemed to reel the idea in for himself. Henry slapped the air, his tongue at once disappearing behind his lips.

"Absolutely, my girl – you are a friend of mine with musical passions like what you have just demonstrated to me," he declared with another yellow grin.

Emma sighed lustfully with the excitement they shared.

"Do you think Doctor Hartmann would listen to me if I brought it up, like you did?" She gave a wide smile.

Finding herself listening, awaiting a reply from the man, a long pause left her bereft of the excitement.

Emma swallowed, shrinking when her shoulders gathered. Gazing upon Henry's face, she reeled when he had frozen up.

Henry's eyes focused on something far ahead of himself, entranced. Breaking from his vision, his head dipped. "Ah, no, he doesn't listen." His voice had dropped, an instant cliff edge plummet to her excitement was announced in the change of his tone alone.

Upon hearing it, Emma focused on the man's features, gauging his hands at his sides, and his expression. How he re-entered the conversation would bounce into Emma, deciding how she would continue the interaction. What an appropriate response would be, the natural flow of a pure emotion having halted at once. Emma felt herself regressing back to mechanical responses at the darkening of the man's mood. Despite her anxious thoughts at the stiffening of her newfound friend, she gave a naïve shot at lightening Henry's mood.

"Why not? I can talk to him, he was my doctor." Emma hoped Henry would become someone to share a common interest in, but he flinched. Unaware, she began to spiral on at him, thinking that he was listening to her still.

"I think I am more than able to have a chat with Hartmann about re-opening the hall and getting it back in shape for use. I could get the nurses in —"

Henry's head snapped to Emma.

"No. You will do no such thing, girl."

Looking upon his face, Emma grew afraid when his eyes became hard, and his eyelids peeled back, giving no leeway for her to avoid his deathly glare.

His lip curled, aimed like a spout when he went to speak again. The man lunged forwards, his hands tensed at Emma.

"Hartmann won't do anything else for you other than he already has. He's a selfish son of a bitch, do you know what he did to me?" Henry exclaimed, spit flying onto Emma's lips from his.

Emma had no chance to back away before he lurched forwards again.

"Those drugs, they're made that way – what they do to you, Hartmann produced them for drug trials, he's killing off patients here, you do know this, don't you, girl?"

Her first reaction to this was horror, and she was afraid to break eye contact with Henry for fear of an escalated reaction.

"Those drugs he gives aren't normal!" he hissed, striking Emma with every word he spat with such a degree of sudden self-assurance. A finger was jabbed in the direction of the double doors to the auditorium. "He – that man – concocts the drugs himself so you become so ill, you question if you ever felt right in your entire life."

Emma's lips twisted but words wouldn't leave her muddled brain when she went to respond.

The same bony finger pointed up high on the stage, Henry straightening himself to elicit the importance of what he was lecturing Emma with.

"Concocts them?" she whispered, more to herself than the old man, but he caught it and attacked her.

Henry fast latched onto the question and threw it back in her face as if the words were alight. Emma's chest rose and fell at a speed which made her feel faint, but her feet refused to move.

She needed to escape Henry's aggressive grip but she couldn't move. His skinny arms had thick green veins popping under his skin as he frothed with anger.

"They ain't normal – they'll cripple you," Henry stated, his bottom lip jutting forward with his profound statement. "He's been giving me 'em for a good while now, all bloody types of them, and I've been in some right states thanks to him."

The man laughed to himself, but Emma was silenced. Her skin prickled, and she felt her spine curve between her shoulder blades.

"Let me be the one to tell you, girl," he continued, but Emma had her eyes on the floor, feeling the warmth in her chest of a flicker of rage.

When she lifted her head to look upon this eccentric old man she scrutinised him, and stared at him with disgust.

Emma next looked upon Henry, who was spitting in her face at the spouting of his sharp words. At the flecks of spit reaching her skin, she pulled away. It was with her blood being violently thrown around her veins under her skin, and gushing through her ear canals that Emma received the man's words.

"Hartmann'll break you. You'll never leave. You're just what he'd like to have stick around."

Her indifference melted away from how it clung onto her skin, and left her raw to simmer and fester with the brunt of Henry's statement. It was as if acid had been poured over her head, shredding away her defensive layers with claws and teeth. She held fire in her eyes when she twisted her heavy glare onto Henry.

Henry gave a snort, then asked "How're you feeling, girl?" He ripped with laughter at his taunting words.

Emma's anger aimed at him like the barrel of a gun, for he had torn her open and her guts collapsed out on the stage. She broke open completely, having no words or thoughts to argue back and was left breathless. She was hollow, broken, but it came with grave danger, as she was now filled with white, seething rage filling her empty chest.

Henry had no clue what danger he presented, and Emma was powered by a fearsome rage, driving her into the pit of some of the most extreme of violent instincts.

Like a woman possessed, Emma's hands wrapped themselves around his skinny throat and at once her shoulders came together to weigh heavy on top of Henry when he collapsed like a pile of sticks under her. Emma's hands worked together to double down the force at which she applied pressure, tightening her thumbs over his larynx.

Henry sputtered and flecks of his spit landed all over the skin of her hands on his skinny neck.

Under her palm as she tightened, she felt his Adam's apple desperately bobbing, poking hard at her. This only drove Emma to squeeze harder to stop its motion.

His forehead broke into an ugly sweat, fists banging at his sides to lift, landing a grip atop her shoulders and attempt to push her off.

Teeth bared, Emma gritted them to gain strength as her muscles tightened throughout her body. Her eyes bore into his, the whites reddened by the upspring of the tiny veins in his eyeballs threatening to roll over. She drew in closer, feeling Henry thrash and push while small gurgles, choking escapes of air, left his throat.

Emma's palms released for a second, allowing the man to gasp, but only to close up his oesophagus tighter when she regained her grip.

Tears of panic streamed down Henry's crow's feet when he sputtered under Emma. His hands scratched at the wooden stage and his limbs kicked out.

In a victorious glower over him, she lowered her face into his with her hands low on his neck. Her jaw opened and then came unhinged over his half-conscious face, and Emma released a blood- curdling scream over him.

The man's eyes closed and tears fell down the sides, blinking hard when they wouldn't stop coming.

Her mouth remained a void out of which came another demonic scream, shaking him by the power she exerted from it. Her eyes focused in on the way Henry lay paralysed as she imagined grabbing his skull and smashing it on the floor of the stage until his brain matter was visible. Much like a demonic monkey, the sight of his brain when she would next lift his skull, may possibly provide her appeasement.

With the consuming thought of his limp body under her, Henry's struggling eventually coming to an end, his gasps, struggles, and kicks no more.

White noise had invaded her ears and no sound could have reached her. Emma felt she had her head underwater. She sucked in to stop her saliva escaping from behind her row of teeth.

She was thrown from her position straddling the man, finding herself rolled on her back on the floor of the stage. Her teeth remained bared, willing to lash out her anger at anyone. She seethed in every aspect, practically convulsing at the power possessing her small body. Emma's eyes were glued to Henry while he was aided to curl up on his knees, choking and coughing. Nurses patted him on the back and held his weak frame.

Emma's arms were thrown out to the side of her, legs spread through hard kicks to her inner thighs, and proceeded to be sat on.

Emma turned away from her choking victim and relaxed under the restraint of nurses holding her arms. Some sat on her legs and her torso was pinned down with various jigsaw pieces of their bodies combined. In the restraint the nurses applied, Emma found herself coming down from the high of her emotions. She tipped her head back before morphing her lips upwards, breaking into a smile. Her teeth bared and lips turned up with nothing but glee. Her ribs began to bounce from the wrack of laughter which washed her over, strung out on the floor. Aloud, and without shame, she laughed and struggled to control her volume. Eyes closed, a healthy, terrifying laugh echoed through the hall, her chin wobbling and bouncing to allow the titters to escape her.

Emma lay in hysterics atop the stage as if in a scene from a

Shakespeare play. She continued to erupt in bouts of giggles and bouncing laughs with a sloppy, lopsided grin stretched onto her face.

The blur of nurses having ambushed Emma were panicked. Unnerved. Their faces were white and some rapidly swallowing, flapping with their hair and uncertain of what to do. They grabbed her limbs and held her tight, unsure of the next steps to take. They reflected the cynical nature of it all, and perhaps that's why Emma found it all so hilarious. The medical professionals all shared looks of fleeting panic and disturbance when they looked upon a co-worker's clammy face. Straying hairs stuck to their skin, eyes trying to stay fixed on Emma's limbs.

The weight of the nurses piled on her did not halt the bouts of hysterical laughter from echoing through the hall. And Emma, not for lack of trying, could not manage to stop herself from displaying the grin that had plastered itself onto her face, neither could she control the wracking laughter that left her in tears.

# Chapter Twenty-Five

"IT WAS TRULY one of the most disturbing encounters. I don't think it would be best seeing her right now, Doctor Hartmann," Mary-Ann stated in the midst of the hall. Her face was flushed and her cheeks glowed red.

The doctor's nose wrinkled at the notion. "Nonsense. It's necessary for me to assess what state Emma is in," he argued, briskly striding past her to signal the end of the conversation.

Mary-Ann stared after him, eyes flitting, and bringing a hand to her temple. She rubbed her fingers against the sweat gathered there. Her chest was still shaking from the disturbing scene she had come into. The eccentric old man, Henry, still hadn't spoken a word about the incident.

He had been difficult to calm down from the attack at first, but was settling down now. As a result, he had stopped talking to the nurses that had been helping him. They weren't sure if it was his ego kicking in to mask his pain or suffering, or going into a type of shock.

In his room, Henry retired into the tall armchair and held a glass of water in his still hand, loped over the armrests and lost in thought, staring ahead. He did not drink the water after being requested to by a nurse. He held the glass wavering over the end of the arm, and she was prepared for him to drop it, but no such thing happened.

The nurses were worried – the scene had thrown their professionalism off course, having never witnessed such severe behaviour.

Word spread around between the barrage of professionals and an undertone became emotionally tense in each shared gaze and the false, passing smiles.

Doctor Hartmann did not speak of it, but he was busy dealing with the outburst's aftermath.

The nurses on Lilypad ward were split in two, one team to wrestle with Emma while the other half tended to Henry alongside Hartmann.

The doctor's mood was dark, but his lips curled into a half-assed smile when anyone made eye contact.

Henry's room door was shut and locked. Around the bed the curtain was pulled from the sides of his headboard to shroud the bed while Hartmann got to work over him.

He had swooped in to finish off where the nurses could go no further.

Hartmann's hands got to work among the multiple beeps and monotone noises in the room. They hurried to manipulate the assorted wires attaching to the board behind where Henry's head lay, yanking the monitor wire from the board.

A tired looking stand at the side of Henry's bed yield a sunken IV bag.

Doctor Hartmann looked from the IV bag, to Henry in the bed. He dug a hand into his coat pocket, touching a plastic, thin object that made him run cold. Rubbing a finger along the plastic, he once more flicked his gaze to Henry, and pulled the object out, having flicked off a cap to remain behind in his pocket.

The plastic of the drained bag was pierced by the neck of a needle, which Hartmann then shot a substance into the mixture that led into the man's bruised, skinny arm.

Henry struggled under the sheet and stammered, straining to turn his head. He clearly wanted to pluck together the strength to sit up, but his muscles felt loose and would not be of any help in his attempts.

Henry, for all of his stammering, was not able to find the words to say to the Doctor, but he would have found his attempts at speaking to be rudely disregarded anyway.

Hartmann avoided eye contact with Henry, only having looked at him in pittance and dismay at the sight of the pathetic elderly man laid up in the bed.

Doctor Hartmann was quick to shove the needle into his pocket, and lifted his head only when leaving Henry's room. Standing in the hallway with pottering residents, Hartmann flicked his eyes up, and then down the hall, with distrust.

Emma, residing in a padded cell at the other end of the Hospital, was raging, and Hartmann was on his way to her.

A vein in her neck had become engorged with the pace of blood rushing through her extremities. Her tensed hands gripped at the roots of her hair and pulled, screaming and throwing herself at the blackened glass. In the room with the cushioned walls, Emma screamed bloody murder, apparently willing the world around her to crumble under the sheer force of her turmoil.

Behind the bulletproof glass, Hartmann flinched to see the girl in such a state, her hair matted and knots visible at the straying, thin ends. Emma's face was beet red, her throat threatening to close up and give her body a rest from the relentless screaming and crying.

Hartmann leaned forwards, humming to himself while Emma threw herself at the walls. His upper lip was stiff and he gave an air of indifference, despite flinching at Emma's behaviour. He watched with an unmoving face while she cycled from hysterical crying to screaming in rage.

The doctor's eyes narrowed. Hartmann was disturbed to view her cycling in such rapid succession.

"I can't have a patient of mine like this," he complained with a tut, his voice sounding weary regardless of his annoyance. Hartmann turned to the door when he heard it pushed open, turning his head to lay eyes on Ruth. With a finger cupping his chin, his eyes returned to Emma.

"Doctor Hartmann," she purred, her voice slimy.

Hartmann puzzled over what to do with the patient in the padded cell. Nurse Ruth's voice only entered his head minutes after she had initially spoken.

"What are you planning to do with her now?"

The doctor wrinkled his lower lip, sucking it over his row of teeth and nibbling. "I have never seen someone go from zero to a hundred like that, medicated, too." He frowned, deep in thought.

When Ruth looked at Hartmann she noticed he had perked, his eyes holding a gleam in them that told her the doctor had an idea.

Hartmann put a hand up when Ruth went to turn and leave, initiating a pause.

Seeing his hand raise, the nurse stopped.

"Ensure you're on hand for me this afternoon."

Without anything but obedience, Ruth was quick to leave the doctor alone in the small observation room.

Hartmann turned to look through the glass again, a fiery determination heating his forehead.

Doctor Hartmann wasted as little time as possible with making it understandable to Emma that he was serious.

He wasn't entering the padded cell to take any messing about from her, he glared down at her to stop her excitement heightening.

Hauled up against the wall, Emma curled into herself to appear smaller, squeaking at the doctor when he strode up to her.

Emma's eyes were jittery, but focused in on Hartmann striding to her.

He pinched the leg of his trousers and pulled the fabric up his leg when his knees came forwards.

Emma stared at Hartmann in front of her, eyes glassy and never moving from the doctor's movements with eyes wide.

"Sit up," he instructed. Emma was slow to react, much to the annoyance of the man. His hand reached into his coat pocket, fingertips gripping the lid of a small plastic bottle.

Upon the small bottle being revealed, he unscrewed the lid and wrangled out a single pill.

"Take this," he said, pinching the pill between his thumb and forefinger. Emma threw her head back into the wall in repulsion.

"Screw you," she spat.

Hartmann sighed and rolled his eyes. He was fast tiring of her tirade. "I won't have you all excitable, you need to take this," he insisted, then lowered his tone.

"What are they for?" she questioned sceptically.

Hartmann was straining to maintain his calmness with the short amount of patience he was dealing with. Under the stress of the observation looming overhead, time wasn't going to be on his side if he did not get the pill into Emma's system quickly. Emma asking a nonsensical question such as that fast got a rise of anger from Hartmann.

He bowed his head in front of her before prodding the tablet into her face again. "Not long ago, Emma, you choked an elderly patient of mine to almost unconsciousness."

She smirked at his words, but caught herself and her face returned to a scowl.

Hartmann's eyes narrowed at her then. He scanned her grinning face and, feeling revulsion at the sight of a hidden smirk, he frowned.

Emma having not done a good job of concealing her glee, gave a shrug.

Upon filling his lungs, he released the air in a huff. An unkind thought passed through his mind.

"Emma," he warned. "You could have killed him. He is in a very fragile condition, I have just come from tending to him."

Emma tipped her head to the side, looking away apparently to hide her feelings, her loping hair covering her face.

Hartmann's eyes did not leave from being focused on her. "Would you listen to me? Emma, look at me," Hartmann demanded of her, taken aback when she followed his instructions.

He swallowed, tightening his jaw when he took in the appearance of the young woman before him.

The darkness under her eyes seemed to have become impactful bruises, a purple tinge under the greying skin. It appeared swollen, like she was never long from having just finished crying. Laid against the off-white damp walls, Emma looked to have been through the wars. It reflected on her face, cheeks having become gaunt and less easy to raise a smile onto.

Her cheeks were patched with small red blotches, these being the same shade as the swelling under her greying eyes. Emma's limbs hung, as if glued in place or she was too tired to move them, hands against the floor and knees stuck out sorely under the hospital gown.

He pulled at his white coat as a small fidget. "You better start behaving yourself, do you understand?" He fought his discomfort to look into her eyes.

Emma gave a feeble nod, her absentminded gaze raising annoyance from the doctor when he saw she wasn't listening.

Hartmann's head fell again.

"Emma, this is no time for games," he started up again. "I warn you against any funny business. It would be wise to ensure you are hearing of that, if nothing else I have said."

Hartmann was not impressed with her smirking, and he seemed to tire after that. He felt completely at odds.

Hidden behind the blackened glass, he watched Emma slump in her place, eyes willing to close at any moment. He saw the slow blinks she gave and thought of the Xanax residing in his coat pocket with a jaded glance downwards. He knew he was getting desperate. When Hartmann stared at Emma once more, he resonated with a reluctance, shaking his head. The lack of any form of drugs in her system gave the doctor a simmering feeling of unease – regardless, he found himself entering the padded cell once more.

"Emma, I will repeat myself this time, but I warn you to listen to me," he threatened lowly, gaining a passing glance from Emma's eyes. He froze, but his gaze remained hard on hers.

Emma smirked, her eyes shining when her lips broke.

Hartmann's chin raised, watching. He was angered by her smirking, Emma being able to riddle the man with apprehension.

He struggled to gauge what she was feeling and forced his eyes to observe every little movement that much harder to make up for his lack of understanding.

When her head sank to her chest, Hartmann saw that her eyes remained glaring at him. He jostled on the spot, as if wishing to rid himself of an uncomfortable itch without picking at himself. Without making his discomfort obvious. Emma remained glaring, and he cleared his throat.

"Not again, Emma," he grumbled, eyes moving to avoid the glower from her sunken ones wishing to penetrate him.

Emma, for the first time, moved, perhaps provoked by his comment. She stretched her shoulders under the gown, edging each one forwards like she was slowly waking herself up. She winced when rotating her shoulders and moving her arms, the muscles contracting, apparently sending a small prickle of pain through her.

Doctor Hartmann continued, having tried to refresh his declining attitude in the quiet. "You are off your medication, as I'm sure you remember our discussion about that." He clipped, pulling at the wrist of his white elastic glove, snapping it against his wrist after stretching it over his hand, inciting a shrivel from the patient.

"I'm going to put the incident with Mr. Allen down to you being left unmedicated, otherwise why would you have become so violent, hmm?" he prodded her.

The room seemed to shrink, the walls souring in the silence that she left Hartmann in. Hartmann's movements becoming jerky, he ran a knuckle upon his goatee, flexing his chin.

Emma stared up at Hartmann, with a mystified look.

"I don't believe you to be the violent type, am I correct in thinking that?" He then gestured with a loosely pointed finger in her direction, looking back at her to watch for a change in expression. It took a delayed spell for the threat to reach her, but when it did she leaned forwards.

"Yes."

"So why did you do it?"

Emma shrugged, eyes to the side. She remained silent.

Hartmann, upon distancing himself from her, even by a few centimetres, saw the miniscule movements she made into his space when he retreated. He flicked his eyes to the tiniest edging she managed, but did not allow himself to linger.

The doctor stood, establishing a confident ending to the one-sided conversation. Emma sized him, fear flashing over her eyes when she tilted her gaze into the light. Hartmann gave a thought just after pulling away from Emma. He stuck his tongue at the roof of his mouth, flicking his eyes to the ceiling for a few seconds.

Emma, looking ahead of herself again, smiled and shook her head. She looked at Hartmann with her chin held high. "You think I care, at this point?" she said with a smile. "I want to tell you why I strangled that man." In the grip of her anger, her face reflected indifference.

Hartmann flinched but decided to entertain the unstable

girl on the floor. He turned to her, nodding to continue, her eyes glued to his face. His arms folded and his eyes grew cold.

"Go on, share," he said with wavering impatience.

Emma smirked, staring up at him. "Because he told me what you're doing, you're murdering your patients. And I believe him now." The words reached his ears, and Hartmann threw a hand to his chest.

He broke out in a grin and threw his head back, bursting out into bouncing laughter. Emma's mouth gaped, going to speak while physically she recoiled, leading her lips to shut again. Her eyes flew over Hartmann. When Hartmann had finally stopped his laughter, he tutted aloud in the padded room.

"Murder? Emma, Henry is a paranoid schizophrenic, he thinks I murder all of the patients I discharge," he said, gesturing with his upturned palms. The entertained glint in his eyes remained, but he adjusted his blasé attitude. The allegation slid from him, there being no shock or horror to his features when she revealed her revelation. Her apparent attempt at getting a rise from Hartmann hadn't worked.

"You, of course, wouldn't know this, but Henry is a man that fails to understand where my patients go after discharge, or rather, what happens at that stage." Hartmann loosely gestured with an upturned palm again. "And you, of all people in my hospital, fell for his lah-de-dah tales and tall stories."

"Liar! What about all of the weird drugs? You make them, and make all the patients sick, like when I was ill after that IV," she accused, the words falling out of her mouth without pausing to come up for air.

Doctor Hartmann remained unanimated, while Emma was outpouring in front of him and when she managed to halt, the air was only filled by the sound of the girl struggling to catch her breath.

Doctor Hartmann paused and tilted his head, sucking his

cheeks. His eyes strayed upwards for a second before returning to her.

"Back in my Germany, my good friends and I, we share a saying," he began, standing before Emma and gazing down his nose at her. "A wise man never knows all, only fools know everything." He feigned inconvenience, understanding his wisecrack had failed to make sense to her when Emma didn't react.

Emma broke eye contact and looked down, defeat no doubt piling atop her with a heaviness on her chest. She gazed at her legs, shrinking under Hartmann's hard, cocky squint. Above her, he loomed with a deep frown.

Emma raised her head, an eyebrow arched. "You're calling a mentally ill man a fool?"

Hartmann's lips wrinkled, then yanked into an ugly twist downwards. "No." He took a breath. "Someone who thinks they know everything is a fool, Emma," he scolded, angered by her misunderstanding, or own take on his belief.

She shrank, feeling the embarrassment shroud her shoulders and make them bunch together. Shrouded by the silence of the room once more, Hartmann picked up where he had left off.

Stood in the midpoint of the box room, he raised his chin to speak while lowering his gaze to Emma who remained crushed, and sat rigid against the wall. She gave a few blinks. Emma looked at the walls, fear on her brow as she squeezed her legs into her chest with a frantic breath. The walls growing tall and bold, edging closer to where she was sat and threatening to fall atop her. She lifted her heavy head to trail up the trouser legs of the Doctor, eventually reaching his eyes.

"I will also add, Emma, I still am wishing to see an improvement in you." His lips pursed, and his eyes dropping over the young woman.

In the glassy mirror of her eyes, Emma stared at Hartmann from where she was leaning against the padded wall, chest rising and falling in an unnerved rhythm. Her body spiked, and she looked at her knees blinking rapidly with the muscles above her eyebrows pulling at her skin.

Unsure of whether to cry or scream, when she looked at the doctor once more she was completely blank.

Hartmann recognised Emma had nothing left to give, nothing to pour out about, there was no fire and she laid up against the wall as if immobilised. He smirked down at her, thinking a gust of wind may blow her away, revealing his feeling to be correct, Emma was splitting at the seams when a single glassy tear rolled down her sunken cheek. Her hand rushed to wipe it away, and that was the fastest she had moved in hours.

The tension between the two sat hard and it stayed, refusing to remove itself, but Hartmann remained with a hard glare on the young woman.

Doctor Hartmann's hands held in front of himself in the neutral stance he began to often adopt.

The doctor parted from standing over Emma, and he stopped watching. Emma quivered when he stepped forwards, her bottom lip shaking. Hartmann then turned before her, the width of his shoulders towering over her.

"Now, understand I have come a long way from medieval methods such institutes used to use on patients," he explained with a gesture out at his side. "But in your case I may have to make an exception."

Emma stared at Hartmann, panic coming over her features. Still staring, Emma's brow dipped upon hearing what doctor Hartmann said, clearly spinning through her head. Her brow hardened but her jaw slacked at his fearful words.

Hartmann's hands were behind his back and he pushed his shoulders back while his chin and chest came forward.

"Why are you being nice to me now?" Hartmann's smile faded.

From sitting on the floor and glaring at the doctor, she

kept her stance and her eyes only flinched briefly. Hartmann remained with his hands behind his back.

"Miss Merrick," he chided. "May I remind you about your behaviour?" He arched an eyebrow to imprint the warning when she did not look away. A mutual understanding of the threat he gave had arrived into the padded room.

If he had wanted Emma to recoil or shrink, impossibly becoming smaller – he remained oppositional to her. He held his stance and the air became thicker between them both.

Emma's glare was only removed from Hartmann when she heard the lock lift behind Hartmann, the door shunting open to reveal Nurse Ruth stepping onto the cushioned floor.

One of Hartmann's hands came swinging from behind, and he gestured freely upwards, towards Emma on the floor "Now, let us transfer the patient."

At once, without any hesitation to handle her and without fear or caution, the two pair of hands launched at Emma.

At once, they were rough with her and pinched her skin when she skidded away to avoid their reaching fingers.

Emma yanked and pulled to writhe herself free from the grip of the doctor and nurse who had formed a grip under her armpits. She glared at fearsomely at both of them.

Hartmann overlooked her distress when she looked up to him.

She was in the hands of nurse Ruth and Hartmann, as they both handled her roughly. She may have had a chance of fighting back if she weren't being held so tightly.

# Chapter Twenty-Six

THE SKIN of Emma's upper arms were beginning to feel the residing hot burn from the friction, like a slow and itchy carpet burn. Combined with the grip both Nurse Ruth and Hartmann had on her, pulling her along while she strained to keep up with their synced marching, it appeared to be an awful deal of effort for Emma to attempt to keep up – albeit it was the straightjacket's fabric making her sweat in its unbreathable fabric. The two yanked and pulled at her, her being barely tall enough to land her feet on the floor.

The two at each side of her seemed to increase their pulling as if having the dual thought of, "Why won't you walk?" with great impatience. The skin of her arms would most likely be left with harsh red marks.

Hartmann gave out directions to a place Emma was becoming fast fearful of, the colour on the walls and murals fading into off-white sent her into a panic. Imagery of cells, isolation rooms or multiple IV stands flooded her mind as both nurse and doctor continued dragging Emma along. She shuddered as she glanced at nurse Ruth walking beside her nonchalantly, with her awful, thin nose high in the air.

Her already pinched lips soured when the three turned the fateful corner to the hallway which had her room situated on the left hand side. The two continued on, seeming to gain pace in their dragging of Emma.

"Stop it, you're hurting me!" Emma burst out, yanking an elbow up in her straightjacket with such irritation her protruding bone knocked into Nurse Ruth's jaw. She clipped the bottom of her jaw with such force, the nurse froze up completely as the pain wracked through her in waves.

While the realisation hit, Doctor Hartmann had continued on with his striding, almost ripping Emma's arm from its socket when he failed to notice Ruth had paused.

Immediately she glued her eyes to the nurse's face when she rotated her jaw in a disturbing fashion.

The nurse's jaw clicked as she did though, and Emma was white with fear that the woman she had accidentally hurt would get her revenge through the use of further torturous druggings, perhaps jabbing her and purposefully missing the vein. It would be like Nurse Ruth to return the favour in a sadistically violent fashion. The images flashed through her mind while blood drained from her face, her bottom lip trembling.

The two pairs of eyes laid on her. Nurse Ruth hissed something in her harsh and aggressive voice. In replacement for Emma being unable to catch what she had said, her hand tightened on her to drive home the temper behind her words. If the anger was all she could understand, she would be content with that. Emma's lips dropped in horror, her bottom lip shivered with her mouth open.

"I didn't mean to hurt you." She allowed her sentence to trail off meekly. Emma sounded false, and her words hung in the air. They lacked meaning when she heard herself speak, and cursed the way she sounded in her own head, let alone to the angry nurse's ears,

Emma had not been taking in her surroundings, being too

fearful to focus on anything other than how badly her arms hurt.

"Let us continue please, the room we want is just to the left here," Hartmann said with a nod ahead of himself. He did not look at Emma, and if he had seen the horror on her face and fear – perhaps he would have been uncomfortable.

Emma was trying to retreat from the strong unsettled feeling in her stomach when the pair clutched her once more to make the final stretch until reaching the room.

On the side which nurse Ruth had gripped her after collecting herself, her hands held her tighter, possessing more of a cruel pinch. Emma did not writhe against her although her muscles tightened and her arms were rigid. She was disturbed, made to become deeply uncomfortable when she felt a wash of sickness come over her. The corners of her world darkened at the sensation, curling up and becoming discoloured, bleached like an old photograph.

The floor felt uneven, the sensation of dread washed over to set her blurred vision on the blue curtain having been already drawn at the sides of yet another hospital bed. Emma motioned up and down, because of the yanking received gave her a strange gait when trying to walk with the two at her sides. Her ears rang and then became muffled, protected from the talk of the two that swirled in the room.

Hartmann spoke fast and in great detail about Emma, but she was not listening. She froze, eyelids slow to blink while her mind pieced together apprehensive guesses on what was about to happen to her. Any coherent thought scrambled from her, letting her writhe in her fast gathering panic.

Emma swayed on the spot while the two pairs of eyes flit from focusing on her and back to the conversation they shared. Before she had time to almost collapse from the weight of her head filling with loud thoughts, a demanding, aggressive voice echoed around her skull.

"Miss Merrick."

"Huh?" she said absently with her jaw slack, without moving her head to remove the loping long locks of hair from her face.

They covered the corners of her eyes' vision, adding a dark fuzz to the corners of the world she saw. Her tunnel vision was interrupted again. Recognising the voice moments as being Hartmann's, she heard him release a heavy tut.

His expression was blank, but he held an impatient undertone to his voice which she recognized with ease. He raised his eyebrows when she did not answer him, surely a prodding reminder of the warning yet again. Her breathing was irregular. No matter how hard she tried, she was denied to take back control of her breathing rate. She picked up the courage to look to the bed, all made up with the corner of the thin sheet folded over. Before her, the bed posed a growing fear, panicked that she may never be able to get up if she laid down. Behind the head of it was a counter with a cream coloured box atop it. There were two dials and above the middle of them both was a dial wielding a needle behind the thin, dirty glass.

The two pair of eyes remained on her every move. Emma rotated her legs up and her spine trailed the hard mattress at the slouched sitting position. Nothing she had ever witnessed happened as fast as Hartmann moving in to the side of her face, scrutinising her. Emma worried that her breathing was incredibly loud, the heat in the room being insufferable. The air was too thick to breathe in and her rapid rate of breath brought a sweat to her brow.

On the opposite side of the bed stood nurse Ruth, who watched with intent to follow Hartmann's upcoming instructions while he flicked on different switches behind the head of the bed. Her head moved wildly between the pair looming like skeletons. Ruth bent to grab something, Emma's eyes searching but not seeing. A thick roll of medical gauze was shoved into her dry mouth, sucking up every last bit of moisture she could have mustered. She tipped her eyes away from the nurse to notice Hartmann leering over her, standing with two flat, white pads in each hand.

Sticking the pads onto her temple, Emma found herself to be held down by Nurse Ruth at her wrists.

At the exchange over her, Emma's heart gave a hard, panicked thud. She was afraid of fainting under her nerves threatening to electrocute her, worsening her fear when her leg muscles tightened and wished to begin a fast exit from the situation's ugly head.

Everything was going far too fast for her to even have a chance of processing it all. Emma pleaded to Hartmann who stood back, and stared at nurse Ruth's hands on her. Spitting out the gauze, Emma held terror in her eyes. "Please, I can't breathe," Emma whispered, moving her head from the pillow, straining to sit up. When she was ignored, her desperation was met with increasing lack of patience as the discarded gauze was balled up by nurse Ruth and shoved deeper into her mouth. The fabric touching the back of her throat brought tears to her eyes as she supressed a gag.

"Let the doctor do his job, Emma," Ruth warned.

Her eyes went to him to plead, beg – for them to stop. Without warning, a hot, zapping current from the applied pads on her temple jumpstarted her body to seize up. Her jaw clamped tight onto the gauze in her mouth, eyes squeezing as her body was wracked by a current of electricity. It showed no mercy, ripping through her as if she'd been struck by lightning. The waves sent her muscles into spasm on the bed, hissing many small releases of breath as her frame contorted. Her back arched, and when it released, it sent her head crashing back to the bed. The current continued to burn her nerves, heat enveloping every inch of her body like a fire set from deep within her skull, ripping through her nerves with all of the ferocity in its consuming method of a bushfire concealed under her skin.

Emma's mouth was dry, and lips chapped. Her jaw slacked,

muscles releasing from their stringent tightness and felt herself aching all over, her tortured muscles screaming in agony.

# Chapter Twenty-Seven

HARTMANN DISCARDED his gloves in the bin, having left Emma to rest in her room after the intense session back in the forgotten part of his hospital. He was basking in his genius in his office, pleased to be contending with a slate which was now wiped clean of all memory, pleasant and unpleasant. He was content, and a small smile was on his lips.

With a strained look, his mind wandered as he exhaled. His fingers absently fingered the cuff of his jacket's arm. A light fluttering sensation tickled Hartmann, threatening to grow and expand to other regions of his body. The doctor was finding it more difficult to control his urge. He had repressed it the last time, but this time he was not so certain of himself being able to do so.

He felt the growing pressure forming, and he pulled hard at the cuff he had been fiddling with, wishing to loosen the irritating fabric. He ushered himself back into his office, locking the door behind him and fumbling with the blind over the window of the door.

He was hasty to yank it down. In anticipation, he almost tripped over himself getting behind his desk. In the darkness of his office, he once more threw himself down into his comfortable chair, throwing his ankles atop his paper strewn desk. He was grateful to throw his head back and allow a ripple of pleasure to cause his breathing to become tremulous, akin to how his hands were when he pinched his thumb and forefinger on the metal of his trouser zip.

# Chapter Twenty-Eight

EMMA'S TWITCHING and flinching did not cease when the doctor left her room. Instead, the shut in feeling of darkness that permeated her mind and caused her squirming intensified. Gloves, those awful white powdery gloves, thrust at her, glowing in the dark which surrounded them like a cloak. When she threw her head back to avoid the grabbing fingers, they halted and spread backwards as if trying to communicate with an animal – meaning no harm. The gloves surroundings lightened, it seeped into her eyes and a scene reared its ugly head.

Emma's back went rigid from her crouched sitting position, edging back as the hand extended out towards her. Emma's eyes shrank when the streaming white light of the hospital room dimmed and her eyes adjusted, leaving the white glowing halo around that of Jason's head. Her jaw fell slack, failing to notice that she allowed the hand to slip around her eyesight and felt a stabbing pain in her upper arm – sending a chill through her arm. Horror froze her body. She fell forward and cried out when Jason leaned back, fiddling with the needle top in his hand, flitting disappointed looks at Emma. She watched as his lips moved, making words she wasn't able to hear. Stiffening again, she straightened and watched with her teeth clamped onto her bottom lip, a small whimper leaving her.

Jason turned away from his examining look at her, and turned to continue with his lips moving, babbling away with a serious expression to doctor Hartmann. He was turned to Emma, his hands clasped and washing with invisible water before her as he nodded and listened to Jason – without taking his eyes from Emma for a second all the while. Emma saw when Hartmann's lips began to move and the men exchanged nods, lips tightening and eyes staring as if she had two heads.

Emma wished to scream out but found herself paralysed. Looking to the upper shoulder of her arm, finding a healthy line of trickling blood pouring from the needle entrance. Emma looked to the two fictitious men above her for help, feeling hot tears blur her vision when she looked up. Their heads shook, and Jason tutted, his brow furrowed by his over-whelming feelings of pity for Emma.

Emma curled her hands and rubbed at her eye sockets, driving her knuckles into her eyeballs to rid the tears that didn't stop flowing. When, in the white of the room she removed her hands, she was met with Jason crouched down to her level. The tears stopped warming her cheeks as the flow halted, jaw slacking and trying to form words.

Emma watched with eyes peeled wide, too focused to dare blink despite her eyes stinging. She did not tear her eyes away from Jason.

Jason tilted his head and rubbed his stubble, giving an audible tut before looking into her eyes slowly, dragging them from the sidewards glance he had been giving her before speaking. Jason's shoulders slumped forwards. "Oh, Emma, when will you get better?" he roused.

Emma's eyes were open before anything else came into motion, like the tears welling in her sockets and fast flooding down her face. She stared at the ceiling of the room. Her chest bounced with the wracking force of her tears, holding flattened hands to her eyes to direct the tears to fall down the top of her hands. She was devastated by the nightmare's imagery coming back into her mind.

A soaked palm curled to a fist and she banged her arms on the bed, turning her head to shake the thoughts, but knowing all too well they wouldn't be rid of easily, they were imprinted into who she was. Her trauma was a part of her, she was riddled with the imperfection.

In the dark surrounding her, Emma feared situations such as these were permanent – that there would not be a day when the nightmares would not creep and pounce upon her.

The idea, let alone the confirmation of the thought, sent her body into trembles.

The IV needle in her arm made it sore. Under the surface, she saw bruising and felt the urge to scratch at her skin. Emma remained crying with her right arm lopped at her side in the dark of her room.

She cried in the silence. She wished not to alert anyone and upon allowing herself to escalate to sobs, she had to hold her breath often to stop her lungs from bouncing so erratically. Supressing her tears brought back the aching of her muscles, feeling like she was back in that dreaded treatment room.

Emma wished deeply, on the edge of praying to God – that she would be forgiven for whatever she had done so wrong. Her final thoughts in the black of her room were that she would be forgiven, and that she was sorry. Apologising with tears, her silent cries for peace all alone in her room.

Emma mouthed the words "I'm sorry," repeatedly, over and over until she was dragged back into an exhausted state of rest.

Her final few tears dried on her cheeks minutes after her eyelids closed.

Waking up to the gleaming light of the morning sun, Emma felt a soreness under her eyes, and winced. She wished to turn her back to the sun and fall back asleep. Her ribs ached, taking in a shaking breath and braving up to the morning feeling rested. Eyes searched the space around her, focusing on the door being shut. The haunting vision of the nightmare she had that night weighed heavy on her chest, feeling floored into the mattress by the power behind her ability to cause so much harm from just a nightmare alone. Understanding the strange vision would haunt her for the remainder of her day, she played off poorly that she was indifferent.

Emma pushed with fists at the mattress to sit, pausing in the quiet to think, but began to strain when the images so vivid hours ago, would not come back to her. Not being able to tap into that memory, but the knowledge of knowing she had forgotten something which she had strained to keep with her. The foggy mess it left Emma in whilst sat up in the white sheets seemed to strengthen the effects of the drugs she was under.

Emma was swimming in a confusing haze. She grimaced, feeling tears well up in her again at the dragging sadness she felt.

She was grateful to be alone at least. Emma did not check how she felt first thing, not setting herself up for failure at the beginning of her day.

She released the straightening in her arms, falling back onto the mattress with an exhale of tensed breath she felt appropriate to release with little care for her volume.

She squeezed her eyes tighter when the flashes of her nightmare came before her in the dark. The gloved, outstretched hands coming at her face – she shot up from the hospital bed and ragged her fingers at her aching skull.

She didn't understand. Only minutes ago the nightmare would not come back to her when she dared to try and re-imagine the horrific scenes of her nightmare, Yet the flashes that disturbed her most would come with ease when she tried to ease herself to a state of comfort.

Emma wasn't trying to be cruel to herself. Not knowing or being able to possibly comprehend what lay ahead for her that day, Emma was unmotivated. Then, the vision of Hartmann leaning over her bed scared her enough to sit up again from the warmth she rolled in.

Emma looked at the IV tubing that led into her arm, and wasted no time in clenching her jaw and letting out an elongated groan when she pulled it from where it was stabbed into her assaulted vein.

Emma slapped her hand over the bleeding hole and felt herself gush harder from the slight adrenaline kick to numb whatever pain she may have been feeling.

Emma understood what would happen, and hurried to the sink at the wall of her room to bend the inside of her bleeding elbow underneath the tap.

The gushing cold water made Emma wince initially.

Her arm stretched out over the sink while she wiped and poked at the wound, awaiting impatiently for the bleeding to stop, or slow to a degree in which it would not be a problem to her. Her blood kept leaking from the small hole in her arm, and the water began to run a faint orange against the porcelain of the sink as it drained away.

Upon relaxing at the cool water easing her itchy, inflamed skin, she paused. She looked at the tap, then reaching to it, and turned the flow off, the tap giving a small, pitched groan as the flow was stemmed.

Emma's eyes flicked to the inside of her elbow, wrapping her other hand around her elbow, just under where the IV had been stabbed in.

She squeezed, and the flow of blood pushed out with force, rolling over her skin and dropping in fat blobs onto the porcelain of the sink basin.

Emma stared at the droplets that came from her arm, mystified by the vivid, bright red colouration.

Against the gleaming white of the sink the deep red looked

beautiful. She was amazed something so bright came from inside her, as if having stabbed a children's cartoon, and the fantastic ink was all bleeding out. Releasing her squeezing grip on her elbow, she leaned in, dabbing two fingers in the pooling of blood, lifting her fingers to her face and rubbing the blood between, until it coloured her fingertips orange.

"Emma, what are you doing to yourself now?" a tired, yet authoritative voice came from behind her.

She straightened from the shock, breaking away from her hypnosis at the hands of her own blood. Emma ducked, trying to shrink and minimise herself from being noticed.

She did not turn around, thrown into shaking at the sight of the blood covered sink. "What've you done?" quipped Doctor Hartmann, pushing up the front of his gelled hair.

Meeting his eyes, Emma saw his gaze drop to her arm.

Emma's vision flew to Doctor Hartmann standing before her, hands behind his back. Her legs had jellied, but solidified again when she felt the urge to escape from the room. Escape and run for her life before the tired doctor had chance to entrap here within it.

Looking angered, as if able to read her mind, Doctor Hartmann's eyes hardened on Emma trembling in front of him.

Hartmann held her frozen in his stare. His head bowed to her arm, which she allowed to bleed freely, as it was merely trickling.

"Medication time, Emma," he announced with an unflinching stiffness.

Never becoming more afraid of those words than that moment, the doctor dug into his coat pocket and produced a small white bottle.

She focused in, narrowing her eyes to clear the tiny writing on the label, but looking back to the man smirking behind the bottle he held in his pinched grip.

Her fear fuelled her to nod feebly between shaking, too afraid to do anything else but comply.

For the next few days, the only emotion Emma held in abundance was fear. The tremendous, clawing fear clouded all vision apart from the lone doctor who inflicted such hell on her.

Emma had begun to separate herself from reality, as she had no grip on it anymore – and so let loose completely. She was coming undone at the seams.

Everything she saw spun around her, blurred with bright and blinding strobes that pierced her skin as if it was translucent. Her way of thinking was simplified, and it became clear to Emma that she would never have control over herself again.

She was asked if she was hurting, in pain, the language used by Hartmann was simple and it altered the way she processed events, facts, whatever she was told.

Before Wednesday, Emma had gone through a phase in which she desperately searched for confirmation that she was real, and in fact alive. Her head rose from the bed and she strained, hurting her limbs that were pinned to her sides. She searched in the eyes of Doctor Hartmann for this confirmation, putting her fear aside to do so. Some sort of comfort no matter how small – but never receiving any. She cursed herself for being so stupid. So naive. And upon never receiving what she craved, she sank into a dreamlike state. With heavy and laboured breaths, her arms weighed her to the bed, Emma had not moved them in so long.

The world outside of Westview General shrank and wilted away, breaking off from the image of the grand hospital in her fogged mind. She figured she would forever be a patient, unable to think for herself beyond her wracking terror of Hartmann. The world in all its wonder became very small to her, words echoing inside her vacant skull when the doctor would speak. She comprehended the words slowly, thinking if she could even understand what Hartmann was saying to her anymore. Sentences had begun to bounce from the walls, messing around – before reaching the point where Emma was able to understand what he commanded of her. She felt like a shell of herself.

When she struggled to breathe, she got panicked so quickly it barely gave the doctor time to react before she reached her highest level of frenzy. Emma was almost convinced that she was being choked – strangled – by an unknown and invisible hand.

And in the evening, with the haunting imagery of Hartmann's gloved hand coming at her from her nightmare, she was vehement to deny a link between the two, even though the idea niggled and itched like a terrible rash, it could not be placed.

Emma's lack of any type of excitement or enjoyment in anything resulting in the numbing of the sensations on her tongue. Everything faded into the background, nothing bringing her forwards much joy or feeling – only pain when she would once again swallow those awful tablets.

On the Thursday morning, Doctor Hartmann offered Emma the opportunity to go outside, although she would be supervised.

She remained with her head to the window of her room, and did not speak nor move. Emma sat in the room armchair with her loping, soaked hair dripping to form cold puddles of water on the floor. She sat among the monotony of her existence, wondering absently about Doctor Hartmann. Her thoughts spun around her empty skull, his name being the only thing to fill her at any point.

She gave a small sigh, leaving an imprint of her breath on the glass.

# Chapter Twenty-Nine

THE FATEFUL SUNDAY morning rolled around.

A voice called out to Emma through the darkness of her eyelids and the fog in her mind. She flitted them open with her slack jaw tightening, putting a stop to the dribble leaving the side of her lips.

"Doctor...Hartmann?" she whispered. Her voice was raw and rough, somewhat fragile. Emma saw the doctor flinch – did he recognise the effects of prolonged screaming and crying on her vocal chords?

The doctor stiffened, cleared his throat and bowed his head to refocus himself on the task at hand.

Emma squinted her eyes at Hartmann when he ignored her. Her eyes remained fixated in the moments he tended to her – thinking to herself, "What's your game?"

In answer, her sight would become foggy when she would look – or it became significantly harder to think and keep her train of thought going. This was not because of the drugs that he had pumped and forced into Emma's system, but the fact that she began to feel herself soften each time she gazed at the man at her bedside.

Her lip edges curled wistfully, eyes fixated in a dreamlike

trance upon his glistening skin, the unshaven stubble lining his jaw when his brow was lowered hard, being so focused.

"I think I've got you where you needed to be all along." He gave a brisk nod, and then a smile. She did not quite understand the sensation his softened tone brought upon her body. When his eyes gazed into hers, she shied away, becoming apprehensive of the eye contact, but she did not pull away her limp wrist from being held by him.

"It was all for the better, hm?" Hartmann smiled, then straightened his back. His palm tensed, and Emma took her wrist back into her side.

Emma's eyes explored the man's face as if she had never seen it before, he was a reprieve to her constant suffering and provided her with a feeling of peacefulness. She felt he reappeared at the perfect time.

She felt her muscles relax and unclench, hypnotised by the man and every little thing he did.

Hartmann walked around her bed and collected wires and wrapped them upon the drip at her side, fiddling with buttons and clips behind her head.

She was curious, almost in a state of child-like wonder, careless to stare at the doctor. Her mind was blank but she was pleased about it. Emma felt he was there, he was back – to make everything okay again.

Her eyes dizzied in her skull from their tiredness despite only having recently woken up. Amidst her dreamlike state in the bed, she pondered his reaction if she would confide in him about her bizarre dream. Toying with the images imprinted in her mind of Hartmann's face changing, his brows raising and lips to part in an oval shape when she would reveal her disturbing dream to him.

She laid herself back, relaxing her spine back against the mattress. Wondering if her Doctor had the same dreams, if the man tending to her at the bedside was haunted by memories that clung to his innermost dark, private corners.

In an almost perverse fashion that overtook her mind, she found herself wanting to dig beneath and pick at his wonderful brain, to be unfiltered when asking questions.

In an appropriate reaction to her thoughts, her skin flushed a deep heat which was released and flooded from her chest cavity.

Emma looked at the ceiling, the white swirls giving her the misjudgement of having a clear mind.

# Chapter Thirty

EMMA BROKE AWAY, staring at the floor with eyes blank. She then arched her spine so she curled into herself. She would straighten her back and sit up as if posing herself to ask a question, and Hartmann would catch her – and she would wilt back into herself again, recoiling when he caught her fidgeting.

In her display of uncertainty, The doctor raised his brow before knitting them together. "Before you scurry off anywhere," Hartmann chided, producing once again the familiar bottle from the never ending depths of his jacket pockets.

After she swallowed the tablet he had dotingly placed upon her tongue, he snapped his gloves off and turned on the spot to discard them. The noise of the bin lid shutting made Emma jump, watching him when he walked away, and focusing again when he turned.

Her memory of all previous events evidently had since faded like features in a bleached photograph through the vacancy Hartmann had never seen before in her eyes. It was now all she held in those orbs.

"Now run along, don't go getting into trouble." He gave a nod sideways, indicating to the door, his fingers clenching around the cap of the bottle and twisting it airtight. His warning was playful in tone, but he had faith she understood he meant it.

Emma was slow to throw her legs over the side of the bed when Hartmann lowered the bars at her sides. She flinched at the clanging of the metal of the bed underneath itself.

She was slow to move from the bed, looking to her bony feet with distrust, relieved she was not able to view the sight of her legs under the gown. Emma was able to make sense of nothing. Links to more than one thought at a time would not be made, her fried brain couldn't handle the capacity for it. Unable to rationalise anything apart from a singular name. Henry. Nothing else would come to her. She felt if she was to then violently bash her skull against a wall, nothing but fluff could be visible between the cracks. She almost broke into a smile at the idea of such random violence.

In between the fluff, though, Emma held only the strange name in highest concern. Henry was the only thing on her mind but she did not understand why. Or who he was, why his name was imprinted on her fogged mind.

But feeling intensely something was wrong with him, and it niggled at her, pulling at her hair like an unknown hand. She was driven, knowing she needed to see this Henry man for herself. Emma wandered the halls, focusing all of her energy on trying to remember the man's name.

Under her breath, she mouthed the name of the eccentric old man repeatedly.

Feeling that tightly wound rope constrict inside her stomach when she thought hauntingly of her hands clamped around the man's throat, him gargling and clawing at her skin having been the only other sensations she felt besides her impulse. She felt acid jump in her stomach at the recollection of what she had done. She looked to her hands in horror, holding them out in front of herself like she had never seen them before.

Emma winced, but found the recollection of her actions within her head to be encapsulating to her. The images fading from her mind, her head rose and she broke into an adrenaline fueled sprint.

"What ward is Henry on?" she shouted to a nurse as she ran.

Frazzled, the nurse looked as if she would calm the sweating girl, her lips jumping. "Miss, you need to return to your ward, let me—"

Emma groaned, eyes rolling at the immediate response.

"I think I tried to kill the bloke," she hissed. "He's old, and I remember I choked him." Emma held a hand before herself that shook, her fingers gathered tight around an imaginary throat.

The nurse clamped her lips shut to stop herself from gasping, eyes widening. Giving a half hearted shrug although a flash of recognition came over her eyes, the nurse stepped back, lowering her tone. "I will get Doctor Hartmann. We should go and consult him as I don't actually know." She pawned Emma off with an enlightened smile appearing, going to put her hand to a shoulder and turn the patient around to retrace her steps.

Emma threw a shoulder forward with disgust, discarding the hand of the nurse from her skin. She lunged and bolted ahead, hurtling like a one-woman stampede through the halls.

The nurse's jaw clenched while her feet scrambled to turn and begin a hastened type of jog herself, holding onto her watch that hung from her breast pocket. A clammy palm slammed into the doorframe before her head could appear, the nurse's hair straying from her ponytail and frazzled by her sweating.

---

The nurse entered the ward breathing heavily. "Doctor Hartmann, Emma has gone to find Mr. Allen," the nurse declared breathlessly.

At once, the doctor pulled at his jacket, the fabric straining as he pulled it in. He was quick to withdraw from the patient sat up in bed, pushing the curtains around the bed aside to barge out into the bay.

Hartmann brushed past the sweaty nurse without uttering a word, while the nurse scrambled to start where Hartmann had left off. The patient in the bed raising his head to gather where the doctor was going with such urgency, rather than tending to him. His palm stretched out in front of himself to allow the doctor to barge through the double doors with a cold glare. There was a sheen of sweat coating his forehead that shone under the glaring lights, a throbbing vein making its appearance under his temple.

---

"Come on," Emma mumbled through her teeth as she eyed the signs over the doorways, giving directions only to places she didn't want to go.

It had increased in importance to her, the more that she ran through the halls, that she apologise to Henry.

A type of self-applied pressure mounted in her mind and intensified the chances of a shred of release from her mental anguish. Emma's legs leaped out in front of herself. She rationalised that the dreams which haunted her would stop, and for the love of nothing more in the world, she wished they would do nothing but stop.

She poked her head into every room which had a doorway she could look through. Failing to find Henry, she spurred on with her head down.

Emma's wandering landed her onto the unknown territory

of Carnation ward, where she burst into Intensive Care reception like a bull.

Emma's eyes met those of the nurses sat neatly behind the reception desk of the ward when she entered.

Standing from her chair a nurse flashed a smile. "Are you lost?"

Emma was too careless to lie. She was too antsy, too desperate to ease her own level of suffering.

"No, I'm looking for an old man, I think he's called Henry, is he on this ward?" she asked between her heavy breaths, a finger pointed between her feet.

The nurse that had not seen Emma before and being relatively young had her brow furrowed. Her confusion was heightened further as to why the young patient wanted to see an elderly man in critical condition with such desperation. Being aware of how Mr. Allen ended up in intensive care, an eyebrow arched.

"I..." The nurse hesitated. "He is in critical condition. We can't allow you to see him."

Emma winced again.

The nurse looked over Emma's shoulder before refocusing her eyes to the puffed out patient.

"You've got to let me, I know how he got here, and please I just need to see him," she pleaded, not removing her eyes from the nurse as she made her plea.

Emma hoped the nurse, who seemed to be less than clued up – would consider Emma's begging.

The nurse blinked before refocusing. She shifted her weight onto a favoured foot. "I do apologise but nobody–"

In that time the nurse took her eyes from Emma's, she knew she had lost any chance of being allowed to see Henry. So, the patient went around the nurse in her way, having done so with a grunt.

"Excuse me!" came the call from behind, but Emma waved her hand behind herself and broke into a sprint again.

In the distance as Emma ran ahead, a tired looking senior nurse picked the phone from its stand and pressed the Intercom button, then leaned into the mouthpiece.

"Henry? You down here?" Emma called out. Becoming increasingly careless, she jogged down the hall, yelling out for Henry.

She stopped dead, her heart switching to flood her body with an onset of the nerves along her spine to spike. Her ears pricked to hear monotone beeps coming from the space between a door left ajar.

Emma stepped into the room, her eyes widening. It haunted her, but relieved her at the same time when she set eyes on Henry in the bed. The imagery flooded back to her again, having not forgotten her unforgiveable actions against him.

"Piano girl," he wheezed, eyelids heavy from the wrinkles piling atop in their folds.

She was right.

Emma hesitated to move any closer, fearing the wires bound into Henry's wrists and the metal plate shoved up his third fingernail would lash out like whips. The wires would wrap themselves around her throat with a great ferocity, wrapping around and around and constricting. Emma never had liked snakes.

"I just knew I needed to see you," she began, growing nervous and swallowing to ease herself, standing in the midst of this man's room.

The machines wired to Henry shouted out in their monotone voices, and they swarmed around her head and tormented her mind to think while the constant mechanical beeps permeated all other functions. Lifting a hand to rub her fingers against her palm, gathering small grey balls of her clammy skin when her sweat was gathered through a show of her nerves.

"I came to apologise for what I did to you," Emma began,

exhaling and rubbing the back of her neck. She bowed her head. "I honestly am, I'm so sorry Henry."

Henry had been a healthy man the day Emma met him, being of a healthy body weight and a pleasant face, although his teeth overlapped and were stained yellow. Compared to then, it was insult to injury – Henry had lost a lot of weight. His cheeks had hollowed out as if done with an ice cream scoop. His hands looked bruised by the penetration of the broad needle and he was a bony frame under the sheet. He looked pitiful. It erupted a great bout of empathy, and deep aching sadness from the pit of Emma's stomach.

Henry's head laid completely still in the middle of the memory foam pillow, eyes lolling about in his skull more out of consciousness than he was in, but between the washes of barely being conscious, he could apparently hear Emma's voice apologising – he shook his head.

"I have to tell you something, my girl," Henry began, Emma watching over his side as the bones of his ribcage rose to make room for the words. He released his gathered breath, curling his fingers and pointing over his stomach.

"Doctor Hartmann has put something in my IV."

Henry's raspy words collided with her chest like a punch with such power that she almost stumbled back. His pointed finger lowered back to his side and Emma clasped her cupped palm to her gaping mouth.

Everything Emma had been certain of came together at Henry's words. Beneath her hand, her jaw closed and she broke into a grin.

"Is that what's made you like this?" she asked, having removed her hand.

"He came in with a needle and left with it, empty," he gasped, breaking out into pitiful coughs. "My girl," Henry regained his breath.

Emma's eyes were affixed on his.

"I fear Hartmann would think you were someone very unwell." He paused for a breath again.

Emma's square shoulders lowered, her muscles striking up her back like an electric current. Her shaking eyes froze.

Henry continued after a long drawn breath. "If you told him my suspicion."

"You don't think I seem unwell?"

"No, you're a nice young lady. Emma, wasn't it?" Henry gave a choking cough, his chest bouncing so hard with the force of his coughs he almost fell out of the bed.

"You are my mirror image in that head of yours, piano girl." Henry smiled, swallowing to wet his throat that itched. He took a breath. "But, that isn't going to ensure you won't end up like me."

Emma took a step back, as if she had been pushed. But her vision dizzied, repeating what Henry had said. Her lips trembled much like her hands had began to.

*End up like you?*

Just as Emma almost fell back into Henry's wardrobe, the door was pushed open, making Emma jump and her nerves to spike. She lunged back to Henry's bedside, resuming her sorrowful position at the ill man's bedside. Fear made her skin prickle all over, but more so the knowledge within her now that she was in grave danger. More danger than she could fathom.

Eyes on her like lasers, her arms went limp at her sides and she panicked, darting her eyes around the room for help, but finding nobody.

The face of Doctor Hartmann was one that looked immediately to the sight before himself with a pair of tightly pulled lips. He stiffened from his sudden entrance, and the door was closed behind him, by the kicking of his heel to ensure so.

"I was apologising, that's all." Emma surrendered, flinching as the door was kicked shut. Seeing the doctor looking betrayed, Emma was wary, her arms firm at her sides but feet fidgety. Emma looked to Henry.

"What have you done to him?" she asked.

Hartmann shook his head, his brow arched hard.

"Remember what I told you in your room?" he reminded, hands disappearing behind his back.

Her dry lips pinched at his words, rejecting his manipulation. Hartmann's eyes dropped to her hands and he stepped forwards, reaching out with stretched fingers.

"What have you done?" Emma squeaked, her voice shaking as she flung her hands away from him reaching for her. "Why have you done this to him?" she pressed, feeling her heart thump, her eyes darting to Hartmann, akin to a cornered animal.

The doctor stopped from lunging at the girl and looked to Henry in the bed with his raspy breathing being the only noise he was making.

"Don't hurt him," Emma interjected, walking towards the bed with her arms outstretched.

Hartmann strode up to Emma and straightened his back as he leered over her with an unimpressed frown.

"Mm. You've already done enough to him," he sneered under his breath, making his voice audible to Emma only.

She looked at the man with her jaw slack, and brows knitted together.

"Get out of Mr. Allen's room immediately, Miss Merrick," he hissed over her head. His words were hard and growled from between his jaw, causing a restriction in Emma's airway.

The doctor hardened his stare when he pulled away. Without forethought, she shook her head, throwing her dishevelled hair about.

Hartmann cleared his throat and made effort to make his voice boom, although he had a smirk on his face. Emma's lips wobbled beneath him, her fear paralysing her under the man who glowered with an underlying rage. Giving a fake, tight smile, the doctor eased. He relaxed, seeming to take a breath he looked at the ceiling of the room briefly. Emma's terror intensified when he churned her stomach with this, having swallowed his fury and hidden it so fast scared her more.

"You are delusional, Emma. You are a danger to yourself, listening to a clearly mentally unwell man like him," he nailed pointedly, lips tight from his pinched fury under the skin.

Emma's chest sank and her throat warmed, ready to scream at his adamance. "I am not! You've done something to him." She wavered in her harsh tone, fighting between the fluctuating emotions of anger to extreme distress. She began to tear away from herself and her face crumpled, her back arching to fold into herself while she helplessly began to sob.

"You need to stop this, all this manic behaviour." The doctor strode to the door and folded his arms.

Emma's tears rolled down her face, dripping from her chin down her neck. She didn't care to wipe them away for they poured from her eyes. Her Feet felt like bricks while unpleasant flashes of Jason ran through her mind amidst her torment.

In the moments of darkness she wanted to cross her arms over her head and surrender to it all that came crashing atop her tiny frame. Her torment threatened to ruin her again, bathing her in humiliation of the imagery of her ex-fiance coming into the scene.

Her tear-strewn face turned away from Hartmann. She grimaced hard and bore her teeth as her insides convulsed with tidal waves of hatred.

Hatred for herself, hatred for her past and being driven demented in Westview. Hatred that dragged her into an endless sinkhole. Emma's hatred, and contempt for her hopeless longing to have a partner.

How she wanted to bellow, rage and scream for everything she absolutely hated with every inch of herself.

"Are you listening to me?" Emma was powerless to stop the

fat tears that poured from her eyes despite them being shut tight. She swayed, and body struggling to contain her convulsing frustration.

The doctor sighed, shaking his head and watching Emma cave, probably thinking she may collapse any minute. He edged forward, eyebrows pinching together. His breathing slowed, taking a moment to himself, his hand outstretched to her shoulder, wrapping his fingers upon her collarbone with his eyes on the back of her head.

"Stop," Emma snapped at him, sniffling when she gripped the door and swung it open. "I knew you were a liar." Lacking no hesitation, Emma then threw herself into the hall, escaping the reaching hands of the infuriated doctor left scowling in Henry's room.

---

He allowed her to run from him, rolling his eyes inside of his skull and giving a delayed exhale through his gritted teeth.

The doctor vowed himself to have patience. His palms curled, and then he released the grip he formed. Hartmann muttered under his breath, top lip curling in disgust when he saw Henry staring up at him. With distaste, he studied the fluid in the IV bag. He muttered to himself again.

Regardless of seeing the doctor's hard and cold eyes, Henry raised his chin and his thin lips parted.

"Doctor, if I may, can I be brought some water?"

Hartmann was miles away and Henry's question faded into white noise of the room, becoming as insignificant as the beeps of the multiple monitors maintaining his status.

"Doctor if you could please just—" Henry repeated.

"You're fine."

Henry shrivelled just that bit more like shedding a skin, any shred of confidence he mustered from within himself to prose his request again fell apart.

294

Hartmann did not look at the way in which the frail man flinched, and his eyes dulled upon looking downwards.

He swallowed what little saliva he could muster from bringing it forward from behind his tongue.

As Henry became unsettled into resting himself, Hartmann scrutinised the entanglement of different wiring. Becoming frustrated with his own jerking movements, he threw his hands down with an exasperated grunt. Doctor Hartmann was brisk to hiss to himself, rushing out of Henry's room and slamming the door behind him.

Once again Doctor Hartmann was storming around his hospital. Nothing could have driven him away from finding Emma, for he was filled with an unrelenting anger.

He thought hard about what would happen when he got his hands on her. His inner dialogue was cruel, and sadistic.

He had to hold on to his infuriation, but he could feel it poisoning his muscles and tightening them, making him run hot.

Doctor Hartmann's eyes hard and accusatory, he thought only of how he would debilitate Emma for the final time.

# Chapter Thirty-One

EMMA YANKED at the door handles of the offices she ran past, finding them all locked when the handle wouldn't budge. At each door that failed to open she felt her stomach jump, fleeing into wards she had not entered before.

Emma hurtled into the open area of the ward's reception desk, not before alarming several patients on her way.

"Police, call the police, I need the police," Emma insisted as she threw herself over the desk top, making pleading eyes with the woman sat at the computer.

"What are you doing on this ward? Get off the desk."

Emma's plea was met with irritation from the receptionist, who clearly had little sympathy for her distressed and alarmed state.

Her eyes widened when the woman ushered her hands from laying on the desk, giving a loud tut. The receptionist remained tutting when Emma turned on the spot.

"I need to use your phone, I need the police, please," Emma tried again with her legs pulsing with an ache. Time seemed to freeze upon the receptionist hearing those words repeated again.

"Why?" She raised a greying eyebrow.

"Because Hartmann has killed a patient!" She exaggerated with a flap of her arms, appearing to be haunted by the knowledge.

Emma watched when the receptionist wrinkled her pruning lips and waved a hand up in the air, flinging her fingers towards her. Emma recoiled, clasping her hands to her head.

"Nurse!"

"No, I'm not crazy, I swear please," she hissed at the receptionist who kept her eyes on a fast approaching nurse, the figure down the hall losing its fuzziness as the professional approached. As the fuzz around the approaching nurse dissipated, it was clear to Emma it was none other than Nurse Ruth. Emma's feet refused to let her stand still, and she kicked herself to escape from the wretched woman behind the desk, who looked at Emma with loathing.

"I'm not crazy, damn it," she sighed, growling to herself with fingers at her heated temples. The fear of hands grabbing at her again ensured she forced herself into a sprint. The fear of Ruth closely linked in with Hartmann had the young woman bolting for her life.

"She's run into Iris ward," Emma heard the receptionist calling to Nurse Ruth.

As she turned a corner, she heard Ruth barking out an order. "Get Doctor Hartmann up here."

Emma fell into an office, throwing her head about to search for a telephone.

The shaking of her wrists made it a valid threat she would drop the phone on the floor, being excessively aware of the likelihood Hartmann was prowling the hospital hallways to find her. Her shaking fingers pressed the three fateful digits, aware that Hartmann and Nurse Ruth were probably hot behind her.

Emma was greeted on the other end of the line by a soft spoken woman.

"Get the police to my location, it's urgent, a doctor here is murdering patients," she blabbed.

"Miss, are you aware you are calling from Westview General Hospital?" The line crackled and fuzzed while the operator hesitated, pulling herself away from the phone with an unintelligible mumble.

Emma leaned in, stammering to get her words in when she felt the woman on the line was not listening to her.

"I am, and I am calling for help, not to be made fun of," Emma insisted with seething impatience, her heart pounding. Her eyes trailed across the floor to the office door.

Hartmann's eyes held an angered glint. He brought his hands forward from behind his back and they curled and gnarled at something invisible before him.

Emma thought her heart may burst, and she gave a squeaking scream of panic when he slammed shut the door behind him.

Emma watched as his jaw protruded and he practically ripped himself open with flames erupting from his mouth. She could almost feel the heat from his anger on her skin.

He took a step forward, and a bent arm pointed his forefinger at Emma's face accusingly. "Your life means nothing," Doctor Hartmann managed through his strangled voice, taking another step.

Emma looked at him in terror as she writhed helplessly against the wall. There was nothing in arm's reach to bat the man away with, so she used her own hands to whack his away.

His hands opened to grip Emma's flailing wrists that battered him away meekly. Once held fast, Emma trembled uncontrollably, falling forwards as her feet stumbled when he yanked at her.

Hartmann's face was level with hers, and he had her wrists held together in a single hand. His neck pulsed beet red and flecks of his awful spit landed on her cheeks.

"You do not do anything without my permission!" he

snarled with an ugly contortion to his features at the conviction behind his spat words, the doctor's bottom row of teeth protruding at her.

"Do you understand what I am telling you?" Doctor Hartmann seethed, back arched with the climax of his pent up anger.

Emma was petrified by his lack of control, pulling back on the doctor and backing away as best she could despite his hold on her wrists. His stubby nails dug into the skin of her wrists and she yelped, desperate for him to release her. She focused on her tiny wrists in his hand, whimpering with tears gathering in her eyes.

If he let go of her wrists, Emma would have had the mind to place her forearms out together before her face for the fear Hartmann would lash out with a flat palm, aiming for the flesh of her cheek.

"Let go, you're hurting me," Emma whimpered with a sob, desperately cowering from the enraged man.

His grip on her wrists grew tighter, and she let out a strangled scream.

"You've killed Henry, you stupid girl – that's what I was trying to stop you from finding out," he finally yelled. The veins in the doctor's large hands bulged under his skin.

"But he's not dead."

"Christ alive." He blinked in disbelief. "Henry Allen is on life support, Emma. What you did to him has cut short the poor man's life," Hartmann spat, pointing to the closed door of the office behind him. Hartmann regained his breath. "What the hell have you phoned the police for?" Emma gave a denying sob, and closed her eyes, shaking her head vehemently. She opened her eyes again to argue, although she was crying.

"You're wrong, I haven't – you saw him," she weeped.

"Stupid girl," Hartmann muttered again, clasping a hand to his forehead. "Why do you never listen?"

"I have listened, I listened to you plenty and I know I did

not kill Henry," Emma insisted, although her voice was breaking from holding back her tears.

Hartmann's eyes rolled in his skull, finger releasing Emma's wrists to drag down the sides of his nose.

"Please, Emma," he begged, screwing his face up. "When the police come, you must explain exactly what you have done."

"What I've done? You can bet I will tell them what you have done. I know that I haven't done anything wrong."

Anger flickering in Doctor Hartmann's eyes again, he looked to Emma's blotchy face. "Oh?" he repeated, looking at her incredulously. "Is that so?"

"I know you're lying to me."

At the emanating bravery from Emma, the doctor hummed with his arms crossing tight over his thrust chest. His eyes slid down her tiny frame as he then swung a leg out in front of the other, sliding up to Emma, who was trying not to show how badly she was quivering.

"Who'll believe you? You're a patient," the doctor revealed with a smirk. "Even more so, you're one of mine, in fact." His arms unfolded to gesture around the empty space in his office.

Emma's jaw was wide, and although she shook, she held her stance firmly, tensing her muscles for fear if she relaxed them she would collapse on the spot.

She went to speak, but as her jaw fell open again the Doctors voice commanded.

"When the police officers arrive I am excited to hear what exactly I have done to you."

"You drugged me, you made me sick," Emma spat in adamance, using her wrists to wipe her tear-filled eyes.

"Emma, that never happened. It is important you know your facts, and I know the officers are going to be very annoyed to see you having wasted their valuable time."

With the belittling tone of Hartmann's voice making her confidence waver, she made great effort not to show it. She felt she could argue with this man until she went blue in the face, but found the silence gave her more of a chance of saving talking for when it would matter most.

"Go. Run off. You better hurry now, Emma, because they'll be here soon," Hartmann spat with an ugly smile, looking up from his watch with conviction in his eyes.

She felt the anger in his growled, low voice which warned her to obey.

Clueless to do anything but escape the fury of the man, she began to step back, without ever taking her eyes from the doctor until the fury in his hard glare had cooled enough that her skin was no longer burning.

# Chapter Thirty-Two

EMMA WAS CONVINCED that she was able to feel the singe of Hartmann's stabbing glare at the back of her head as she escaped him. Despite the swarming intensity of her actions, she strode along the walls, attempting to convince herself she was relaxed, and content with the consequences of her actions. Most of all, convincing herself that she was calm.

Emma froze to see Hartmann was not behind her. Half twisted at the torso, palms beginning to sweat, the burning at the back of her skull like two great lasers faded just then.

Racking her mind, she found it a near impossibility to have lost the man in such a short amount of time.

Poking her head out beyond the dipped greying heads, and wrinkled complexions, the girl broke out into a run.

Peering through the droplet-patterned glass panes, she was barely wary enough to stop herself running over the patients that fumbled and struggled to move out of her way. "Shit," Emma mumbled, seeing a police car's unmistakable bright bonnet approaching from beyond the metal fence of the garden.

Emma stumbled, almost toppling over herself in her attempt to dash again. She was exhausted. Her lack of co-ordination reflected her state well. Hands coming out in front of herself, the young woman barged once again past fumbling patients.

"How rude," an annoyed woman remarked when Emma had unsuccessfully slid herself past the walker she was using, her hip bashing into the metal, having knocked the woman to the side.

Other patients saw the look in her eyes and moved themselves out of the way, shuffling to the sides as if for an out of control emergency vehicle to barrel through.

Nothing could touch Emma, for she was only feeling the incredible pounding of her heart within her chest that threatened to erupt.

The uncoordinated patient practically raced the police car through the walls of the hospital.

They drove up to the hospital entrance and she bolted through the hallways. She told herself again that poor judgement had not gotten her to this stage. Emma toppled against the automatic doors that failed to open for her, twisting her head up and around to look for a button to press. Her sweaty hand bashed the disabled access button at the wall but the doors failed again to slide open for her.

"Open, come on," she breathed, slamming her hand into the button multiple times.

A nurse from the reception desk approached with hands ready to hold Emma at her shoulders, and paused upon Doctor Hartmann coming into the reception area with a palm to her face.

"Leave her."

The nurse froze where she stood, turning immediately back to the reception desk with her head bowed.

Hartmann walked up behind Emma in the doorway, and she almost fell through the doors when they opened.

"Fuck." Emma stumbled, glancing at Hartmann bristling,

standing tall beside her. Her hands flattened the fabric of her gown, picking at the multiple creases.

Hartmann strode ahead, standing down a few steps to greet the officer. Emma did not look at Hartmann again until the policeman was making his way up the steps, hands held in place firmly around the shoulder straps of his heavy duty vest. The man's lips were straight, not moving to smile when Hartmann outstretched a hand.

"Good afternoon."

"Afternoon." The officer nodded at Hartmann. His lips straightened and remained, his eyes moving from Hartmann when Emma stumbled out in her gown.

"My name is Officer Chester Alwan," he said with fingers grooming through the dark hairs of his sizeable beard.

Emma released a smile, unsure of herself in the state the policeman would have formed a first impression which was inaccurate.

Under his vest his stomach bulged low, his shirt visibly straining with the weight.

"I apologise for my patient, she warrants that her delusions are worth wasting your time."

"They aren't delusions," Emma argued with all of the indignance of a sulking child, on the verge of tearing her hair out at the endless back and forth.

Hartmann turned to her with the police officer stood beside him, looking at her with a tilted glance into her wide eyes.

"Emma, if you would, explain to the policeman what you were worried about." He folded his arms with a nod.

She shifted her weight from one foot to the other and drew in a breath. Both set of eyes were then on her.

"This doctor is murdering patients." As soon as she spoke, she was met with a hard glare from the officer, who raised his bushy brows.

"That is a very serious allegation," he noted.

Emma nodded multiple times, gesturing to Hartmann who stood with a glum, un-entertained look upon his face, but directing it at Emma.

"Please follow me, come inside if he has nothing to hide he would let you in, isn't that right?" Emma stared at the officer, egging him for a nod or agreement.

"I wasn't even a patient at the beginning. He admitted me here against my will. I didn't sign a bloody thing." She steamed with confidence, her voice unwavering throughout her fuelled rambling at the officer, who struggled to take it all in as quickly as the woman was throwing at him.

The officer's lips pulled thin, eyes squinting at the poor sight before him. He saw the cuts and scattered bruises that decorated her legs, probably wondering, with a tilt of his head, just how they got there.

"I don't think that would be the appropriate action right now," came the voice of Officer Alwan.

Emma did not falter in her demanding nature, pointing through the sliding doors to the reception, glaring again at the officer.

He picked up on what she said as it replayed in his head.

"Please, I can show you, I need you to see for yourself, otherwise I know I sound absolutely–" Her sentence trailed off as her voice faded, failing to finish. Emma dropped her arm and she curled it back to the side of her ribs.

Mad.

In the silence Emma left herself in, Doctor Hartmann scoffed, shaking his head at the woman while taking a step to interject.

"I do apologise again."

The police officer's gaze was amiss from Hartmann's when he spoke, and he instead gazed at Emma, slumped with his thoughts. Officer Alwan then stood tall, jerking himself to raise his eyes. "You were not a patient here, in the beginning?" he questioned Emma.

She sighed, but gave a nod. "Yes, I was in a car accident but I did not need admitting," she explained. With a vindictive pointed finger, she threw it at Hartmann. "He admitted me, and drugged me to make me unwell, or prolong my stay or something." She waved her hand, and upon looking at the smirk on Hartmann's face, she blew up in rage. "He's full of shit!" she exclaimed, her hair thrown about by the rapid turning of her head.

Hartmann looked at her with mild disgust, rolling his eyes when Officer Alwan looked from Emma to him.

The officer smacked his lips, Emma stood staring at him, not letting his eyes escape hers for a second.

Every move he made was under close scrutiny by her, unsure of what to make from the contrast of Emma's high energy versus the doctors disappointed looks.

With a frown, Officer Alwan shook his head. "I don't think I'm getting the full story here," he deduced.

"The allegation you have made against both the hospital and this man before me, means you need to come back to the station," he briskly informed, his hands still clutching the shoulders of his weighted vest.

Hartmann stared at the man's face, silenced by the outcome.

His eyes flew immediately to land on Emma's, who had brightened significantly. Her energy heightened, giving the officer assuring nods.

Emma could not handle her elation. Finally, something was working in her favour and it left her with a lopsided grin on her face.

The officer had words with Hartmann over her head, and she couldn't care to listen. She heard the way Hartmann argued, and gestured to her with an open, flat palm with eyes locked on Officer Alwan.

It clearly took Hartmann a great deal of effort to restrain himself from continuing to argue with Officer Alwan, and so he adopted a prim, tight pull at the corners of his lips. All Emma wanted was to watch while the very sight of Westview faded.

Once placed in the back of the police car, she turned with glee to watch as Hartmann stood and his prominent features became difficult to make out. He became a streaky blob of white and brown.

The road wound out under the car like a grey tape, and the building of Westview got smaller. With a smile forming on her lips, Emma raised a hand and wiggled her fingers through the boot window.

The last thing she saw was Hartmann's look of disdain as the car drove out of view.

## Chapter Thirty-Three

THE OFFICER PULLED up the car's handbrake after parking outside the doors in a designated bay.

Emma absently stared at the building, unaware of the officer watching her in the rear view mirror. Officer Alwan was the first to jump out and pull the boot open, closing it and then pulling her door open, holding a folded blanket in the crook of his other arm.

"Here, put this over your shoulders," he said, unfolding it wide.

"Thank you."

The officer smiled, and Emma pinched the corners of the fabric at her collarbones to ensure it did not fall away from her, and grateful for it covering the sight of her awful hospital gown. Her stomach rumbled as she walked up to the door of the station, confronted again by an immediate bustling of officers.

"Right this way, please." Officer Alwan opened the door wide to introduce Emma into a small room with couches and a coffee table in the middle. There was a camera in the corner of the box room, the red light glowing under the glass.

"I am going to speak to my seniors, alright? Sit tight and I'll be back." He said as Emma sat, giving a nod.

"Do you want some water?"

Emma nodded again, giving a smile. "That'd be nice, thank you," she said, fidgeting on the couch.

"Good. I will be back soon."

Emma's toes touched down on the blue carpet, tickling her feet.

She lowered the blanket from her shoulders and exhaled, releasing the tension from within her chest. At her prolonged release of air, she fell back onto the leather couch and stared at the ceiling of the room. Willingly, her eyes closed, her ribs lighter at the knowledge this was her big chance to tell all – to finally relieve herself of the dysfunction at Westview.

"Miss Merrick, this is Officer Daniels. He is going to be helping me with your questioning, okay?"

Emma nodded, smiling at the man. He sat on the couch at the side of her, being careful to leave a good few feet between himself and Emma.

"Now, if you are not already aware we are going to be recording this for recollection of events, and it's a standard practice, as I am sure you are aware." The man smiled at Emma who was slow to react, delaying a smile in return.

"Yes, that's fine," she said, looking to the pair.

The two men situated themselves on differing areas in the room and poured Emma a glass of water from a jug they had brought in. She sat with her bruised legs showing in contrast to the black leather of the sofa, and the officers were careful to avoid being caught looking.

Officer Alwan was stating the details, the date at the time and explaining to an absent minded Emma about the recording of both audio and visual in the room while under questioning.

"There is no appropriate adult present."

"The time on my watch is now eleven fifty-eight, and the

date today is Saturday the eighteenth of July and the year is two-thousand and fifteen. We are currently situated in St. Gridgevey police station, and for the purpose of the tape please tell me and officer Alwan your full name."

"Emma Lily Merrick." She stiffened.

"These are just formalities, Emma," Officer Daniels said with a smile.

Emma felt herself shaking with nerves bundling inside at the sets of examining eyes on her.

Officer Daniels lifted his leg and rested his ankle over the other leg that remained in front. As he shifted on the couch, she noticed the permeating smell of the leather tickling her nostrils for the first time.

She knew she was only here to tell the truth, and recall events to help the officers gain an understanding of events – but she could not help but become nervous under the pressure the two men applied on her weary shoulders. Shrinking her shoulders over in the chair, she pushed her hair behind her ears and cleared her throat, raising her head. Emma commanded herself to hold eye contact, and to have a presence in the room.

"Now, following on from the admission you made to me earlier, can you repeat what you told me please Emma?"

"I believe Doctor Hartmann has drugged a patient of his, with intent to kill him," she said.

"What evidence can you provide to back up your statement?"

"The man, Henry, the victim, he told me himself. Hartmann injected something into his IV fluid."

Officer Alwan looked to Daniels with a raised brow, seeing his colleague engaged with Emma's admission. His arms folded, raising his chin.

"You did not see this happen?"

She shifted in her chair, and felt pressured to maintain her eye contact.

"No," Emma said, balancing her toes on the floor. "I know that sounds ridiculous, but before Hartmann got hold of him, he was so much healthier, physically. You could see the difference in him."

Alwan's arm stretched to the back of his balding head, scratching his skull. "And who is this Henry, is he a patient?"

"Yes, he was," Emma's eyes glanced sideways. "He's probably dead now, thanks to Hartmann." Her tone had dropped, visibly stiffening Detective Daniels in his chair.

"Right." Officer Alwan initiated a pause. "And is this man the only credible witness?"

"Yes officer, he is," she nodded.

"What did Henry tell you, Emma?"

She looked to the ceiling for a moment to think back to those few moments of being in Henry's hospital room. Emma strained to think clearly.

"He said Hartmann had come into his hospital room with a needle. He put it into the bag on the stand and left, with the needle empty, he told me."

Detective Daniels raised the wrinkles in his forehead, and Emma's eyes dropped away from the pair as she was filled again with fear of the man.

She raised her head and her voice was hoarse, her throat burning, unable to speak above a whisper. "He was terrifying sometimes," she whispered. "Henry was like a bag of bones in the bed laid up with massive purple veins bulging from his tiny arms." Emma's hand ran up her own arm when she spoke, glancing to her skin, her eyes had glazed over as she fixated on the imagery.

"Who was terrifying? Do you mean Doctor Hartmann, Emma?"

Her head remained staring down at the skin upon her arm. "Yes, when he got angry. I was petrified he would hurt Henry when he found me in his hospital room."

"Weren't you supposed to be in there?"

Emma tiptoed around how she was going to answer, resting her trailing fingers on her arm. "No, patients aren't allowed to mix in different wards."

"Why were you in Henry's room if you weren't allowed to, Emma?"

At once she felt a heat rush under her skin, breaking her out into a clammy sweat. Fleeting to her thoughts that hid, she stammered on her words when her lip trembled. Small exhales of breath left her, as if having held a hot coin in her mouth and tossing it around to cool it down, while trying not to incur an injury.

Detective Daniels narrowed his eyes, leaning forwards at the sight of seeing her stammer and hesitate to answer a question for the first time during the questioning.

"I was in his room to apologise."

"Apologise for what, Emma?"

"I had become upset, and I had put my hands around his throat." The room quieted, and Emma felt the rawness at the back of her throat become acidic, and burn her. She wanted to reach for the glass of water on the coffee table, but dared not outstretch her arm to take it, wanting to shrink and become pitiful.

Officer Alwan cupped his chin, his eyes narrowed on Emma while Detective Daniels' were wide, and his face egged her to go on.

"And what did you do with your hands around this man's throat, Emma?"

"I..." She hesitated, drawing a breath to steady herself in the chair. "I squeezed."

Sitting himself straight, Daniels pressed her, suspicion showing on his face that she was not telling all of the details after her elation at the hospital.

"How hard, Emma? You need to tell us what you did to Henry."

A tear rolled down her cheek when she began to shake

uncontrollably, and she used her wrist to wipe the droplet from her cheek with her head bowed into her sunken chest.

"I wasn't in the right mind. I'm never violent, I promise – I was so drugged up and unwell, I lost my temper and flew at him," she sobbed, fat tears now falling from her eyes and dripping onto her gown.

"Did you make him lose consciousness?"

Emma shook her head. "No, he only struggled under me."

"And then, did he fight you off or did you get tired, what happened?"

"Nurses pulled me off him."

"Okay." Detective Daniels nodded while Emma dried her tears. Sitting back again, he let Emma have a moment.

"Now, what had upset you in the first place?"

"Henry had said something," She sniffled in her pause. "He told me that the drugs, the medicines that Hartmann gave to me would do me harm, on purpose, rather than to make me better."

"Now how is that possible?" Detective Daniels asked her pointedly.

"I don't remember," Emma admitted with a shake of her head to the officer and detective. She put a hand in front of herself and waved her wrist. "Henry was angry, but he told me about drug trials, and the killing of patients, too."

The two men looked at Emma, and she only cried upon feeling she had unloaded onto them in such a way that their heads may explode. She cried for the helplessness of her situation, and the sobs wracked her tiny ribcage, feeling every single sob throughout her body. Now having unfolded at least part of some backstory, it was a haphazardly guess as to what Emma would admission onto the two next.

Trying not to look as overwhelmed as he felt, Detective Daniels pressed her again. "So he was the one that told you about these initially?"

"Yes, but I had seen and experienced horrific events myself, too. What Henry told me just confirmed my previous suspicions," she said. "It was only after seeing Henry in bed and so sick for myself and linking it to what he told me, I realised that he had been right."

Detective Daniels gave a slow nod, lips parted, licking his teeth before asking further.

His colleague jumped in. "You had experienced... events?" Officer Alwan questioned her with a hard glare.

Emma nodded, her tears having dried, building herself up in confidence when the questioning began to steer correctly again.

"I had only been in Westview after a car accident, a minor one." She paced, slowing her words to almost make sense to herself, earning watchful looks from the men who observed her closely. "Hartmann's a liar, is what I am trying to tell you through all of this." She breathed shakily.

Officer Alwan leaned back in his chair. "You see, that's why we need to know what you experienced, alright?"

Emma tucked her loping hair behind her ear.

"Hartmann told me I was sick, very unwell, and needed treatments to fix." She struggled to find words and gestured in front of herself. "Whatever it was he saw wrong with me."

The officers allowed Emma to continue, both completely silent while she painted the picture for the two.

"And I got sick from the treatment he gave me. He ran tests, and told me again I was unwell and was to stay at the hospital."

"Right." Detective Daniels gave a squint of his eyes, Emma narrowed her shoulders. Looking at Detective Daniels filled her with unease on whether he believed what she was saying or not. Emma, knowing that was not an option to give them, went into more severe detail to ensure they were convinced of her suffering not being fictionalised.

"Over time, Hartmann was treating me more extremely, using straightjackets, and there was a padded room."

"A what? You mean with cushioned walls and the floor?"

Emma gave a nod.

Neither of the men looked half convinced. They looked at her like a liar – she recognised the look immediately.

Holding a palm up in the air and stammering to stop her, Detective Daniels leaned with his elbows on his knees.

"Going back to what you said earlier, before we go any further ahead – why do you think Doctor Hartmann wanted, or had tried, to murder Henry?"

Emma sighed. She was disappointed the admission of straightjacket useage had failed to ignite a reaction of horror. Shaking her head with her brain rattling around, she shrugged.

"I don't understand why, I don't know, honestly I wish I did." She began to shake again, unravelling at her lack of reasoning that formed a massive burning hole in her plan.

"Emma, you must have been admitted into an asylum for a reason."

In response, she grew increasingly tired causing her fingers to rack against her skull, getting entangled in her hair.

"It's a hospital," she corrected, bristling on the couch. Beginning to feel a tightening in her throat, Emma observed that the detective and officer had agreed on an unspoken agreement to battle against her. "I apologise, but–" Emma gritted her teeth, growing in her desperation. She ripped into an argument, battling the two enquiring men before they had chance to ask her anything more. "Hartmann basically kidnapped me, I never signed bloody anything," Emma searched the pair of blank faces before her.

"You have already told us that Miss Merrick."

"But I haven't told you about the electro-shock therapy yet."

"That's enough."

"But you're not listening to me," she argued, raising in her chair. "I assure you, my mind is perfect, I have only been unwell or acted violently under the constant drugs and–"

"Emma, hold on here." Officer Alwan held his hand on her face.

She stopped, her sentence left hanging midair and staggering down from her state of battling the two men off.

"Chester, get this nut job out of our station." Daniels shook his head.

Increasingly desperate, Emma began to bounce a leg under the desk, her top row of teeth clamping down on the beaten flesh of her bottom lip. "He must have got my signature somehow, I assure you I did not sign a damn thing," she argued.

"How can we believe you did not sign an admission form of some sort?"

"Because I handled no paperwork which needed my signature."

The officers leaned away from her, and she leaned in, having taken a breath this time, gathering herself and adjusting her harsh tone. She turned her head to the floor and squeezed her eyes shut.

Emma spoke clearly when she looked at the men from her eyes at her lap. "How would I have signed anything, before or after, with or without memory of doing so?" she calmly explained, slowly feeling the possibility of a breakthrough with both the officer and detective. To drive it home, she stated, "Either way, can you understand that Hartmann has done something under my nose, here?"

Officer Alwan gave it a thought and hummed, looking to his colleague, who looked less than impressed. Furthermore, he looked much less than convinced. In a manner that relayed again her state of franticness, Emma's eyes flitted from one man to the other and would not remain still. They may roll out of her skull if she for one moment allowed herself to relax. Emma was ready to fight the right battle.

# Chapter Thirty-Four

OUTSIDE OF HENRY'S ROOM, overworked nurses hurried about like flies. Hartmann's body seized up with tension. "What did I tell you repeatedly? What had I insisted, multiple times to ensure?"

"That Mr Allen was to be checked on every thirty minutes on a ro–"

"No! What had I told you about his condition?" he asked her again. The nurse looked pained. "He was to be dosed on at least sixty mil."

"And you failed, evidently." The exasperated Doctor gestured around himself, as if the wrongdoings of the nurse were written on the walls. Her eyes barely strayed from watching his hands.

"I have handled the situation now myself, and as such, I am making that of which you failed me, your last. Get out of my hospital," he said, pointing to the door.

Presented with the problematic failings of his staff following his strict instructions, the doctor did not look to himself when things went wrong. Instead he flung out with a venomous tongue at those who worked under him. Humiliation swarmed over the man and he was furious, lashing out immediately, blaming every other person that he had to deal with for the stinking fumes of his own fire.

Hunched over his desk, the doctor's broad shoulders rose and fell while he took large, deep breaths, steaming with his fury.

With flared nostrils and a heat of rage bubbling under his skin, Hartmann stared at the wall when he stuck that same arm out in front of himself and ragged his arm across the piled high desk.

Using such force that his computer was yanked free from the wire and smashed, spewing out shards of plastic and glass onto the floor, along with the descending sheets of paperwork that flew around before landing on top of the trashed office floor ever so softly.

———

Hartmann had only calmed himself moments before the police arrived at the hospital once again, having been pulled by Nurse Ruth – the only one brave enough to approach him during his rage.

From the reception he seethed, resenting the sight of the foreign car sitting itself comfortably in the carpark.

Officer Alwan approached across the gravel road, where Hartmann awaited for him at the top of the steps.

"Ah, good afternoon again, Officer, what news do you bring me of my patient?" His eyes peered over the shoulder of the officer to see the backseat of the car was empty.

Hartmann's eyes returning to the officer, he cleared his throat, a poor vent for his residing irritation.

"Miss Merrick is at the station. She is safe, don't be worried." Officer Alwan flashed the doctor a reassuring smile when his face dropped.

"Oh." His tone darkened, trying not to look dismayed. "I

see." He hesitated arguing, and tried to perk. But he bit his viper tongue on telling the man Emma was far safer here – with him.

"We would like you to come back to the station with us, as we have now some questions to ask of you." The small smile remained on Officer Alwan's face.

Doctor Hartmann's lips pulled thin and he took a sharp inhale of the afternoon air. "I am bunkered down, I am afraid you would need to come inside." He gestured, indicating the doors behind himself.

Officer Alwan put his hands behind his back. "Afraid not, you have to come with me by law, this cannot be handled outside of the station."

Hartmann lowered his arms and straightened his back, having hunched as he would naturally to meet the eyes of the officer who was quite a bit shorter than himself.

Officer Alwan watched with an unmoving face at Hartmann's brow dipping and the corners of his lips souring. Hartmann noticed him scrutinizing him intensely, stiff and unmoving. Hartmann's hands became heavier at the slow motion of them returning to his side, and felt the urge of something akin to wanting to give the officer a punch in the face. He knew he would land it right on the end of his round, bulging chin.

"I will have to have a talk with my nurses, then," Hartmann said. His eyes lowered to meet with Officer Alwans'. "Wait here, would you? I won't be but five minutes."

Hartmann was glad the officer let him speak with his nurses. His rage was seething under the skin and Hartmann feared he may lash out at the policeman if he hadn't.

Having caught Nurse Ruth two minutes up the corridor, he called to her. She twisted at the urgency in his voice.

"Ruth, ensure Henry's room is sorted, and I will be less than an hour, at most," he hissed into her eager, leaning ear.

She nodded. "Of course, I'll handle it. What about Emma?"

Hartmann rubbed fingers against his temple. "Nothing, just get rid of everything, clean the rooms, both of them." He shook his head and Ruth nodded again as he began to pace backwards. With the lasting glare Hartmann gave her, she made a beeline for Lilypad ward.

## Chapter Thirty-Five

HARTMANN WAS NOT PROVIDED A BLANKET, but if he was offered one he would have shunned it anyway.

The multiple differing professionals within the walkways of the station gave smiles to the doctor as he followed Officer Alwan, before finally coming into a compact, uncomfortable room.

Entering, he was met with a foldable desk with a chair at each side, and a third tucked behind the door, revealed only after the door closed. Throwing himself comfortably down in the desk chair, he placed his ankle atop his knee, facing both the officer and the detective. His confidence beamed, and it came as little surprise from the two men that sat opposite him. Getting through explaining the audio was being recorded and a camera filming the room at all times, Hartmann gave a noncommittal but understanding hum.

"Beside me here is Detective Daniels. He is assisting me with the questioning of you today."

Doctor Hartmann was barely listening, but pretended to pay the utmost attention. He only was paying attention when being asked to say his name for the recording.

Clearing his throat, Officer Alwan began with the questioning. "Now, Miss Merrick."

"My patient, Emma, yes." His tone was flat, unrelating to the officer in front of him. Officer Alwan eyed the man.

The silence stood at the interruption.

"Yes, now, she has stated to us that you have acted multiple times out of practice."

"Regarding what?" His words collided with the chest of the officer, and he struggled to wager his feeling of control inside the interrogation room.

"Did she sign any admission papers?"

Hartmann cleared his throat, then leaning in to cough into his balled hand. "Of course she did. I have them in my office filed like every one of my patients."

The officer and detective twitched in their chairs.

Hartmann looked fed up already, but Officer Alwan, being of the hardened type of policeman, disregarded the look he saw upon the doctor's face.

"She claims she didn't sign a thing, and on the evening of any paperwork being handled it was of nothing requiring a signature."

"Emma is an alcoholic, I soon discovered when I looked upon her history afterwards of the accident," Hartmann explained, looking at the two. "She did tell you about the accident, didn't she?" He raised an eyebrow suggestively.

Both the detective and officer nodded. "She did, but not in a lot of detail."

Hartmann sighed, looking to the desk. "Well, she got herself upset that evening after drinking too much, and threw herself out into a busy road." Hartmann rubbed at his stubble. "She represented, and continues to represent, a great danger to herself," he said.

Tilting his chin upwards, detective Daniels quipped in. "What about the admission papers?"

"She signed them, but probably will not remember so, as

she was still in a bad state the next morning. But I assure you, she signed them herself, with full knowledge of what the papers meant." The doctor looked to the inquisitive detective. Sitting back in the chair, it gave a creak.

Detective Daniel's brow pulled up at the gaze of the doctor, who broke his eyes away to absent-mindedly pull at the wrist cuffs of his shirt.

"A major concern of hers, was around a man she seemed to have befriended. Do you know what we're talking about?"

Hartmann winced. He pulled at the wrinkles on his brow and fidgeted in his chair, detective and officer watching intently.

"Yes, I do. His name was Henry."

Detective Daniel's brightened. "Yes, now this is where—" But he paused, letting a particular cold term settle on his shoulders. "Was?" he repeated. He looked to his colleague, who was just as gobsmacked to hear the doctor speak in the past tense.

Hartmann looked to the men with a furrowed brow. "Now this will only make sense if you have been told the truth by my patient."

Officer Alwan leaned in. "What happened to Henry, Doctor?" having slowed his pace of speech.

"After Emma strangled him, he took a turn for the worst, and he has since passed away."

Officer Alwan bristled uncomfortably. "When did this happen?"

"After the incident, he suffered a stroke and deteriorated to the point of having passed during a nap."

Detective Daniels scratched the side of his cheek. "She murdered him, didn't she?"

Hartmann stared at the officer, the shine of sadness in his eyes having disappeared. "No," he said. "I'd never have my patient as the type to murder anyone. Don't be jumping to such conclusions."

"But the old fart's dead, Doctor." Detective Daniels noted.

"My patient did not intend to kill him." Hartmann was adamant.

"This makes quite a difference. She had not told us this, you see." The detective waggled a finger, smiling to himself with the new information introduced.

The doctor straightened in the chair, giving a sigh.

"I had hesitated telling her, as her mental state is very fragile right now. She didn't need to know about the consequences, I would have brought it to her attention possibly later." He rambled on, making circles with his wrist atop the table.

From that point, the questions wound themselves down and led the detective and officer down a long winded route, slowly becoming more able to piece together both lies, and then gaining the truths.

A ball of lies from Emma was unravelled like an ugly, maggot-infested shag carpet. The image both the detective and officer held of the small woman changed, having spoke about an evolving violent streak being present before the incident with Henry. Detective Daniels felt he and his colleague had been manipulated, and would later be scolding his colleague for not listening to him when she said about Emma being a crazy woman.

The doctor scarcely moved himself about in discomfort and was not afraid to be met with hard eye contact, often being just as intense himself or more so. The two who were asking the questions would be breaking it off more than he himself would need to. It gave him all the more reason to maintain his confidence, but upset at having his time away from the Hospital wasted.

Hartmann's palms motioned and he looked to the ceiling upon thinking back, recounting the times Emma caused him worry, almost being so comfortable, and confident to unload his thoughts onto the officer and detective.

The enquiry into the murder of Henry was kept brief in conversation, but there was an understanding that both Alwan and Daniels would need to do some investigative work into the scene of the crime.

Hartmann was more than happy for the nosy pigs to snoop around his hospital.

"That's absolutely fine, I will accommodate you anyway I can in your investigation," Hartmann said, standing from the chair with an effortful noise as his knees creaked after sitting for an elongated period of time.

"Gentlemen, if I may discuss a pressing matter with you." Hartmann looked at the two remaining in their chairs. He did not sit back down.

"Yes George, what is it?" Officer Alwan asked.

"In regards to arresting her, I request you not to."

They looked at the doctor as if he himself was suffering the same insanity Emma represented. Suffering from the same dregs of some form of immoral madness with the calmness at which he asked such a strange thing.

Rebuffing a scoff at being unable to be entertained at what he disbelieved to have heard, Officer Alwan stood from his chair and leaned on the table.

"That's not how it works, we may need to arrest your patient," the detective announced slowly.

He watched when Hartmann looked to him with a frown.

"She is best spending her time remaining at the hospital, where I can continue treating her for her various..." The doctor's hands spun at the side of himself, unable to find the correct word, but being met with the patient gaze from the two.

"We understand you have concerns, but we need to keep her with us until we can charge her."

Hartmann poked the table with his finger. "Emma is much safer in an environment which can maintain her mental state on a manageable level," Hartmann advised the men. "Unless you can accommodate her in a secure facility, with mental health professionals for her." His finger lifted from the table after a final poke.

"With the utmost respect, she has murdered somebody."

"With the utmost respect, my Emma is not a criminal. She needs my facilities, not to be behind your bars. I am seriously concerned for her ongoing state. And unless you are able to pay for her ongoing care, she will be going unmedicated, and I warn you against that severely."

Shifting in his chair, Officer Alwan leaned into Hartmann's space, shaking his head.

"How's that been working for you, Doctor?" He almost spat at the man.

Hartmann lowered his gaze honestly, deciding to bite at the reel he was being fed. Keeping his gaze on his knuckles resting atop the table, he spoke. "I will admit, not very well. She is challenging with me, and has escaped my hospital before now."

Officer Alwan glanced at Hartmann. He continued. "She was found at the train station, and had tried to convince a couple waiting there to phone the police."

The men sat opposite Hartmann sat stiff.

The doctor looked up. "Friends of yours, see?" He gave a small smile, but his eyes were sad. "This is not her first incident of trying to gain the attention of the police." He gave a frown, pulling back his knuckles.

Rubbing at the prominent wrinkles on his forehead, Officer Alwan smacked his hand on the table.

"She has told us half-truths, here," the flustered officer seethed, eyes wide and looking ready to pop with the accumulation of pressure atop his brain.

"I apologise. She lies to me too. Quite often," the doctor mumbled with a tilt of his head, exposing a sympathetic side towards the officer.

Hartmann eyed the red-faced officer with disregard,

shaking his head when heat crept up his neck. He shook it off, jostling himself to gain some air.

Staring at the forlorn, exhausted face of his colleague, Detective Daniels scoffed. Hartmann decided to sit back down. The folding chair gave another creak.

"The crime she has committed is far too serious for her to be in the company of the general public in your hospital, doctor. She is clearly at a risk for flight, manipulation, and violence." He explained without breathing.

"You fail to realise what my hospital provided for Emma," Hartmann grumbled. "Stability, for the first time in her life. She went out of her way to do other things and speak with other patients and found out she didn't like it, and so unfortunate events have happened, yes," he explained with his hands gesturing atop the table.

Hartmann took a breath. "But within the boundaries we set for her, she will become better. That is all I want for her, and it won't happen being thrust into the prison system.

Being left speechless, the arms of Detective Daniels folded and his lips morphed into a tight scowl.

"Doctor, I cannot allow Emma to be released back into your Hospital."

Hartmann's chest collapsed, his palms became increasingly clammy, the room immediately having become too hot for him. His palms warmed as if a rope was slipping through them, and burning his hand as it left his grip. Hartmann was not a man who was blown off. Straining not to come across as a man who would not have himself listened to, he gave the men across from himself a small smile, and folded his hands comfortably over atop his stomach. Flicking his eyes to theirs, he took a breath before he next spoke, in the most crystal clear voice he could muster.

# Chapter Thirty-Six

IT WAS ANOTHER PLEASANT, summery day late into the month of July. Through the glass windows throughout West-view hospital, the sun beamed through in rays of yellow light.

When the sun's beams reached skin it was a warm embrace, the beams like arms stretching from between the clouds.

Patients set themselves up along the decking to simply tip their heads back, content to bask in the embrace.

Beyond the open doorway, out in the garden, every colour was fluorescent and appeared to glow – multiple hands replacing sunglasses, thrust out in front of the wrinkled eye sockets to gain clear sight.

But they smiled, bright and without thought or considera-tion for reason why. Pollen clung to the white gowns, and it hung in the warm air, a gentle wind periodically tickling the many flowers laid in their beds to carry it in the wind.

Patients were delighted when the blades of grass tickled between their toes, having discarded their slippers upon the decking, too gleeful to be able to ditch them. The sound of bouncing laughter added to the joy of the summer days at Westview, the nurses offering out glasses of fresh lemonade atop trays they carried, and the clinking of the tall glasses which followed thereafter. Chatter regarded the zip of the citrus beverage along the greying tongues, causing bouts of pleasant excitement. Behind the garden, atop the roof of the ground floor were the multiple open windows of the residents' bedrooms, all open to ensure the summer air could to flow around and throughout the entirety of the hospital.

Only from one room was the window left closed, and it was noted to be a small, ghostly figure looking through the glass. The arch of her spine was visible under the skin of her neck, hunched in the chair she had pushed, and then dragged across the floor, not having the strength to exert herself to lift it.

She sat, hunched in the chair at the window she stared out at the garden, completely still. Her eyes only moved to focus in on a particular individual out on the grass before they disappeared. Although the scenes outside were infectiously joyful, Emma's eyes were dull upon watching. Her room was filled only by the deafening silence, in which she found a great comfort. The sound of chatter and the displays of happiness in the garden were muffled, and her lips twitched and she withdrew when the sound became loud enough to reach her ears.

On the arms of the chair her arms had fallen, and remained. Floppy wrists allowed her hands to hang carelessly over the edge, fingers curling inward. Emma was exhausted, but had slept through the night for the first time in what felt like forever, if she had the mind to ponder about it. She didn't.

The nightmares had come less frequently, and she wondered to herself yesterday if it was down to Doctor Hartmann.

---

Hartmann, that morning, had bought Emma a bouquet of flowers, his choice being pure white lilies. He explained that they were what Melissa had been delighted with the most. He left them in an engraved glass vase atop her bedside table. She did not regard them.

Instead, sitting in the armchair, Emma pressed two fingers into the bruises that resided at the inside of her elbow. They were a deep purple and red from where Emma drove her fingertips into her skin, feeling the way it brought upon a dull ache. She would wince, and give herself a rest, but then go back moments later and push even harder.

Emma's pattern of breathing did not change when a hand placed itself down onto her shoulder. Her eyes remained staring straight ahead as if hypnotised, being unable to break her gaze away. She scratched at her wrist where the hospital band was causing her skin a slight irritation.

"Open up for me, my love."

The words took seconds to sink in. Her lips parted, and her pink tongue pushed out flat. Pills rattled in the bottle of Hartmann's pocket, focusing on the one he had pinched in-between the space of his thumb and forefinger. Hartmann was careful and slow to place it onto her tongue, and he watched with a smile spreading across his face when Emma pulled her tongue in, and his eyes dropped to her delicate throat. Under the skin he watched her motion of swallowing. Satisfied, the doctor tugged up the thigh of his trousers and dropped himself at the knees before her.

"Look at me, Emma," he requested softly.

Her dull eyes met with his, and he met her with the corner of his lips tugging upwards, reaching forwards with outstretched fingers to hold the locks of her hair.

"Do you feel better?" Hartmann proposed, a hopeful glint in his eyes, searching her face with a lustful smile. His cheeks turned a shade of pink at the beginning motion of running his fingertips through her hair. He looked at her again, searching her eyes.

His voice waned. "Melissa, did you..." He shook his head, but did not cringe. A small smile spread halfway across his lips before restraining it going any further. "Emma." He began afresh. "Did you hear what I just asked you?"

Emma remained silent, only giving her doctor a small few nods of her head. At watching, the sparkle in the doctor's eyes had reason to remain.

As he stood up, he exhaled sharply through his teeth, loosening his tie. "Let's try and remember what I told you yesterday, hmm?" he chided, his fingers now palming at her skull, encountering knots in the straggles of her hair. His paced, heavy breaths fell against her chest.

---

She felt as if there were grooves being moulded into her skull by his fingertips repeating the motion, and her head fell to the side.

A song she had never heard played in the back of her mind, eyes glazing over at hearing it. She swallowed, her sight falling into her lap. She spoke in barely above a whisper. "I had a dream last night."

The doctor's face broke out into a smile, giving her a reassuring nod with his eyes focused in on hers that absently gazed through him. He ran his fingers through her hair lightly again in the tender moment.

"You can tell me all about it later, alright?"

# Epilogue

STANDING tiny amidst the wary eyes of the faceless gown wearers, her hand floated in front of herself. She began to follow her hand when it glided out and then gently upwards. Her mind was empty, barren from thoughts to hinder her motions. Emma posed on the front of her bare feet, the grass soft under the hardened skin. Her bruised skin was warmed by the sun, and under the rays she kicked a leg out, and followed it with a willingness, eyes shutting to let herself flow without hindrance. She began flowing with elegance to music only she could hear. Arms flew up above her head and then floated down to her side as she spun on the grass, her gown flowing in the gentle releases of warm wind. Emma's head tipped back and she continued to dance under the rays that warmed her entirely, hearing the keys of the beautiful, dust coated piano ripple through the air.

The smile on her face remained wide as she spun in glee, tipping her head to the bouncing rhythm of an accompanying, hypnotic violin. The grass was never ending under her feet and wherever she started to dance, she found it to be so soft.

The patients stirred and stretched up, tall and their bodies hardened, growing brown and arms breaking to erupt into branches from the sleeves of their gowns. The branches reached out and strained for the others touch their leaves, to have fingers intertwine and hold the other, swaying in the wind and not ever growing apart.

Gently, the tiny feet of the smallest birds would land upon the fingers of the trees, and they brought Emma their beautiful songs, harmonising to the piano keys falling and the violins melody bleeding together. From the grass between her toes, flowers raised their heads, lured out by the seduction of the commanding sun. The joyous beams became yellow ribbons flying in the gentle wind of the high noon, Emma's hands swaying and fingers tickled, only to try and grasp the ribbons in her fingers. Oh, how she could dance under the sky of ribbons forever, the triangular flags attached to the head of the pole, the crude, bright colours bleeding through her eyelids.

Her face held a proud, peaceful beam in the bright sun of the afternoon's peak.

How she never stopped or heeded her dance, becoming entangled with the ribbons entirely, and to the flowing of the bouncing fiddle's song.

How she craved, she hungered from deep within for the violence of the sun to never cease her wanting to bask in it.


Fin.

## About the Author

Elley Fletcher resides in the U.K and is twenty one years old. She is an avid and passionate creator and fan of all things True Crime, horror and thriller related. Planning to publish many more books, she is pursuing her career in education while remaining passionate to make time for her writing. This is her first novel and her second book.

You can find and connect with Elley on her social media channels:

Facebook: E.V. Fletcher – Author

Instagram: elley_writing

Professional enquiries can be made to the author at author.elley@hotmail.com

If you enjoyed *Around the Maypole and Back*, please consider leaving an honest review on Amazon, Goodreads, or your favorite review site. Thank you!

## Also by Elley Fletcher

Recipes for a Murderer

Printed in Great Britain
by Amazon